WHEN NO ONE'S HOME

As Sydney hit the buttons on the microwave, she heard a floorboard creak in the living room behind her.

Sydney frowned. "Krista? Joel?" She stood for a moment and heard nothing but silence and the whir of the fan inside the microwave. The interior of the house was cast in shadows, lit only by the small copper lamp over the kitchen sink and by a nightlight in the hallway near the master bedroom. She walked into the dark living room that opened directly into the kitchen, where she halted and listened.

Sydney glanced around the cabin. Something didn't feel right. Was she just being paranoid?

She stood quietly and listened again. She tried not to think about Eshey and stared up the dark staircase that led to two bedrooms and a full bath. Could someone be upstairs?

Her head filled with images from horror movies. The images were superimposed with Eshey's face. Could he be here?

Cold fear seeped down her spine. She rested her hand on the rail. Did she go upstairs? Did she run out the front door and down the drive?

Just then Sydney caught a movement out of the corner of her eye, and she screamed. . . .

And then they laughed.

"I love you, Mom," Krista said.

"I love you, too, Krista." And when Sydney looked into her daughter's eyes, she saw Marla.

Epilogue

Krista jutted her hip and rested her hand there. "Mom, do I *have* to?"

Sydney stood outside the door of her mother's nursing home and plucked the headphones from her daughter's ears. "You have to come in and say hello. You don't have to stay. You can wait in the lobby and *read your book*. School will be starting again in no time."

Krista turned to Marshall. "I think this should be illegal."

He never cracked a smile; Sydney was proud of him.

"What's that?" Marshall said as they walked through the automatic doors into the lobby.

His arm was still in a sling, but his shoulder was healing nicely. He'd lost a little weight during his week-long stay in the hospital, but he looked great to Sydney. Pretty close to delicious.

"Making young impressionable women like me see their grandmothers," Krista huffed. "You know, people like her give kids nightmares."

Sydney rolled her eyes. "Got your grandma's burgers?"

Krista dragged her feet after her mother, holding up a greasy brown bag decorated with king's crowns. "Got 'em. Yuck. Does she know how bad meat is for her? Does she realize they have to kill cows to make these burgers?"

Krista was recovering amazingly well, according to a psychologist Sydney had taken to her after their encounter with Dorian and Darin at the cabin. She was dealing as well as expected with the loss of her father. There had been great floods of tears and almost as much anger at Joel for abandoning her by dying, but with time, Sydney knew Krista was going to be all right. She was already sleeping better and continued her interest in softball. Her team had won the state championship and lost in the regional competition. And now she was looking forward to school beginning again. It was astonishing how resilient kids were.

For Sydney, it was all going to take more time. She was still having a difficult time sleeping. After learning the details of what the FBI had found at Dorian's house, she dreamed about pigs eating bodies. Marshall was trying to help her work through it.

She smiled and slipped her hand into his. After his hospitalization, he had returned to New York, but had been back in Delaware a week later. It was too soon to tell where the relationship would go, how they would manage long distance, but she was happier than she had been in years. Maybe ever.

Sydney walked into her mother's room. Cora was in her easy chair in front of the TV that was blasting, as usual. Today it was *Bonanza*. What was it with her mother and cowboys?

"Hi, Ma." Sydney walked over and kissed her mother's cheek. It was her new ritual. She had come out of that cabin with a new appreciation of life and an acceptance of those around her, including Cora. Cora was who she was, and Sydney couldn't change that. She couldn't make her mother love her or treat

her in a particular way. What she could do was con
trol her own behavior.

Cora ignored the kiss.

"Ma, there's someone here I want you meet. A
friend of mine." Sydney glanced at Marshall. "His
name is Marshall King. You might remember him. He
interviewed you right after Marla died. He wrote a
book about her and about Eshey."

"Bring me something to eat?" Cora held out a
gnarled hand, her gaze locked on the tube.

Hoss was chasing a lone calf into dangerous territory.

Sydney sighed, giving Marshall an apologetic look.
"Give your grandmother her burgers, Krista."

"Hey, Grandma." Krista, standing as far from her
grandmother as she could, offered the bag.

Cora turned her head suddenly. "Marla!"

Krista took a step back, giving her mother that I
told-you-so look.

Sydney came between them. "No, Ma. That's Krista.
My daughter. You remember Krista."

Cora's hand tightened around the paper bag,
crushing its top as she stared at Krista. "'And you shall
sound the alarm of the trumpets so that you may be
remembered before the lord your God and be saved
from your enemies,'" she quoted.

Sydney gave Krista's shoulder a squeeze. "Yes, Ma.
Krista's safe."

The old woman shocked Sydney by smiling. "I read,
you know. I read the papers. I knew Marla was safe.
Read they all died. Got what they deserved."

"I'm out of here," Krista said, backing out the door.
"You coming with me, Marshall? 'Bye, Grandma."

Marshall met Sydney's gaze. "I'll wait for you in the
lobby." He caught her hand, gave it a squeeze, and let
go.

Sydney bent down by her mother's chair and looked

nto her cloudy gray-green eyes. "Ma, that wasn't Marla
he paper was talking about. It was Krista. Eshey's sons
ried to kill Krista. It was my daughter, Krista, who was
aved."

The old woman's eyes filled with tears and she
hifted her gaze to meet Sydney's. "Don't you think I
now that?" she whispered. She watched as Krista dis-
ppeared down the hallway, her strawberry blond
onytail swinging. She looked back at her daughter.
I know Marla is dead. I just like to pretend she's still
live sometimes. Nothing wrong with that, is there?"

Sydney threw her arms around her mother. "Of
ourse not, Ma."

Cora pushed her away, scratching at the burger bag,
er gaze locked on the TV again. "So how many bur-
ers you bring me?" she whined. "An old woman
ould starve in this place."

Romantic Suspense from
Lisa Jackson

Contemporary Romance by
Kasey Michaels

__Can't Take My Eyes Off of You
  0-8217-6522-1   **$6.50US/$8.50**
East Wapaneken? Shelby Taite has never heard of it. Neithe
the rest of Philadelphia's Main Line society. Which is pre
why the town is so appealing. No one would ever think to
for Shelby here. Nobody but Quinn Delaney . . .

__Too Good To Be True
  0-8217-6774-7   **$6.50**US/**$8.5**
To know Grady Sullivan is to love him . . . unless you're
Kendall. After all, Annie is here at Peevers Manor trying to
she's the long-lost illegitimate great-granddaughter of a toilet
tycoon. How's a girl supposed to focus on charming her way
an old man's will with Grady breathing down her neck . . .

Call toll free **1-888-345-BOOK** to order by phone or use
coupon to order by mail.

Name_____

Address _____

City_____ State _____ Zip ____

Please send me the books I have checked above.

I am enclosing $_____
Plus postage and handling* $_____
Sales tax (in New York and Tennessee only) $_____
Total amount enclosed $_____

*Add $2.50 for the first book and $.50 for each additional bo
Send check or money order (no cash or CODs) to: **Kensington Publis**
Dept. C.O., 850 Third Avenue, New York, NY 10022
Prices and numbers subject to change without notice.
All orders subject to availability.
Visit our website at **www.kensingtonbooks.com.**

THE OTHER TWIN

Hunter Morgan

ZEBRA BOOKS
Kensington Publishing Corp.
http://www.kensingtonbooks.com

ZEBRA BOOKS are published by

Kensington Publishing Corp.
850 Third Avenue
New York, NY 10022

All Kensington titles, imprints and distributed lines are
available at special quantity discounts for bulk purchases for
sales promotion, premiums, fund-raising, educational or
institutional use.

Special book excerpts or customized printings can also be
created to fit specific needs. For details, write or phone the
office of the Kensington Special Sales Manager: Kensington
Publishing Corp., 850 Third Avenue, New York, NY 10022.
Attn. Special Sales Department. Phone: 1-800-221-2647.

Zebra and the Z logo Reg. U.S. Pat. & TM Off.

First Printing: August 2003
10 9 8 7 6 5 4 3 2 1

Printed in the United States of America

For my own softball player, Red.
Don't get any ideas . . .

Prologue

"Where is he?" Sydney sat on the back seat of their father's '66 Chevy Impala, her thin arms crossed impatiently over her chest. "I've got to get home. I have to study for my English test."

From the front seat, Sydney's twin, Marla, glanced over the top of her social studies book. The twelve year olds weren't identical twins, but everyone thought they were. Marla had green eyes, Sydney had blue. "You know where he is, and you know he won't be back until he's out of money."

A tractor-trailer without the trailer drove by slowly, stirring up a slight breeze on the hot afternoon. The driver smiled and waved as he rolled by.

Sydney huffed and flung herself back on the torn car seat. Little puffs of mottled stuffing came out and stuck to her sweaty elbow. "Damn him. I knew we shouldn't have let him pick us up from school. I knew this would happen." She struck the front seat with her hand. "Lousy drunk. What did we do to deserve a lousy goddamned drunk for a father?"

"Sydney, please don't say those words. God'll strike us dead."

Sydney gave her sister the eye as she wiped the

sweat that dribbled down her temple. Though it was after five, it was still incredibly hot. Her shorts and T-shirt were damp and stuck to the fake leather of the car seat. She picked up the book she had been reading, *The Count of Monte Cristo*.

"Ma would say we deserve him," Marla said quietly. "Our conception was polluted by sin."

"Well, he can sit in that bar and get drunk off his ass. I'm not sitting here and waiting on him." Sydney shoved opened the car door, and it groaned as if it was going to come right off the hinges. She grabbed her book bag.

Marla leaned out the window. "Sydney, please don't go." She was angry with Dad, too, but she had never been able to express it the way Sydney could. "Please don't leave me here. You know this is a bad part of town."

Sydney stood in her wrinkled T-shirt, which was damp beneath the armpits. Her breasts were just beginning to swell. Sydney thought she and Marla both needed bras, but so far Ma wouldn't bite. She said they would only lead her girls down the path of sin. Sydney didn't know if she meant the breasts or the bras, but she didn't ask because she'd knew she'd get her mouth washed out with soap for talking smart.

Sydney glared at her sister.

Marla's lower lip trembled as if she were going to cry. She was always the good girl. She never cursed, never talked back to their mother.

"Please don't leave me," Marla begged.

Sydney immediately felt guilty.

"Come back," Marla said. "And if he doesn't come in another thirty minutes, we'll go into the bar together and see if we can get him out. He's only been in there a little more than an hour."

Sydney glanced up and down the seedy street. Most

of the businesses were closed, and the brick apartment building across the street was boarded up. There were a few cars parked, but little traffic. She glanced back at her sister. "You think he'll come out if we ask him?"

Marla smiled. "I think so."

She sounded so hopeful. Marla was always like that, always wanting to believe in the best in people. Not like Sydney, who saw the truth for what it was.

With a groan, Sydney threw her book bag into the car through the window and climbed into the back seat again. She slammed the door behind her.

"Hey there, little lady."

Startled, Sydney leaned back as a man in a blue plaid shirt stuck his head in the rear window. "I was wondering if you could tell me how to get to Poplar Street." He smiled, and Sydney noticed that he had a front tooth that was black on the end. His hair was short and bristly like a porcupine's and he needed a shave.

He hooked his thumb in the direction of the tractor parked just ahead of them on the street. It was the one she had seen pass them a few minutes ago. "I'm s'posed to pick up a trailer of auto parts on Poplar and haul it to Caroliney." He had an accent like their neighbor, who was from Georgia or somewhere down south.

Sydney shook her head, the hair on the back of her neck rising up. She didn't like strangers. She didn't trust them. "I . . . I don't know where it is. You could ask our dad. He'll be back in a minute."

"Oh, he will?" He smiled, showing the bad tooth again. "That be the case—"

The stranger clamped his hand over Sydney's arm, and for a moment she froze. She didn't know what to do.

Marla had turned around in the front seat and was

up on her knees. Sydney's gaze met her sister's. It seemed to take both of them an instant to realize something was wrong. Very wrong.

The man swung the rear door open and reached in with the other hand to drag Sydney out. She thought she screamed, but barely a croak came out.

"Sydney!" Marla sobbed.

The man was trying to pull Sydney out the door, but Sydney somehow managed to wedge one stained white Ked against the door so he couldn't pull her through. "Let me go! Let me go!" She kicked her free leg.

"Shut up, you little bitch," he growled. "I'm not gonna to hurt you."

Sydney opened her mouth to scream, and he leaned in and slapped her hard in the face. As he hit her, she bit down and caught his finger between her teeth. The man yelped in pain, and Sydney gave a kick, flinging herself backward, flat onto the tattered car seat. It was enough to get free of him. She kicked again and stretched, reaching for the other door, thinking maybe she could slide out the other side. She was still flat on her back when she saw him jerk open the front car door.

Sydney screamed again. This time the sound came out. She saw Marla's strawberry blond hair fall forward and her mouth open as the man hauled her out of the car, but no sound came from her sister's mouth. It was almost as if Sydney screamed for her.

She scrambled to get up, to get out the door, as the man pulled Marla out of the car. But as he moved away with the silent Marla in his arms, he kicked the back door hard. It slammed on Sydney's ankle and fiery pain shot up her leg. Her head seemed to burst into sparks of light and agony. "Marla!" Sydney cried, trying to sit up. "Marla!"

Sydney managed to get out of the car, but the moment she put pressure on her foot, the pain shot up her leg again, making her dizzy and sick to her stomach at the same time. She was going to throw up. Through a blur of tears, she saw the man step up into the blue truck and shove Marla in ahead of him. As Marla disappeared inside, Sydney caught one last glimpse of her sister's face. Marla was so terror stricken that Sydney could *feel* her fear deep in the pit of her own stomach. She could feel the little short gasps of breath Marla was taking.

The truck started up with a great rumble, and Sydney threw herself forward, trying to run. "Help! Someone help," she screamed. She tripped and fell forward on the rutted asphalt, and the last thing she saw before her chin hit the pavement was Marla's face in the rear window of the tractor as it sped down the street.

One

The present

"OK, your turn," eleven-year-old Carrie said.

Her twin sister, Cassie, spun the spinner on the game board.

The girls were up in the tree house that their dad had built in their backyard. It had been a present before he left. Carrie wished her dad hadn't moved out and was divorcing her mother. She really missed him, but she liked the tree house.

Cassie jumped up and headed for the wooden ladder.

"Where you going?" Carrie frowned. She was winning. She didn't want her sister to quit now. "You didn't hop yet."

"I'm going to bathroom." Cassie turned to back down the ladder. "I'm hungry. I'm going to make a peanut butter and J sandwich. You want one?"

Carrie twisted a blond pigtail. "No. Just cookies."

"Mom'll get mad. We're not supposed to eat cookies in the middle of the day."

Carrie began to count the paper money she had already won. "So don't tell her." She stuck her tongue out at her sister.

Cassie stuck out her pink tongue, too, and disappeared down the ladder.

Carrie was just starting to count her twenties when she heard a man's voice call her name from the far side of the fence. She thought she heard a puppy bark.

Was it her dad? He wasn't supposed come today. Had he bought her a puppy? They had always wanted a puppy, but Mom always said no. Now that he was gone, their dad was always buying them things Mom said they couldn't have. "Dad?"

Carrie shimmied down the ladder and stood at the gate for a second. Her mom would be mad if she talked to Dad today. It wasn't their visitation day, and her mom got really hyper about visitation days. The puppy yipped again.

Carrie pushed the gate open and stepped out of the yard.

Sydney padded barefoot across the kitchen floor, the wood cool on her feet. As she poured herself a cup of freshly brewed coffee, she gazed out the window of her ocean-block house. The sky was a hazy blue; it was going to be another scorcher.

"Going out to do drills, Mom," Krista called from the front of the house.

The door slammed, rattling a picture frame in the front hall, and Sydney smiled. With her thirteen-year-old daughter occupied, she could enjoy her coffee in peace before she went downstairs to her office to start her workday, without a confrontation with the little she-beast she had given birth to. She had an August deadline for her next book, *A Fool's Guide to the Family Vacation,* and she needed to get her ever-expanding butt in gear. She'd never missed a deadline since the first *Fool's Guide* had come out nine years ago, and she wasn't about to miss this one.

Sydney carried her favorite mug to kitchen table

and tucked one bare foot under her as she sat down.
Sipping the hazelnut coffee, she flipped through yesterday's mail. Bill, junk, bill, something from her
publishing company, a weekly news magazine. She
didn't have time this morning to read the whole magazine cover to cover the way she liked to, but she
thought she would treat herself to the political car-
toon page before she headed downstairs. As she
flipped through the pages, a headline caught her eye.

TRAGIC COINCIDENCE, it read. Sydney didn't have time
for anyone's tragic coincidences this morning. She
needed to call one of her researchers before she started
the chapter on finding the right hotel, and she was already short on work hours today. Krista had a dentist
appointment this afternoon and then softball practice,
and there was the obligatory visit to her mother to get
through as well.

Sydney took another sip of coffee and ran her hand
over the glossy page, folding it back.

Another child kidnapping. *Shit*. Did she have some
kind of sick radar or something? How did she always
find these articles?

Every time she read about one, her heart stopped.
There was so much depravity in the world these days
that it was a wonder her heart could keep starting
again. The little girl, a twin, was missing from near
Annapolis—an hour from Sydney and a world away.
But the story wasn't about the kidnapping; it was
about the coincidence.

She set the cup down, the coffee suddenly bitter in
her mouth. She heard her ex's voice in her head as
she skimmed through the article, her heart beating
faster: *If that shit bothers you so much, stop reading it.*

He was right, of course. But she couldn't help herself.

According to the article, the coincidence was that
the missing child, Carrie Morris, who was a political

activist's daughter, was also the daughter of a woman whose twin sister had been kidnapped and murdered almost thirty years ago.

Sydney suddenly felt sick to her stomach, and for a moment she thought she was going to throw up.

The woman's twin sister had been kidnapped and murdered in 1972—two years before Marla's kidnapping.

Sydney couldn't catch her breath. She wanted to put the magazine down, but she couldn't stop reading.

While no one was ever charged with the murder, it is widely believed that recently paroled Charles Eshey, 62, was responsible for the murder. Eshey was tried and convicted for the 1974 murder of twelve-year-old Marla Baker.

Recently paroled?

Sydney dropped the news magazine on the table as if it were anthrax tainted. She pressed her hand to her pounding heart. Charles Eshey paroled? That son of a bitch.

It was impossible, of course; the article had it wrong. They were always screwing up, and then the following week the error would be noted in a little box near the editorials.

Charles Eshey couldn't have recently been paroled. He had been sentenced to life in prison. He'd served less than twenty-nine years. Sydney bent over, realizing she was hyperventilating. Her heart was pounding out of control and she felt dizzy.

There was a sudden explosion behind her, and she shot out of the chair as lines spidered across the picture window before the glass fell to the floor in fragments. A softball hit the floor with a thump and rolled to a stop against the refrigerator.

It was enough to snap Sydney back to reality. She leaned against the refrigerator, pressing her hand to her pounding heart. She heard the back door open and Krista run up the steps from the laundry room.

The door in the kitchen opened and Krista stepped in, halting in her cleats. No cleats on the hardwood, it was a rule. The green-eyed strawberry-blond teen stared at the window and then at her mother. "Oops. Sorry about that," she said sheepishly from under her teal visor.

Sydney exhaled and took in a deep breath. Somehow she managed a little laugh. "Your screwball?"

"Not screwing this morning," Krista said hesitantly, testing the maternal waters.

Just seeing her daughter safe and sound made Sydney smile. Right now she wouldn't have cared if Krista had broken every window in the house. She had an overwhelming urge to run barefoot over the sticky glass and throw her arms around Krista, but she didn't dare, knowing her daughter would rebuke her. Krista was at that age where moms just didn't hug daughters often—especially when they'd just shattered a window with a softball.

"Get the broom," Sydney said, heading for the stairs that lead to her office below. "I'm going down to work. I'll call the insurance guy." She turned on her heels. "You might as well turn off the air-conditioning on the whole floor. No sense in cooling the entire Atlantic coast."

Krista tossed her glove on a chair and raced to the hall closet in obvious relief. "I'll take care of it, Mom."

Sydney closed her office door and made a beeline for the phone. On the way down the steps she had considered calling Joel. If what the magazine said was true, if Eshey was out on parole, if a child had been kidnapped and there could be a connection with Eshey, Krista's father had a right to know.

But she knew Joel too well. He would tell her she was overreacting. Overextrapolating. He would say it was too far a stretch to suggest that if Eshey was out, then, as the daughter of a twin whose twin was murdered by Eshey, Krista could be in danger.

Sydney slid into her leather chair behind her desk and reached for her electronic Rolodex. She brought up New Jersey Victims Services and punched the number into her phone. She received yearly updates on Eshey, and last she had heard, he was still in jail. He wasn't even supposed to be eligible for parole for more than a year.

"Victims Services, may I help you?"

Sydney tried to calmly relate what she needed, and she was put on hold while her name was verified. Elevator music played in her ear as she tried not to let her imagination run away from her. She doodled on her blotter, drawing circles that spiraled inward. Eshey wasn't out. Even if he was, the missing girl in Annapolis was just what the article said, a coincidence.

"Mrs. MacGregor?"

She dropped the pen and it rolled under the desk. "Yes?"

"You were sent a letter on February fourteenth notifying you of Mr. Eshey's parole hearing and then another on, let's see, March twelfth notifying you that Mr. Eshey was being released on parole on April nineteenth. The note cites good behavior and a heart condition as extenuating circumstances."

Good behavior? Good frigging behavior? He killed Marla, for God's sake.

Again Sydney felt short of breath. "No. I never received such a letter."

"It says right here that notification of all hearings are

to be sent to Mrs. Sydney MacGregor, 701 Seagrass, Albany Beach, Delaware—"

"Not 701," Sydney interrupted. "107. You had the address wrong."

"Hmm," said the woman on the other end of the line. "We just had our computer system updated before Christmas, what with all the new 911 addresses. Let me make that correction now."

"Make that correction now? How the hell is that going to help me now?" she demanded. "He's out!"

"Yes, ma'am," the woman said patiently. "Released on April nineteenth, as stated in the letter."

Sydney sat back in her chair. This was the stuff nightmares and bad movies were made of. "Is . . . is there any other information you can give me? Where is he?"

"Well, he's in the state of New Jersey, because parolees must remain in the state. I can't give his address, of course. That's confidential."

Sydney wanted to ask her what right a man who had raped, tortured, and murdered a twelve-year-old girl had to confidentiality, but she had dealt with this bureaucracy long enough to know she'd be wasting her breath. "What about his parole officer?"

"Ma'am?"

"The name of his parole officer." Sydney grabbed a pen from a tin can Krista had made for her years ago, decorated with colored yarn. "I want the name and number of his parole officer."

"Let's see. Yes, I believe I can provide that information."

Sydney jotted down the name and phone number. A woman. She hung up and called the number immediately. She got a voice mail message. "Hello, this is Cynthia Carmack, please leave your name, number, and a brief message as to how I can help you."

She sounded like a bank manager or a doctor's receptionist instead of a parole officer whose clients were thieves, pedophiles, and murderers. Sydney left a clipped message with her home and cell phone numbers and disconnected. She punched Joel's office number.

"MacGregor and Patterson. This is Sue."

"Hey, Sue, it's Sydney. Joel in?"

"Sure is, hang on," she said sweetly. Too sweetly. What Sue didn't know was that Sydney knew Joel had been doing her even before the divorce.

The line clicked. "Hey, Syd, what's up?"

Tears welled suddenly in her eyes. She was well over Joel. She had loved him once, but the hell he had put her through with his drinking had been too much. The love hadn't survived. Still, hearing his voice brought a lump of emotion up in her throat. "He might be out," she croaked.

"Who?"

"Who?" Sydney leaned forward, resting her head in her hand, her elbow propped on her messy desk. "Eshey."

There was a silence on the other end of the phone.

"Joel, did you hear me? He's out. The son of a bitch is out on parole for good behavior. Can you fucking believe it?"

"What about your New Year's resolution?"

It was Joel's attempt at a joke. He had given up booze and she'd given up her favorite swear word. They had both agreed that such language wasn't good for an impressionable teenager.

"It gets better, Joel. He was released almost two months ago, but there was a screwup with victims services so I was never notified." She got up, taking the cordless phone with her. She was too edgy to just sit. "There was a kidnapping in Annapolis last week. The daughter of a woman whose twin sister was probably murdered by Eshey before he killed Marla."

"I know where your head is going, but, Syd," he said calmly, "it's just a coincidence. A terrible one, but—"

"A twin," she said, hating to say it aloud. "The little girl who is missing has a twin sister."

Joel was silent again for a moment.

Sydney reached out and adjusted the lamp above her bonsai tree on a bookshelf.

"Well?" she demanded.

"You need to stay calm, Syd."

"I am calm. I'm so fucking calm I want to take a pen off my desk, drive to Jersey, and sink it into the man's heart. Calmly, of course."

He made a sound in his throat, and she exhaled heavily.

"I called his parole officer, but she wasn't in."

"Hell, he's got to be now, what, pushing sixty?"

"Over sixty," she said. "With some kind of heart condition. Supposedly, part of the reason he was released was because of his poor health."

"Well, maybe you coming at him with a Bic will put him over the edge and he'll die of a heart attack."

"Joel! This is not funny." Her tone bordered on the edge of hysteria.

"I know," he said gently, in that voice that had once made her toes curl. "But remember, you said a long time ago that you weren't going to live your life in fear. You vowed you weren't going to raise Krista in that kind of shadow."

Sydney leaned against the bookcase and closed her eyes. She could hear Krista upstairs going down the hall, then the sound of one of the heat pumps kicking off.

"She busted the window in the kitchen this morning. The one next to the sliding doors."

"Screwball?" he asked.

"Not screwing this morning." She had to smile, despite herself. Krista was an excellent softball player and was really coming into her own, pitching. She was consumed by the sport—ate, slept, and drank it—and Sydney was glad for the sense of direction in her teen daughter's life. It kept her mind off boys and drinking and drugs and all of the temptations the world had to offer young girls these days.

"You want me to come over? Hold your hand? Be your punching bag, even?"

She shook her head. "Nah. I'm going to make some calls about the window, do a little work, and then take her to the dentist and then softball practice. I'll go see Cora while she's practicing."

"That's who you ought to take your Bic after."

She laughed, but without any real humor.

"You sure you're OK?" Joel said softly. "Because if you're not—"

"I'm OK. I'll talk to the parole officer and let you know what she says. You're right, of course. It's just a coincidence." She brushed back her chin-length strawberry blond hair. "Call you later?"

"I'll be in meetings, but I'll tell Sue to interrupt." He paused. "I can take Krista tonight, if you want."

"No." She said it more adamantly than she had intended. "I need to have her here. You know it's all I can do to leave her at practice."

"Call me if you need me."

Sydney hung up and returned to her desk to look up her insurance agent's number. If she just kept busy, she knew she'd be all right. Joel was right. Eshey was in New Jersey, an old man with a failing heart. It was just a sick coincidence.

* * *

"Jesus H. You see this, Steinman?" Jessica Manlove walked into her fellow FBI agent's cubicle and opened the newspaper on his desk. She liked Carl Steinman. He was an excellent agent and a good man to boot. They weren't as easy to find in the bureau as one would think. "You see this guy with the bombs tied to his ass? He thought he'd blow up the White House on his way to work as a dental hygienist." She shook her head, because no matter how long she was on the job, she still couldn't believe this kind of stuff went on.

Sandy-haired Carl glanced up at her from his whole wheat bagel and egg-white-only breakfast sandwich and reached for his coffee. "Could you spare me the news until I finish? You know how I hate hearing about bombs tied to people's asses before breakfast."

She glanced at the institutional clock on the wall of the cluttered Baltimore field office. The room, divided into cubicles and called the bullpen, was shared by the special agents assigned here. "It's after ten. Breakfast *is* over."

"It is now." He wadded the half-eaten sandwich up in the paper and tossed it into the waste can beside his desk. "So what does Crackhow have for you?"

"Us." Jess pulled the file out from under arm. It was thin. A new case. "Kidnapping. A little girl. Eleven years old, out of Annapolis."

He frowned. "When did she disappear?"

"Be a week tomorrow."

He glanced up in disgust. "And they're just handing it to us now?"

"Barker did the initial crime scene interviews when we were on surveillance at the bar." It had been a long week of surveillance that resulted in nothing but boredom and the realization that the information on the killer they were looking for was incorrect. "He concluded there was a good chance it was the non-custodial father."

"So where's this father?" He rubbed his temples.

"Don't know."

Jess knew Carl hated child kidnappings. Homicide, suicide, armed robbery, bombings; he'd take any of them before taking a case involving a child. Jess, on the other hand, was pleased to have been transferred to the Violent Crimes unit. She had a good head for this kind thing.

"Barker's got local police looking for the father, who is supposed to be vacationing in Florida."

Carl groaned. "Anyone check Disney World? If I napped my daughter, I know that's where we would go if she had her way."

"He's not registered under his name in any hotel on site or in the area, but we're talking a big area. Oh, and this case is being considered high profile. Dad's some kind of lobbyist." She began flipping through the pages. "This is where it gets interesting. Why Crackhow really wants us on this case." She read on. "The girl's aunt was kidnapped at about the same age. Murdered."

"Sick world. They catch that one?"

"No one was ever officially charged, but it was believed that Charles Eshey killed her." Jess looked up at Carl over the edge of the manila folder. "You remember him? The one who killed twins, only he just did one. Never killed both, even if they were together when he snatched his vic."

Carl loosened his tie. "No, I don't remember any Eshey. How long ago?"

She ran her finger over the notes sent over by the Maryland state police. "He was arrested in '74. This girl's aunt disappeared two years before."

"How do you remember all of these sickos?"

She stared at the folder, surprised by the sudden well of emotion that bubbled up in her throat. It was so unlike her. She was usually so good at staying emotionally disconnected. It was the only way agents could do their jobs effectively year after year.

"Believe it or not, my dad worked the Eshey case out of the Newark field office."

She'd been too young to know what her father had been working on at the time, but just before he died, right after she had graduated from the FBI academy, he'd actually sat down and talked to her about his career. He'd told her about some of his cases that he had never been able to quite get over. The Eshey case had been one of them.

Her father had died three weeks later of a massive heart attack.

Jess swallowed the lump in her throat. "So Crackhow said to check with you. He wants us to look into the Eshey angle. Let the others who are already on the case deal with the actual missing kid." She lifted her gaze. "You in?"

Carl stuck out his hand. "Let's get started. We'll read the file and then we'll go start the reinterviews. I want to talk to the mother myself." He shook his head. "Sweet Mary, I hate kidnappings on Monday morning. Ruins my whole week."

"Not as much as it ruined this little girl's . . ."

Two

"Mom?" Krista called down from the top of the stairs.

Sydney stepped out of her office into the ground floor hallway. The beach house was a tri-level, with the utility room, laundry room, and her office on the lower floor, the living areas and the master bedroom on the middle floor, and three more bedrooms on the upper floor. She called it "the house the fools built" because the astounding success of her fool books had paid for the house, mortgage-free.

"Yeah, babe?"

"Glass is all cleaned up and I'll take out the kitchen garbage. I'm going out to finish my drills and then down to the beach to read, if it's OK."

Sydney's first impulse was to shout up the stairs, *No, you can't go to the beach. You can never leave my sight again.* She bit her tongue and gave what she knew was the right response. School was almost out. Today was an in-service day for teachers, but summer vacation started at the end of the week. She couldn't keep Krista in all summer for fear some killer was on the loose.

"Be back in the house and ready to go by noon. You've got a twelve-thirty dental appointment." Sydney looked up at her daughter, who was standing on the top step. Her strawberry blond hair was pulled back in the usual ponytail. She had Marla's green eyes. Sydney fought the lump that rose in her throat again. "We'll grab some lunch and then I'll take you to softball."

"So I miss the Grandma interrogation?"

Sydney grimaced apologetically. "'Fraid so."

Krista made a fist, thrust her arm skyward, and jerked it down enthusiastically. "Yes."

"If you go for a swim, be sure you're in front of the lifeguard stand."

"Yes, Mom," Krista groaned. "Later."

Krista closed the door and Sydney stood in the hall fighting a sense of panic that suddenly pounded in her chest. She didn't want to let Krista out of her sight. It was ridiculous notion, of course. Joel was right. She had decided a long time ago that she would not live in fear.

If only her father hadn't let Marla out of his sight. . . .

Sydney checked her cell phone in the outside pocket of her purse again. Still no call from Eshey's parole officer. If the woman didn't call by the time she got home, Sydney would call again. She'd keep calling until she got some answers.

Sydney took a deep breath, girded her loins, and pushed though the door to her mother's private room at the high-end nursing home where she'd resided since her stroke three years ago. Sydney forced a smile. "Hi, Ma." She walked to the recliner where her mother spent all of her waking hours. The TV was on. As far as Sydney knew, it hadn't been off since Joel took it out of the box when Cora moved in.

Her mom made no response, but stared straight ahead at the 27-inch TV. *Gunsmoke.* Sydney didn't realize the show was still in syndication. "I brought you a cheeseburger. Krista said to tell you hi. She wanted to come, but she had softball practice." Sydney set down her purse and pulled the burger out of the bag. "Want to eat it now while it's still warm? I can get you some apple juice."

Cora stared straight ahead, her mouth pursed, seemingly frozen in time. It was the same scowl Sydney remembered from her childhood. Her father had been a drunk, but at least he had known how to smile. If anyone else had entered the room, they might have thought Cora was deaf, but Sydney knew better. She heard her daughter loud and clear. Cora was simply ignoring Sydney, as she had since birth. Marla had been the favored child. Quiet, well-mannered Marla.

"Cheeseburger, no onions." Sydney unwrapped the burger and set it on the table beside the recliner. She pulled up a chair beside her mother.

Cora grabbed the burger with her good hand without taking her eyes off Marshal Dillon.

Sydney glanced at the door, half tempted to get up and leave. What was she doing here? She couldn't deal with her mother today of all days. Would Cora even notice? To her surprise, tears welled in her eyes. What was with this need to be loved by a woman who was incapable of loving anyone? Any ounce of motherly devotion Cora had once possessed had died with Marla.

"I didn't think you would remember." Cora chomped loudly on the burger, smacking her lips the way old people did. "I'm hungry. I'm always hungry."

"Ma, we've been through this." Sydney fished an emery board out of her purse and attacked a chipped nail. "You wouldn't be *hungry* if you would *eat* the meals that are brought to you. Hell, the food is better here than at my house."

"'Curse God and die,'" her mother quoted. Ketchup oozed out of the corner of her mouth, which had been left lopsided by the stroke. "Job. Don't remember which chapter."

"My good old friend Job," Sydney remarked sarcastically, reaching out with a napkin to wipe her mother's mouth.

Cora shifted her gaze from bank robbers riding off in a cloud of dust, to Sydney, and back to the outlaws threatening Miss Kitty. "I told you, I can't eat here; it's not safe. They're trying to kill me."

Sydney exhaled, knowing this conversation, like most with her mother, would be pointless. Cora thought the nurses were poisoning her Ensure. How could you argue with that kind of reasoning?

She decided to change the subject. "Krista's pitching well these days. Her private coach is pleased with her progress. If you like, I can take you to a game sometime. We could take that wheelchair for a spin in the fresh air and sunshine." She forced a little laugh.

Cora shoved the remainder of the burger into her mouth. She talked with her mouth full. "What's wrong?"

Sydney blinked. "What?"

"You're my flesh and blood. I suffered the agony of childbirth to give you life. You think I don't know when something is wrong?" she sneered. "The stroke damaged my body, not my brain."

Sydney leaned forward in the chair, resting her elbows on her knees, her face cradled in her hands. "Eshey's out," she said softly.

She didn't know what had made her say it. She'd

come here with no intention of mentioning it to her mother.

Cora shook a bony finger, her voice like a crow's. "'I looked and there was a pale green horse! Its rider's name was Death, and Hades followed with him; they were given authority over the earth to kill.'"

The quote was from Revelation, of course. Cora didn't have to tell her that one. It was her mother's favorite book of the Bible. It amazed Sydney that the stroke had taken away her mother's ability to walk, to write, sometimes to reason, and yet that tortured mind could still quote word for word verses she had learned as a child from her Southern Baptist father.

"A child's been kidnapped in Annapolis," Sydney said, unable to stop herself from going on now that she had started. "The girl's aunt was murdered by Eshey before Marla was. I know Joel's right—it's just coincidence. A crazy, sick coincidence because this is a crazy, sick world, but—"

"Not a coincidence. He's out and he's killing again," Cora said, her eyes lighting up with a fire. "'And then the dragon stood before the woman who was about to bear a child, so that he might devour her child as soon as it was born!'"

The quote was irrelevant. They usually were, but that fact was of no comfort. "Great." Sydney threw up her hands. "So what you're saying is that Krista is in danger from this maniac?" She stared at her mother, wishing just once that Cora could offer *some* maternal solace. She looked up through her hands. "Mom, what did he do to her?" She didn't dare mention Marla's name. "You never told me."

Cora returned her gaze to the TV, the light in her eyes dying. She lifted the remote and turned up the volume so loud that the gunfire was earsplitting.

Sydney picked up her purse, her heart suddenly

pounding in her chest. She had to get back to the ball field. Had to see Krista, just to know she was safe. "See you tomorrow." She walked out of her mother's room without waiting for a response. Without expecting one.

Three

"You've been here more than an hour." Krista tossed her bat bag into the back of Sydney's SUV, slid into the front seat beside her mother, and reached for her seat belt. "Grandma get to you?"

"I was watching you practice. Nice job on the pop fly drill."

Krista snapped her seat belt, glancing sideways at her mother. "You never watch me practice. You usually read if you have to wait."

"So maybe I should watch more often." Sydney smiled and slid the truck into reverse.

Krista grabbed the water bottle her mother had brought for her. "Can I spend the night with Katie tonight?"

"No." Sydney couldn't help herself. She just couldn't bear the thought of letting Krista sleep elsewhere.

"Why not?" Krista's voice took on the whine that grated on Sydney's nerves.

Sydney kept her eyes on the road. "You were there last weekend."

Krista chugged the water, her tone edged with teenage confrontation. "So?"

Sydney cut her gaze to her daughter, signaled, and pulled into the Chinese restaurant parking lot. "Besides, you have school tomorrow." She pulled a bill from her purse. "Now go in and pick up dinner and stop arguing with your mother."

"Soon as you start making some sense," Krista muttered as she climbed out of the car.

"What was that?" Sydney leaned over to look at Krista standing beside the vehicle.

"Nothing."

The door slammed, and Sydney sat alone trying to catch her breath and get her thoughts straight. She probably should have told Krista she could spend the night with Katie. She was just being paranoid. The missing child in Annapolis had to be a coincidence. It had to—

The cell phone rang, startling her. Sydney fumbled with her purse. Two rings. Three. She couldn't get hold of the thing. She hit the "receive" button at last. "Hello."

"Mrs. MacGregor?"

Sydney hated being called Missus. Always had. "Yes, this is Sydney MacGregor."

"Cynthia Carmack, here."

"Thanks for calling me back." Sydney glanced up. Krista was standing in line, her hip jaunted out to one side in one of her favorite "I'm bored" teenage poses. "I'd like to get some information on one of your parolees"—she hated even to speak his vile name— "Charles Eshey."

There was no response on the other end of the line.

"Look," Sydney ground into the phone. "That son of a bitch ripped my sister out of the front seat of the car while I sat in the back. He kidnapped and raped her and then he murdered her."

"I'm sorry," said the voice on the other end. The young woman sounded no older than Krista. She was, no doubt, one more starry-eyed recent college graduate who believed all men and women could be rehabilitated. "How can I help you? We're allowed to provide only certain information, even to victims."

"So it's true? He's been released."

"Yes, ma'am."

Sydney's voice trembled. "So he's out, eating, sleeping, working?" *And Marla is dead and buried in the cold ground.*

"He has secured a job, yes. And is doing quite well, I might add."

"Don't add," Sydney snapped. "I was supposed to be notified of the parole hearing; I wasn't. I was supposed to be notified if he was ever released. I wasn't."

"Mrs. MacGregor, let me assure you, you are in no danger from Mr. Eshey. He's elderly and his health is poor. He could pass away at any time."

Sydney's heart was racing again. She glanced up to see Krista moving up to the cash register to offer the bill in exchange for the brown bag on the counter. "Do you know that a child has been kidnapped in Annapolis? A child whose aunt was killed by Eshey?"

"Mrs. MacGregor, Mr. Eshey was convicted of only one count of murder."

Tears filled Sydney's eyes. Just one murder. Just Marla. She wiped her nose with the back of her hand. "How far from Annapolis is the bastard?"

Young Cynthia's voice took on an adversarial tone. "Mr. Eshey is required by the state of New Jersey to remain in the state. He checks in regularly with his parole officer. Me. He has not left the state, I can assure you."

"So what you're saying is that you're personally guaranteeing that my daughter is safe. Is that what you're saying?"

Again, silence.

Sydney took a deep breath. This wasn't accomplishing anything and she knew it. "So he has to check in with you regularly? What, he just calls in to say hi?"

"We have phone contact, and Mr. Eshey is also required to see me in person once a week." She paused. "Look, Mrs. MacGregor. I'm sorry for your loss, I truly am. But this is a rehabilitated man if I ever saw one. He's old; he has serious heart disease. He's of no threat to anyone."

Krista pushed through the glass door of the restaurant and walked toward the car with the paper bag in hand, scuffing her feet in her new cleats.

"Thank you for returning my call, Miss Carmack." Sydney rubbed her temple; her head was pounding. "Should there be any developments, will you call me?"

"I don't expect any trouble from Mr. Eshey," she said, "but certainly."

"Thanks." Sydney hung up as Krista slid into the front seat.

"Who was that?"

"Wrong number." Sydney kept her gaze downcast as she punched a number into the phone.

Joel answered the phone himself at his office. Working late, no doubt.

"Hey, it's Sydney."

His voice was immediately filled with concern. "You OK? Krista?"

She glanced at Krista, who was staring straight ahead, her arms crossed stubbornly over her chest.

"We were wondering if you wanted to join us for dinner. We just picked up Chinese."

"I'll bring the Diet Pepsi," he said without hesitation. "See you in a few minutes."

Krista glanced at her mother as Sydney dropped the phone on the seat and started the SUV. "Who was *that*?"

She threw the truck in reverse and laid her right

arm on the seat to back out of the parking space. "Your dad."

Krista broke into a grin. "Cool!"

"So what do you think?" Carl Steinman sat behind the wheel of the company car, as he called it. It was a light blue unmarked Crown Victoria that screamed "cop." They were still parked in front of the Morris house. Pricey, nestled right in old Annapolis. They had interviewed Lorraine Morris, Carrie's mother, and come out knowing nothing more than they had known going in.

Jess stared at the brick sidewalk that wound through the tree-lined neighborhood. "I think Dad's probably got her. His office is expecting him in on Friday. It's hard to believe he didn't leave them an emergency number."

"Not if he was planning on abducting his daughter."

She nodded. "I guess you're right, but there's something here." She shook her finger. "Something that just doesn't seem quite right."

"What, because the mother says she doesn't think the dad would take one little girl without the other?"

Jess lifted a shoulder. She was dressed much like Carl in a blue suit, and she was hot in the car in the jacket. "Twin sister had just gone into the house to go to the bathroom. Maybe Pop meant to take both, got scared and just took the one."

Carl watched her carefully. "But you don't think so?"

"I don't know," she said slowly. "My intuition is telling me something isn't right here."

"Well, we've got half of Florida looking for the father. We'll find him." He started the engine. "In the meantime, what do you want to do?"

She glanced at him as they pulled away from the curb. "I'm thinking we interview Eshey."

"Think Crackhow will go for that?"

"I don't see how he can argue. Carrie's mother mentioned her sister's death today. We can hardly ignore her inquiry. And Crackhow did put us on this case to look into Eshey."

"You don't just want to send anyone from the Newark field office to do the interview?"

She unhooked her seat belt, slipped out of her suit jacket, and snapped the belt again. "I think I want to see him for myself, Carl, if that's OK with you." She thought about her father and how he had said the man had haunted him because he had seemed too pleasant, so incapable of such a horrific murder. It had always bothered her father that he had not been able to get Eshey on any of the other kidnappings and murders.

So did Jess want to do this for Mrs. Morris—or for her dad?

"I'm not trying to trivialize your concerns, here, Syd, but I really think we've got nothing to worry about." Joel leaned back in the chair, his cigarette glowing in the dark. They were out on the second floor redwood deck that ran the length of the house on the ocean side. A cool breeze blew in off the water, and they could hear the crash of the outgoing tide.

Sydney pulled her bare feet up and tucked them beneath her on the cushioned glider. She clutched the zip-up gray sweatshirt, not sure if she was cold or if fear made her shiver. The left side of her brain totally agreed with Joel. It wasn't right that Eshey was out. It wasn't fair. But he was a sick old man. He was no danger to Krista. What happened in Annapolis—just a terrible coincidence. But the right side of Sydney's brain, her maternal instinct, felt a darkness that she couldn't shrug off. Something deep in the pit of her stomach told her she should be afraid.

Sydney reached for her Diet Pepsi, took a sip. She could hear the TV on in the living room. Krista was watching a Brad Pitt movie. Her daughter had every one he'd ever made on tape.

"You're right," Sydney said. "I know you're right." She looked across the balcony at the man she had once loved passionately. "But what if you're wrong?"

He gazed out toward the ocean. "If it will make you feel safer, I'll move back in."

She pressed her lips together, thinking that was all she needed right now. She was just learning how to be on her own, to depend on herself. She and Krista were just getting so that they could have breakfast together without getting into a shouting match over why Sydney had kicked her father out of the house. "Joel—"

"A hundred fifty-seven days, Syd. Not a drop in a hundred fifty-seven days."

His tone was close to begging, and she didn't want to make him beg. Didn't want to hear him beg. "Joel," she said softly. "Let's not get into this tonight."

He put out his cigarette in his empty soda can and came over to sit beside her on the glider. He slid his arm around her shoulder and she didn't shrug it off. Right now, she could use the hug.

"I didn't mean in your bed," he said quietly. "Though that would be nice, too."

He was grinning like the college boy she had fallen in love with her sophomore year at the University of Delaware. He was so damned handsome. Could be so charming. He had also nearly destroyed not just his own life but hers and Krista's with his drinking, over-spending, and womanizing.

"No, it's all right," she said. "I know you're right. I have nothing to be afraid of. How could Eshey know where we are? Know where the little girl in Annapolis was? He's been out only a few weeks." She shook her head, trying desperately to convince the pit of her stomach that what she said was true. "Just coincidence. Tragic coincidence," she repeated, as if she could convince herself by merely speaking the words.

Krista appeared in the light in the doorway. "I'm going to make popcorn. You guys want some?" She was smiling. She loved having her dad around, especially now that he was sober.

Sydney wished she could slide out from under Joel's arm, but she couldn't without making it obvious. She hoped that Krista couldn't see that well in the dark. "No thanks, hon."

Joel made no attempt to move away, and Sydney felt as if he was playing her against their daughter. He knew how badly Krista wanted them to be together again. "None for me, slugger."

Krista rolled her eyes and went back into the house.

Sydney jumped up. "Well, thanks for coming over." She backed up against the balcony railing, drawing the sweatshirt around her again. As she stepped back, her foot struck a softball and she stumbled.

Joel stuck out his arm to steady her. "That your subtle hint for me to go?"

She kicked the softball out from under her foot and it rolled under the glider. The damned things were all over the house. It was one of the dangers of living with a thirteen-year-old softball fanatic. She lifted one shoulder. "I didn't get a lot of work done today. I think I'll go downstairs and see if I can peck out a few pages."

What she really wanted to do was go on-line and see what she could find on Eshey. On the details of her sister's murder. She'd only been twelve when it had happened, and her parents had rightfully hidden most of the particulars. But Sydney needed to know them now. It was the only way to protect Krista. Knowledge, after all, was power. And she was feeling powerless now, as powerless as she had that hot June afternoon when the bastard had carried Marla off.

"All right. I'll go, but you'll call me if you need me. Even if you just need to talk."

He smiled that handsome smile of his, and she had the irrational thought to ask him to stay the night. Not just in the house, but in her bed. God how she missed him in her bed.

So maybe she wasn't as over him as she thought she was . . .

"'Night." Sydney remained in the dark listening as Joel said good-bye to their daughter. Since he had moved out more than a year ago, he had become Krista's hero, while Sydney had become the wicked witch of the west, Freddy Kruger, and the Borg all rolled up into one.

The self-help books Sydney had read on divorce stated this was not uncommon. Custodial parents were normally the ones left with the responsibility of homework, chores, and discipline. It was only natural a child would like the noncustodial parent, the fun parent, better.

That didn't mean Sydney had to like it.

She waited until she heard the front door open and close and then headed downstairs to her office.

Charles Eshey sat down on the single chair at the table and carefully folded back the page from the news magazine he'd stolen from the mini-mart where he worked. He chuckled to himself as he ripped it carefully out and smoothed the page on the rickety table in the one-lightbulb room he rented in Hoboken. Staring at the page, he reached for the bottle of Mad Dog and took a swig.

Slowly he eased out of his chair, staring at the face of the pretty little blond girl. He carried the article to the refrigerator, where he used a carrot magnet left by the previous renter to secure it.

"That's one," he muttered to himself proudly. He tipped back the bottle of Mad Dog and took another swallow, wiping his mouth with the back of his hand. He was so proud. He just couldn't stop grinning.

Four

Sydney pushed her reading glasses up onto the bridge of her nose and reached for her soda can, not taking her eyes off the computer screen. She had found very little on the Marla Baker murder on the Internet; just dates, vague details she already knew, and information on Eshey's conviction. What she did find was that a book on her sister's death, authored by a Marshall King, had been published in '77.

Twin Murders.

"You gruesome son of a bitch," Sydney muttered, hitting the search button on the on-line bookstore site. What kind of man profited from the murder of a little girl like this? As the computer searched for the book title and its availability, Sydney pulled off her glasses and rubbed her eyes.

She'd set the security alarm on the house and checked it since Krista went to bed. She knew they were perfectly safe. They had neighbors on both sides of them and an elaborate alarm system that even had motion detectors. She didn't own a gun, but she wondered if she ought to take some sort of training and buy one. The only gun she knew about was a Glock pistol, and she was only familiar with it because one of her favorite authors always put them in the hands of the characters in his books.

The cover of the paperback bestseller *Twin Murders* popped up on the screen. Sydney grabbed her glasses and peered closer. There was a picture of the cover: the front grill of a tractor-trailer covered in blood, which was stupid. Eshey hadn't run over his victims. That much she knew. He only used the tractor to carry them off.

She scrolled down the page to see a photo of the author. He was good looking, with dark hair, dark eyes, and movie-star smile. Of course, it was taken twenty-five years ago. The man was probably bald by now and being fitted for dentures.

She stared into his eyes on the computer screen. Where did he get enough information to write an entire book about the murders and Eshey? She didn't recall her mother ever mentioning being interviewed by a writer. That didn't mean Cora hadn't given an interview—especially if she'd been offered cash.

Sydney made a mental note to ask Cora about it on their next visit. She doubted her mother would offer any information, even if she remembered anything, but it was worth a try.

Sydney located a brief description of the book at the bottom of the screen. "A gripping tale of the life of a killer and the death of innocent girls," it read. Her stomach flip-flopped.

She read to the bottom of the screen.

The book was out of print. Of course it was.

"Ah hell," she muttered. She tried to find a used copy, but to no avail. "Must have sold like wildfire," she muttered. "Or they only printed a thousand copies . . ."

Next she typed in the author's name on her favorite search engine and came up with a web site. There was a brief description, with covers of several true-crime books he'd written, and it contained an e-mail address.

She switched screen names to the one she used for fan mail; she liked her privacy. She typed a quick note.

My name's Sydney. Twin Murders *tells my sister's story. May I ask you some questions?*

She stared at the screen for a moment wondering if she really wanted to open this can of worms, then hit "send."

She put her computer into sleep mode, flipped off the lights, and went upstairs in the dark. The kitchen light was out, but an outside security lamp cast a ring of dim light on the hardwood floor. Now what? she wondered. Write out bills? Clean out a cabinet? Watch something mindless on TV?

None of her choices sounded appealing, but they were all better bets than actually getting some sleep tonight.

The task was done. He was proud of his work.

They were proud.

Now the body had to be dealt with. He knew the previous MO, what the police called the method of operation. It was how the cops found you. How they arrested you, convicted you, and threw you into jail to rot through the best years of your life. But if the MO was altered—if you were clever enough—there was less likelihood of getting caught.

Of course there were reasons for the MO. These were not random, spontaneous killings. A long time ago the bodies had been left to be found, but that was risky.

That was why he had changed the MO. He could outsmart the local police. The FBI, when they were called in.

There would be no body for evidence. The body would just be gone.

He picked up the limp, cold body that seemed to weigh nothing more than a sack of groceries. It was beyond rigor mortis now and quite flexible. As he turned in the darkness, he felt the blond hair brush his arm and he shivered.

He didn't like the feeling. It rattled him.

He quickly put the body down with a thump and looked around for an old towel. Finding one, he wrapped the head in the towel and picked up the body again.

He knew exactly how he would dispose of it so that there would be no evidence. He would do it the way he had done the last one—an experiment that had been a success. Not a speck left when he was done.

He smiled at his own cleverness.

Sydney tucked her Annapolis *Times* under her arm and balanced her cup of black coffee while she unlocked the car door. She'd dropped Krista off at school because the thought of putting her on the school bus hadn't been acceptable this morning. Now she was headed home to work, but not before she scanned the newspaper.

She slid in behind the wheel, put down the cup that was hot despite the paper ring, slammed the door, and locked it. She spread open the paper and scanned quickly. Nothing on the front page. She flipped the pages, the smell of ink mixing with the rich scent of her coffee, making her glad she hadn't eaten breakfast.

Her stomach lurched as she found the headline she'd been looking for. LOBBYIST'S DAUGHTER STILL MISSING.

After a week of searching, authorities still have very few clues. Her father, Edward Morris, recently divorced from custodial parent Mrs. Lorraine Morris, is thought to be on vacation in Florida. Police are currently attempting to contact Mr. Morris.

The article did not say police suspected Carrie's father of kidnapping her, but it went on to cite the statistics on the kidnapping of children by noncustodial parents.

Sydney tossed the paper aside. Maybe her father had taken her.

But why would he take her out of the back yard where she'd been playing in her tree house? Why take her without any of her clothes or toys? Most parents who kidnapped their own children did so while exercising their visitation rights. Had Edward Morris taken his daughter and just made it look like a kidnapping so he wouldn't be a suspect? If so, why only one daughter? His favorite?

Sydney knew about favorites. Marla had always been her parents' favorite. She had been well behaved, never difficult the way Sydney had been. After Marla was gone, Sydney had spent many a night lying alone in the bed she had once shared with her sister, wondering if her mother and father wished it had been her Eshey had taken and not Marla.

Sydney forced herself to set those memories aside and think of Carrie again. If the father had taken her, what kind of sick fuck was he, to do that to the mother of their child?

Or was it Eshey?

Sydney felt a chill of fear. She knew it was unfounded and unreasonable, and yet she couldn't shake it. She gripped the steering wheel in indecision. Irrational as it was, her first impulse was to go back to school and pick Krista up. This was the last week of school. What harm would it do? They weren't doing anything, anyway.

But if she picked up Krista, she'd have to give her daughter some explanation. She wasn't ready to do that. Krista knew her mother had had a twin sister, but Sydney had told her she had died, not been murdered. It had seemed perfectly logical at the time—the little white lie. Now it seemed overwhelming.

Sydney pressed her forehead to the center of the steering wheel, her heart pounding in her ears. She breathed deeply.

She thought about what the news magazine she'd read earlier in the week had said about the incident being a tragic coincidence. It was what Joel said, too. And she wanted to believe it. Sweet Mary, Mother of God, but she wanted to believe it.

As her heart slowed to an acceptable pace, her reasoning took over.

Of course she couldn't take Krista out of school because some little girl had been kidnapped in Maryland. That wouldn't make sense to anyone; it didn't even make sense to her. That kind of crime took place every day in metropolitan areas. That was why she had settled in little old humdrum southern Delaware to begin with. It was a safe place to raise her daughter.

Sydney started the car, backed out of the doughnut shop parking lot, and roared down the street, her thoughts racing. So what did she do now? Should she ignore the whole thing, chalk up this feeling in the pit of her stomach to paranoia, and get to work on her book? Should she take Krista out of school and go to Europe? She'd thought about taking a trip to England in August. Maybe they should go for the whole summer. Or should she choose the middle of the road?

She liked to think of herself as a middle-of-the-road kind of person. Paranoia wasn't really her style. But then, letting a murderer like Eshey get his filthy hands on her child wasn't, either.

By the time Sydney got home, deactivated the security alarm, and got down to her office, she'd come up with what she thought to be a reasonable plan. She'd talk to Krista about safety again without mentioning Eshey, and she'd let Krista go about her activities while keeping her on a tight rein.

She didn't want to scare her daughter. She didn't want her daughter growing up frightened of her own shadow the way she had. Hell, Sydney hadn't slept in the dark after Marla was taken until she started sleeping with Joel in college. All through her teen years, she'd been convinced that Eshey would get out of prison and come after her . . . take the girl he *should* have taken to begin with.

No, Sydney wasn't going to do that to Krista. But she wasn't going to stick her head in the sand, either. She'd continue her investigation into the murders, not just Marla's, but those involving children Eshey had been suspected of taking but hadn't been convicted of killing. She'd learn everything she could about Eshey. About how he worked, what his motivation had been for killing those little girls. *Know thy enemy* came to mind as she sat down to her computer and logged on to the Internet.

Sydney flipped through her mail at one address, then changed her screen name to the one she had used to write to the author Marshall King. She scrolled down the list of twelve e-mails, all titled things like "loved your book." She broke into a grin. The very last e-mail was from an M. King. He must have sent it this morning after she checked her mail before taking Krista to school.

Sydney—
I'm intrigued by your note. Can you verify that you are, indeed, Sydney Baker?

M. King

Sydney's first reaction was anger. She let out a string of curses and stared at the e-mail. Proof? What kind of proof did he want? Then she realized that if he was any kind of journalist, he would certainly ask for some sort of proof. She was pleased to see that he wasn't willing to talk with just anyone about her sister's murder.

Sydney stared at the flat screen computer monitor, trying to keep a distance from the memories, but feeling herself being dragged in. Taking a deep breath, she forced herself to type a reply to M. King.

*It was a hot day. I remember the stench of the baking asphalt through the open window of the car. My sister was in the front seat, wearing a sleeveless T-shirt. Pink stripes. It was tight, thin, and worn. I was in the back seat of the car reading a book I'd gotten from the library—*The Count of Monte Cristo. *I never finished it. When Eshey opened the car door, the metal screeched like an animal. Marla didn't even scream. I screamed for her.*

Sydney wiped the perspiration from her upper lip and went on.

I tried to get out of the car. To save her. But he slammed the door on my ankle. He broke it in two places. They gave me a cherry popsicle at the emergency room. I walked on crutches for weeks. I remember her pale red hair stuck to her sweaty cheek as he carried her off. Hair the same color as my thirteen-year-old daughter's.
I need your help.

Sydney didn't read what she had written. She didn't even sign the note. She just sent it. Then, unsure if she could deal with his answer right now, she went off line and pulled up the next chapter of her book. Work. Work was what she needed. It was the only way to keep the ghosts at bay.

Five

Marshall King poured himself a cup of black coffee from the coffeemaker and crossed the room of his Village loft to his desk. He had an article for an amateur detective rag to get in and he'd been up half the night going over the next scenes in his novel. He was hoping to break into the suspense market, but so far, the going was slow. Thank God for the royalties on the true crime books he'd written in the seventies and eighties. Otherwise he'd be living with his parents in Jersey City.

Marshall set his mug on the small hot plate beside his keyboard and rested his fingers on the keys. But instead of pulling up the article he needed to finish, he flipped to his Internet screen. He only had one phone line, so when he left the computer on-line no one could get through. Not that it mattered. There wasn't anyone he particularly wanted to speak to.

He had two ex-wives who called only when the child support payment or the alimony was late. A shit for a son who worked for a computer software company in California during the week and got high on the weekends. Then there was the daughter in high school in Miami, but she rarely called and then it was only to thank him for a birthday gift or to ask for money. Marshall had been seeing a woman for a couple of months, but Lorna was in Connecticut this week, moving her parents to a nursing home.

It was a pathetic little life, but it was his.

He heard the familiar sound of *you've got mail* and vowed to take the time to figure out how to shut it off. He was hoping for a note from a woman who had e-mailed him claiming to be Marla Baker's surviving sister. He doubted it really was her. With twelve successful true crime novels, he'd run into his share of nut jobs over the years. This was probably another, but still, he was curious. He hadn't gotten mail in years for *Twin Murders*. Its last reissue had been more than a decade ago, so unless the woman dug up an ancient copy at a yard sale somewhere, she might just be for real.

He scanned the list of e-mails, and sure enough "Sydney" had responded. She posted under the name Fool366. He chuckled as he opened the post; sometimes the nut jobs were just so damned obvious.

Marshal groped for his reading glasses on a pile of unopened mail. As he read the letter through the lower edge of his bifocals, he reached for his cup of coffee. The hot liquid burned his lip as he took his first sip.

The first words of the e-mail gave him chills.

My sister was in the front seat, wearing a sleeveless T-shirt. Pink stripes. It was tight, thin, and worn.

He set down his coffee and reached to the right of his desk where there was bookshelf where he proudly displayed his published books. His first published novel, *Twin Murders,* hadn't been a best-seller, but *Axe Man* and *Darkness Waits* had. He quickly flipped through the pages of the book to the description of the twelve-year-old Marla's clothing. He had described the shirt as a pink K-mart—but nothing about stripes. He dropped the book on his desk and returned to the e-mail.

They gave me a cherry popsicle at the emergency room.

There was something so eerie about her simple words that it made him shiver. He could almost taste the popsicle. Sweet. Cold. He could feel the terror that she did not speak of, but which he knew lay just below the surface of her innocuous words.

The popsicle wasn't a detail he'd put in the book. Not a detail he'd even known. Was it for real? He'd researched the Marla Baker murder for a year, followed the trial day to day, and never heard anything about a cherry popsicle. In truth, he'd gotten very little about the sister, Sydney. The hag of a mother hadn't been willing to talk about the surviving daughter, not even for the money he had provided her up front before the book was sold.

I remember her pale red hair stuck to her sweaty cheek as he carried her off. Hair the same color as my thirteen-year-old daughter's.

Goosebumps rose on Marshall's forearms. He didn't get spooked easily. He'd interviewed rapists, serial killers, even a man who had chopped his wife up into little pieces, put her into Ziploc bags, and clearly marked them with indelible ink before freezing them. But this spooked him.

I need your help.

Marshall hit reply. He'd never done this in his life; he was always so careful to protect his own privacy. *Call me.* He typed his number, sent the message, and logged off to free up the line.

Marshall paced the loft, finished up his short story, printed it, and paced some more. He did a hundred fifty sit-ups and forty military push-ups. He'd had to drop the health club membership a few months ago to cut costs, but he was still trying to stay in shape. He ate a little Chinese take-out left over from the previous night and paced some more.

The phone rang around six. He let it ring twice, giving himself a moment to collect his thoughts, before he picked it up. "Marshall King." He didn't know why he said his name; he didn't usually. Didn't know why he was suddenly nervous, either.

"Mr. King, this is Sydney MacGregor . . . I was Sydney Baker."

She had a sexy voice, husky. If this really were Sydney Baker, she would be about ten years younger than he was. Marla was killed in '74 when the girls were twelve, so that made her about forty now.

"Thanks for being willing to talk to me," she said. She sounded as if she'd been running.

He carried the cordless phone to the window so he could look down on the street below. Taxicabs honked. New Yorkers, all dressed as if they were going to funerals, hustled up and down the sidewalks. How many people still smoked, considering the proof that it would eventually kill you, still amazed him. He'd never smoked. He had other vices.

He listened to the voice on the other end of the line, trying to get a feel for her. She didn't sound like a crazy so far. "What can I do for you, Mrs. MacGregor?"

"Sydney," she said softly as if someone were listening in. "It's just Sydney."

"Okay, *Sydney.*"

She exhaled and the line was quiet for a moment, so quiet that he wondered if she had hung up and he hadn't heard the click. He was getting that creepy feeling again.

Then he heard her inhale. She took a great swallow of air and talked rapidly. "I'd like to get some information from you on my sister's death. You see, my parents never told me much." She took another breath. "Mr. King, he's out. Did you know that? Eshey has been paroled."

"Holy shit," he muttered without thinking. He grimaced. "Pardon my language."

She laughed a husky laugh that seemed laced with an odd mixture of relief and sheer terror. "It's OK. My New Year's resolution this year was to cut down the use of the f-word. It's my favorite word, right after ice cream."

He found himself chuckling with her. "So how you doing on that New Year's resolution?"

"Not as well as I was. Not since I found out about Eshey."

Marshall walked to his desk and grabbed a notepad and a pen. He didn't know yet how this had anything to do with him, but his instinct told him to pay close attention. "You say he was paroled. When? How? He got life. I know that doesn't mean life, but I didn't expect him out so soon. I didn't even know he was even eligible for parole yet."

"Me either. The state victims services somehow screwed up. Something about the new 911 address changes and an entry error. I was never notified about the parole hearing or his release. He was let out in mid April, according to his parole officer."

"I know the news has to be unsetting to you," Marshall murmured, feeling a strange connection with this woman he had never met.

"It gets better." She paused again. "I see from your number that you're in New York City. You probably don't get much local news from the Baltimore/Washington area there, but a little girl was kidnapped in Annapolis."

He grimaced, his nutball alarm going off in his head. "So?" he wanted to say. Sad fact was, little girls were kidnapped every day. What did that have to do with Eshey?

"I know," she said seeming to hear his thoughts.

"Little girls disappear all the time. Except that this little girl's aunt, Patricia, was kidnapped and murdered in 1972, two years before my sister. Eshey was suspected in the crime."

He knew Patricia Brown's name as well as he knew his own. She was right; Eshey was suspected of killing the eleven-year-old girl. Victims' names always stuck in his head, even years later. Even though he wished they wouldn't.

"And you think Eshey kidnapped this little girl? How old is he? Like a hundred?" He didn't mean to sound so cynical—it just came out that way. Maybe because he *was* so damned cynical.

If she took offense, he didn't hear it in her voice. "He's sixty-two and supposedly has some kind of heart disease. That's part of the reason he was paroled early."

"That and prison overcrowding and the fact that he's been *rehabilitated*, right?" Marshall muttered sarcastically.

"Exactly, Mr. King. You ought to be working for our prison system. You have precisely the right attitude. Everyone deserves a second chance to kill." Her tone was equally biting.

Against all reason, Marshal liked this woman. She was tough, gritty, and clever. "I think you'd better call me Marshall," he said.

"All right, Marshall, listen. Right now the papers are suggesting the girl's father took her. Apparently her parents recently divorced and the mother got custody. Now, no one has come right out and said it, but the police are looking for him. He's thought to be vacationing in Florida." She took a deep breath. "I don't know. The whole idea is crazy. I know that." There was suddenly desperation in her voice. "But what if the father doesn't have her?"

"Sydney, I don't mean to discount the pain you've been through, but—"

"Marshall, the little girl who is missing, she has a twin, too. The twin was left behind, the same way I was left behind."

He cursed again.

"Yeah," she muttered. "I'll drink to that. Find last week's *Newsweek*. There's a little article in it about the girl. They say this is a tragic coincidence, her mother being a surviving twin."

"But you don't think so?"

She exhaled. "Marshall, I don't know. But I have a daughter. Did I tell you that? She's thirteen and she's my whole life, and I am not going to let that son of a bitch take her from me. I'm not going to let him do this to me again. *I won't be a victim again.*"

The force of Sydney's last words made him wish she were here in the room. Wish he could touch her. Comfort her in some way. "I don't know what to say," he said after a moment. "Have you talked to the police?"

She took a deep breath and when she spoke, she was totally in control again. "I talked to his parole officer, who insists Eshey is safely in New Jersey. He works and is now the *model citizen.* I have absolutely no proof. Right now if I went to the police, I'd just sound like a paranoid mother." She was breathing easier now. "So what I need from you, Marshall, if you're willing, is some information. This really could all just be a coincidence, but I'll feel better if I have more details. If I know what I'm up against, or if I really am up against anything. Once I'm more knowledgeable, then I'll contact the police if I still think this could be Eshey."

He nodded, looking down at his notepad. He'd written Sydney's name, Eshey's name, and a list of the victims' names he still knew by heart after all these years: Tracy Ponds, Patricia Brown, Anna

Paulie Carpenter, Mary Elizabeth Truitt, Maureen Naples, and Spring Jackson. There were seven girls in all over four years' time, Marla Baker being the last. But there wasn't enough evidence to charge him with all seven kidnappings and murders and he never confessed to any of them, so the state had decided just to prosecute on the Baker case. It was the twelve-year-old Sydney's testimony in a closed courtroom, her detail of Eshey, his bad tooth, his buzz haircut, his West Virginia accent, that had sent him to jail for what was supposed to be a life sentence.

So what if Eshey *was* killing again? Hell, a story like that would put him on the *Times* list for twelve weeks straight.

He immediately felt guilty for having thought such a thing. But truth was truth.

"Tell me how I can help," Marshall said. He told himself it was just for the book. But the truth was, there was something in Sydney's voice that made him want to help her.

"I guess the first thing I need is a copy of your book. I can't find one on the Internet." She gave a little laugh. "I know that's pretty bold, but if you send me one, I can send you, let's see . . . *A Fool's Guide to Planning Your Wedding*, *A Fool's Guide to Picking the Right Summer Camp*, and, if I make my deadline, *A Fool's Guide to Planning Your Next Family Vacation*."

He dropped his pen and reached to the floor to grab it. "You write those? You're kidding me! You're Mallory Moore?"

"My alter ego."

"Hey, I'm impressed."

He thought he could hear her smile.

"If you could send me a book, that would be great," she said. " I mean it's fact, right? You don't make crap up?"

He smiled, not in the least bit offended. "I don't make crap up, not for the true-crime books. I have always been careful about the facts in all of my books." He shrugged. "Maybe I added a little drama to the text, but it's all true, to the best of my ability."

"So where'd you get the information?"

"Most was common record. I had just dropped out of college and was hungry. I followed the newspapers, talked to the local cops and the FBI. Sat in on the trial."

"Did you talk to my mom or my dad?"

"Your father never agreed to an interview, not with anyone."

It was her turn to curse. "So my mother sold out to you. Good ol' Cora, always looking out for herself."

"It wasn't that much money," he said quietly.

"Marshall, if I had come to interview you after your daughter had been kidnapped, raped, tortured, and then left to die in a hotel room while her kidnapper went out for fried chicken, would you have talked to me?"

"Not in a million years."

She was quiet on the other end of the line for a moment. "So after I read the book, maybe we can talk?"

"Definitely." He scribbled *Sydney MacGregor* on the notepad. "Give me your address. I'll overnight it."

"I can't tell you how much I appreciate this."

He copied down her address. The call was pretty much over, but he wasn't sure how to end it. Didn't really want to.

She did it for him. "Well, thanks Marshall. I'll call you."

He hung up and stared down at the street below. He had been hoping, no praying, for a break to kick start his stale writing career. Now he felt sick to his stomach. If there was any truth to Sydney's suspicions . . . God help them, he wouldn't have wished this on anyone.

Marshall dialed a phone number and waited.

"'Lo."

"Have I got John or James?" The two boys sounded so much alike that he couldn't tell them apart on the phone.

"James," the teen said on the other end of the line.

"Mom home from work?"

"Sure, Marshall. Just got home. I'll get her."

He heard a clunk as the phone hit the counter. A second later Renee picked up. "Hey," she said. "Long time no talk."

"Yeah, well, I've been busy. You know, the book and all." He walked to the window and pulled the drapes. "Which is why I was calling."

"Uh-huh? John, get the milk."

"James said you just got off work. I was thinking you might like to come down for a glass of wine after the boys go to bed."

"That would be nice."

"See you about nine?" he said.

"See you then."

Marshall hung up the phone and went to kitchen to grab a cheap bottle of chardonnay out from under the cabinet to stick in the fridge. He had invited Renee up for a glass of wine, but she knew what she'd really been invited for. A quick roll in the bed, a little fun, then back to her own apartment with her boys.

Marshall liked Renee. She was in her mid-thirties and a single mom who worked long hours at St. Mary's hospital as a nurse. She didn't have the time or the energy for a relationship. She just needed a warm shoulder and a good lay once in a while to combat the loneliness.

It was the perfect arrangement, especially on nights like tonight, when Marshall didn't want to be alone, either.

Six

Marshall King's book arrived two days later, and Sydney read the whole thing in one sitting. By the time she arrived at school to pick up Krista, she'd already started taking notes. Her head was pounding when she pulled up in front of the school, her stomach queasy. She'd thrown up her breakfast ten minutes into the book and had managed to get nothing else down all day but some hot tea and a few Saltines.

Sydney had been so horrified, so angered, so disgusted by all she had read that, at the moment, she felt absolutely nothing. She was spent. Numb. The details of King's book were gruesome. She would have liked to have thought they were embellished, played up for effect, but she feared he had simply done what he had claimed. Told the truth.

The bile rose in Sydney's throat as mental pictures of Marla and Eshey flashed through her mind. Terror. Blood. Pain. She fought the images, concentrating on thoughts of the beach at dawn. She breathed, panting the way she had been taught in Lamaze class all those years ago when she had prepared for her own daughters' births. The nausea passed.

There was a sound at the car door, and Sydney nearly leaped out of her skin.

"Can I stay with Katie tonight?" Krista jumped into the car, throwing her backpack over the seat. She didn't even realize she'd startled her mother. "Go home with her after practice?"

Sydney swallowed hard and her heart settled back into her chest cavity where it belonged. "Well, hello to you, too." She waited for Krista to buckle her seat belt, then locked the doors with the automatic button at her fingertips, and pulled out onto the street. "My day? It was great. How about yours?" She glanced at her daughter.

Krista rolled her eyes and muttered something under her breath. She spoke as if she were being held at gunpoint. "Hi, Mom. How was your day?"

"It sucked."

Krista frowned. "Hey, hey! Watch your mouth. I thought you gave up cursing."

"Suck isn't cursing. I heard Pastor Mike say suck last Sunday in his sermon."

"I'm not allowed to say suck."

Sydney signaled and turned onto Route One, the main highway through town. "You're right, you're not. And no, you may not spend the night with Katie. It's a school night."

"For criminy sakes! Tomorrow is the last day of school! Mom, we don't even take our backpacks." She crossed her arms over her chest, where tiny breasts seemed to have popped up overnight.

She was changing so quickly, Sydney's little girl. She was so difficult to deal with sometimes, but Sydney loved her so much. Loved her more than anything on this earth.

Sydney bit down on her lower lip, glad she was wearing sunglasses so Krista couldn't see the tears in her eyes. She had to get a grip on herself.

"You argue with me over the Katie thing and you'll

spend the entire summer under my roof." Sydney waggled her finger. "Vacation has not officially started, and the rule is no sleepovers on school nights."

"What's with you?" Krista grumped. "PMSing again?" The teen stared straight ahead. "You're being totally unreasonable. *Again.*"

Sydney knew that Krista was closer to the truth than she wanted to admit, but she couldn't let her daughter out of her sight. Not today. Not after she'd read what Eshey had done to Marla.

Sydney bit down on her lower lip as her stomach did flip-flops again. God, she wished she hadn't read King's book. Thank God she had. Now she knew just what an animal Eshey was.

"But because summer vacation officially begins tomorrow, I did want to ask you what you would think about going to England. Maybe Paris."

Krista glanced sideways at her mother as if she'd grown horns. *"When?"*

Sydney thought of the little girl who was missing. She thought about what she learned from the book. If Eshey had kidnapped Patricia Brown's niece, Sydney could only imagine what he had done. The book had discussed some of the other killings that had been attributed to him. His MO had been similar each time, but he was a creative man. Had he become more inventive in the years he had spent thinking about little girls, socializing with other child murderers?

Sydney forced herself to focus on Krista and the conversation at hand. She tried to sound casual. "I don't know. I'll have to check the Internet for tickets."

"What about your stupid book?" Krista muttered. "I thought you had a deadline."

"I could take my laptop, work at night in hotels."

Sydney forced a smile, trying to make the whole idea seem appealing. "We could make a whole summer of it."

"Are you nuts?"

Sydney flashed her daughter a look that even from behind sunglasses Krista would recognize as proof she'd crossed the line.

Krista looked down at her tennis shoes. "Sorry. It's just that I'm sure I'm going to make All-Stars. Mom, it's what I've always wanted. You know that."

Sydney gripped the wheel tighter and groaned. Krista had worked hard to improve her softball skills. She didn't have as much natural talent as some of the other girls her age, but she seemed to make up for it with her bullheaded determination. She practiced longer than the others, harder, and it was paying off. Even Sydney, who had known nothing about softball before Krista became involved two years ago, could see it.

"Well, I'll check the prices, see what's available, and then we can talk about it. When are All-Star picks?"

"The regular season runs another two weeks. You know that. Picks aren't 'til the end of the season." Krista reached over the back of her seat to her back-pack and pulled her personal CD player out of the pocket.

When the CD player came out, Sydney knew she was about to be formally dismissed. "I said we'd talk about it."

"You mean *you and Dad* will talk about it." Krista pushed the ear buds into her ears. "It's not like I have any say, anyway." She hit the play button on the CD player and rock music rang out of both of her ears.

Sydney gripped the steering wheel tighter. She needed to talk to Joel. She'd get him to read the book, and then they could talk. She was afraid she was too emotional now, too close to the whole mess to see anything clearly. Right now, she was going home for beer.

"Mr. Eshey, come in." The blond woman with pale blue eyes pointed to a chair in front of her desk.

She'd be prettier if she wore makeup. Charlie shuffled in and sat down. He had gotten good at the walk, watching other old folks. A man's walk could be so telling. So misleading, too, if you were clever enough. "Afternoon, ma'am." He pulled off the tan ball cap that was part of his work uniform. His mother had raised him to be a gentleman. It had been beaten into him with a stick in the hills of West Virginia. "I want to thank ya for lettin' me change my appointment the other day. Like I said on the phone, had to cover for a guy who got sick."

She flipped though some files on her desk. He could see his name and Social Security number neatly printed on a folder. Purple ink. "I appreciate your calling and changing the appointment rather than simply not showing up. You understand that by not making an appointment with me, you'd be in violation of parole. New Jersey's parole program is strict, Mr. Eshey. You could be sent back to prison for missing a single appointment with me."

"Yup. Yup, I understand that perfect, ma'am. That's why I called you. When they said Fred was sick and I had to come in, I said to my supervisor, I said, 'Mr. Devane, I got to talk to my parole officer first.'" He glanced at a bowl of miniature chocolate bars on her desk.

"Oh, please, help yourself." She smiled.

Pretty teeth. Nice titties. Perky, but small. He liked 'em small. Just a mouthful was enough.

He took a Hershey candy bar. He liked Hershey milk chocolate, too. There were all kinds of fancy new candy bars out these days, ones that had come out all those years he'd been in prison. But Hershey he knew. He let the chocolate melt in his mouth, warm and sweet, savoring every bite. It was a lot easier eating with these nice new choppers the state had given him.

"So how is your job, Mr. Eshey? Are you enjoying your position as a janitorial engineer?"

He bobbed his head. "It ain't bad. I push a broom. Pick up trash people throw in the grass. I hate people who litter, don't you, Miss Carmack?" Truth was, he despised the job. He hated cleaning up other people's crap. Hated scrubbing urinals that other people had pissed in. But he liked being at the turnpike rest stop. He liked seeing all the little girls come and go. Liked seeing the trucks pull in, fuel, and pull out headed for only the Almighty knew where. It reminded him of the days when he'd been a truck driver. He'd loved being a truck driver. The open road. The freedom. He longed for those days again.

"And you're making out fine with your apartment?"

"Twice as big as my cell." He grinned. "I near get lost in the night trying to find the john."

She smiled at his joke. "And you're following the routine we planned together? You've not left the state, of course?"

He chuckled. "My driver license expired back in '75. I take the bus to work. Take the bus home. I walk to the market. Bought myself a half pint of Mad Dog the other night." He winked.

She smiled, charmed. He'd always been able to charm the ladies. That was his mistake with Marla.

He'd gotten overly anxious and snatched her instead of just luring her into his truck with his charm, the way he usually did, and then the other one had started screaming. He didn't make many mistakes, but he'd regret that one till the day he looked St. Peter in the eye.

"Keep in mind, Mr. Eshey, overindulgence leads to bad choices."

"Oh, I ain't much of a drinker. Just had a mind for a taste. " He took a deep breath, adding a little wheeze to it. Truth was, he felt good. Better than he had in years. But the young missy didn't have to know that. He pressed his hand to his chest.

"Mr. Eshey, are you all right?"

He took another wheezy breath and nodded.

"Just fine, ma'am." He licked his dry lips, going on as if he were feeling much better now that he had caught his breath. "I got me a cat. I tell you that?"

"No, you didn't."

She pressed her clean white hands on the desk and leaned toward him, flashing a little skin at the V of her shirt. She had freckles. He liked freckles, but not on women. Liked them on little girls.

"I have a cat myself," she told him.

"Do you, now?" He smiled the smile he knew women liked. It showed off his new false teeth. "Make nice friends, don't they? I found her in the alley behind my place. Poor wee thing had been left to die. Call her Tangerine, you know, 'cause of her color."

"I think having a pet is an excellent idea, Mr. Eshey. Responsibility for another leads us to responsibility for ourselves." She wrote something on a paper in his file with her purple ink pen and closed the folder. "Well, I think you're doing quite well." She glanced up, suddenly seeming a little nervous. "There's just one more thing I need you to do."

He waited patiently, because he was good at waiting.

"There are two FBI agents waiting outside who would like to speak with you."

Seven

The FBI? Charlie fought a flutter of panic in his chest. What did they want? He didn't need the f'in FBI in his business.

Miss Carmack didn't make eye contact with him, but pretended to be busy shuffling the files on her desk. "There's been a . . . an incident in Maryland, and they'd like to talk about with you."

"Maryland?" He gave a snort. She'd taken him off guard there for a second, but he was all right. He was calm. All he had to do was stay calm. "I ain't been in Maryland in, well, near on thirty years."

"I understand, Mr. Eshey. But you know how things work with law enforcement. They have to be thorough."

She believed him. It was his smile.

He slid forward on the chair, feeling in complete control again. In fact, at this moment he felt more alive than he had in years. They thought he was an idiot. A stupid, uneducated hick from West Virginia. Well, he was from West Virginia and he certainly was uneducated, but he was not stupid. Not just any man could have killed ten little girls and gotten away with it. He frowned, looking concerned. "You said an incident in Maryland. You mean a murder?"

She rose from her desk. "I think I'd better let Special Agents Manlove and Steinman address that, Mr.

Eshey." She came around from behind her desk in her short skirt with her knobby knees. She pushed open the door. "We're ready for you." She opened the door for a tall, slender man and a short, chunky woman with short, bright orange hair that didn't come natural on God's earth.

Miss Carmack stepped out of the room and closed the door behind her.

The two FBI agents seemed to fill the small office. The woman perched on the corner of the desk right in front of Charlie. She was wearing a navy suit that would have looked like a man's if she'd been wearing a necktie. He wondered if she was one of them queer women.

"Mr. Eshey, I'm FBI Special Agent Manlove and this is Special Agent Steinman. We're out of the Baltimore field office, and we'd like to ask you a few questions."

Charles nodded politely. "Afternoon to you." He met her gaze. "How can I help you? Miss Carmack said you wanted to know 'bout an inc-i-dent in Maryland." He gave a little laugh. "Used to run trucks through there, deliverin' south as far as Richmond. 'Course I ain't been there in a coon's age." He gave her his *smile for the ladies*. They always ate it up. Miss Carmack had, hadn't she? "And you know jest where I been all these years, don't you?"

The cop lady responded the way he expected her to. She just looked back over her shoulder at the man and back at him. She had to be queer as a three dollar bill. "Mr. Eshey, have you left the state of New Jersey since your release from prison?"

"No ma'am. Got no way to leave if I wanted to."

"And you understand that if you left the state, you'd be in violation of your parole and you'd be returned to prison?"

He nodded his head. "I know the rules, ma'am. You

can look fer yourself in my records. 'Course, I know you already done that. I'm what they call a *model prisoner.*"

She didn't take her eyes off him.

"Did you kidnap Carrie Morris from her home in Annapolis, Maryland?"

Charley felt his heart skip a beat. He felt empowered. It was almost like the old days all over again. "Look at me," he said trying to sound sad. He gave a little wheeze for effect. "I'm an old man. Old man with a bum ticker. I couldn't wrestle no flea to the ground, no less kidnap a little girl."

"Answer the question, Mr. Eshey," the tall, quiet one said.

Eshey lifted his head to meet the man's gaze. He wondered why a nice looking man like Special Agent Steinman would let a queer woman wear the pants in the family, so to speak. "No, sir, I did not kidnap no girl named Carrie Morris." He liked the taste of her name on his tongue. Sweet, like that Hershey bar.

The woman looked over her shoulder yet again, then back at him. "That will be all for now, Mr. Eshey, but if we have any more questions for you—"

"Miss Carmack knows jest how to get ahold of me." He stood slowly, like his bones ached, and watched as the two agents left the room. "Good day to you both," he called after them.

Miss Carmack stepped back into office, but left the door open. "Well, I think that's all for today. I'll see you next week?"

"That I will. Now, you have yourself a good day, ma'am." He nodded politely, put his hat back on his head, and shuffled out of the tiny office. As he went down the stairs, he slipped his hand into his back pocket and touched the clipping he'd cut out of the newspaper. It was a school picture of Carrie Morris. Sweet thing. Her aunt had been cute as a button, too.

When he closed his eyes, he could still see the way she had looked at him with her big, frightened blue eyes.

They'd never find Carrie if they hadn't found her by now.

Now, he wondered, how long would it be until the next?

Eight

"You want to take her to Europe?" Joel frowned.

Once upon a time, he would have shouted the words. Maybe thrown something—an insult, at the very least. But Sydney's ex had softened in the months since he stopped drinking and had started going to counseling. She could tell that he was trying to be understanding right now. Trying to be the sensitive ex-husband. She would have almost preferred if he'd thrown something. That she could deal with.

"Sydney," he continued in his sensitive-guy tone, "we agreed we would discuss any major decisions concerning Krista. You might be the custodial parent, but I'm still her father."

She got up from the dining room table and picked up her plate to take to the dishwasher. Krista had already left the table and was sitting out on the deck talking to a friend on the phone.

Sydney slid the glass door to the deck shut so Krista wouldn't hear them. "I didn't say we were going. I said we were thinking about it."

"Don't you think this is a little drastic?"

Sydney knew he was thinking *paranoid*. She flipped on the faucet to rinse her spaghetti down the garbage disposal. She hadn't been able to eat more than a few bites. She gritted her teeth, fighting the terrifying images King had painted in her mind, images that seemed to become more indelible with each passing hour. "I want you to take the book home and read it and then tell me I'm being drastic in thinking I should get my daughter the hell out of here." Her voice cracked with the last word.

"She's our daughter. Remember?"

She couldn't meet his gaze because tears welled in her eyes.

"Ah, hon." Joel walked up behind her and put his arms around her waist.

Her first impulse was to push him away, but right now she needed the hug more than she needed to be strong. She set the wet plate on the counter and leaned back against him, closing her eyes. He felt so big and warm. So protective. That was what she really wanted right now; to be protected, to have Krista protected. She didn't want to do this alone.

Joel had lost weight since he'd quit drinking. Started going to the gym. She could feel the changes in his body. Good changes. She felt a stir of desire and was surprised. It had been so long since they had sex that she could barely remember what it was like.

"Syd, I don't want to read the book," he said softly, his breath warm in her ear. "I don't need to know the gruesome details."

"No, you do need to know what that sick fuck did to Marla."

Joel gently turned her in his arms until she faced him. She let him, because at this moment, she didn't have the strength to fight him. To fight herself.

The faucet continued to run.

"I'll read it if you want me to," he said quietly. "But I think we're moving too quickly here. There is no proof that Krista is in any danger. None whatsoever."

"Haven't you heard anything I've said?" Her voice

was meek. Desperate. "Weren't you listening? The little girl is gone and they have no idea where."

"That does not mean that Eshey killed her, Syd. You
said yourself that the father could have taken her."

"Taken her and not her sister? It doesn't make any
sense."

Sydney pressed her hands to Joel's chest and leaned
her forehead against his chin. She had forgotten how
good he felt.

The glass door slid open and Krista walked into the
kitchen off the deck. Sydney spun around, out of
Joel's arms, and reached shakily to finish rinsing off
the plate.

"Hey, you two making out?" Krista said, walking to
the far counter to hang up the phone.

Joel didn't say anything. It was a conspiracy between
father and daughter. Krista wanted them to get back
together. Joel wanted to get back together. They
played their best hands whenever an opportunity
arose.

"We were not making out." Sydney jerked open the
dishwasher.

"'Cause if you were, I wouldn't be that grossed out,"
she said hopefully.

"Krista, can you excuse us? Your Mom and I were
talking about something important."

"Sure. Whatever. I think I'll go for a walk."

"No," Sydney snapped, turning around. "It's already
after dark. I want you inside."

Krista's gaze flew to her father. "Do you see what
I'm talking about? She still thinks I'm two."

Joel returned to the table to grab the salt and pep-
per and grated Parmesan cheese. "It won't kill you to
stay in."

"I'm not going *out* out. Sheesh! I just wanted to take
a walk around the block. Maybe up onto the beach."

"Not tonight," Joel said firmly.

"Fine!" Krista threw up her arms. "I'm going to my room. Tell me before you go, Dad." She walked out of the kitchen, shouting over her shoulder. "And tell her I'm not going to Europe. Not if she if she ties me up and puts me in the cargo hold in the belly of a plane."

Joel waited until they heard Krista's door close upstairs. "You have to hand it to her. She can be dramatic." It was a teasing tone. He was trying to make light of Krista's antagonism and Sydney's irrational fear that a serial killer was stalking their daughter.

It wasn't working.

Sydney shut off the faucet and reached for a dishtowel to dry her wet hands. "I'm not saying I have to take her out of the country. I'm just saying it could be a possibility, that's all."

"And I'm saying you're moving way too fast." Joel walked to table to bring the bowl of pasta and sauce to the counter. Sydney pulled out plastic storage containers and he began to dump the food into them.

"I mean, don't you think the police have already thought of Eshey?" He looked at her with those dark brown eyes that had once touched her soul. "Don't you think they've talked to him?"

"I don't know what to think." She threw up her hands. "All I know is that it's my job to protect that child." She pointed at the ceiling. "Do whatever I have to do to protect her."

"You sound like a she-lion."

He was teasing her again. She didn't smile.

"Oh, come on. Think about it." He pushed the leftovers containers into her hands for her to put in the fridge. "If Eshey was going to kill again—which apparently he doesn't have the ability to do since he's already got one foot in the grave—would he go after the same families? It doesn't make any sense. He's on parole and being watched. He'd be bound to get caught, and he knows it."

"I don't know why he would do such a thing! I don't know why he would kidnap and rape and murder little girls in the first place." She pressed her lips tighter, closing her eyes. She should have known there was no use in talking to Joel about this. He was a CPA, a man of numbers. Of hard facts. She had no hard facts, just a sickness in the pit of her stomach.

"You're probably right," she said suddenly. To Joel, she knew she would sound as if she were conceding to him the way she had for most of the years of their marriage. In those days, she had wanted so badly to be loved by him, *protected* by him, that she had been willing to sacrifice herself and her beliefs to keep him. But tonight she wasn't giving in. She just didn't want to talk about it anymore. Tomorrow she'd call King. She had a list of questions for him two legal-size pages long. She'd get her facts. She'd get the facts straight and then she would call the police. She'd make sure someone had looked into Eshey.

She added a tablet of dish detergent to the dishwasher, closed it up, and hit the start button. "Why don't you go tell Krista good night?" she said.

He stood in the archway to the hall, looking damned fine in a pair of jeans and a gray T-shirt. "I could stay," he offered.

She gave him a half grin. "Good try, but no go. I've got work to do." She passed him and turned to go down the stairs to her office. "Set the alarm on your way out."

Sydney checked the clock beside her bed. It was 11:45 P.M. She'd been in bed more than an hour. Beside the clock was *Twin Murders.* Joel hadn't asked for it when he left, and she hadn't forced it on him. What was the point? She couldn't *make* him read it.

She looked at the clock again. She really needed to get some sleep, but she couldn't relax. She'd tried reading a favorite mystery, even gotten up and made herself a cup of hot chamomile tea. But the tea sat on the bedside table cooling, untouched. Nothing could induce her to fall asleep. She couldn't get the names, the black and white images from the book of Eshey's victims out of her mind. She needed to talk to King.

It was 11:50 now. Way too late to call a man she didn't know. He was probably asleep.

She picked up the phone, hesitated, and then punched the numbers. She had never been a math wizard like Joel, but she had a good memory for numbers. Phone numbers, addresses, her SAT scores from high school, and the stats on the Orioles last season.

Marshall heard the clang of the phone and opened his eyes. He must have drifted off for a minute. It was almost midnight. Who the hell was calling him at midnight?

He thought of his aging parents. His dad hadn't been feeling well. Heart attack?

The phone rang again.

The woman in bed beside him didn't stir. He picked it up. "Yeah?"

"I'm sorry to call so late," she said apologetically. It was Sydney MacGregor. Her voice was soft, hesitant.

As she spoke, her words on the computer screen typed out in his head, letter by letter. *Marla didn't even scream. I screamed for her.*

"But I read your book," she said, "and—"

"You can't sleep," he finished for her, feeling a tenderness that was completely unlike him. He slipped out from under the sheets and left the woman sleeping in his bed. Her name was Leslie. A waitress from a bar down the street.

Marshall walked naked into the bathroom and shut the door. "It's OK," he said into the phone. "After writing as many of these books as I have, you never sleep."

There was a pause on her end. He waited.

"I have some questions."

"I knew you would."

"You sure it's OK if I call so late?" She sounded stronger now. More confident.

"I'm serious when I tell you I don't sleep much. I've had insomnia for years." He put down the toilet lid and sat down. The seat was cold on his bare ass, but he didn't want to go out into the loft. It wasn't that he didn't want to wake up Leslie; it was time she went home anyway. Call it crazy, but he just didn't want to share his call with Sydney with anyone else. It was his, and his alone.

"So tell me what you need to know," he said. "I've got some other info for you, too, on the Carrie Morris case. Apparently the custody battle was pretty ugly. Supposedly, Mom has a little drinking problem."

If *Mom* had experienced what Sydney had as a child, actually witnessed her sister's abduction, this didn't surprise her.

"OK, great." She paused again. "Hell. I don't even know where to start. I have so many things I need to know."

"Then I've got a better idea. Why don't we meet?" He didn't know what made him say it. Why did he want to meet her? This could get messy. Complicated, considering these weird feelings for her he was experiencing. Marshall didn't do messy.

"Meet?"

"Yeah, get together. I mean, if you like. It might be better doing this face to face."

"Well. Yes, that would be better. If you don't mind."

They agreed to meet in Cape May, New Jersey, the following day at noon. She'd take the ferry across the bay. He'd rent a car. Marshall hung up and stepped out of the bathroom. "Hey, Leslie," he called. "You'd better get going."

He picked up a pair of black denim jeans off a chair and pulled them on, then walked to his computer screen and flipped it on as the naked woman climbed out of his bed and began picking up her clothes off the floor.

Marshall sat down in the chair in front of the computer, titles for his new book racing through his head. This whole thing with Sydney was probably just parental paranoia. But if it wasn't, she was going to make him a best-selling author again.

Nine

Sydney waited nervously on the front step of the bed and breakfast in Cape May where she had agreed to meet Marshall King. On the first floor was a great tearoom that always featured a nice view of the street and a decent lunch.

The house was one of those big Victorian homes with the wraparound white porch and grand porticos that had been remodeled to look the way it had at the turn of the century. It was a peachy pink color with the most beautiful turquoise trim and shutters. Only the Victorians could get away with painting a house such brilliant hues.

It had been one of those places she would remember forever. The Carter House. She and Joel had stayed here when they had first married, a lifetime ago.

She spotted Marshall walking down the sidewalk toward her and recognized him immediately. She was pleasantly surprised. He looked just like his picture on the book jacket. He hadn't changed a bit in all these years. Inky black hair, touched with a little gray, now. Intense dark eyes and a strikingly handsome face. He really was movie-star good looking. Tall. Six-two, maybe -three. Good build. But he didn't act like he knew how good looking he was, the way some men did. He didn't have that saunter.

"Sydney MacGregor?" He must have recognized her from one of her book jackets or some national ad campaign her publishing company had run. He walked directly up to her and offered a broad, warm hand. His smile was even warmer.

A charmer.

"Marshall." She shook his hand. "I'm glad you could make it." She felt awkward. Almost shy. Like this was some kind of date instead of a business lunch. Business lunches she could do, but not dates. Sydney didn't date.

"I asked for a table on the back porch, if outside is OK with you." She walked across the wide porch without waiting for him to respond. Inside the front door, the hostess greeted them.

On the back porch, Sydney and Marshall ordered iced teas and club sandwiches while they stumbled over the niceties of initial friendly conversation.

"How's your daughter?" he asked, folding his linen napkin on his lap. "She's thirteen, right?" He shook his head. "A hard age."

She nodded. "Yes, thirteen. Her name is Krista. She can be a handful."

"Your only child?"

"I'm divorced." Sydney dared a peek at him. He was dressed in khakis and a designer polo. It was a little faded, but it fit him like a glove. She had noticed he had no wedding ring. She couldn't ever recall looking for a ring on a man before. "You?"

"Divorced times two." He gave a laugh that was husky . . . intriguing. "I'm not sure if that's good or bad."

She nodded because she didn't know, either. He made her feel strange. Self-conscious. "So how was your trip down?"

"Fine. The Jersey Turnpike. You know how that is."

The waitress brought their iced tea and Marshall

studied her intently across the table. "So—enough chat?" he asked.

She leaned forward, frowning. "Pardon?"

"I was wondering, you know, if we've had enough casual conversation?" He gestured with his hand. "I want to talk about Eshey. You want to talk about him. I know neither of us wanted to dive right in, but—"

"But here we are," Sydney said, appreciating his straightforwardness. She pulled her notepad out of her bag. "I think we're ready to talk."

An hour later, they had eaten their sandwiches and the waitress had served them each a third glass of tea. "Enough of the gruesome details," Sydney said, sipping her tea as she glanced at her pages of notes. She was getting better at distancing herself from the facts. Not thinking so much about Marla. Now the words on the pages were just words and not bloody images. "Eshey's background is a little weird, isn't it?"

"For a serial killer?" Marshall lifted a dark brow. "Unfortunately, not at all. Most of his history is pretty typical for this kind of killer." He squeezed fresh lemon into his iced tea. "There's evidence of him killing small animals when he was a kid. Starting fires. He was abused by his mother—emotionally, for sure. Probably physically, too. Supposedly a very religious family. Pentecostal type, snakes, fits on the floor. He was picked up on Peeping Tom charges twice as a young man, long before the murders began. These kinds of characters don't just wake up as killers one morning. They work their way up the ladder."

"And he had a twin brother?" Sydney glanced up at Marshall over the rims of her zebra-striped reading glasses. They had been a gift from Krista last Mother's Day, meant to be a gag, no doubt. But Sydney liked them. To her, they shouted, "Forty and proud of it!"

"Yes. His twin died in some kind of farming accident when they were fourteen. I couldn't find much in the way of details. I actually went to West Virginia several times to do interviews, but those folks aren't exactly the friendly type. I don't think that in all my years of doing personal interviews, I've met any community so tight-lipped. Most people are dying to spill the beans."

She lifted her gaze to meet his. "You mean like my mother?"

"I didn't say that." Marshall watched her with those dark eyes of his. "All I know is that it was a horrific farming accident," he continued. "There was dismemberment involved. The family buried him the next day on the family farm."

"You're kidding me. " She scribbled Eshey's name and drew a horizontal line and wrote the word *twin*. "And then Eshey's wife gave birth to twins?"

"Twin boys. But she was his girlfriend. He never married her. The kids weren't born until after he was in jail awaiting trial."

She flipped through her legal pad. "I guess there's no need to wonder why the obsession with twins."

"Well," he said sipping his tea. "He was obviously obsessed with them, you've got that right. But I never figured out why he killed one of each set of twins. Something to do with losing his brother, I suppose. He was alone—wanted other twins alone. Something like that. I don't know. And of course he never confessed to any of the murders, even Marla's, so I never got any of the juicy details from him."

She looked up at him in response to the word *juicy*. She didn't appreciate it.

He grimaced. "Sorry. I don't mean to make light of what happened to you or your sister. It's just that you get a thick skin, writing about this kind of stuff. Have to."

She exhaled and looked down again. Though she still thought that what Marshall wrote about to make a living was a little sleazy, she was impressed by how well educated he was in the minds and habits of pedophiles, rapists, and murderers. She surmised that he probably knew more about criminal behavior than many law enforcement officers.

"So the twins were born after he was in jail, waiting for trial?" she asked.

"That's right. The girlfriend took off and left the boys with Eshey's mother. She was a druggy. Turned up dead a few months later in some seedy motel in Wheeling. Had been hooking and apparently a john got carried away with the fun."

"They've got hookers in Wheeling, West Virginia?"

He chuckled. "You really have led a sheltered life, haven't you, Miss Mallory Moore?" He leaned forward and she could smell his cologne. It was something musky . . . and expensive. "Sweetheart, they've got hookers in every town in this grand country of ours."

She flashed him a grin that was daringly close to flirtation. Then she was appalled with herself. She hadn't flirted with a man since her college days. She made a point of studying her notes. "OK, so Eshey goes to jail, the girlfriend bails, and Granny takes the twins."

Marshall nodded. "They moved to Maryland. A poor suburb of Baltimore. "

She looked at him over the rims of her crazy glasses. "What then?"

"I don't know. I never followed up. Eshey had been convicted and sentenced. End of book."

Sydney sighed as she pulled off her glasses and rubbed her eyes. "I'm sure I've got more questions, but I can't think any more right now." She checked her watch. "And I'd better get going if I'm going to catch the ferry. It's my daughter's last day of school.

We always do some summer shopping and supper out somewhere." She glanced at him across the table.

He was watching her.

She looked down at her neatly manicured hands. "I want to thank you for meeting me like this. Being willing to talk to me."

"I'm sorry I didn't have time to find any up-to-date info on Eshey. I'll see what I can dig up. I'll see what I can find on his family, too."

"I don't know how much help that will be, but sure. Why not? If you don't mind. I'm swamped with this deadline, and, honestly, I'm not good at this kind of research." She tucked her pen and her glasses into her purse. "I don't know how you collect all of this personal information."

"You'd be amazed by how much is out there lying around. Especially now with the Internet. Our private lives aren't nearly as private as we think."

"I suppose that's true." She tucked her notepad into her khaki-colored Kate Spade purse and stood. She stuck out her hand. "Thank you, again."

"I'll call you when I have more," he offered, rising to his feet.

His grip was strong. Lingering.

"You sure? You don't mind? I'll be happy to pay for the calls."

He waved her away, smiling. "Nice to meet you, Sydney. Talk to you soon."

She smiled back as she slipped on her sunglasses and walked out of the tearoom and onto the street.

Ten

"Mom, I'm going to be late for practice. If I'm late, I have to run laps." Krista followed Sydney into the nursing home waiting room, tossing a softball as she walked. She was practicing her wrist snaps.

"I won't be long."

Krista slumped into a flowered upholstered chair. "I don't understand why you couldn't just drop me off at the ballpark," she whined.

"And I don't understand why you can't walk down the hall and say hello to your grandmother."

"Because she doesn't like me." Krista continued to toss the bright yellow ball in the air, catching it each time.

"If it will make you feel any better, she doesn't like me, either." Sydney passed Krista. "Now stay put. I'll be five minutes." She carried the greasy white paper bag down the hallway toward Cora's room and entered without knocking.

The TV was on and her mother was seated in her reclining chair, her eyes closed. "Ma?" Sydney called softly.

Her mother made no response and Sydney took a step closer, "Ma, it's Sydney."

Cora's pale eyes flew open. "Thought I was dead,

didn't you? Thought you were finally rid of me," she snapped.

Sydney rolled her eyes. Dealing with her mother never got any easier. It just never did. "I didn't think you were dead." She dropped the bag on the table beside her mother, not in the mood for her nonsense today. "I can't stay. Krista has practice and I thought I'd watch."

"Saw it on the news." Cora nodded her pointed chin toward the TV. The paper bag rattled as she dug for her cheeseburger, reminding Sydney of an old rat with that pointed chin of hers, whiskers and all.

"Saw what, Ma?"

Cora opened the paper on the burger and took a bite. "That little girl missing. They say missing, but she's dead. It's him, Sydney. Charles Eshey come back to finish us off." She raised the burger skyward. "'And then the slayer shall return home, to the town in which the deed was done.' Joshua 20. Don't remember which verse." She took another bite.

"Ma, that wasn't what they were talking about. You're always taking the verses out of context."

"You'd do better to listen to the word of God, girl. If your father had, we wouldn't be in this mess we're in today. The whole world wouldn't be crumbling around us."

Sydney crossed her arms over her chest. She hadn't had a chance to go home and change out of her khaki slacks into shorts after meeting with Marshall King, and she was hot. "You're right Ma. It's Pop's fault. The crime, the unrest in the Middle East. Hell, global warming is probably due to his drinking and gambling. The fact that he's been dead twenty-five years doesn't really matter."

"I don't know where I went wrong." Cora shook her head, eating the last of the burger, talking with her mouth full. "I tried to raise my girls to be God fearing. To respect the Almighty and the power of his wrath."

Sydney ran her hand through her hair, thinking she needed a cut. A really short one. She wondered why it was that when things got bad, women always wanted to cut their hair.

"Ma, why didn't you ever tell me that when they found Marla near the hotel, she wasn't dead yet?" Sydney fought tears that suddenly burned the back of her eyes. She hadn't even been thinking about Marla or what she had read in Marshall's book. It had just come out of nowhere.

Sydney turned away so her mother couldn't see her face. She wouldn't cry. She wouldn't let her mother see her weakness, because Cora had always preyed on weakness. "Why didn't you tell me that she lived two days in the hospital before she died?"

"Dead is dead. What does it matter?" Cora rattled the fast-food bag. "You only brought one? I'll starve on one sandwich a day."

"I'll bring you two next time." Sydney started for the door because she couldn't hold back the tears. "I probably won't be by tomorrow, but maybe Sunday after church."

"Bring me two next time," Cora called after her.

Sydney hurried down the hallway, ignoring the old folks in wheelchairs who rolled toward her, holding out their arms, calling to her.

"Jane? Jane, that you?" an old man hollered from the doorway, where he was strapped into a wheelchair.

Sydney darted into the waiting room and passed Krista. "Let's go."

Krista popped out of her seat, still tossing the ball in the air. "Wow, that was fast." Her tone changed as she hurried out the door after Sydney. "Mom, you OK?"

Sydney choked back her tears.

"Mom, what's wrong?" She touched Sydney's elbow, prompting another flood of tears. It was so infrequent that her daughter touched her these days; it was as if Sydney had the plague.

"Get in the car."

"Mom, what's going on that you're not telling me? And don't say nothing. You've been weird for days. Weirder than usual."

At the car, Sydney clicked the remote key entry on her key fob. "Get in."

"Mom!"

Sydney slid in, waited for Krista to climb in beside her, and locked the door. "Krista, I need to tell you something."

Sydney had not intended to tell Krista about Marla until she was older. Even in the last few days, she had still hoped to keep her daughter innocent. Now, suddenly Sydney knew she had to tell her. There was something in the pit of her stomach that told her Krista had to know the truth.

"Can you miss practice?" Sydney said. When she looked at her daughter, she made no attempt to hide her tears.

"Yeah, sure. We just need to ride by and tell Coach." Krista scrunched up her forehead. "Did someone die or something? Is Grandma dead?"

"She's not dead." Sydney yanked on her seat belt and backed out of the parking space. "We'll go by the ballpark so I can talk to your coach and then go to Taco Rio's." It was Krista's favorite restaurant when she wasn't avoiding carbs.

"OK, Mom," Krista said, her old sweet pre-thirteen self for once. She kept staring at Sydney. "Whatever you want."

An hour later, they sat in a booth at Taco Rio's.

Sydney had a beer. She wanted another. Hell, she wanted another half dozen, but she was driving, so she nursed the bottle slowly.

"Wow, I can't believe all of that happened to you," Krista breathed, crunching on a third veggie taco. She wasn't in the least bit upset. Kids today were like that. The world was so filled with daily horrors that there was no innocence. Nothing seemed to shock them. "It's like out of some kind of horror movie or something."

"Something like that." Sydney sipped her beer.

"You said there was a book about your sister and the guy. Can I read it?"

"No, you can't read it." Sydney took a breath. "I'm sorry for not telling you about your Aunt Marla sooner, but I . . ." She stared at a large multicolored sombrero hanging from the ceiling. "I didn't want you to grow up afraid . . . the way I did," she finished quietly.

Krista wiped her mouth with the napkin. "It's OK. I understand. What I don't understand is, why now? Did Grandma say something to get you upset?"

Sydney made herself look at Krista. In so many ways she was still just Sydney's little girl. But in other ways, Sydney knew she was nearly all grown up. Krista could handle the truth, even if the truth was that her mother was paranoid.

"The man who killed Marla was a guy named Charles Eshey. He was released on parole a few weeks ago."

Krista pushed the remainder of the taco into her mouth. "They let him go? I would have thought they'd have fried him in the electric chair for something like that." She was so matter-of-fact, as if she didn't really understand the finality of capital punishment.

"There wasn't much frying in electric chairs in those days. And he never confessed, so execution wasn't really an option."

"And now he's out." Krista shook her head. "Bastard."

Sydney frowned at her daughter's choice of language.

Krista offered her mother her most contrite "oops" smile. "Sorry 'bout that."

Sydney nodded. She felt better now. She didn't know why, but she felt stronger. She felt as if she and Krista were a team now. "I don't want to scare you, but his being out scares me. And I want you to be sure you're following our rules. Rules that keep us both safe."

"Sure, Mom. I'm not stupid, you know."

Sydney glanced away, feeling the tears on the backs of her eyes again. She and Marla hadn't been stupid, either. She made herself look at her daughter again. "I'm sorry I had to tell you about all of this. Sorry you have to know, but I feel better."

Krista pressed her lips together. "I'm glad you feel better, Ma." She sipped her soda. "Can we have some fried ice cream?"

Eleven

Jess adjusted the gooseneck lamp over the pages of the file she had spread out on her desk. It had been sent over to her office from NCIC—the National Crime Information Center. Besides its database of information on license plate numbers and stolen vehicles, stolen and recovered weapons, fugitives, missing persons, and stolen securities, the NCIC also provided access to criminal histories.

As she dug for a paper clip in a drawer, she heard a key in the front door. She grabbed up the grim photographs on the desk and stuffed them into a manila envelope.

The front door swung open. "Hi-de-ho? You here, Jess?"

"In my office." She rolled her chair to the doorway and leaned back to catch sight of Meagan coming through the door, her arms loaded with groceries.

Meagan was an attractive African-American woman in her late thirties, with creamy cocoa skin, sleek, dark hair, and brown eyes that sparkled with an incredible brightness and love of life. Her inner spirit was a good contrast to Jess's dark side.

Jess closed the office door behind her and went to the kitchen to help her put down the bags.

"How was your day?" Meagan asked. She was way too cheery for the mood Jess was in tonight.

"Shitty. Yours?"

"Delivered a healthy baby girl and then went back to the office and did about, oh, I don't know, half a dozen pelvics." She leaned across the kitchen counter to kiss Jess.

Jess closed her eyes, needing the warmth of Meagan's mouth against hers. The old photos of Eshey's victims taken at the scene had given her the chills, and she'd not been able to shake them. Mr. Morris had shown up in his office this morning, and his ex-wife had been there waiting for him, along with the Maryland state police. Turned out he had gone to Florida, but with one of the secretaries from his office. A married woman. Ed Morris's steps would be traced, but Jess had already contacted the hotel where he'd stayed in Key West, and no one had seen a little blond girl. Just a buxom blond in her mid-twenties in very small bikini. Now there were no leads.

Jess held up her hand, switching gears, thinking of Meagan and her gynecological exams. "Spare me the gory details," she muttered.

Meagan laughed, pulling away. "Sounds like you *did* have shitty day."

Jess reached into one of the bags and pulled out toilet paper, a roll of paper towels, and two boxes of tissues. She folded the paper bag carefully, running her finger along the creases.

"Hey, what's wrong?" Meagan left the package of chicken on the counter and came around into the dining room, where Jess had perched on a stool. She opened her arms and drew Jess into them.

Jess rested her cheek on Meagan's breast for a moment and let her eyes drift shut. "A bad case. Missing girl. We hoped all week that her dad had her, but he didn't."

Meagan ran her hand over Jess's short-cropped hair, smoothing it soothingly. "You want to talk about it? Sometimes talking it through—"

"No. It's OK."

Meagan stroked Jess's cheek. "I understand that it's a case, confidentiality and all, but—"

Jess shook her head. "No, it's not you. I need to let this all stew a while. This little girl who is missing had an aunt who was murdered years ago." She paused. "Pop was on the case. It was one of those cases that always bothered him. You know, he never talked much about work, but he actually told me about this guy Eshey who killed all these little girls and then was convicted of only one murder."

"And you think it could be the same guy?" Meagan's bright eyes grew round. "He's not dead or in jail?"

"Out on parole and as old as the hills. I think it could be the same guy, yet I don't see how."

"Then why is it bugging you?" Meagan studied her. "What's telling you there's something *not right*?"

"I don't know," Jess mused, glancing up at her. "My dyke intuition?"

Meagan laughed and kissed Jess's forehead. "So trust it."

"I'm trying. But a case like this takes a lot of footwork and usually ends up with a lot of dead ends. I'm not sure my supervisor is going to go for too lengthy an investigation based on my dyke intuition and no facts."

"Well, just don't sell yourself short. You think you're right, you stick to your guns." Meagan playfully tapped Jess's holstered .45-caliber Thompson.

Jess couldn't resist a smile. "Carl is with me on this one. He's letting me run with it. I've already interviewed the obvious suspect. He can probably be ruled out, but we're trying to track down some prison records and some family members. Just to verify what the old geezer is saying."

Meagan grabbed the tissues and toilet paper off the counter and headed down the hall. "I was going to throw the chicken breasts on the grill. You want to make a salad?"

Jess got up, already feeling better. "Boobs on the grill? Sounds good to me, but only if there's wine."

"You bet there's wine," Meagan hollered from down the hallway. "Give me a minute to change and I'll meet you on the deck."

Jess smiled, thankful to have someone like Meagan to come home to.

Twelve

"You told her?" Joel snapped. "What do you mean you told her?"

Sydney glanced at the lady sitting next to her on the bleachers, who seemed more interested in Sydney's and Joel's conversation than the Little League softball game. The score was three to five, with Krista's team up by two in the bottom of the third.

Sydney gave Joel a push, indicating that she wanted to speak with him privately. He climbed off the bleacher and held out his hand to help her jump down the three feet to the grass, but she ignored him. It had taken her too long to realize that she had been depending on him too much to start asking him for help again. For anything.

"You should have discussed this with me first," Joel said, meeting Sydney's gaze.

She tossed her empty water bottle into a garbage can beside them. Krista was on deck to bat and she didn't want to miss it. Krista had the second highest batting average on the team.

"After talking to Marshall . . . and to Mom," Sydney confessed, "I decided I would rest easier if Krista knew about Marla."

"Oh, so your crazy mother and some guy I've never laid eyes on are now making decisions concerning my daughter?" Joel's mouth was pinched. He spoke again before Sydney could respond. "And what do you mean, *you'd* rest easier? Will Krista rest easier knowing her aunt was raped and butchered by some crazy the state has now deemed rehabilitated?"

The batter ahead of Krista made it to first on a nice single grounder between the third baseman and the short stop, and Krista stepped up to bat.

Joel continued. "No thirteen-year-old girl needs that kind of information." He stared at the ground. "I suppose you told her about the missing girl in Annapolis, too? About how you think Eshey is on the rampage?"

"Of course not. And I didn't give her any of the details of Marla's death. What kind of mother do you think I am?"

"Oh, well," he said sarcastically. "I suppose there's something to be said—"

"Hush a minute," Sydney interrupted. "I want to see her hit."

And she did want to see Krista hit, but she also wanted to take a breather. Joel was putting her on edge, making her question herself. She knew she had done the right thing in telling Krista about Marla. Krista wasn't even that upset. Kids these days seemed to take violence in stride so easily. Whether it was the movies, the music, or just the fact that kids were affected by violence more these days, she didn't know.

It was hard for Sydney to have Joel so annoyed with her. It was hard for her to go against him, even when she knew she was right. She'd spent their whole marriage trying to make things right at any cost, and old habits were hard to break.

With two balls and two strikes, Krista slammed the softball up the center for a long drive. Sydney jumped up and down and clapped as Krista rounded first base and made it to second with time to spare. The girl on second came in to home for an RBI for Krista.

The ball returned to the pitcher, and the next batter stepped up to the plate. Sydney turned back to Joel. "In retrospect, I think we should have told her sooner than this."

"Why? What good would the information do her, except to give her nightmares?" He clenched his jaw. "Because, Sydney, I've been patient long enough with you on this. Krista is not in any danger. Charles Eshey is not killing a second generation of twin girls, and I do not want you filling our impressionable teenager's head with this kind of bullshit."

"What good did my telling her do?" Sydney demanded softly, but with an edge to her voice. "It gave her some honesty. Her mother was being totally honest with her for once. That will be important as she gets older, Joel. She needs to know that what we say to her is truthful."

"I think you're way off base here, Syd."

"Look," she reasoned. "What if there's media coverage as the investigation of Carrie Morris's disappearance progresses? What if, God forbid, the kid turns up dead, which you know very well is a good possibility at this point." She took a breath. "If Krista does hear anything on the news or reads the paper, she won't learn about her mother's past from some reporter for *The Washington Post.*"

"She is not going to pick up any newspaper or watch CNN." Joel totally snapped, losing his calm demeanor. Now this was the Joel Sydney knew. "When was the last time Krista read anything voluntarily that didn't have to do with friggin' softball?"

Sydney crossed her arms obstinately over her chest. The June afternoon was overly warm and the sky was hazy. It reminded her of the day in the car with Marla.

Once she would have crumbled when Joel snapped at her, but not any longer. "Lower your voice," she warned. "Or I'm walking away."

"I want to know exactly what you told her about Eshey." Joel poked his finger at her. "Because I'm not going to have my little girl afraid for her life because her mother—"

Sydney held up her finger to interrupt Joel as the cell phone hooked on her belt loop rang. She was thankful for the call; she didn't want to hear what he had to say anyway. She didn't care if he thought she was crazy. Her motherly instinct told her she had done the right thing.

"Hello."

One of Krista's teammates hit the ball into the outfield and all the parents leaped up from the bleachers, hollering and clapping.

Sydney turned away from Joel and the others and stuck her finger in her ear so she could hear better.

"I'm sorry. I called you at a bad time," the male voice said on the phone. "This is Marshall King."

She had already recognized his voice. Sydney smiled. "No, no, not at all. It's OK."

"It's Saturday," he went on apologetically. "I should have known you would be busy."

"I'm not busy," she insisted. She hadn't expected to hear from him so soon. They had just met yesterday. But she was glad he called. Glad to hear his voice, for some reason. "Well, I'm at a softball game, but it's the second this week. Fifteenth this season." She chuckled.

Joel took a step closer, obviously interested in who had called her. She walked away from him. "So what's up?"

"Um. I haven't been able to get anything more about the Carrie Morris case other than what you've probably gotten off the news. I do know the FBI is involved. I don't think they're looking at the father anymore. Let's see," he sounded as if he were reading off a piece of paper. "Special Agents Manlove and Steinman, out of a field office in Baltimore, have been given the case."

"It's been more than a week," Sydney said quietly. "They think she's dead, don't they?"

"No one's saying anything, which is what worries me," he confessed. "I think I'll give the agents a ring Monday morning. They'll probably refuse to talk to me, but I'll give it a shot."

"Should I call them?"

"Honestly, I think they might take me more seriously. They're likely to assume the worst of you—a paranoid mother."

Sydney gripped the phone. Marshall was right. She knew he was, but somehow it didn't seem right that she should do nothing at all. "OK. Well, let me know what they say."

"I did find some information on Eshey's daughters. Or should I say surviving daughter."

"Daughters?" Sydney glanced at the ball field and then turned her back on it again. "I didn't know he had any daughters."

Marshall made a sound. "Something I uncovered today. I'm really embarrassed to say this, but I got it wrong in the book. Eshey's twins were *girls*, not boys. Whatever source I obtained the original information from was apparently wrong, and I guess I never double checked. I feel like a jackass for making such a stupid mistake."

"Minor detail," she said, wanting to make him feel better. "It really doesn't make a difference. But you said there's only one alive? Has she had contact with her father before or after he was released?"

"Not as far as I know. I had a friend check the Jersey state prison visitation information, and apparently

Eshey never had a single visitor, not in all the years he was in the slammer."

"Hmmm. Not even his mother, who took the kids?"

"Well, that's part of what's so interesting. This poor family is cursed or something. Wait until you hear this . . ."

Sydney glanced back to see the fielders running in. Krista walked onto the field to pitch. "Hey, Marshall, listen, can we talk later tonight? Or tomorrow if you've got something going on?" she added quickly. "Krista's is about to start pitching her fourth inning, and I'm getting the evil eye from my ex."

"Oh, you can call me later. No problem. Call as late as you want."

Sydney smiled again and she didn't know why. "What, no hot date tonight?"

He laughed. "Just me, my computer files, and a chicken caesar salad."

She laughed with him. "I'll call you later. Nine-ish?"

"Talk to you then, Sydney."

"Who was that?" Joel asked as she hung up.

She felt like telling him it was none of his damned business who it was. "Marshall King—the author of the Marla book. He had some more information for me."

"Getting pretty friendly with a man who used your family's tragedy to make a buck, aren't you?"

Sydney studied Joel's face for a moment. If she didn't know better, she'd think she heard jealousy in his voice. "He offered to dig up some info on Eshey for me, and he was calling me back, that's all." She walked to the fence. The umpire had just called for the first batter.

"What? Is he hoping Eshey's on another murder spree? Hoping to cash in on *The Twin Murders, Book Two*?"

Sydney frowned. She hadn't really thought about

Marshall's motivation, but she had no intentions of discussing it with Joel. "No," she answered. "He's just being nice."

Joel rolled his eyes. "Sydney, you're so naive. No man does something just to be nice. He either wants to get into your shorts, or he's hoping to cash in on you somehow."

"That's ridiculous."

Krista had thrown two strikes and a ball.

"Not any more ridiculous than your refusing to consider the possibility."

Another two balls. Full count.

Sydney closed her hand into a fist. "Come on, baby," she whispered. "You can do it. All together, now."

"Strike," the umpire grunted.

Sydney clapped. "Atta girl, Krista!"

Krista glanced at her mother by the fence, grinned, and shifted her gaze to the next batter.

"Listen," Joel said, obviously trying to make an effort to speak more calmly. "I'm not trying to tell you what to do. I know better than that. But I think you're getting a little obsessed with this missing girl and with Eshey. You need to take a step back and take a good hard look at what you're doing. Maybe you need to talk to someone."

"I thought you weren't going to tell me what to do." She continued to gaze over the fence, refusing to meet his eyes. "You think I need a shrink?"

"Syd, forget it." He scuffed his sneaker in the grass. "Can I take Krista home to spend the night?"

Joel had shifted the conversation just like that. He did it all the time, and it made her crazy. "Nope," she said.

"Syd—"

"She's going with Katie for dinner and ice cream after the game. It's Katie's little sister's birthday. She won't be done until ten. You can have her tomorrow for the day, as planned."

Joel said something under his breath.

Sydney glanced at him. "You know I hate it when you do that. If you have something to say, speak up, damn it."

He raised both hands to her as if surrendering. Hands that had once stroked her body. "Let's just table it for now. OK? I'm not going to stand here at the ballpark and argue with you over whether or not a serial killer is after my daughter. It's too ridiculous. I'm going for a Coke."

She watched him stomp away, and a part of her wanted to follow him. She stayed where she was.

Thirteen

"Hey," Marshall said when he picked up the phone.

Sydney stretched out on her back on her bed and tucked her arm under her head. She had changed into an old T-shirt and gym shorts and ditched the bra. "Hey, yourself. You have caller ID?"

"You said you would call at nine-ish. It's nine-ish."

She chuckled.

"So how was the game?"

She was amazed at how easily she could talk with this man who was practically a stranger. Sydney had never been comfortable with people she didn't know, which was a little ironic considering what she did for a living. Millions of people all over the US depended on her to help them make decisions on their vacations, the homes they bought, even their weddings. She received fan mail all the time saying what a lifesaver she was, how readers thought she was a like a best friend. Yet she really was a loner. "It was good. Krista's team won eight to four."

"She a good player, your daughter?"

"Pretty good, or so I'm told. Her fastball has some kind of natural curve to it which is apparently great." She kicked off her sneakers. "You like softball?"

"I'm not much of a sports fan," Marshall confessed. "Never quite understood the nuances of baseball."

"I love baseball and softball. Always have." She rolled onto her side on the unmade bed. "So tell me what you found out. What's with Eshey's family?"

"They must have bad luck or a curse on them or something. Listen to this. Eshey's twin girls were called Dorian and Darin."

"Dorian and Darin?" Sydney groaned. "These poor girls are born the daughters of a serial killer, and they have names like that? They didn't have a chance in hell."

"Apparently Darin didn't have a chance in hell. She died when she was eighteen. Just graduated high school."

"You're kidding. How?"

"House fire. Poor neighborhood. No functioning smoke alarms. The other sister was able to get out. The grandmother and Darin died in the fire."

"That's awful. Where is Dorian now?"

"Get this. She's a schoolteacher in Baltimore."

"A schoolteacher?"

"Fourth grade."

Sydney was fascinated. "And she has had no contact with her father?"

"Not as far as I can tell," Marshal said. "At least not while he was in jail."

"Huh," Sydney mused. "Well, she's a teacher, so she obviously went to college. She's made a life for herself. If my father was a pedophilic serial killer, I know I wouldn't be running to maximum security to visit with him." She sat up and sipped from a water glass by the bed. She checked the clock. It was nine-thirty. Krista would be home soon. She knew she'd had to let her go and keep up at least the appearance of normalcy in her life, but she'd be glad when she had her safely in the house.

"So what else did you find out?" She stretched out on the bed again.

"Not much. A little more on the family background, but nothing that really pertains here. Let me run by my notes and see if anything jumps out at you."

The next time that Sydney checked the clock, it was ten-fifteen. Ten-fifteen and Krista still wasn't home. Suddenly she got nervous. Marshall was telling her an interesting story about the son of a murderer he had interviewed once and the facial tick he developed whenever his father's name was mentioned. She cut him off as she walked to the window to gaze out on the dark street in front of their house. "Hey, Marshall."

"Yeah?"

"Krista's not home yet."

"You said she went out for ice cream with a friend."

"I know." Sydney fought the fear that was beginning to build in her belly. Was this the way it had started for Carrie's mother last week, an inkling of panic as she went through all the logical explanations why the little girl was in her back yard one minute and then gone the next?

"The friend's mother said she'd have her home by ten. She knows I'm a stickler for being on time, at least when it involves Krista." Sydney padded barefoot into the dark hallway.

"Maybe Krista tried to call to tell you she was going to be late."

"No. I have call waiting. Mainly just so she can never give me that excuse." She checked her watch. "What if something . . . something terrible's happened?"

"I think your ex is right," he said in a teasing voice that she might have found, in any other circumstances, teasing in a different way. "You are paranoid."

"Please don't say that. You have no idea what it's like to live with this totally irrational fear that he's going to come back."

"You're right," he said instantly contrite. "I don't understand. I can't possibly."

She walked up the dark hallway toward the kitchen that was lit by a lamp over the stove. Her bare foot struck something hard and she gave a yelp, leaping up.

"Sydney?" Marshall said. "You all right?"

She pressed her hand to her heart, which was suddenly racing a mile a minute. "Shit. Yes, yeah, I'm fine." Realizing what she had struck, she kicked the softball down the hall with her bare foot. "Ouch, damn it," she muttered, hopping on one foot.

"You sure you're OK?" Marshall's deep voice was warm with concern.

"I'm fine," she said, suddenly feeling strangely distracted. Detached. She wondered if he knew how sexy he sounded on the phone. "I've gotta go."

"I'm sure she's fine, Syd."

She managed a half smile. "I know. Call me Monday if you get to talk to the FBI agents?"

"Talk to you Monday."

Sydney hung up the phone and walked into the kitchen, flipping on the lights. She walked back down the hall, stepping over the softball that had come to rest in front of the bathroom door. At the door, she checked to be sure the lights were on outside. She pulled back the filmy drapes on the sidelights of the door and gazed out. Just her burgundy SUV.

She went back to the kitchen, found Katie's number on the refrigerator, and called the house. She got the answering machine on the fourth ring.

"Hi, this is George, Catherine, Katie, and Patsy," the message said, each family member cheerfully stating their own name. "Leave your name and number and we'll get back to you," Katie finished.

Cheery answering messages annoyed Sydney. Hers was all businesslike, and she would certainly never let

Krista leave the message. She would never want a stranger calling to know there was a teenage girl in the house. It just wasn't safe these days.

That sounded so bizarre. Was Joel right? Was she paranoid?

The answering machine's tone was long and irritating. "Catherine, this is Sydney. I was checking on Krista." She tried not to sound concerned as she walked back to the kitchen. "If you need me to come by and pick her up, just let me know. Thanks."

She hung up the phone and dropped it on the counter. Then she paced the hardwood floor in her bare feet, her gaze straying to the beachfront below. She thought she saw someone walk by, close to the house. Had he stopped to look up at the house? Could he see her?

Idiot. Of course he could see her. She was standing in the middle of a fully lit room, and he was standing in the dark. She ran to the wall switch and flipped off the lights.

She stood there for a minute in the darkness, not moving. She could feel her heart in her throat, yet at the same time she could feel it pounding in her chest.

She walked slowly to the sliding glass doors that led onto the second-story balcony. She reached out with one hand to be sure the doors were locked. They were. Her gaze shifted to the beach dune below. He was gone.

If there ever was a he. . . .

Oh, God, but what if he had walked around to the front of the house? What if she hadn't heard Krista come in? She raced down the hallway and jerked back the curtains on the door. With relief, she saw no car but her own in the driveway. Krista wasn't home yet. Catherine knew not to pull out until Krista was safely in the house.

Sydney dropped the curtain and leaned against the door, unsure what to do. Krista was never late coming in. Never. She knew her mother had a thing about it, and now she knew why.

Sydney stood for a moment in the dark hall, her heart pounding in her ears. She didn't know what to do, and she hated the feeling. It was almost worse than the fear. She checked her watch. It was ten-thirty-two. Krista was only half an hour late. Catherine might have had to take someone else home first. The Dairy Queen could have been backed up tonight. It had been a warm evening. Sydney knew Krista was OK. She'd be home any minute. She walked back down the hall to the kitchen, grabbed the phone and dialed.

Joel picked up. She didn't even give him a chance to speak.

"Joel," she said, tears running down her cheeks, "I don't know where Krista is. She never came home. Can you come over?"

Thankfully, he didn't launch into a speech about overprotective mothers. He didn't even mention Eshey or Sydney's ridiculous fear that the killer was killing again. "I'll be right there."

Fourteen

Sydney waited at the front door, peering out the sidelight. The minute she saw Joel's green Jeep pull into the drive, she unlocked the door. He met her on the steps with his arms open to her. Nothing seemed more natural than to walk into them.

"Don't worry," Joel whispered, resting his chin on the top of her head as he closed her in his embrace. "She's fine. I know she is, Syd."

"But she's never been late before." She pressed her cheek to his gray T-shirt. She could feel his heart beating steadily. He wasn't upset, and he was Krista's father. If something were wrong, wouldn't he instinctively know? "I don't know if Catherine has a cell phone. I tried operator assistance, but they were no help."

"Let's go inside." He ushered her in the door and up the hallway. "We'll grab a cup of tea, and then I'll try Katie's house again."

"I don't want a fucking cup of tea," she said desperately. "I want Krista! I knew I shouldn't have let her go. I knew I should have talked to the police. Did you know they've called in the FBI to investigate that little girl's disappearance? I think they know it's Eshey. They just don't have the evidence yet."

He halted in the center of the hall and pulled her

into his arms again. She was on the verge of hysterical tears. She was so frantic she couldn't think.

"It's all right," Joel whispered, holding her close, talking in a calm, low tone. "Just take a deep breath."

"I'm sorry," she whispered, clinging to him. Suddenly she realized how much she missed Joel. How much she missed his touch. God, it felt good in his arms again. "I know I'm being ridiculous. Acting nuts. It's just that—"

He smoothed her hair with his hand, holding her against his chest in the dark hallway. "You went through a terrible ordeal as a child. Krista is just a little older than you were when Marla was murdered. You're not crazy, sweetheart. You're under a lot of pressure—just divorced, a book deadline, trying to raise a teenager. This is natural for you to worry about her right now."

He was saying all the right things. The things she needed him to say. "Thank you," she breathed, still holding him tight.

Headlights flashed through the sidelights of the front door, partially illuminating the hallway. Sydney let go of Joel and whipped around to run for the door.

"Sydney, don't," he called after her. "You'll scare the bejesus out of her."

She grabbed the doorknob, but caught herself before she yanked it open. She was panting hard, her heart pounding in her ears. She made herself take a long, cleansing breath. He was right, of course. She took another breath before she allowed herself to open the door in what appeared to be a calm manner.

Krista met her on the steps with pixie-like Catherine Denny right behind her.

"I am *so* sorry," Catherine gushed. "Ice cream place was packed." She talked so fast that Sydney had to pay close attention to catch it all. "I left my wallet at home and had to run back for it." She waved her tiny, ringed hands. "We had a flat. Triple A was slow to come, my cell phone battery went dead." She lifted both hands in the air, then let them fall. "You know how these things are sometimes. One thing goes wrong, and then it's a dozen."

Sydney was so relieved to see Krista that she couldn't be angry with Catherine. She was right, of course, sometimes things did go wrong. And when they did, that didn't mean a serial killer had kidnapped your daughter. She forced a smile. "It's OK, Catherine."

Sydney brushed her hand on Krista's back as she darted under her mother's arm to slip into the house. She just had to touch her, if only for a moment, to be sure she was real. "Krista and I have been talking about letting her have a cell phone—just for emergencies, of course. Maybe it's time we talked about it again."

"Well, thanks for being so understanding." Catherine scooted down the driveway toward her car. "'Night."

"Good night," Sydney called cheerfully after her, so happy she wanted to jump up and down. She went into the house and locked the door behind her.

"What are you doing here so late?" Krista was asking her father in the kitchen. "Please tell me Mom didn't call for backup."

"Nah," Joel lied. "Just stopped by and we got to talking."

"Cool." Krista dropped her bat bag by the back door. "Well, I'm going to bed. 'Night."

"Good night," Joel and Sydney said in unison as they watched their daughter take the staircase up to her third floor bedroom.

"I feel foolish," Sydney said when she was out of earshot.

"Don't," he murmured.

Joel stood in front of her, close enough so that she could smell the faint scent of his aftershave. It was different than Marshall's. Spicier. But there was something inherently familiar about it that made her feel warm all over.

She glanced up at him. She didn't know what she did next, whether it was the way she lifted her lashes to look at him or something she did with her mouth. Next thing she knew, he was kissing her.

She hesitated. There had been no sex between them in a long time. After he moved out, out of loneliness mostly, they had made love a few times. It was almost as if she had had to wean herself from him. After all, the sex had always been good between them, even when his drinking was at its heaviest. But she had been determined the last few months not to let it happen again. She didn't want a relationship with Joel anymore. He had hurt her too much. Taken too much of her *from* her.

But she found herself kissing him back. Somehow, in the heat of the moment, she couldn't stop herself. She parted her lips, took in his tongue. His hand slid up beneath her T-shirt and she moaned. With no fabric between them, she could feel her breast grow goosepimply.

They stood in the middle of the dimly lit kitchen necking like college kids. He pushed her up against the counter, and she wrapped one leg around him, pressing her groin to his.

Sydney was the first to pull away, breathless, her head spinning. She couldn't think. Didn't want to.

What the hell, she thought. It had been too long since she'd gotten laid, and she was, after all, at forty, just hitting her sexual peak, wasn't she?

"You want to stay?" she whispered.

He kissed her again. More gently this time. "You know I do."

They kissed as they moved down the hallway. Groping. Stroking. Krista called it swapping spit. She brushed her hand over his jeans and felt him hard for her.

"You have to be gone before she gets up in the morning," she warned between kisses. "It's not fair to Krista."

"I swear"—his tongue teased her upper lip—"on a stack of Bibles."

Just inside the bedroom door, he pulled off her T-shirt. She shoved the door shut with the heel of her hand. He pushed her backward toward the bed, and when her calves hit the side of the mattress, she bent at the knees and let him push her onto the bed.

He straddled her, resting on one knee as he pulled his shirt over his head. He looked good. Lean. More muscular than when they had been married.

"Been working out?" she murmured, her eyes half closed.

"Trying." He stretched out over her, his hand sliding down her bare thigh.

The sex was fast. Hot. She came twice with little foreplay. Damn, was she *that* horny?

The minute she was done and he slid off her onto the bed beside her, she regretted letting him into her bedroom. She was giving him the wrong signals. It was as bad for him as it was for Krista. The marriage was over. The relationship had to move on to something beyond occasional sex.

Sydney closed her eyes and lay naked on the rumpled sheets. Despite the heat pump that hummed, blowing cool air, she was hot and sweaty. "You should go now," she said quietly. "Then you don't have to worry about getting up early in the morning before Krista."

He rolled onto his side and with a finger traced an invisible line between her breasts. She wanted to push away his hand, but she didn't. She felt so damned guilty for using him this way. The moment it was over and she was done with him, she had realized just how done she was with him. She really didn't love him any more. Well, she loved him because he was the father of the only child she would have. But she was no longer *in* love with him.

"I wish I could go back," Joel said quietly as he painted his thin lines on her breasts. "I wish I could take back all the hurt I caused you."

She caught his hand and brought it to her mouth to kiss one finger. "I'm done with the bitterness, Joel," she said. When she opened his eyes, he was looking down at her. He was still in love with her; she could see it in his hazel eyes. And now she really felt like a shit.

"I wish you could forgive me."

She released his hand. "I have."

"But you can't forget? Give me another chance?"

She didn't answer, because he already knew what the answer was.

Joel sat up in the bed and reached for his boxers on the floor. He pulled them on and stood up to slip into his jeans. She just lay there with her eyes closed and listened to him dress.

When he was ready to go, he leaned over and kissed her cheek. "I'll let myself out and set the alarm. I'll be by to pick up Krista in the morning."

She didn't answer and then he was gone.

Fifteen

He opened the scrapbook by the dim light of a single bulb and slid his hand over the second page. The newsprint was faded and the corners of the articles had curled at the edges with age. He stared at the face of the little girl dead all these years and then compared it to the new clipping and the face of Carrie. There was definitely a family resemblance. Same twinkling blue eyes? He couldn't tell if Auntie Pat had blue eyes; the photo from a school picture in 1971 had been in black and white. Carrie's eyes had been blue. Dark like blue pools of water. Same smile.

He smiled back then and glanced at the previous page. It was too bad there were no clippings of the blond-haired teen to place there. But no one knew that one had met with foul play, apparently. Thought to be a runaway. No one would ever know it was them. Pity.

He turned the page to study the next newsprint photo.

The surviving twin Anna Marie Carpenter had never married, apparently. Little possibility of a twin. He stared at the picture of her and her dead sister, Anna Paulie Carpenter. A shame Anna Marie hadn't married and had children of her own. With identical twins, the likelihood of giving birth to one's own twins increased significantly.

He turned another page in the scrapbook. Smiled again. Norma Jean Truitt, sister to Mary Elizabeth Truitt. Norma Jean had married a Jose Lorenzo in 1986. Lived in Pennsylvania, just outside of Philadelphia. Gave birth to a son, a daughter, and then twins, ten years ago. But boys. He didn't like boys. Nothing could be done about that.

Here the path would simply have to stray.

Sydney walked out onto the upper deck with the phone in her hand and sat in her favorite chair. She tucked one bare foot beneath her. The sun was bright and hot, but a cool breeze blew in off the ocean. It was Sunday afternoon, and she had let Joel and Krista talk her into letting Krista stay an extra night. Sydney wouldn't pick her up until tomorrow morning, so she knew by all rights she ought to be hard at work in her office, starting the next chapter of *A Fool's Guide to the Family Vacation*. It was the kind of day that Sydney ordinarily looked forward to, when she could have a twenty-five-page day.

But she couldn't work. She couldn't think. Not of family vacations at Yellowstone or Disney World or a dude ranch in Montana. She couldn't think of anything but the missing girl and Eshey. And Marla. This morning, over a cup of coffee, she had finally pulled out the few pictures she had of Marla. She had promised Krista she would do it two days ago, but she hadn't worked up the gumption until today. She was shocked by how alike Marla and Krista looked right now. Shocked and frightened. If Eshey ever came upon Krista, he would know in an instant who she was related to.

Sydney knew she had to do something. She just wasn't sure what. She stared at the phone in her hand.

Her only ally was Marshall right now. Should she call him?

It was times like this that Sydney really missed having a good friend. She had always been a loner, but when she did make friends, it never seemed to work for long. When Krista was a baby, before they moved to Delaware, Sydney had made friends with Kim, a neighbor down the street. Then Kim's husband cheated on her, the couple divorced, and Kim moved with her four-year-old daughter back to Iowa to live with her parents. Sydney heard from Kim on her birthday and at Christmas, but they didn't even talk on the phone anymore. They had just grown too far apart.

Then there had been Mary Ann. Sydney had met Mary Ann in a local bookstore five years ago. She had a daughter Krista's age and was also a single mom. They had swapped books, shared tea, laughed, and cried together. Then two years ago, Mary Ann discovered she had ovarian cancer. She died seven months later. Since then, Sydney had had no friend to confide in, no one to ask advice from. She was on her own, and today she had never felt more alone.

She wanted to call Marshall. He was as close to a friend as she'd had in a long time. But then she thought about what Joel had said about her being naive. About Marshall wanting something from her. She found it hard to believe, and yet titillating at the same time, to wonder if it might be her body. She was more concerned that it might be something else. Marshall hadn't really said why he had been so willing to help her out. Was Joel right? Was this about money and the outside hope that Eshey was killing again?

She stared at the phone cradled in her hand. Marshall had the name and number of the FBI agents in Baltimore. After the scare last night, Sydney knew she had to pursue this. She knew she would have to talk to someone who could guarantee Krista was safe. Hell, she'd talk to Eshey himself, if it would give her any peace.

She punched Marshall's number.

"Hello?"

"Hey, it's me . . . again."

"Hi, Again." Marshal covered the mouthpiece and leaned out to meet Lorna's kiss as she went out the door. She was back from her parents' place in Connecticut and had spent the night. They had slept in late and shared the Sunday *Times* over bagels and lox and freshly squeezed grapefruit juice. In the past, he would have considered it nearly a perfect day, but today he had been restless. Sydney was making him restless. Sydney and that bastard Eshey.

"Talk to you tomorrow," Lorna said.

Marshall waved and closed the door behind her. "So what's up?" he asked into the phone. "I take it Krista arrived home safe and sound."

"She was running late. But Christ, she gave me a scare."

Sydney paused and he listened. He walked to the window to gaze down on the street. Lorna looked up from the sidewalk and waved and smiled. She was a good fifteen years his junior, and she looked twenty with her bleached blond hair and sassy smile. He waved back and watched her disappear, wishing he cared for her as much as she cared for him.

"That's why I'm calling," Sydney said hesitantly. "After that scare last night with Krista, even though she was perfectly safe, I realized that I couldn't just let this go and depend on the police to let me know if I needed to be concerned." She gave a humorless laugh. "I can't keep listening to Joel tell me that I'm crazy. I'm not crazy, Marshall."

"You didn't hear that out of my mouth." He walked

to his bed to stretch out on it. It still smelled of Lorna's floral perfume. He'd go to the laundromat this afternoon and wash his sheets. "You and I have both come face to face with Eshey. I've met other men like him. We know a side of humankind that most don't," he said quietly, truly feeling her desperation.

"I think I'd like to talk to one of the FBI agents myself, Marshall," she said. "Just to check in with them. Be sure they've looked in on Eshey and ruled him out."

"I don't know that they'll tell you anything, Syd. Not with an ongoing investigation."

She smoothed back her hair and got up out of the chair, restless. "I think it's worth a shot, don't you?" In the kitchen, she paused at the table, where she had set out three pictures of Marla. One was of the two of them sitting in the grass, arm in arm. There were in jean cut-offs and tank tops. Little scrawny arms and bad haircuts done with Cora's dull scissors. The sight of their smiling faces brought a lump up in her throat. "I have to try, Marshall," she said softly.

"I understand. Let me give you their names and number, but please don't say where you got them from. Anyone traces this back to my friend, and I've got one less friend."

Sydney jotted the information down on a pad of paper meant for the weekly grocery list. That done, she gripped the phone, needing to say something more, but not sure how to broach the subject. "Thanks for the number," she stalled.

"Sure. Let me know what they say."

Sydney plunged in. "I need to know something else, Marshall."

"What's that?"

She walked back to the open doorway to gaze out at the ocean. Sunbathers dotted the beach with bright towels, umbrellas, and bathing suits. She wished she was out there today in her tankini soaking up the sun and reading a good book. "Will you tell me why you're doing this?"

"What?"

She could tell that she had caught him off guard. "Will you tell me why you're helping me?"

He didn't respond right away and she waited, fearing Joel was right, not wanting him to be.

"The truth?" Marshall said.

Her tone took on an edge. "Of course, the truth."

"Well, when you first contacted me, I thought to myself that on the outside chance there might be some truth to your suspicions—"

"You'd have another best-seller on your hands," she said sharply. Joel was right, and she hated it when he was right.

"But, Sydney," Marshall continued firmly, "that was just the reason I initially spoke with you. I'm ordinarily kind of a loner. I don't reach out much."

She listened to him, not wanting to. Feeling her own loneliness in his.

"It's more than that now," he said. It's, it's . . . ah, hell," he breathed. "I don't know what it is. It's you."

A charged silence hung between them.

Sydney wondered if she ought to just say good-bye and hang up. He was in it for the money. He was helping in the hopes that that bastard *was* killing little girls again. He had said so himself.

But that wasn't all, Marshall had said.

What if he was telling the truth? What if it was her, too? God, she could use a friend right now. Maybe even a lover.

"You have to believe me, Syd, when I say I don't want to see anything happen to Krista," he said quietly.

"You don't even know her."

"No, I don't. But I feel like I know you. Like I know you better every time we talk. And I sure as hell know Eshey and know what he is capable of doing."

"OK," Sydney heard herself say, nodding. Joel always saw everything in black and white, everything in numbers, positive and negative. But she knew things were never that simple. "Fair enough. I'll believe you until I see evidence to the contrary. If he's killing again, the book's all yours." She raised her finger as if he were there on the balcony with her. "But if you, for one moment, put my child in any danger, any threat of danger, I swear to God, Marshall King, I'll come to New York and rip your balls off and shove them down your throat. You understand me?"

She heard him chuckle, and she smiled.

"I'd put you up against an army of killers any day, Sydney."

"I'll let you know if I get anything out the FBI." She was still smiling when she hung up.

Sixteen

Mid morning, Jess let Carl ring the doorbell while she studied the neat bungalow in the suburb of Baltimore. It was the home of Charles Eshey's only living relative. His daughter, Dorian Eshey, age twenty-eight, was an unmarried teacher. Taught the fourth grade in an inner-city public school. The only other family had been Eshey's mother and Dorian's twin sister, both of whom had died in a house fire ten years before.

Jess knew that twins were hereditary, but she hadn't known dying could be, too. The report on Eshey she had read had stated that he had also had a twin who was killed in a farming accident when he was a teenager. An official police report was being sent from some archives somewhere.

Jess glanced at Eshey's daughter's house. It was a single story with shuttered windows and nice cedar siding. There were two narrow windows on either side of the front door along the foundation that suggested there was a full basement below the house. The grass was cut as if by a pair of manicure scissors. Bright pink geraniums thrust their heads from pots in windowsill boxes. It looked like a schoolmarm's house—either that or the inviting cottage Hansel and Gretel wandered into before they met their fate in the fiery oven.

No one answered the door. "Ring again," Carl said.

"Car's in the driveway. She's probably here." They hadn't called Dorian Eshey, because it was common procedure not to give people time to prepare for an interview with an FBI agent. This way, if the interviewees had anything to hide, they had to think on their feet.

Jess impatiently checked her watch. It was Monday morning and her desk was stacked with work. She needed to get through this obligatory interview and get back to the office. Carrie Morris was still missing, and with the father eliminated as a suspect, Jess would have to talk with Mr. and Mrs. Morris and admit they had no leads. After this long, there was little chance of finding Carrie alive, and that thought made Jess sick to her stomach.

Jess reached around Carl and punched the doorbell again.

"I think a telephone interview would be enough," Carl said. "You saw the visitation records. She never went to see her father in all these years."

"I like to do personal interviews when I can." Jess glanced at the flowerbed that ran the length of the brick walk. There were perfect, neat rake marks in the dark soil. Impatiens grew in bright clumps, with coxcomb staggered between them. She couldn't remember to water plants; she couldn't even keep a cactus alive. "Besides, they could have written. Or she could have talked to him since he was released."

"I'll check around back." Carl hooked his thumb in the direction of the six-foot wooden slat fence that ran beside the small house. "See if I can see anything."

The front door opened, and a tall, thin woman smiled. She was dressed in elastic-waist jeans with a flowered knit shirt. Her mousy brown hair was pulled back in an appropriate schoolmarm bun, making her look a good fifteen years older than she was. She had on rubber gardening clogs and flowered canvas gloves.

"Good morning," Carl said. "Are you Miss Dorian Eshey?"

"Yes, I am." She clasped her gloved hands.

"I'm Special Agent Carl Steinman of the FBI, and this is Special Agent Jessica Manlove."

She brought a glove to her cheek. "Goodness, how can I help you?" Jess noted that she didn't sound as surprised by the appearance of FBI agents on her doorstep as should have been. Usually the introduction shook people up.

Dorian Eshey wasn't shook up.

Jess watched her closely as she spoke. She was an odd duck for sure, but how could she not be, considering the gene pool?

"We'd like to ask you a few questions, ma'am," Carl continued. "It will take only a couple of minutes."

Dorian Eshey was by no means an attractive woman, but she had a pleasant voice and clear blue-green eyes. Her make-up was laid on a little thick; pink rosebud mouth, rouge on the apples of her cheeks. Jessica's fourth grade teacher had suffered from the same ailment.

"Do come in. I was out back doing a little gardening. We can sit on the patio," she said as she led them through a small living room.

She was friendly. Most people weren't so congenial when they didn't know what the agents wanted with them. But maybe she was just lonely. They got that, too.

The shades were drawn in the living room they passed through and it was cool inside. Nondescript flowered furniture. Old beige carpet that had been well maintained. Jess followed the Eshey woman and Carl through the kitchen.

It looked like Jess' mother's. Avocado appliances from the seventies. Fifties-style gold-speckled Formica top table. But the room was squeaky clean and smelled strongly of pine disinfectant. The linoleum floor shone like an ice rink. Not a thing out of place. Not a dirty dish in the sink. Not a toaster crooked on the counter. As Jess passed through, she wondered where on earth the woman had gotten an avocado-colored dishwasher. Could it really be thirty years old and still running?

She also noted a large red plaid dogbed in the corner of the room. She hadn't heard a dog bark. She hated dogs. She'd been bitten by a neighbor's chow when she was three or four and had required stitches. Ever since then, she and dogs had preferred to keep their distance from each other.

They walked out onto a small stone patio, and Miss Eshey offered them a chair at a wrought iron table. Above it was a yellow and green striped umbrella.

"Please sit. Can I get you something to drink?" she asked kindly. "I just brewed some fresh iced tea."

"No thank you," Jess answered for both of them as her gaze swept the tiny back yard. It was boxed in completely with a six-foot-high fence. Very private. A small shed, green grass, and flower beds that were as neat as the house. Like the kitchen floor, Jess probably could have eaten off the sidewalk, it was so clean.

She spotted a small area fenced in with wire beside the shed. She still hadn't heard the dog bark.

Miss Eshey followed Jess's line of vision. "A pig," she explained in her teacher's voice.

"Pardon?" Jess said.

"The pen. It's for my potbelly pig, Jessica. She must be asleep in the shade of the shed. I can show her to you, if you like. She's very friendly."

Jess caught Carl's eye and she knew he was chuckling to himself. He knew what Jess must have been thinking of a pig called Jessica. She didn't crack a smile. "Thank you, but that won't be necessary."

"They're really quite neat animals. Far more hygienic than a dog, and they make excellent pets," Dorian Eshey explained. "But you didn't come here to ask me about my Jessica, did you?"

" 'Fraid not." Carl pulled a small notebook from the breast pocket of his navy suit. When they worked together in the field, it was usually his job to take notes, while Jess analyzed the situation. His notes were detailed beyond fault and she had a sixth sense that was rarely wrong. They made a good team.

"Are you aware that your father, Charles Eshey, has been released from prison?"

"So that's why you're here." Not a flicker of emotion on her face. "I am aware he was released, yes."

"Have you had any contact with your father since his release from prison, Miss Eshey?"

She folded her garden-gloved hands neatly in her lap and stared at them. Now it was the stern teacher's voice. "I have not, sir."

"There is no record of you visiting him while in prison."

"As far as I know, I have never met my father in my life," she said coolly.

Jess watched her, using her fourteen years of fieldwork experience to analyze the situation. She was probably telling the truth, but Jess had learned a long time ago that truth had many levels. "And no other contact with him before or after his release from prison? Phone call, letters, e-mail?"

Dorian Eshey shifted her gaze to Jess. "I assume you know what he did, otherwise you wouldn't be here. You wouldn't be checking up on him," she said softly. She stared into Jess' eyes, almost as if challenging her, which surprised Jess. "Would you visit him if you were his daughter?"

Jess let her gaze wander to the neat flowerbed that

ran the length of the patio. She spotted a gardening trowel beside the flowerbed. It was shiny clean. The woman had to have some obsession with cleanliness. No one was this clean.

"I'm sorry we had to ask," Jess said, looking back to Dorian. "But we're investigating the disappearance of a child."

"And you think he had something to do with it?"

"I don't know if you're aware of it, Miss Eshey, but your father is ill. There's no evidence he had anything to do with the kidnapping; we're simply doing our jobs."

Dorian Eshey lowered her gaze to her hands again. "Was it a little girl?"

"I'm afraid it was." Jess rose from her seat. There was nothing out of the ordinary here, but the woman still creeped her out. Probably the neat freak in her that was giving Jess the heebie-jeebies—mostly because her own housecleaning skills were not the best. "Thank you for your time. If we have any more questions—"

"Please don't hesitate to call." The schoolteacher rose from her chair. "I'll give you my number."

"We have it," Carl said.

"Of course you do." She gave him a close-lipped smile as she pushed her chair in and then squared it off to the table. Jess and Carl did the same. They followed her back through the kitchen and into the dark living room, parting at the front door.

The agents walked to their car and climbed in. It was Carl's turn to drive.

Dorian Eshey waved one hand and went back into the house. She closed the door. Locked it. Realizing that the strawberry patterned doormat was askew, she

stepped off it and straightened it so it ran perfectly
parallel to the front the door. Then she walked into
the kitchen, where she removed her gloves and laid
them on the counter. She opened the far top drawer
where she ordinarily kept office supplies: pens, a pair
of scissors, scotch tape, and the like. She removed a
photocopy of the newspaper article and a magnet
she'd dropped hastily into the drawer before she
answered the door.

At the refrigerator, she placed the clipping on the
freezer, wishing she had the first one. She'd have to
do some research at the library; now that school was
out, she would have time. She methodically adjusted
the slip of newsprint exactly one inch from the top
and one inch from the handle. Carrie Morris stared
at her, smiling in her school photograph published by
the paper.

Dorian smiled back

Seventeen

"Check this out." Jess tossed a pink "While You Were Out" slip of paper in front of Carl at his desk. "It's from Sydney Baker."

He picked it up. "Sydney Baker?" He tossed it back. "Don't know her."

"Didn't you read the file?"

"What file?" He pushed at a towering stack of folders on his desk, some thin, some thick enough to be a dictionary. "I've got more files here to read than I've days left on this earth."

Jess grabbed the slip of paper and sat in her chair again. "The Charles Eshey file NCIC sent over." The National Criminal Investigation Center saved agents hundreds of hours a year by providing them with information pertinent to their cases.

"You took the file home over the weekend. I couldn't read it."

She frowned, staring at the message slip. "I took it home to read it because I knew you wouldn't."

"It's Little League season." He said it as if no further explanation was needed.

"Her sister was the last one killed. The one he was convicted for. Yanked her right out of a car where the two were waiting for their father who was drunk in some bar." She fluttered the pink slip. "Sydney Baker testified against Eshey. Identified him as the man who carried her sister off."

"In court?"

"Taped. Her father refused to allow her to actually testify in court with Eshey there. But apparently the tape was convincing enough to get him even though he never confessed."

"Wonder what she wants." Carl picked up one of the files on his desk and slid his computer keyboard a little closer. He had shed his suit coat and loosened his tie. He was digging in for an afternoon of paperwork.

"My guess is that she made the connection between the missing Morris girl and her aunt. Probably read that *Newsweek* article."

"You going to call her?"

"I guess I should."

Carl reached for a Styrofoam coffee cup on his desk. "She's probably just checking to see if we're doing our jobs."

Jess reached for the phone. "Someone should be."

Sydney picked up before the phone rang a second time. Krista and Katie were upstairs watching a movie. She didn't want Krista to know she had called the FBI. She didn't want Krista to know any more about any of this than she absolutely had to. "Hello."

"Sydney Baker?"

"Yes." It had to be the FBI agent. She had said Baker. Sydney had left her name as Sydney Baker, though she wasn't sure why.

"Miss Baker, this is Special Agent Jessica Manlove with the FBI, returning your call."

"Actually I'm Sydney MacGregor. I was Sydney Baker before I married."

"What can I do for you, Mrs. MacGregor?"

Suddenly Sydney wasn't sure where to start. Just thinking about diving into this conversation made her doubt herself. This was the FBI, for chrissakes. They probably didn't take kindly to paranoid mothers. "I called because—" She stopped, took a breath, and started again. "I called because I read about Carrie Morris, the girl who disappeared, and how her aunt was murdered by Charles Eshey back in the seventies." She took another breath, going on before she lost her nerve. "My sister was killed by Charles Eshey, Agent Manlove."

"I know."

Sydney was taken off guard. "You know?"

"I've already read the file, Mrs. MacGregor."

"So you've already looked into Charles Eshey?" Sydney felt almost weak with relief.

"Yes, ma'am."

"So you're sure it wasn't him? I mean, I know the world is full of coincidences, but he *was* recently released."

"Mr. Eshey is elderly and ill, Mrs. MacGregor. He's of no threat to anyone."

Joel had said the same thing, but somehow having an officer of the law say it made her feel better. Still, she just had to be sure. "I know he's in New Jersey. And you're sure he hasn't left or anything?"

"I really can't discuss this, but rest assured, we were aware of Mr. Eshey's release from the beginning, and we've been in contact with his parole officer."

Suddenly Sydney didn't feel so confident. She gave a little laugh. "You mean Miss Carmack? I hope you didn't take her word for it. She sounded to be all of about sixteen. I can't see her up against a killer like Eshey."

"You talked to Eshey's parole officer?" It was the first time Sydney heard a spark of personality in the agent. Suddenly she had an edge to her voice. She obviously didn't care for the thought that Sydney was doing a little of her own investigating.

Let her get edgy. Special Agent Manlove hadn't been in the car when Eshey took Marla. She probably didn't have a thirteen-year-old daughter, either.

"So do you have any leads on Carrie Morris?" Sydney asked.

"As I said, I can't discuss the case."

Sydney felt a tightening in her stomach. She was reading into the agent's tone, but her guess was that there were no leads. "Look, Agent Manlove," she said, not caring if the woman thought she was pushy, "I need to know for sure that Eshey wasn't involved. I have a thirteen-year-old daughter. You understand where I'm coming from?"

"I understand your concern, Mrs. MacGregor. Carrie Morris has not yet been found, but I can tell you there is no evidence to support any suspicion of Eshey."

Sydney knew there was nothing more to say. Marshall had been right. The FBI wasn't going to talk to her. At least not tell her anything. But she had made this connection with the agent and she wouldn't just be connected to an old photo the agent had in a file. "Thank you for returning my call," Sydney said. She wanted to say that if anyone began to suspect Eshey, she wanted them to let her know, but she wasn't sure how to put it. How not to sound like a crazy woman.

"I don't anticipate any further information on the Eshey angle," the agent said, "But should anything come up, I'll call you. How would that be?"

"Thank you," Sydney gushed, suddenly uplifted again. "That would be wonderful."

"You have a nice day," Manlove said, and her wish sounded genuine.

"Thanks. You, too."

Sydney hung up the phone and dialed Marshall right away. She didn't take the time to consider why she was calling him first instead of Joel. "She called me back," she said as soon as he picked up the phone.

"Who?"

"The FBI agent. It was a woman. She was very nice; didn't treat me like I was a nut. She knew who I was. She said there was no evidence to believe Eshey had been involved in any way in the girl's disappearance. But she promised she'd call if anything concerning him comes up."

"So are you satisfied?" he asked.

He sounded distant to her. Not as warm as he had been.

"I think so," she said firmly. "Now maybe I can get some writing done." She paused. "Of course, this means no book for you."

He laughed. "I've got plenty of work to keep me busy. My novel is going well."

"Is it? Great." The conversation was over, but she wanted it to on. There would be no need to call Marshall again. "So . . ." she said.

"So good luck with your deadline." He knew they were done, too.

"Thanks again, Marshall." She felt almost wistful, wondering if there could have been something between them. Which was, of course, ridiculous. When did she have time for a relationship? Better yet with a man who lived three states away. "Take care," she said.

"You, too."

Sydney hung up the phone and sat for a moment before calling Joel with the good news.

Eighteen

"Good day to ya," Charlie said, with a polite nod.

The truck driver ahead of him was paying for a soda and a bag of chips in the rest stop mini-mart. Charlie had himself a Hershey bar.

"Hey," the truck driver said, nodding back. He wore a plaid shirt and a stained yellow Caterpillar ball cap.

Charlie knew he had to catch him before he turned away again. "So where you headed?"

"South."

They moved ahead in the line. Some foreign-speaking guy was trying to ask Frances, the cashier, for directions or some such crap. Charlie hated his type. "I used to be a driver myself," Charley told the truck driver, all friendly-like. He tapped his chest. "But I got a bum ticker now. Lost my commercial license a while back."

"Too bad." The driver was next in line.

"So," Charlie said, trying to keep up the conversation between them. "You lookin' for a little company? In your rig, I mean."

The truck driver gave him the once-over. "You lookin' for a ride?"

Charlie smiled. He knew he looked harmless and frail. This driver didn't know he felt better than he had in years. Heck, Charlie doubted there was anything wrong with his heart at all except that it had gotten shriveled and dry in jail.

Charlie nodded. He'd got up this morning thinking a Sunday afternoon ride might be nice. "My Mama's sick, down Richmond way. I was thinkin' of catchin' a ride in that direction."

"I ain't goin' to Richmond," the man grunted.

Charlie knew he wasn't going to Richmond. He'd listened in on a conversation between him and another truck driver in the cafeteria. Didn't matter. He only needed to get south of here. "Oh, that's no problem. I can always get out at any truck stop and catch myself another ride."

The man pulled his wallet out of his back pocket and paid Frances with a five. "Headed for Wilmington, Delaware. Reckon I could take you that far." He accepted his change.

Charlie grinned, genuinely pleased. He had tried so hard when he first got out to follow the rules. He knew he was supposed to stay put, and he didn't want to go back to jail. But he just couldn't help himself. He couldn't hold back his urge to ride. Couldn't restrain the urges that had been pent up inside him all these years. And now that he'd had a taste of the freedom again, he couldn't stop himself. "I thank you much." He offered his hand. "Name's Charlie."

"Buck." He accepted his plastic bag from Frances. "Let me take a piss and I'm meet you around the side where the rig's parked."

"All righty, then." Charlie nodded and stepped up to pay for his candy bar. It was Sunday; he was off until Wednesday, and he had nowhere to be but that dark apartment. No one to keep him there but the cat, and half the time he didn't come in at night. A road trip was just what Charlie needed. He grinned as he walked away, opening his candy bar. Biting into the sweet, warm chocolate.

It was good to be travelin' again.

Nineteen

"Stop it!" Jason shouted at Jacob. "Stop it or I'm going to tell Mom." He splashed his identical twin brother.

Jacob paddled after him, supported by one of the neighborhood pool's kickboards. "Baby!"

"Crybaby," Jacob's friend Kyle chimed in. "Jason Lorenzo's a big fat crybaby!"

Jason hurled his own kickboard across the pool, and the lifeguard lifted her finger, giving him a mean look. If she did it again, he knew he'd have to take a time out and sit beside her on the cement deck. Then his brother and his brother's friends really would tease him.

Jason climbed up the ladder and out of the pool. School had just gotten out last week and he really wanted to stay and play, but not if Jacob was going to be a butt head. Jacob was always being a butt head.

"Where you going, crybaby?" Jacob shouted. "Get water in your eye? Boo hoo."

Jason grabbed his towel off a chair and slipped his feet into the new Adidas sandals he got for his birthday last week. He was ten now and too old to be called a crybaby. "Going home," he shouted.

Jacob paddled over to the edge of the pool. "You're not allowed to walk home without me," he taunted.

"You're going to be in big trouble when Mom gets back from the grocery store."

Jacob didn't care if he did get in trouble. He wasn't going to stay here and get picked on. He walked into the boy's changing room and out the front door of the pool house. At the sidewalk, he turned left toward home. It was only two blocks. He wasn't a baby. He could walk home two blocks and let himself in the house. He knew where the key was—under the stone turtle in the flowerbed by the front door.

He'd glanced at the waterproof watch his best friend had given him for his birthday. If he hurried, he'd be home in ten minutes, in time for *Spongebob* on Nickelodeon.

Twenty

Sydney stood barefoot in the kitchen, boiling teabags for iced tea. Joel had given her one of those brewing machines for Christmas once, but she liked making it the old-fashioned way. She liked adding the lemon and sugar and stirring it. OK, so now it was sugar substitute, but it tasted better just the same.

As she rolled a lemon on the counter, she gazed out onto the beach below and spotted Krista in her turquoise tankini. It was after six, and they'd be in soon looking for supper. Sydney was marinating chicken breasts to cook on the grill.

On the beach, Katie stood a few feet from Krista; they were playing some kind of game with a tennis ball. Sydney smiled to herself. She'd had a good week since she talked with Agent Manlove. Krista was happy to be out of school and had actually been very pleasant to be around. She was busy with softball practices and games and spent a good part of each day with Katie out on the beach.

Sydney was getting a lot done on the book. Max, one of her research assistants, had sent the info she needed on hotels in the Orlando area and she already had the chapter blocked out. Once she was done with Disney World, it was on to Yellowstone National Park.

All week, Sydney had made a conscious effort not

to think about Carrie Morris and her parents. She had read in the paper that there was a nationwide search on for the little girl, but so far there were no leads. Sydney tried to not think about how that poor mother had to feel right now. She tried not to think about the days following Marla's kidnapping, before they found her. She couldn't think about how their father had gone on one of his drinking and gambling binges and come home with a broken nose, a black eye, and cracked ribs after being gone overnight.

That was the first time Sydney had become aware that her father had a gambling problem and that sometimes he owed the wrong people money. Sydney sliced the lemon. It was probably the gambling that had been her father's downfall, rather than the drinking. He had been missing a week when Cora got the call. Sydney had been seventeen, a senior in high school. He'd been found dead in an alley in Newark, shot through the forehead with a large caliber pistol. There were no suspects, but neighbors had whispered the word *mob*. To this day, William Baker's murder remained unsolved.

So much tragedy in her life. If she had the time, she might feel sorry for herself. She didn't.

As Sydney squeezed the lemon into the pitcher, she saw Krista and Katie begin to gather up their things. Five minutes later, the shower under the house came on. Sydney went out on the deck to start the barbecue. After the girls showered and dressed, she'd get them to make a salad, and they'd have dinner outside on the deck, where they seemed to live in the summer time.

By eight o'clock, dinner was cleaned up and the girls were parked in front of the TV with another Brad Pitt movie. A Brad Movie Marathon, Krista called it.

Sydney headed downstairs, hoping to get a few more

pages in. On her way, she set the alarm. She knew Krista was safe. She knew she could put the whole Eshey thing from her mind, but she just couldn't bring herself to totally relax. She probably never would. Close to nine, the phone rang. Sydney let Krista get it.

The door at the top of the stairs opened. "Mom," Krista called. "It's someone from the nursing home."

Sydney picked up the phone, her heart giving a little trip. Had her mom had another stroke? She'd just seen her yesterday and she'd seemed fine—as sour as ever.

"Hello."

"Mrs. MacGregor?" a female voice said.

"Yes."

"This is Jane Roshell at Sandy Beach. Your mother has had a little episode, and we were wondering if you could come over."

Sydney closed down her chapter on the computer and started for the door, taking the cordless phone with her. "An episode? What do you mean? A stroke?"

"No, no I don't believe so. She had a nightmare, I think, but we can't get her calmed down. I really am sorry to call you out at this time of the evening, but she's asking for you."

Sydney felt a strange flutter in her heart. Almost a tenderness. Her mother had always been a difficult woman, a woman who was hard to love, but she *was* Sydney's mother. And she needed her.

"It's not a problem," Sydney said, hurrying up the stairs. She went down the hall to her bedroom to find her sneakers. She was dressed like a bum in running shorts and an old T-shirt, but what did she care? "I'll be there in twenty minutes."

"I'll tell her," the nurse said. "Maybe that will help until you get here."

Sydney hung up as she scooped up her sneakers

and started back down the hallway. "Krista, there's something wrong with Grandma. We have to go to the nursing home." She walked into the dark living room. Brad Pitt was on the TV screen, looking thoughtful somewhere in Tibet.

Krista popped up to a seated position on the couch. The room smelled of popcorn. "Mom," she moaned.

Katie, on the floor, picked up the remote and froze the screen.

"I have to go," Sydney said impatiently. She tried to sit down on the end of the couch, but Krista didn't move her feet. She moved them for her. "Now grab your shoes, both of you."

"Mom, the movie's not over yet," Krista whined. "We just got our pj's on."

Sydney glanced at both girls. They wore shorts and T-shirts that looked to her like the same articles of clothing they had been wearing at supper, but what did she know? "I'm not leaving you here alone," she said firmly.

"Mom," Krista drew out the word into multiple syllables. "Katie's mom leaves her home alone all the time. Doesn't she, Katie?"

"I baby-sit the two year old next door to us, Mrs. MacGregor." Katie peered through her oval glasses. "I took the baby-sitting course at the hospital and was certified." She said it with such seriousness that Sydney almost laughed out loud.

"Please, Mom," Krista begged. "You can set the alarm on auto. It'll go off the minute any of the doors open with or without a key. You can just call from your cell when you get home and I can let you in."

Sydney hesitated. She didn't how long she would be at the nursing home. It did seem silly for the girls to go with her. And Katie had a good point. If she was old enough to baby-sit neighbors' children, surely she was old enough to stay alone in the house with another thirteen year old.

But what good did a baby-sitting certificate do against a serial killer?

Sneakers on, Sydney stood. She knew she had to get on with her life. Had to get beyond Eshey. Otherwise he really had won all those years ago, hadn't he? She hadn't beaten him at all by fighting back. He might as well have taken them both.

But she couldn't give in. Not this time. Her gut instinct told her that she just couldn't.

"This is nonnegotiable. Get in the car." Sydney pointed.

Krista muttered something under her breath and heaved herself off the couch.

Sydney was close enough to see the smoothness of Krista's cheek that she knew was still baby soft. But her daughter smelled so grown up. Shampoos, deodorant, mouthwash—teenager smells.

Sydney pointed again, wordlessly.

Krista flounced out of the room. Katie shut off the TV and followed her friend, avoiding eye contact with Sydney.

It took the girls a full five minutes to come downstairs with their shoes in their hands. They hadn't even bothered to put them on yet.

Sydney didn't care how they came, barefoot or in snowboots, in pj's or stark naked.

She opened the front door and waited for Krista to take her time walking out. They rode all the way to the nursing home in silence, with both girls in the back seat. Krista had to be really angry not to ride shotgun. Sydney didn't care.

At the nursing home, she waited for the girls to get out of the car and locked it. She strode toward the pneumatic front doors. "You can wait in the lobby. I don't know how long I'll be."

"And exactly what are we supposed to do while you're in there?" Krista used her best snotty teenager tone.

"I don't care. Just stay inside the building." Sydney offered an exaggerated smile. "Watch TV. Just like you were doing at home." She indicated the large screen TV showing a movie of the week.

"Mom, we were watching *Brad.*" Krista fell into the nearest chair and slid down until she looked good and sulky.

"I'll be back as soon as I can." Sydney checked on the security guard posted near the front door, then headed down the hallway toward her mother's room.

The place was quiet at night, dark except for the blue light and the shadows from the TVs that bounced off the walls. It was almost creepy. She stopped at the nurse's station. "Good evening," she said to a nurse she didn't recognize. She wasn't here often this time of night. "I'm Sydney MacGregor. Someone called me about my mom, Cora Baker."

"Mrs. MacGregor, I'm Jane." She offered her hand in a warm handshake. "I called." She came around the big desk. "Thanks so much for coming."

Sydney followed her toward her mother's room. "Of course I came. She's my mother."

Jane flashed a frown over her shoulder. She was a plump, short woman, but she had sparkling brown eyes. Compassionate eyes. "You'd be surprised how many people can't be bothered."

"So exactly what happened?"

"We put her to bed at eight, as usual," Jane explained. "Lights out, TV on."

"She doesn't like the TV off ever," Sydney agreed.

"About an hour later, we heard her scream. I was

next door with Mr. Jacobs, so I reached your mother's side in a second. She had dozed off and had a bad dream. It happens sometimes with our patients, only I couldn't calm her down." Jane halted just outside Cora's door and lowered her voice. "She insists a man is trying to kill her daughter."

Sydney met the nurse's gaze and she felt a tightening in her chest. Her mother was afraid for her. Her mother cared. Somewhere in her dark, sour heart, she did care. She hurried in. "Ma, Ma, it's Sydney."

Cora lay in the hospital bed, her face paler than usual. Her translucent eyelids fluttered open and she thrust out her hand. "Sydney, Sydney!"

"I'm here, Ma." She grabbed Cora's good hand and Cora crushed it in her bird-like claw.

"Sydney," she panted. "I saw them. I *saw*. They're going to murder my Marla."

Sydney felt her heart drop and for a moment she didn't breathe. It was Marla Cora was afraid for, not her . . . Sydney knew it was silly that she felt hurt. It was just the ranting of an old, senile woman. She was hurt just the same.

"Ma," Sydney kept her tone low and gentle. "No one is going to kill anyone."

"But I saw them," Cora insisted, her eyes wild. "They took Marla and they . . . they did terrible things to her, Sydney." Tears ran down her paper-thin cheeks. "Please don't let them kill my Marla."

Still holding her mother's hand, Sydney grabbed a chair and dragged it beside the bed. She sat down, covering her mother's hand with hers. "It's all right, Mama. It was just a bad dream."

"You don't understand," Cora murmured. "No one will listen to me. Everyone thinks I'm just a crazy old woman." Her eyes drifted shut.

"That's it, Ma, rest your eyes now. I'll sit right here

with you." Sydney glanced up to see the nurse standing in the doorway. She smiled and nodded, letting Sydney know that she was available if she needed her.

Sydney rubbed her mother's hand in hers and talked softly. Slowly Cora drifted off to sleep, leaving Sydney alone with the pain of emotional abandonment that she knew would never quite go away.

Twenty-one

"Holy shit," Jess said crossing the room between her cubicle and Carl's. She halted and stared at the piece of paper in her hand. It was notes her supervisor had just handed her. It was turning out to be another shitty week in a series of shitty weeks. Carrie Morris had been gone over two weeks and still, there were no leads.

"What?" Carl looked up from the cup of coffee she had brought him from the local gourmet coffee shop. Left to his own devices, Carl drank doughnut shop coffee—worse yet, the coffee here in the office.

"NCIC just spit this out of their computers and sent an e-mail to Crackhow." She stared at the paper, her mind spinning. Another coincidence? Was that possible? "A little boy has turned up missing outside of Philadelphia. But get this, his aunt disappeared in '72 and was found dead a week later. Eshey was thought responsible for her death."

Carl glanced up at her, his face ashen. "Don't tell me the missing boy is a twin?"

"Bingo." Jess walked back to her desk for her coffee. She had a sick feeling in the pit of her stomach. She'd been convinced that the Morris girl's disappearance after Eshey's release was just a sick coincidence. But this missing little boy made the hair on the back of her neck stand up. They had no suspects for the Morris girl yet.

It was like the girl had simply vanished. Jess and Carl and other agents had spent days interviewing neighbors, friends, even workmen who had been in the Morris house in the last three months. Were two coincidences a good indication that the coincidence theory was wrong?

Carl put out his hand. "Let me see."

Jess hated to give it to him. She knew how much these kid cases upset him. She had this silly wish that she could protect him from them. She handed him the information sheet.

"When did he disappear?"

"Monday around noon."

"It's Wednesday," he mumbled.

"Philly field office did the preliminary investigation. Honestly, it's a miracle anyone put two and two together this soon. Kids disappear every day." She hated the words that came so matter-of-factly out of her mouth.

"How *did* anyone make the connection?" Carl grunted, scanning the paper.

"There's a note at the bottom with a name, address, and number. Apparently this sister of the abducted boy's father works in D.C. and heard about the Carrie Morris's case through some friend of Mr. Morris's. She knows the history of the sister-in-law and contacted the state police." Jess set her coffee on Carl's desk, untouched. "Crackhow says we can interview the family of the missing boy as well as the aunt in D.C. A copy of the whole file is coming from the Philly field office today. They're handling the actual case, but we can look into it, see if we can find any connection with the Morris girl."

Carl threw the paper down on the cluttered desk and stared at it. Jess knew he was as sick to his stomach as she was.

"So what does your dyke intuition say, partner?" he asked quietly.

Jess grabbed the sheet to phone the aunt. "It says we interview the aunt and the family tomorrow, and then we make a little stop for a burger on the Jersey turnpike."

"Please come in." Norma Jean Lorenzo met them at the front door.

Jess and Carl had already met with the aunt at lunchtime in D.C. Now they would interview the missing boy's mother. They would stay the night in a hotel, and Friday morning, they would see Parole Officer Carmack and then pay Mr. Eshey a visit.

The Lorenzos lived in a large upper-class neighborhood northwest of Philly. Nice Cape Cod with bicycles in the driveway. As Jess walked up to the house, she wondered which was Jason's. He'd been missing almost four days, so she knew, according to statistics, there wasn't much chance it mattered by now. After twenty-four hours, the chances of finding an abducted child alive were dramatically reduced.

"We're sorry to have to put you through all these questions again," Carl apologized as Mrs. Lorenzo ushered them into a formal living room. Somewhere in the house, a TV blared cartoons.

Mrs. Lorenzo shook her head. She was a petite woman in her early forties, with silky blond hair that fell just above her shoulders. She looked fragile, as if she would crack at any moment. What mother with a missing child wasn't fragile?

"The local, state, and federal agencies do multiple interviews," Jess explained, "because, while we're thorough, we like to be sure we haven't missed anything."

"So you're here because of Eshey," Mrs. Lorenzo said, sitting on the edge of an upholstered floral chintz chair. She folded her professionally manicured hands and stared at the carpet. Her voice was barely a whisper. "The little girl, Carrie Morris who disappeared a few weeks ago. Her aunt, like my sister, might have been murdered by Eshey, too."

"Mrs. Lorenzo, we've interviewed Mr. Eshey and I can assure you—"

"Why did you ever let the bastard out?" Mrs. Lorenzo shouted suddenly, leaping to her feet. "Why?" Tears trickled down her cheeks, smudging her dark eyeliner. "Why did you ever let him go?"

Jess glanced at Carl. This interview was going to be a rough one. He hadn't responded because he was too professional, but she knew his stomach was in knots.

"Mrs. Lorenzo, I understand how distraught you are, but—"

"You understand?" she shrieked. "How can you possibly understand?"

"Because I had a child abducted and murdered fifteen years ago," Carl said without moving a muscle. "My Dani was four."

Jess wanted to reach out and touch him, brush his jacket with her fingertips, squeeze his hand, something. Instead, she stared straight ahead at Mrs. Lorenzo, who was taking her seat again.

"I'm sorry," she murmured, quickly docile again. Carl's revelation had shocked her. It shocked Jess, and she knew about it. Carl didn't talk often about his little girl. Very few of his co-workers even knew once he transferred to the East Coast.

"I'm sorry for your loss, Agent Steinman," Mrs. Lorenzo murmured, "as well as my behavior."

"It's all right." Carl reached into his breast pocket

and pulled out his trusty notebook. "Now, if we could just ask a few questions, we'll be out of here in no time."

"Certainly." She folded her hands again. "Anything."

With the interview back on track again, Jess forced herself to focus on what the woman was saying. As she listened, thoughts of Eshey went round and round in her head. Was that sick bastard really at it again? Or was this just what the *Newsweek* article had said—a coincidence?

"Miss Carmack, thank you for seeing us on such short notice." Carl offered his hand and the parole officer shook it, obviously uncomfortable with the FBI's second visit to her office.

"I'm, of course, willing to help in any way, but I am confused by your call." She returned to her chair behind her desk, not offering the agents one. "Why are you investigating Mr. Eshey? Is there some evidence he's committed a crime?"

"No, not at all. What we think we have here is happenstance, but we're obligated to investigate all angles. Two children have been abducted in the last month," Carl explained. "Both are still missing. Eshey was suspected of murdering both children's aunts." He shrugged. "Eshey is released from prison and suddenly twin children of surviving twins begin to disappear. Parents are frightened, and they want to know we're keeping an eye on Eshey."

"So the children are missing, not dead?"

"Officially, yes, but you know very well, I'm sure, ma'am, the statistics on missing children. We don't usually get ten year olds back this late in the game."

"I have to confess the thought that you might be-

lieve Mr. Eshey is killing again is rather laughable."
She almost smirked as she spoke. "You know his old
MO. He killed and dumped the bodies within a week;
he didn't kidnap and then disappear with the children." She twirled her pen. "Have you considered the
possibility that these could be some type of copycat
abductions?"

Of course we've considered that, Jess wanted to snap.
But she kept her mouth shut and let Carl carry the interview.

"Right now we are only conducting an initial investigation," Carl said calmly. "As to looking into Mr.
Eshey, MOs have been known to change."

Either Cynthia Carmack's tone didn't bother Carl
or he was a better man than she. Jess didn't like her.
Not her pink lipstick, her pen-twirling, or her know-
it-all attitude. She was too smug, too sure of herself for
a woman who didn't know who the hell she was up
against in this lousy world. Jess wondered how confident she would be if she was given the opportunity to
see the old crime scene photos of the little girls from
the Eshey case. Even in black and white, they were
shocking.

"As my partner said, Miss Carmack," Jess broke in.
She just couldn't stand it any longer. "We're checking
up on Mr. Eshey because it needs to be done. These
families already went through hell once, and now
they're going through it again. It's the least we can do."

"But you said yourself Mr. Eshey was only convicted
of killing Marla Baker. He never confessed to any
other abductions or murders."

Jess studied Miss Carmack's diploma on her wall.
University of Delaware, in Criminal Justice. The ink was
barely dry. "He never confessed to the Baker murder,
either."

Carl got out his pad of paper and Jess noticed his

hand tremble slightly. Poor guy. After their interview with Mrs. Lorenzo, he'd been on the can half the night with a colitis flare-up. Jess sat up in her own room half the night in case he wanted to talk about his little girl. He hadn't.

"Has Mr. Eshey reported regularly to you?" Carl asked.

"Yes, sir."

"His appointments are made on time and not changed?"

"He comes on time, as scheduled. He's really a very sweet man."

Jess frowned. "So was Bundy."

Carl scribbled in his notebook. "And you've talked to his supervisor at work? His landlord? No problems at work or on the home front?"

"I haven't spoken to either recently. After all, Mr. Eshey is no longer in prison. But they have my number and they know they can call me if there's any problem at all."

Carl asked a couple of more questions, and he and Jess were out of there.

"He sounds clean to me," Carl said, tossing her the keys. Her turn to drive.

"Little bitch," Jess muttered as she unlocked the car.

Carl frowned, watching her over the roof of the car. "I thought maybe you thought she was cute," he teased.

"Yeah, right. Big tits, little brain."

"Touchy. Homesick?"

Jess did miss Meagan. They'd certainly been apart for more than a day or two before. In the three years they had been together, Jess had worked cases in South Carolina and Georgia. She'd been five weeks on a bombing in Virginia, but something was different these days. She needed Meagan, needed her steady head. Jess guessed she was just old—that or getting burned out.

"Shall we get this over with?" Jess said as she slid in behind the wheel. "And then maybe we can both get a decent night's sleep."

Twenty-two

"No ma'am. He's a good employee, " Harry Devane, Eshey's supervisor, said. "Comes to work on time. Personal hygiene is excellent. Does what he's supposed to. Doesn't shirk his responsibilities."

Carl and Jess stood in a coffee room used by the turnpike rest stop's employees. It was a typical small break room with a table, a few chairs, an old refrigerator. An ancient coffee machine sat on a microwave cart spitting and sputtering as fresh coffee dripped into the crusty pot.

"So he's a model employee?" Jess asked. It was all she could do to keep her sarcasm in check.

"You could say that. He gets a little winded once in a while and has to sit down and rest. But he's probably the best one the state's sent me in years, you want to know the truth," the short, balding man said. "Most we get, they can't find their way to work and when they do, it's to sit on their asses out back and smoke. They usually end up back in jail in a matter of months. Dope, robbery, parole violation of some kind." He lifted one thick shoulder. "Don't matter much to me. By then, they're not showing up for work anyway."

"We appreciate your taking the time to speak with us." Carl flipped his notebook closed. "We just need one more thing from you."

"Happy to help." Devane seemed impressed by Jess's and Carl's status as agents.

"We need Mr. Eshey's work schedule for the last month. His days off, what days he worked and when he punched in and punched out."

"Well, I can tell you he was off Sunday, Monday, and Tuesday this week, but I can't tell you previous to that."

Jess met Carl's gaze. The boy had disappeared Monday around noon. She wondered if Eshey had an alibi for Monday and if anyone could vouch for him.

"He's just part-time because of his health. We don't keep time records here on site," Devane explained. "But I can get them for you."

"Here's our card." Carl handed it to Devane. "If you will fax us the information, we'd greatly appreciate it."

"Can do." The man checked his watch. "Charlie ought to be here any minute. Never late."

"If you don't mind, sir, we'd like to speak briefly with him when he gets here. Then he can get to work."

"Take whatever time you need." The man studied the card. "Charlie's not in any trouble, is he? I'd hate to see him in trouble."

"We don't think so," Carl replied. "Just a routine interview."

" 'Cause he's a nice man," the supervisor said, walking down the tiled hallway. "Real kind."

Jess looked at Carl and grimaced. "Real kind?" she said softly. "You saw the photos of Marla Baker. She had lost so much blood that her skin was translucent." She shook her head, a metallic taste in her mouth. "Amazing how deceiving we humans can be, isn't it?"

Carl nodded with a sigh as he glanced around the room. There were lockers lined against one wall with "Eshey" printed on a piece of masking tape and slapped across one of them. "I suppose one could make the argument that he was rehabilitated. He did, after all, spend almost thirty years in prison."

Jess met Carl's gentle brown-eyed gaze. "Carl, come on. You took the same behavioral science classes in college that I did. You've been to Quantico and heard the profilers speak. You and I both know that psychopaths are never rehabilitated. They have no sense of right or wrong in the way most humans do. No remorse. They kill as long as they are allowed to. As long as they get away with it."

Carl walked to the coffee pot and grabbed a Styrofoam cup. "Want some?"

Jess shook her head. She backed up to lean against the end of the table. "You know, this is probably just another wild goose chase. We ought to be back at the office going over all the evidence. Trying to see if there's actually any connection between the missing boy and Carrie other than the past."

Carl added sugar to his coffee, tasted it, and added some more. "Most of our interviews are wild goose chases," he said mildly. "It's what we do. Chase gooses and occasionally catch the fox."

Jess heard a door open at the end of the hallway and angled back to see if it was Eshey. An elderly man glanced up, meeting her gaze.

Eshey.

His face was blank for a moment, unreadable, and then he smiled, acknowledging that he recognized her. He shuffled toward her the way old men did.

Was he putting her on? He was only sixty-two; by today's standards, he was still young. Maybe it was the heart condition that left him so pale and thin. Jessica made a mental note to request a copy of his medical records. She'd been told he had a heart condition, but she hadn't seen any proof of that yet. Heart problems were sometimes hard to pinpoint. They were easily mistaken and easily misdiagnosed. Even Jess knew that; her father had been as healthy as an ox until the day he had fallen over dead of a massive heart attack.

"Special Agent Manlove." Eshey offered his thin hand and pumped hers. His grip was cool, not overly firm, but not soft, either. Jess's father used to say you could tell a lot about a man from his handshake. She could see how people could be charmed by Eshey, especially women. Some women were such fools when it came to men, so easily deceived. She wasn't. It was that intuition again. She hadn't figured Eshey out yet, but she knew he wasn't what he appeared to be.

"Good morning, Mr. Eshey." A part of Jess wanted to wipe her hand on her pant leg to clean off his touch. Even after all these years, the man *had* to be tainted by the evil he'd committed. She pushed the old crime scene photos from her mind and concentrated on Eshey and his behavior. "You remember my partner, Special Agent Steinman."

"Yes, ma'am, I do." He reached for Carl.

Carl switched his coffee to the other hand and accepted Eshey's greeting.

The older man then shuffled to his locker, opened it, and slipped a wrinkled brown bag in on the top shelf. Lunch, obviously.

Jess checked out the locker; nothing there but a newspaper and a ratty blue sweater. Cardigan type.

"So how can I help you folks?" Eshey took his time in slipping out of his jacket. It was tan canvas and matched his uniform. An embroidered patch on the breast pocket said "Charlie" in red cursive.

"We'd like to ask you a few questions, Mr. Eshey." Carl put down the coffee. It must have been bad for him to find it undrinkable.

"Checkin' up on ole Charlie again, are ya?" Eshey

chuckled in a good-natured way. "Well, check away. I got nothin' to hide." He closed his locker and eased into one of the plastic chairs at the lunch table.

"Mr. Eshey, have you left the state of New Jersey since you were released from prison?"

"Ain't left the fine state of Jersey since the day they locked me up, sayin' I kilt that little girl." Eshey met Jess's gaze. "Been a long time. You wouldn't have been much more than a little girl yourself."

Was he trying to flatter her, or just making conversation the way old men did?

" 'Sides, how would I get anywhere? Got no license or car. Guess I could take the bus." He looked down at his knobby bird-knees covered by wrinkled beige work pants. "But then that would be violatin' my parole." He lifted his gaze to hers and she made note of it. Men who had something to hide were less likely to make eye contact.

"And I don't want to go back to jail, Agent Manlove," he said firmly.

That one statement she believed.

"Can you tell me where you were Monday of this week?" Jess continued to study him, maintaining eye contact.

"Day off." Eshey grinned slyly and waggled a bony finger. "Course I bet you already knew that."

"We'd like to know where you were," Carl said.

"Home. Watched TV. I got me a little black and white, but it don't pick much up. I been thinkin' about savin' for one of them satellite dish things I see advertised. You got one?"

"Did you go anywhere? See anyone?"

Eshey screwed up his face thoughtfully. "Went down to the laundrymat before *McHale's Navy* come on. 'Bout three, maybe."

"Anyone see you there? Neighbors?"

"Maybe. Guess you could ask around." He glanced at Carl. "But I don't remember no one bein' there. That's why I go that time a day. They only got one good washer that don't eat up your drawers."

He was pretty convincing. Too convincing?

"Mr. Eshey, you have not come into contact with any children, have you?" Carl asked.

It wasn't only the questions that were important in an interview like this. It was how the suspect handled himself. Of course, Jess couldn't call him a suspect. She had no evidence whatsoever to indicate Charles Eshey had anything to do with Carrie Morris's or Jason Lorenzo's disappearance. Only coincidence and the possible argument that there could be a copycat murderer out there and Eshey could be the connection.

Still, something struck Jess as not right about Eshey. Somehow he seemed deceitful. She just couldn't figure out how he was deceiving them . . . or why.

Carl asked Eshey a few more questions. When those were exhausted, he tucked away his notebook. "I think that's all we need for today, Mr. Eshey. We appreciate your cooperation."

Eshey rose from the chair the way an old man with arthritis did. The same way Jess' grandmother had moved. He went to the time clock near the door and punched in.

"We apologize for keeping you," Jess said.

"Jest ten minutes." Eshey tucked his card back in the slot. "I'll jest stay my extra ten minutes at the end of the shift. Don't make no difference. I ain't got nobody home waitin' for me but an old fleabag cat, anyway."

"Have a good day," Carl said.

Jess followed him out of the room.

"So what do you think?" Carl asked when they reached the privacy of their car. "He capable of getting to Philadelphia, kidnapping and killing a boy, disposing of his body, and then getting back in time to make work? He didn't have to be back here until yesterday."

Jess stared at the stone rest stop building as she slid into the seat of the sedan beside Carl. "He doesn't look strong enough to harm a cat, does he?"

"Nope." Carl threw the car into gear and followed the signs pointing the way out of the rest stop. They were going to take the turnpike to the next exit and stop by to meet with Eshey's landlord, just to check things out there. Maybe someone could vouch for Eshey. If he was home for three days, surely someone saw him.

Carl glanced at her as he reached for his plain black sunglasses on the dash. "But you're not satisfied."

Jess was wracking her brain, but so far she hadn't come up with anything to point any fingers at Eshey. Not a single speck of evidence. "I know we need to consider the whole copycat thing, but I'm not seeing it that way. " She raised her finger. "That man knows something." She studied Carl. "Do you think he could have an accomplice?"

"Who?" Carl merged with the traffic that was moving at seventy miles an hour. "He hasn't been out of the joint too long. It's not that easy to find a partner you can kill with and trust not to give you away. Usually those kinds of partners are long-time friends—at least acquaintances."

"I don't know." She ran a hand over her face. She was tired. Not enough sleep last night. "Maybe an old friend from the pedophile unit in prison?" Jess knew that pedophiles were kept separate from other inmates to prevent the general population from killing them. On one hand, it kept them alive. On the other hand, it gave them a lot of free time to mingle with men like them.

"You mean they hooked up after being released?"

"It's possible," Jess sighed, frustrated. "I don't know. Anything is possible."

"I'll check his prison record again. See if anyone is mentioned as being friendly with him. I'll put in a call and see if there are any guards who might be able to tell us something about him."

"You think this is a waste of time, Carl?" She studied him. He always reminded her of a young John Wayne. He had such a noble, all-American face. "You think we're chasing the wrong goose?"

"If you ask me what my gut feeling is," Carl said, speaking honestly as always, "my bet would be that Eshey is not involved. But you know me." He flashed a grin. "I follow your dyke intuition. It's never steered me wrong yet."

She couldn't resist grinning back. Carl was a good man. She was fortunate he'd been available to team up with her. Even though the FBI had had women in their ranks since the seventies, and she'd been one of them for fourteen years, Jess still felt she was treated differently than the guys. But not by Carl.

"All right, cowboy." She slapped the dash of the blue government-issue Crown Vic. "Let's get this interview done with the super of Eshey's building and go the hell home."

Twenty-three

The phone rang after Jess and Meagan had gone to bed. They had spent most of Saturday working on their lawn, mulching flower beds, and cutting the grass, so they were both beat. They had eaten take-out from a local Chinese place and watched an old Katherine Hepburn movie together before putting out the lights a little after ten.

At the sound of the ringing phone, Jess rolled over sleepily. Meagan wasn't on call tonight; why was the phone ringing? She opened her eyes and glanced at the clock. Five after eleven. Who the hell was calling them after eleven if it wasn't the hospital?

The phone was on Meagan's side of the bed.

Jess heard her hit the lamp, groping for the phone in the dark. "Dr. Cartier," she said, sounding amazingly awake considering the fact that she had been fast asleep a minute before. It was what Jess called her doctor voice.

"Sure, hang on. Just a sec."

Meagan laid back on the pillow, phone in hand. "Jess, you awake? It's for you."

Jess half sat up, reaching for the phone. "For me?"

"Carl."

Jess ran her hand over her face, trying to come fully awake. "Carl? What's wrong? Kids OK?"

"Kids are fine," he said in his quiet, steady voice. "I'm sorry to call you this late, but I just got a call from Crackhow."

"On a Saturday night?"

"The Lorenzo family has been putting up missing posters all week. A call came in this evening. Tuesday night someone spotted two men who they think were with the Lorenzo boy in Philadelphia at a fast-food joint."

Jess sat up in the bed, completely awake now. Two men? Eshey and an accomplice? "Shit," she said.

"What's wrong?" Meagan touched her elbow.

"Crackhow didn't have the report on the description of the men, but the witness saw only one of the Unsubs, anyway. You know, it was dark, et cetera."

Unsubs, unknown suspects. Carl spoke like a cop even half asleep. "You want me to meet you in the office tomorrow?" Jess asked Carl.

"I can't. It's April's birthday."

She could hear the frustration in his voice. "We've got Barb's parents coming. Mine. Like a hundred five year olds. We're doing this barbecue thing after mass."

"It's OK, you enjoy the party. I'll go in, get things organized so we can tackle it Monday morning."

"Why don't you come over to the house tomorrow? Bring Meagan. Have a hot dog. I can grab a few minutes to talk."

"OK." Jess lay back against the pillow again.

"Sorry again about calling you this late. I was already in bed, too," Carl apologized, "but the story probably made the press deadlines. I didn't want you reading about our case on the front page tomorrow morning."

"Don't stress, Carl. Get some sleep. We'll get him. Them. Whoever is responsible for snatching these kids, we'll get 'em."

Jess passed Meagan the phone and fell back on her pillow. "Fuck," she said.

"What's wrong?" Meagan hung up the phone and flipped on the light.

Jess squinted. "Someone spotted my second missing kid with two men in Philadelphia."

"*Your* kid?"

Jess cut her gaze to Meagan. "You know what I mean."

"I do. And I know I don't have to tell you not to let yourself get too close to this case." Meagan rested her head on Jess's pillow and draped one arm over her waist. "Because I know that you know you can't hold yourself responsible for your father's failings."

"He didn't fail," Jess snapped. "Eshey went to jail for thirty years." The minute the words were out of her mouth, she regretted them. An agent had to care about each and every case; it was the only way to do the job. But an agent also had to know where to draw the emotional lines in the sand. Was she stepping over the line here because Eshey had been one of her father's perps?

"So do you think the little boy is still alive?" Meagan changed the subject. She knew Jess well enough to know she had made her point. And she knew enough not to go on about it.

"I don't know." Jess brushed her fingertips over Meagan's bare arm. Jess hesitated to tell her any more. She didn't usually share cases. When she came home, she just wanted to relax and forget about work. But this case was bugging her. She was missing something, and she couldn't for the life of her figure out what it was. "Maybe he's still alive. Statistically speaking, probably not. The question still remains, is Eshey responsible?"

"And you think that's possible?"

"I interviewed him Thursday for a second time. I'd already met him after the girl disappeared." She stared at the dark ceiling. "The man made my skin crawl."

"Because of what you knew he did thirty years ago, or because you fear what he might be doing again?"

Jess hesitated, tempted to tell Meagan the whole story. She already knew much of it, stuff she'd picked up in bits and pieces, but maybe Meagan could help. Maybe she could see something through her eyes that Jess was missing.

Jess quickly related the whole story, filling in the details she'd not told Meagan before. She also included Jason Lorenzo's aunt contacting her and the call from Sydney Baker.

"OK, so it sounds crazy," Meagan murmured. They lay side by side on their backs, temple to temple. "I haven't seen the medical reports, but it doesn't sound like Eshey could kill anyone. I mean, it takes a pretty strong person to subdue a ten year old."

"But he could have a partner," Jess mused aloud, "which would explain the sighting of the two men with the boy."

"Serial killers do that? Have partners?"

"Not often, but it can't be ruled out. If they do, one man is the mastermind. The other is the physical force behind him."

"Man? You know it's a man?"

"Statistically, most likely. Only approximately two percent of all serial killers are female. Of course, that only applies if we have a serial killer here, which has not yet been determined. So far, I have no evidence there's a serial killer. You know it usually takes years to make that assessment. Eshey killed girls for four years at a rate of one or two a year before the FBI caught on. All I have now is two missing kids—simple kidnappings. I've got no connection to Eshey at all that's not thirty years old, other than coincidence and similarity of cases."

Meagan was quiet for a moment. "So are you going to call the woman?" She pushed up on one elbow, and her dark hair brushed Jess's cheek. She smelled good, like shampoo and a scent that was uniquely hers.

"What woman?"

"The woman who testified against Eshey when she was a little girl. You said that you told her not to worry. That her daughter was safe. She doesn't know this little boy has been kidnapped."

"I don't know what I'm going to do." She stared at the dark ceiling. "I told her I would call her if anything came up."

"But you don't want her to panic," Meagan offered. "And you really don't have anything."

"Nothing but another missing kid. It's just so crazy." Jess closed her eyes. "Christ, I can't think about this any more."

Meagan kissed her cheek tenderly. "So give your mind a rest and get some sleep." She rolled over and shut off the light and then rested her head on Jess' pillow again. "You going into the office tomorrow?"

"I'm sorry. I know you wanted to work on painting the garage floor."

"It can wait." Meagan traced Jess's jaw line with her fingertip. "This is more important."

One of the best things about Meagan was that she said what she meant. Jess knew it really was OK to skip helping with the garage floor so she could get in a couple of extra hours at work.

"It's little April's birthday tomorrow." Jess continued to stare at the dark ceiling above them, as if answers would come to her straight from heaven. "Carl and Barb are having a barbecue and want us to come."

"You up to it?" Meagan continued to stroke her face, easing the tension from her muscles.

"It would give Carl and me a few minutes to talk. I don't want him coming in to the office, not on Sunday. Not on his daughter's birthday."

"So we'll go." Meagan leaned over Jess and kissed her on the mouth, her fingertips brushing Jess's breast.

Jess was deathly tired, but right now, feeling close to someone was more important than sleep. She needed to feel good, if only for a few minutes. She needed to feel good about the lousy, rotten world. She rolled onto her side and faced Meagan, slipping her hand under her T-shirt. Her skin was warm and soft. Her nipple puckered under her touch. "You know I love you." She gazed into her companion's dark eyes. "I don't always show it. And I know I don't say it often enough." There was a catch in her throat. "But I do love you, Meg."

Meagan smoothed Jess' hair and kissed her, her tongue flicking out to tease her upper lip. "I know what's in your heart," she murmured. "And that's what matters."

Twenty-four

"Do I have to?" Krista groaned.

"Yes, you have to. You haven't actually been in your grandmother's room in weeks. Just go in for a minute, say hello, and then excuse yourself. You can grab a Coke at the soda machine and wait for me in the lobby."

Sydney and Krista stood outside Cora's door, whispering. They'd just gotten out of church and were stopping for a quick visit before going home. Joel had gone to the cabin in Maryland to crab and Krista had decided at the last minute that she didn't want to go.

"Oh, Mom. Don't make me go in there. She so creeps me out with all that Bible stuff. She sounds like those guys shouting on TV about repenting or burning in hell."

Sydney grabbed Krista's hand firmly and walked into the room, pulling her daughter with her. Krista gave a squeak, but put up no resistance.

"Ma, good morning. How was the Reverend Holiday this morning?"

Cora sat in her easy chair in front of the TV. On Sundays, the nurses kept the TV tuned in to an evangelist station that ran church services all day. Holiday was one of her favorite TV preachers.

"Going to hell, that's how he is," Cora grumped. She raised a bony finger, evangelical style. "'And the wicked, they shall be turned unto hell as in all nations that forget God!'"

Krista turned to her mother, giving her the eye.

Sydney gave her daughter a little push. "Krista brought you a cheeseburger."

"Two, Grandma, because Ma said you really get hungry in this place. What with all the exercise you get." She offered the bag, giving a little half laugh.

As Cora reached out to take bag, she lifted her lashes to stare at Krista. "Marla?" she croaked.

Krista took a step back, obviously startled. This couldn't have been worse timing. Sydney had just this week shown Krista the pictures of Marla and she, too, had noticed that she actually looked more like her aunt than her mother. "No, it's Krista, Grandma. I'm your granddaughter, Sydney's daughter."

"Marla?" Cora reached out with one claw-like arthritic hand.

Sydney went to her mother's chair and crouched beside her. "No, Ma. That's not Marla. It's Krista. Sydney's Krista."

The burger bag fell to her lap. "Oh, sweet Jesus. It's not too late," Cora groaned. "Not to late to save her."

"I'm getting out of here." Krista spun on her tennis shoes and ducked out of the room.

Cora motioned frantically toward the empty doorway. "Marla? Don't let him hurt my Marla. Please." She looked to Sydney, her cataract-thickened eyes filling with tears. "Please help me. Please help me save my baby."

Jess walked around the moon bouncer Carl had rented for the back yard. It was a brightly colored tent filled with little girls squealing with laughter as they bounced up and down and fell into piles like puppies.

"Hi, Auntie Jess," April called, poking her head out of the doorway. She was wearing a yellow sundress and her hair was in two neat braids. Well, they probably had been neat earlier in the day.

"Hey, sweetie. Happy birthday."

"Thank you for my present! I can't wait to go to the pool and try out the swimmies."

"You're welcome."

Meagan had bought the gift. She did birthdays and Christmas. She wrote the thank-you notes and sent the mass cards, too. Anything that had to do with sentiment was Meagan's job. Jess liked to think it was because that kind of crap didn't matter to her. Meagan said it mattered too much and that was why Jess couldn't do it. It was Meagan's theory that Jess was not a cold fish, but a woman so filled with emotion that if she didn't keep it at bay, she'd lose her mind. Meagan thought it was the job. Meagan had a lot of theories for a woman who had a degree in obstetrics rather than psychiatry.

"Where's your daddy?" Jess asked April as she bounced away.

"Cookin' dogs." She pointed toward the house. "Watch, 'cause he burns them."

Jess smiled and walked away. The neat, well-manicured back yard was busy. Clumps of men and women dressed in shorts and T-shirts stood here and there. Carl's old golden retriever, Jake, slept under the shade of an elm tree near the back gate. Jess spotted Meagan chatting with Barb Steinman. Meagan waved with her diet soda.

Jess nodded.

Carl was right where April said he would be, the command post of any picnic—the barbecue grill. She climbed the steps to the deck. He lived in an attractive two-story colonial south of Baltimore, a nice house for a family.

"Want a hot dog?" he said as she approached.

"April says you burn them."

"What's she know? She's five." He pushed a hot dog in a bun into her hand. It smelled good. The whole back yard smelled good; charcoal and burgers, freshly cut grass, warm sun. Happiness. Jess was glad Carl had all these things. He deserved them.

"Ketchup, mustard, and relish are on the table."

"No thanks." Jess bit into the hot dog. It was all beef. Kosher. Carl was right. April didn't know what she was talking about; it was delicious. "I take mine straight up."

"Always a purist at heart," he teased. "Beer?"

"Sure. Meg drove." She nodded as he fished two out of a red and white cooler full of ice.

Carl flicked some of the water off the brown bottle, popped off the lid, and handed the bottle to her. She took a drink; it was icy cold and perfect on a hot Sunday afternoon.

"So you went into the office?"

Jess took a seat in a green plaid lawn chair on the deck. "Yup."

Carl sat in the one next to her. "And?"

She chewed on the hot dog, choosing her words carefully. She didn't want to ruin Carl's day. He didn't need to think about these cases right now. He needed to enjoy his day off with his family. "Crackhow left the preliminary report. The guy the witness actually saw couldn't have been Eshey. Description doesn't fit; he was in his thirties. But the witness did not get a look at the driver. All he saw was a man in a ball cap hunched up at the wheel. Could have been sixteen or six hundred. And we're still not sure if it was Jason who was spotted. This boy was a plump Latino-looking boy about the right age. Clothing didn't match, but we know that doesn't mean much. "

"So do you think it could be our buddy up in Jersey?

You think he killed Carrie, disposed of the body, and then went after Jason?"

Jess finished the hot dog and licked her fingers. "With a partner, you mean?"

Carl sipped his beer thoughtfully. He was dressed in a yellow polo shirt, docksider shoes, and what Jess called Nixon shorts. They were plaid and went to his knees. "Two men with a boy, if it was our boy. Works."

Jess knitted her fingers together, lost in thought. "OK," she said, looking Carl in the eye. "What do you think, partner? White, heterosexual, Judeo-Christian male gut instinct? Do we have a true connection here between these cases and Eshey, or are we just talking about crazy coincidence?"

"Could be coincidences," Carl sipped his beer. "You remember that man who killed his wife for the insurance, only to find out that his brother, who he hadn't talked to in years, had done the same thing four states away on the same day?"

"Or the woman who happened to be dicing up her husband on the kitchen table when John and Mack went to interview her about her co-worker's mail fraud."

"Exactly. Every agent in the office can tick off a number of crazy coincidences they've encountered on the job." Carl chuckled. "World's crazy. Crazy coincidences. Sick ones, too."

Jess set her beer on the deck. He had just stained it a few weeks ago. It looked nice. "But I don't think it's coincidence, Carl."

"You saying this because you don't think so, or because your dad's originally being on the case is coloring it?"

Her gaze narrowed. She wasn't angry. She could never be angry with Carl. But she could sure as hell

To start your membership, simply complete and return the Free Book Certificate. You'll receive your Introductory Shipment of 3 FREE Zebra Contemporary Romances, you only pay $1.99 for shipping and handling. Then, each month you will receive the 3 newest Zebra Contemporary Romances. Each shipment will be yours to examine FREE for 10 days. If you decide to keep the books, you'll pay the preferred subscriber price (a savings of up to 20% off the cover price), plus shipping and handling. If you want us to stop sending books, just say the word… it's that simple.

FREE BOOK CERTIFICATE

Yes! Please send me 3 FREE Zebra Contemporary romance novels. I only pay $1.99 for shipping and handling. I understand that each month thereafter I will be able to preview 3 brand-new Contemporary Romances FREE for 10 days. Then, if I should decide to keep them, I will pay the money-saving preferred subscriber's price (that's a savings of up to 20% off the retail price), plus shipping and handling. I understand I am under no obligation to purchase any books, as explained on this card.

Name _____

Address _____ Apt. _____

City _____ State _____ Zip _____

Telephone (___) _____

Signature _____

(If under 18, parent or guardian must sign)

Thank You!

CN083A

Offer limited to one per household and not to current subscribers. Terms, offer and prices subject to change.
Orders subject to acceptance by Zebra Contemporary Book Club. Offer Valid in the U.S. only.

E E PLU
OF BOOK CLUB
MEMBERSHIP

- You'll get your books hot off the press, usually before they appear in bookstores.
- You'll ALWAYS save up to 20% off the cover price.
- You'll get our FREE monthly newsletter filled with author interviews, book previews, special offers and MORE!
- There's no obligation — you can cancel at any time and you have no minimum number of books to buy.
- And—if you decide you don't like the books you receive, you can return them. (You always have ten days to decide.)

Zebra Contemporary Romance Book Club
Zebra Home Subscription Service, Inc.
P.O. Box 5214
Clifton , NJ 07015-5214

get annoyed with him. "You've worked with me long enough to know me better than that, Cowboy."

He raised one broad hand. "Sorry. I had to ask. Anything else you dug up today?"

"The fax finally came from Eshey's boss. We already know he wasn't scheduled to work the day Jason was taken. He was off the day Carrie was taken, too."

Carl scowled.

"But," Jess continued. "That's circumstantial. The man only works about three days a week to begin with. No court is going to think that makes Eshey a prime suspect. Hell, you were off the day Carrie was taken, too. That was the day you went on that school field trip to the Smithsonian with April."

He nodded. "OK, so the work schedule won't help us now, but it could later. So let's say for a moment that there is a connection between him and the missing kids. If it's not Eshey and possibly a partner, it's someone who knew him, or at least knew the cases, right? We just need to break this job down to manageable size. Why don't I get John and Mack in on the Lorenzo and Morris cases with me? John has some experience with kid-snatching. You start going over the whole Eshey case with a fine-tooth comb. I don't mean just our files either, but the court stuff, too. And didn't you say there was one of those true crime books? We need to get a copy of that."

She lowered her head, staring at the deck, and then looked up. "I can take the boy's case if you want, Carl."

"No. I'm fine." He met her gaze, his eyes warm. "Jess, you don't have to treat me with kid gloves with these cases. Sure, I hate anything having to do with kids involved in crimes, but Dani was a long time ago."

"You never get over losing a kid, Carl."

"Of course not, but you get on with life. Your heart

gets filled with other children who you love just as much as the one you lost. Maybe appreciate more. I'm a lucky man, Jess. I lost Danielle, but I still have so much more than most people."

They were silent for a moment, and as that comfortable silence stretched between them, Jess realized that she loved Carl. She loved him as much as she had ever loved any man in her life.

"All right, you take the Lorenzo and Morris cases," she agreed. "I'll start going over whatever else NCIC can dig up. I'll order copies of the court records out of Jersey and get my hands on the physical evidence, if anyone saved it."

"There's probably an entire room of records. It'll take you months to get through them."

He was warning her they could be in for a long haul, but she knew that. She knew they might not ever find Carrie and Jason, alive or dead. If there was a serial killer at work, Eshey or someone else, it could be years before they had enough evidence even to say it was a serial killer.

"So it will take some time." She stood up with a shrug. "I'd better get to work. See you tomorrow?"

He didn't get up, but reached for another beer in the cooler. "See you tomorrow, babe."

She smiled. She liked it when he called her babe. He was usually too professional for such endearments. She turned back to him. "Hey, Carl."

He tipped the brown bottle to his lips. "Yup?"

"The Baker—MacGregor—woman," she corrected herself. "You think I should call her back? I told her that I would let her know if there were any developments in the Morris case."

"Crackhow won't like it. We've got no proof these two missing kids have anything to do with her or her kid."

"I didn't ask you what Crackhow would think. What do *you* think?"

He shook his head. "Close call."

She hesitated for a moment. "Well, you're a parent and I'm not. If you were Sydney Baker—"

"Call her."

"Will do." She tipped an imaginary hat. He was, after all, senior to her at the Bureau. "See you in the morning."

"Thanks for coming," Carl called after her.

She waved over her head and walked off across the freshly cut grass to find Meagan.

Twenty-five

Sydney heard the phone ring, heard Krista pick it up, and a second later her daughter screamed with obvious delight.

"Yes! Yes!"

Sydney could hear her jumping up and down on the kitchen floor. The walls shook.

"Mom!"

"In my office," Sydney called.

A second later, Krista charged down the steps and into the office. "I made it! I made it!"

Sydney looked up from her computer screen, suppressing her smile. "Made what?" she asked blankly. She, of course, knew exactly what. The All-Star team. The managers had met Friday, and Krista had been waiting all weekend to hear the results. Sydney guessed it was the real reason she had decided not to spend the night with her dad last night and go crabbing with him at their cabin.

"Made what?" Krista bounced into the air, spun like an out of control ballerina, and knocked a book off the shelf as she came back to earth. "The All-Star team, that's what! I made the All-Stars!" She spun again. "I can't believe it."

"Well, of course you made the All-Stars," Sydney teased.

Krista ceased her dance in the middle of the blue and green oriental carpet. "What do you mean, of course? Mom, do you know how many girls were trying for those twelve spots?"

"Wouldn't matter if it were a thousand." Sydney got out of her chair and rounded the desk. "I knew you were going to make it." She threw one arm around her daughter and Krista gave her a half hug.

"Oh my gosh!" Krista raised both hands to her cheeks, her eyes widening. " I have to call Dad. He's going to be so happy."

"He's probably not home yet, but you could try his cell."

She wrinkled her freckled nose. "But half the time he doesn't even turn his cell on when he's at the cabin. It's makes him mad that the static is so bad that he can't hear."

Sydney had to bite her tongue. She'd been telling Joel since they built the cabin that he could have a phone installed if he wanted. She wasn't going to do it because she didn't need a phone there. That was why she went to the cabin in the first place—to get away from ringing phones.

"You can try and call him," Sydney said. "Or leave a message on his machine at home and tell him to call you when he gets in."

Krista began to bounce again. "And I have to call Katie." She stopped mid leap. "But what if she didn't make it? I don't want her to think I'm bragging or anything."

"I'm sure she made it. She's a good ballplayer, but even if she didn't, I know she'll be happy for you."

Krista grabbed her mother's hands. "I have to be at practice tomorrow at five-thirty and you have to be there, too. Mandatory parents' meeting. Practice every day. Sometimes in the morning, sometimes at night. And pitchers will have extra practice." She let go of Sydney and ran for the stairs. "I can't believe this! I just can't believe it."

Sydney smiled, her heart swelling with pride as she walked back to her desk. She was just pulling up her chapter back up when the phone rang again. It was probably Katie calling Krista back. Sydney let Krista answer it.

A minute later, "Mom, it's for you," Krista hollered down the stairs.

Who was calling her at this time of evening? She half hoped it was Marshall. She'd been thinking a lot about him. Too much. Maybe he was just calling to say hi.

"Hello."

"Mrs. MacGregor, this is Special Agent Manlove. We spoke a week ago."

Sydney rose out of her chair, gripping the phone. She felt as if the floor was falling out from under her and she was spiraling downward. In her heart, she knew what the FBI agent was going to say, even before it was out of his mouth.

The silence stretched out, yawning until it was a great canyon. Sydney couldn't seem to catch her breath.

"Mrs. MacGregor, are you there?"

"Yes." Sydney leaned forward, her elbow on the desk as she propped her forehead on the heel of her hand. Waves of nausea washed over her. She just knew they had found Carrie's body. She knew the little girl was dead and she knew Eshey had done it.

"Mrs. MacGregor, this is very unusual for me to be making this call on a Sunday night. It's not how we do things." The agent paused.

Again the silence, but shorter this time.

"It's OK," Sydney heard herself say. "I . . . I was just working in my office."

"I don't just mean calling on Sunday," the female FBI agent explained.

She had begun the conversation very businesslike, bordering on cold, but something had changed. Sydney thought she could detect some emotion in the voice, though what emotion, she didn't know.

"I mean calling you at all."

"It's Carrie Morris, isn't it?" Sydney lifted her gaze to the doorway. She didn't want Krista overhearing this conversation. "You found her body, tortured and murdered like my sister, and you think Eshey is killing again."

"No, no, ma'am, we didn't find Carrie. And there's no proof Eshey has left the state of New Jersey. I personally saw and spoke with him this week."

"So why are you calling me on a Sunday night?" Sydney didn't mean to sound so sharp, but if they hadn't found Carrie, why was she scaring her half to death like this?

"Were you aware that another family possibly connected to Eshey had a child kidnapped this week?"

"No," Sydney whispered. Again, the falling sensation. "I wasn't."

"The family remained pretty quiet about the whole thing. They never revealed to the press that the boy's aunt had been kidnapped and murdered as a child. And we got lucky, if you can call it that. There was other news this week with all that crap going on in the Middle East. No reporters looked into the family and made the connection."

Sydney didn't want to know the details of the missing boy and yet she couldn't *not* ask. "You said a boy is missing. I'm so sorry. What happened?"

"His name is Jason. He was kidnapped in the suburbs of Philadelphia on Monday. He was walking back to his house from a community pool."

"Oh, God. So long ago." Sydney whispered. She hadn't read much of the paper this week; she'd been too busy. But even if she had and there was a reference to the boy, she would never have known he had any connection to Eshey unless the article said so.

"Eshey was suspected of killing this little boy's aunt in '73, Mrs. MacGregor. Never formally charged, but of course, you know that."

Killed in '73. Sydney knew the names by heart now; Mary Elizabeth Truitt and Maureen Naples had been killed in '73. "Whose nephew was he?" she asked.

"Pardon?"

"The little boy whose been kidnapped. Was he Mary Truitt's nephew or Maureen Naples's?"

"Mary Truitt's."

Sydney thought about Krista. Pat Brown, Carrie's aunt, had been Eshey's second victim. Mary Truitt had been his fourth. There seemed to be no pattern there. But a second child missing? How could that possibly be another coincidence?

Sydney's lower lip trembled as she fought tears. She was dizzy and felt slightly disoriented. But she couldn't fall apart. She wouldn't. She had to be strong for Krista. "So what makes you say it's not Eshey? If Carrie's body, or she," she added quickly, "hasn't been found, it doesn't fit the MO. Eshey always left the girls in plain sight once he was done with them." She felt a sudden spark of hope. "And they *were* always girls."

"I agree with you. The MO doesn't match. And I've interviewed Eshey twice. He has congestive heart failure. He's thin, hunched over, has difficulty breathing at times. This little boy who is missing was big for his age, ma'am."

"Not easily overpowered, you mean." Sydney thought back to the hot afternoon in her father's Impala. She had kicked that bastard with everything she had to get away from him and she didn't know, to this day, if she would have gotten away from him if he hadn't decided to go after Marla.

"Exactly. Kids by this age usually put up some struggle at some point, even if it's not during the actual abduction."

"So if you don't think it's Eshey, who could it be?" Sydney's gaze strayed to the bookshelf where her bonsai tree sat. It needed water. She got up without thinking and picked up her atomizer. "Who else would know the victims' families?"

"Unfortunately, if there is a present correlation, which there may not be—you'd be surprised how often this kind of thing turns out to be nothing. Turns out there is no correlation except the crime itself. But if there is, just about anyone curious enough to look into it could have found these families. During the trial, the names of the missing or dead children he was suspected of killing were well published." The agent's tone was cool again, as if they were speaking of something ordinary; the weather, soda pop. "There was also a true crime book."

A glimpse of Marshall's handsome smile flashed through Sydney's head. "I know," she said. "I just read it."

"Do you mind if I ask how you got it?" The agent seemed surprised. "I haven't been able to locate one."

"I got it from the author," Sydney confessed. She misted her tree lightly with the water. "I'll send it to you."

"Thank you." The agent provided a downtown Baltimore address and Sydney went back to her desk and jotted it down on her ink blotter.

"So you've actually talked to the author?" Manlove asked.

"Yes. I realize this sounds silly, but I knew very few

details of my sister's death. I needed to know what happened, and Mr. King was very cooperative. " She sat behind the desk again. The nausea had subsided. Now she just felt numb.

"I'll be ordering court records of the Eshey trial," the agent continued. "Once I look through those, I'll have a better idea what we've got here. I'll be looking into the theory that we could have some sort of copycat killer."

"How likely is that?" Sydney asked.

"Very unlikely. But my experience, Mrs. MacGregor, has been to check every angle. We're trained to see what others sometimes don't see. What usually happens with this kind of assignment is that we thoroughly investigate and conclude that the crimes are not linked."

She felt a flicker of hope. "So Eshey's release and these kidnappings still *could* be just coincidence?"

"Could very well be." She halted. "Listen, Mrs. MacGregor, I have absolutely no proof that your daughter is in any danger. That's not why I called you. I just contacted you out of courtesy. Because I told you I would."

"And now what am I supposed to do?" Sydney fought not to sound confrontational. It would do no good to anyone if she started shrieking at this woman. She might need her help at some point; she didn't want to piss her off.

"You're not supposed to *do* anything."

"But how can I just sit here and go about my daily life? What if it is Eshey?" She gripped the phone. "I *have* to do something, Agent Manlove."

"Then I suggest that you do what any mother should do. Keep an eye on your daughter. Go over safety rules with her. You know; no talking to strangers, in person or on the Internet. Don't get into cars with people you don't know, no matter what they say. Never enter a public restroom without a companion. Common sense."

"All right." Sydney took a deep breath. "I've been over all that a hundred times with her, but I can do it again." She opened the drawer where she had hidden the book, *Twin Murders*, and ran her finger over the pages. Words blurred by. Black and white images of Marla. Of other little girls. "Are you going to contact the others?"

"You mean the women whose sisters may have been taken by Eshey?"

"Yes." Sydney reached for a mailing envelope in the bottom drawer of her desk.

"Honestly, I don't know, Mrs. MacGregor. That's a pretty gray area in law enforcement—remember, Eshey was never even officially accused of killing those other little girls. I have to talk to my supervisor. Even if we find it necessary, it will take some time to track them down."

"Apparently *someone* was able to track them down."

There was a pause on the other end of the phone.

"I'm sorry," Sydney said. "That was uncalled for. I'm just . . . I'm just scared to death, Agent Manlove. I understand it's unlikely there's a connection, but what if there is?"

"It wasn't my intention to frighten you. As I said, I called not because I think you have any need to worry, but because I told you that I would if there were any developments in the case. I want to emphasize that I have no evidence that your daughter is in any danger. Both missing children were twins, by the way, so your daughter doesn't fit the profile."

Sydney felt nausea rise in her stomach again. Tasted her own bile. She had guessed the little boy was a twin, but she hadn't wanted to think about it long enough to ask. Two twins. Would Krista be next?

"I'll send you the book right away." Sydney got up from behind her desk, suddenly feeling overheated. She could feel the flush on her cheeks and she was perspiring heavily. She headed for the powder room down the hall. "Thank you for calling."

She hung up on the FBI agent without waiting for a response, ran to the bathroom, and vomited into the toilet bowl.

Twenty-six

"Mom?" There was a knock on the bathroom door. "Ma, you OK?"

Sydney slowly rose from the cool tile and flushed the toilet. She turned on the water in the rose-colored porcelain sink and splashed her face with cold water. "I'm OK," she said weakly.

"Are you sick?" Krista sounded worried.

"Must have been something I ate." Sydney opened the door to gaze on her red-haired daughter, who looked so much like her dead sister that it brought tears to her eyes. For Sydney, Marla would always remain this age, still innocent and yet on the cusp of womanhood.

Krista stared at her, looking confused and a little frightened. "Ma?"

Sydney managed a laugh and reached out to touch Krista's cheek. "I'm OK. Really."

Krista took a step back. "That was Dad on the phone a minute ago. He caught some crabs. Can he bring them over for dinner tomorrow night after practice?"

"Sure." Sydney started up the stairs to the main level of the house. On an empty stomach, she seemed to be thinking more clearly now. "Walk around and check all the windows."

"Why?"

"Just do it. You should have seen the electric bill last month. I'm tired of paying to air-condition the entire beach block."

Krista went one way down the hall toward the kitchen; Sydney went the other way. Sydney had set the house alarm earlier tonight, but she checked it anyway. Green lights shone on the main panel near the front door showing that all systems were operational. She went back down the hall to the kitchen to make a cup of tea for her queasy stomach. She had to settle down if she was going to figure out what she was going to do.

"Windows are all shut and locked," Krista declared, coming into the kitchen.

Sydney carried the kettle to the sink, trying to appear as normal as possible. "Thanks."

"So I'm going to bed."

Sydney glanced at the oak-framed clock on the wall. It wasn't quite ten. "So early?" She wasn't sure she wanted Krista out of her sight yet.

"Big day tomorrow. My first All-Star practice." She kissed her hand and threw the kiss to Sydney the way she had done when she was younger. "Love you, Ma. Mean it."

Sydney had to turn away to hide her fresh well of tears. "I love you, too, sweetie. See you in the morning."

As Krista's footsteps on the staircase died away, Sydney attempted to get hold of herself emotionally. "I've got to think through this calmly," she murmured to herself. "Krista's in no immediate danger. Eshey never took a child from her home. Carrie and Jason were both alone when they were kidnapped. As long as she's with me or Joel or even Katie's mom, she's safe."

She didn't know if she believed that entirely, but it was something to cling to.

Sydney turned on the burner under the kettle and leaned against the counter. Her gaze strayed to the phone. The first thing she needed to do was call Joel. Maybe this time he would listen to her.

Marshall walked around his loft picking up the clothes he'd shed in the heat of the moment. He tossed them into the laundry basket and pulled on a clean pair of gray boxer briefs from his dresser drawer. He took the two wine glasses from the bedside tables and carried them to the kitchen sink.

Yvonne had just left. She had to be at work early tomorrow morning for an editorial meeting at the fashion magazine she worked at, and she wasn't ready. Lorna had introduced them at a party a couple of weeks ago. He actually felt a little guilty about seeing Yvonne. Not guilty enough not to sleep with her, though.

Marshall ran water in the wine glasses and swirled it around to rinse them out. He'd been feeling edgy the last week. He had thought he might be growing bored with Lorna, seeing her two or three nights a week, which was a lot for him. That was why he had given Yvonne a call. She was a redhead. He was partial to redheads.

But when he had met Yvonne at the corner pub for a beer, when she had greeted him with a warm smile and a kiss, it hadn't been Yvonne he had seen in his mind's eye. It was another redhead.

Sydney.

He couldn't get her out of his head and couldn't for the life of him figure out why. She wasn't really his type. Way too independent. Too old. With the exception of Renee, he rarely dated women older than thirty-five.

Marshal shut off the water and walked to his computer and flipped on the screen. Maybe he'd work on his book for a few hours.

He sat in his chair and stared at the screen. Who was he kidding? He hadn't worked on the book in days.

The phone rang, startling him. He hoped it wasn't Lorna. She knew he saw other women, but he didn't want her to know about Yvonne. He didn't want to hurt her.

He walked to the bedside and picked up, glancing at the clock. Five after ten. "Hello?"

"Marshall."

It was Sydney. He knew it even before she identified herself. Sydney with a small voice that sounded far away.

"Sydney, what's wrong?"

"I'm sorry. I should have called Joel, I know. This isn't your problem, but—"

He felt that tenderness again that seemed to overcome him only when Sydney was concerned. "Tell me, Sydney."

"Marshall, another child disappeared this week." She almost sounded like a little girl, lost and forlorn. Like twelve-year-old Sydney Baker.

"Disappeared?" Marshall wished he wasn't he wasn't so far away from her. Wished he was close enough to put his arms around her. Would she have let him?

"Kidnapped. I don't know any details," she said. "Just that it was Mary Truitt's ten-year-old nephew."

Her words were chilling. "Another twin?"

"Uh-huh."

He sank down on the edge of the bed, gripping the phone tightly. This had to mean another book. It had to.

Did it also mean Krista MacGregor was in danger?

Of course, she wasn't a twin, so maybe she was safe. But this missing child was a boy. That didn't follow the MO, either. "OK, calm down and tell me what you know," he said. "Tell me how you know it and then we'll discuss your options."

"I knew you'd know what to say." She sounded more like the Sydney MacGregor he had met in Cape May now. "I knew you'd know what to do. I guess that's why I didn't call Joel. He's not going understand. He's going to say I'm overreacting."

"Just tell me what happened," Marshall plied.

Sydney told him word for word what Special Agent Manlove had said. He made her go down to her office and take notes. He told her to list the possible explanations for the two kidnappings beyond Eshey's killing another generation of children. The only two possibilities were random coincidences or some kind of copycat killer. On another page, she wrote her options if he was killing again. Marshall did the same on his own notepad.

"I guess my first option," Sydney said, "is to sit and wait patiently. I could trust the FBI and the state police to do their job."

"I'm assuming that's what the agent wants you to do."

"You assume correctly. Of course that option didn't exactly prove to be an effective in the past, did it?" she chided. "Eshey killed six girls before he snatched Marla from the car, and at that time, he hadn't even been a suspect."

"What else can you do?" he asked. "What about taking a trip? Getting out of here."

She sighed. "Thought of that. I considered buying plane tickets to England tomorrow and taking Krista as far from here as possible." She hesitated. "But I can't do that."

Marshall sketched a picture of an airplane on his legal pad under his list of Sydney's options. "Why not?"

"Krista just found out that she made All-Stars. She would be devastated if she lost the chance to play," Sydney groaned. "I know it sounds silly, but this is so damned important to her. And what if I'm wrong? What if she isn't in any danger? Would she ever forgive me? Worse, would she ever get over it? When a girl is this age, Marshall, her dreams are so important to her."

"Well, I guess that leaves you with only one option." Marshall got up and walked to the window to look down on the dark street. "You and I can form a united front. We'll conduct our own investigation. We'll see for ourselves if Krista is in any real danger."

"You can do that kind of thing?" Sydney sounded so hopeful that he would have done anything for her at this moment. Jumped out the window, met her at the altar.

"Well, it is what I've done for the last twenty-five years," he said trying not to sound boastful. "It's not like the police hand me their reports. I know you didn't read *Axe Man*, but I actually interviewed the killer before he was a confirmed suspect. I was cited by the Chicago police as having actually aided them in catching the killer."

"So you're good at it?" Now her voice had taken on a softer, huskier tone. Sexy.

"I think so."

"Well, I guess that's my only option. Unless, of course, I drive to New Jersey tomorrow morning and put a bullet through Eshey's head."

"Nah. Not really a good alternative," he said lightly. "You don't have a gun, and even if you did, you don't know how to shoot it."

"Yeah, good point," she agreed, playing along. "And if I did kill the bastard, I'd spend the remainder of my daughter's teenage years in jail and Joel would be raising her. Bloody day in hell I'd let that happen."

"OK, so definitely scratch that one off the list."

To his relief, she chuckled. He was glad she didn't really think that killing Eshey was a viable option. It wouldn't have been the first time someone would have tried it. Frightened people could behave in desperate ways.

"All right," Marshall said, going back to the notepad on his desk. "So it's decided. We'll let the FBI continue their investigation, we'll stay out of their way, but we'll look into it on our own. Eshey's on parole. He can't be too hard to find."

"Deal," she said firmly, sounding much stronger and in control now. "So where do we start?"

"Well, I'm going to start by paying Mr. Eshey a little visit."

He heard her breath catch in her throat. "You think he would talk to you?" she whispered.

"Might. He did before when he was on trial. He never told me anything, of course." Marshall shrugged. "But he was more than willing to talk to me. The pervert was actually friendly."

"If you're going, then I'm going with you," she said, surprising the hell out of him.

Marshall slammed his Mont Blanc pen on his paper. "Absolutely not."

"Marshall, I have to see him."

She had that desperate sound in her voice now, the kind that made rational people do totally irrational things. He was scaring her. She suddenly sounded so determined.

"I'm not even going to discuss this with you, Sydney. If the man is killing, do you know how dangerous this could be? Would you want to draw attention to yourself? To Krista?"

She was silent for a moment. He was afraid she was crying. He didn't know what he was going to do if Sydney cried. Any other woman and he would have just hung up. He didn't do female crying jags. But Sydney wasn't any other woman.

"Marshall," she said after a moment. There was no sound of tears in her voice, only that rock solid determination. "Marshall, there's something you need to know. Something not even Krista knows."

He waited.

"She's a twin."

He wouldn't have been any more surprised if Sydney had said Krista was an alien adopted from Mars.

"What?"

"She's a twin. Her sister died at birth." Sydney's voice caught in her throat, ragged and full of emotion. "Krista's umbilical cord was around the baby's neck. We never told Krista because we didn't want her to feel guilty that she lived and"—Sydney halted and then started again—"Kayla didn't."

He didn't know what to say. "Sydney, I'm so sorry."

"It's OK," she murmured. "Really. It was a very long time ago. It was probably a bad decision on my part not to tell Krista, but back then I still felt so damned guilty that I survived and Marla didn't. I didn't want to put Krista through that."

"It's not exactly the same thing," he said.

"No, of course it isn't, but I was a new mother and . . . and, hell, I didn't know any better. Joel went along because he didn't want to deal with the pain of losing Kayla. So we just went home and pretended there hadn't been two babies. I know it sounds crazy, but—"

"It doesn't sound crazy."

She took another breath, calmer now. "So don't you

see? Don't you see that I need to lay eyes on him for myself? If I see this sick, pathetic old man that the FBI is trying to tell me Eshey is, then maybe I can accept that Krista is safe from him."

"Sydney—"

"Listen to me, Marshall." He could hear her grit her teeth. Her voice was stronger now. "This isn't your choice. Either I'm going with you or I'm going alone. I can find him just as well as you can. You can't stop me."

He was tempted to just hang up. Tell her to forget the whole thing. But he couldn't—not now, knowing that Krista was a twin. Besides, a part of him could understand why she would want to see Eshey. Maybe this would put an end to what had been a very long nightmare for Sydney. Maybe seeing Eshey the way the FBI portrayed him would at last bring some closure. Because while Sydney pretended not to be affected by her past, he saw it in everything she said. Everything she did.

"I'm totally against this," he said firmly. "It would be damned unprofessional of me to take you."

"Thank you," she breathed.

She'd won and she knew it. She knew he wouldn't let her meet the sick bastard on her own.

"You're not meeting him face to face."

"M—"

"This is nonnegotiable, Sydney," Marshall interrupted. "You go with me to this turnpike rest stop where he works. You sit in a booth across the room and you drink your Diet Coke and you bring absolutely no attention to yourself. You understand?"

"Marshall, all I want to do—"

"Because if he recognizes you and something happens," he said sharply, "you understand you'll have drawn attention to yourself and to your daughter. You understand you'll have to live the rest of your life knowing that."

"That's pretty harsh, Marshall."

His tone softened. "You're right it is. I'm not saying it to hurt you or to scare you. I'm just telling you the truth."

There was a pause between them. "You've got a deal, Mr. King."

Marshall exhaled, feeling as if he had been through some battle. "I'll see what I can find out about exactly where on the turnpike he is and what days he works. I'll call you tomorrow."

"If I'm not here, you have my cell."

"'Night, Sydney."

"'Night, Marshall."

He hated to hang up. He wanted to talk longer with her, to keep this connection he felt to her going. He hung up anyway.

Sydney shut out the lights in her office and went upstairs to check the doors one last time. She stood at the glass doors leading onto the deck and stared at the circle of light cast by the security lamp outside. She couldn't believe she had told Marshall about Kayla. She'd never told anyone. And she couldn't believe she had just made arrangements to see Charles Eshey again. She hadn't thought she'd meet him until kingdom come.

God, could she do it? Could she walk into the same room with him? Could she look at him? Should she? Marshall implied she was being selfish in wanting to see him. A part of her knew he was right. She was taking a risk in having any contact with Eshey whatsoever if the police were wrong and he was killing again. But Agent Manlove seemed certain, and Sydney felt compelled. She had to know that he was as harmless as the FBI thought him to be. It was the only way she would be able to find any normalcy in her own life again, provide any to Krista.

Sydney gazed out over the lonely, dark beach. It was after midnight. She could just see the white froth of the waves, illuminated by the moon as they washed up on the sand. It was hard to believe that on an earth so beautiful, there could be such ugliness in the forms of pedophiles and murderers.

She flipped off the kitchen lights climbed the stairs to the third floor to look in on Krista. Quietly, she peered into the dark bedroom. The teen lay asleep on her side, an old stuffed bear wrapped in her arms. Not such a grown-up girl yet.

Sydney pressed her lips together to fight the wave of emotion she felt, and then quietly closed the door.

It wasn't until she was in bed, contacts out, and teeth brushed that she realized she hadn't called Joel. She rolled over, pulling the sheet with her.

Tomorrow she'd tackle her ex.

Twenty-seven

Bright and early Monday morning, Charlie shuffled into the public library, putting on a good face. He hadn't made it all the way to the big polished desk when the woman behind it looked up.

He smiled. "Good morning to ya."

She smiled back, obviously flattered. She was ugly, with a wrinkled face like a sow's and a body that looked like someone needed to let out some of the air. "Good morning. May I help you, sir?"

Still smiling, he leaned on the desk. He let himself get a good breath. The walk from the bus stop had actually winded him a little, but not as much as he was letting on. "I was wondering if I could get a look-see at some old newspapers," he told the pig-librarian. "I been gone a long spell and I was hopin' to find out a little about my loved ones."

"Separation from those we love is so difficult, isn't it?" She rounded the desk. "If you tell me what papers you're interested in and the years, I can certainly help you . . ." She paused obviously waiting for him to supply his name.

"Charles Patterson," he said. Again, the lady's smile. "But you can call me Charlie. All my friends do."

"Well, Charlie, I'm Mrs. Moore, the librarian here. Ida Moore. Now, you let me take you back to the microfiche and computer room and I'll show you how to find what you're looking for."

She led him toward the back of the small library. She was wearing a flowered dress and orthopedic shoes like his mother used to wear. They squeaked, just like his mother's. Charlie ground his teeth, remembering that squeak, remembering how badly he had wanted to end the squeaking. Permanently. Just the way he had ended his brother Clyde's never-ending whining.

Apparently old granny's squeaky shoes had gotten to Charlie's offspring, too. He smiled to himself, thinking of the new clipping he had tucked inside his jacket. Terrible fire in '93. Burned up an old granny and one of her grandchildren. Tragic, was what the headline had said. It had been mailed to him just this week. An old clipping, carefully preserved. The sender hadn't written a note, or even a return address, but Charlie knew who had sent it. And he couldn't have been prouder.

"Now," the librarian continued, "I have to keep an eye on the front desk, but if you need me, you need only to give me a holler."

Charlie stopped at the door that led into a small, dark room. He waggled his finger at her. "You're from Virginny, ain't ya? Maybe even over the line into West Virginny."

Her piggy face wrinkled even more and flushed bright red. "Born and raised in Charlotte, but I haven't been there in years. Husband got work here when were young, God rest his soul."

Someone rang the little bell on her desk. She ignored it.

"I knew it." He clicked his fingers together. "I'm from West Virginny, myself. Little ole' town called Red Dragon. Ain't been there in years, neither."

The bell rang again. She glanced at the desk in

obvious annoyance. "Charlie, I have to see to that young lady."

"You go right ahead." He walked into the room and flipped on the light. "I'll make myself comfy and you get back whenever you can." He already knew how to use the computer; he'd learned in prison. But he didn't have to tell her that. He hobbled into the room. "I got all day."

"I'll be right back," she murmured, pressing her hand to his arm.

He watched her hurry back toward the desk, her fat jiggling. He was tempted to take her back to his room and kill her just to see if he could. He guessed she lived alone. Had no friends. Otherwise she wouldn't be so nice to him. She wasn't to his taste, though—too old, too gristly.

But the thought did cross his mind.

Twenty-eight

"An FBI agent called you on a *Sunday* night?" Joel's tone bordered on suspicious.

Sydney glanced at the door that led from the deck to the kitchen to be sure it was shut. Krista was supposed to be doing her chores. Then they would head for the outlets, a quick visit with Cora, and then softball practice. Until Sydney figured out what to do, she wasn't letting her daughter out of her sight unless Krista was with Joel or Katie's mother. Not for a minute.

She struggled against her rising anger. "Are you calling me a liar?"

He groaned on the other end of the line. "No, of course not. I'm just not sure you interpreted the call right."

"What's there to interpret?" Sydney heard the pitch of her voice rise and checked it. She had to remain calm. She knew it was the only way to protect Krista. "Special Agent Manlove called to say that a little boy who is Mary Truitt's nephew has disappeared."

"And this Mary Truitt was supposedly killed by Eshey."

Still that infuriating tone of his. "There's no *supposedly*," Sydney shot back. "Everyone, the FBI, the police, the lawyers, they knew he killed those other little girls.

The state decided to prosecute him only for Marla's abduction and death because they had me as a witness." She gave a kick, pushing the glider she sat in, and she drifted backward. "Mary Truitt was the fourth girl to die. She was walking home after getting an ice cream with her sister. The sister ran back to the ice cream shop for more napkins. Mary was never seen alive again. She turned up in a dumpsite ten days later. It was April of '73. If you had read the book like I asked"—she couldn't resist a little sarcasm—"you would know that."

"So this FBI agent said Eshey was a suspect with these kids who are missing now?"

Sydney's first impulse was to lie. She brushed back the hair that had fallen in her face. She'd had one cup of black coffee this morning, but she sorely needed another. She should have known better than to think she could deal with Joel before ten in the morning with only one shot of caffeine.

"No, the agent didn't say that Eshey was a suspect, but sometimes these things are complicated. You have to have a certain amount of evidence to consider someone a suspect."

"So if Eshey isn't a suspect, why the hell did she call you in the first place? First you make friendly with the guy who wrote that sick book and now you're buddying up to this FBI agent. Syd, do you know how this sounds?"

She knew how it sounded. Like she was losing her marbles. Or, at the very least, like she was hung up in her past, unable to get away from Marla's death and wanting to relive it over and over again. She was glad she had decided not to tell him she was going to see Eshey with Marshall.

She chose to ignore his comment. "The agent called," she said, forcing patience into her tone, "because I asked her to."

"Wait, you've lost me now."

Sydney knew Joel well enough to know he wasn't really listening to her; that's why he was lost. All he was trying to do was antagonize her. He didn't want to hear what she had to say because he didn't, for even a moment, want to consider the possibility that Krista could be in danger. Typical male response—head in the sand. He'd been the same way about their marital problems and his drinking.

"Agent Manlove called me because last time we spoke, she said she would let me know if anything unusual developed with the Carrie Morris disappearance."

"Unusual?"

"Well, I'd say this is pretty fucking unusual, wouldn't you? A pervert is accused of killing seven little girls who are all twins. He goes to jail. The killings stop. He gets out and suddenly a niece and a nephew of the dead girls disappear?" She shouted the last words into the phone.

Joel didn't say anything right away. When he did speak, it was in the manner one used with a blithering idiot. "You said there was a boy missing. Eshey sexually molested girls. How could it be Eshey? He killed *girls*, Sydney."

She was tempted to just hang up on the ass. This was going nowhere. "So maybe the MO has changed," she snapped. "It happens, you know."

Joel made a sound into the phone that signaled the call was just about over, which was fine with her. She had told him about Agent Manlove's call because she felt it was her responsibility to keep him informed. She hadn't really expected him to believe her when she said Krista could be in danger. She hadn't expected him to believe in her instincts. He wasn't a mother, and he wasn't a mother who had fought Eshey off in the backseat of an old Impala. How could he understand?

"So exactly what is it this FBI agent wants you to do with this information?" Joel asked.

"Nothing." She spoke quietly, feeling amazingly calm. She wouldn't be calling Joel again about any of this. She was on her own. "She just wanted me to be aware that Mary Truitt's nephew was missing. She said I should be sure that Krista understands about being safe." She paused. "And I think we need to consider telling Krista about Kayla."

"Absolutely not," Joel shouted into the phone. "We agreed."

"We were kids. We agreed not to say anything because we didn't know what to say."

"We are not telling Krista," Joel repeated. "Don't you think she's got enough going on right now with her pitching and All-Stars and—"

"Her crazy mother?" Sydney cut in.

"I didn't say that. You're stressed out, too. You know, I've been wondering, this thing with Eshey, do you think this all could be just some kind of separation thing with you? You know, Krista's getting older. She needs you less than she used to."

"Are we back to discussing whether or not I actually spoke with the FBI agent?" Sydney raised her voice. "She called me, Joel."

"Fine. Did you tell Krista about this call?"

Sydney glanced through the glass doors into the kitchen. Krista had appeared. This morning she was dressed in gym shorts with her school name printed across the bottom and a T-shirt, and her hair was tied back in a bright green bandana. She looked so young and innocent as she put cleaning supplies back under the sink.

"Of course not." Sydney got out of the glider and walked to the rail to gaze out over the ocean.

The beach was already beginning to come alive with

activity. Kids running after Frisbees. Seniors staking out
a good spot on the beach early, before it got crowded.
The funny thing was, they always put their umbrellas
forty feet off the shoreline. Sydney had always wondered what the point of sitting on the beach was if you
couldn't see the ocean.

"Well, you'd better not say anything to her about
Kayla or this missing boy," Joel barked.

So much for Mr. On-The-Wagon-And-Full-Of-
Understanding. This was the Joel she knew. The Joel
she had known she could not live with for the rest of
her life.

"And I'm warning you, you scare her," he went on,
"and I'll have you back in family court rethinking this
whole custody thing."

She had known that was coming. *Known* it. "Have a
good day." Sydney hung up. "And I hope you enjoyed
that fuck the other night," she ground out, now speaking at the phone in her hand, rather than into it.
"Because it was your last, buster."

The door slid open and Krista stuck her head out.

Sydney slapped the phone down on the deck rail,
trying not to look too guilty. At least Krista hadn't
caught what she had just said.

"Hey, Ma. Where's the toilet bowl cleaner? I thought
I'd do the bathrooms while I was at it."

Sydney couldn't resist a smile. It wasn't often that
her daughter voluntarily offered to do anything extra
around the house. Usually there were threats involved
in even getting her to pick up her room. It had to be
the good news about the All-Star team that had her
pumped. "Under the sink in my bathroom, I think."

"OK." Krista slid the door shut, and disappeared
into the house.

Sydney stared at the phone on the rail for a minute.
She wanted to make another call. Did she dare?

She dialed.

"Hello."

"Marshall, it's Sydney. You busy?"

"Pretty busy drinking coffee."

She smiled to herself. Just hearing his voice made her feel better. What did she care if Joel believed her or not? Marshall did. "I know you said you'd call me. I know you couldn't have found anything out yet."

"You can call me any time," he said. "I told you that. What's up?"

"I just talked to my ass-ex."

"And?"

"He's not going to listen to me. He doesn't even believe Manlove called me." She left out talking to Krista about Kayla because that whole subject was now so raw that she didn't want to deal with it for the moment. "I think he thinks I'm having some kind of breakdown. Something about anxiety over separation from my teenage daughter."

"So he's not going to be much help?"

She leaned against the salt-treated railing, and it pressed into the small of her back. She wondered just why she was calling Marshall. What did she want from him? Did she just want help trying to figure out if Eshey really was a threat to Krista? Or did she want something else from him? Something more personal? The thought scared and titillated her at the same time.

"He's definitely not going to be any help. He doesn't believe Eshey has anything to do with the missing kids."

"Even if Eshey doesn't," Marshall reasoned. "That doesn't mean *someone* isn't after these kids. It doesn't mean that Krista couldn't become an intended victim."

Sydney pressed her lips together. "I wish you wouldn't say that out loud."

"I'm sorry." He was immediately contrite. "I'm not

saying we have to panic. But I think it's safer if we consider the possibility, don't you?"

She closed her eyes for a moment, letting the heat of the morning sun beat down on her. "Joel's at least partially right, you know. I have been an overprotective parent."

"You don't have to give me an explanation," he said. "Remember, I've read your testimony. I know what you went through and I've met Eshey."

"Thanks," she said softly.

"You bet. Now listen. I was just about to call you. I already found him."

"Eshey?"

"Yup. I found which rest stop on the Jersey Turnpike."

"Which one?"

"I'm not telling you," he said.

"Why not?" She pretended to be offended, but she wasn't really. She knew why he didn't want to tell her.

"Because I tell you where he is and you might try something crazy like going to see him on your own."

"I don't have to. You're going to take me."

Sydney couldn't tell if he was smiling or scowling.

"Anyway, he's off today and tomorrow. What's Wednesday look like on your calendar?"

Sydney licked her lips. She couldn't believe she was going to do this. But she was. "Krista is supposed to spend all day Wednesday and then Wednesday night with her dad. They're going crabbing at our cabin in Maryland, then coming back for practice. They wouldn't have to know where I went."

"Wouldn't have to know you met me?" he teased.

She felt her cheeks grown warm and was a little startled by her reaction. Was Marshall flirting with her? "That too," she said truthfully.

He chuckled. "Fair enough. Now how about if we meet somewhere and go to this rest stop together. I don't want you even driving into that parking lot where he's working."

"OK," she agreed, knowing he was probably right.

They made arrangements to meet on the turnpike Wednesday at noon. Marshall was going to take his chances that Eshey would actually be there and that he would talk to him. In the meantime, he was going to begin phone interviews with as many of the families of Eshey's suspected victims as possible.

"So I'll see you Wednesday," Marshall said. "After I talk with him, I'll take you out for something to eat." He hesitated. "I've been wanting to see you again, anyway."

"Ah, so this is just a ploy," she heard herself say. She was definitely flirting now. "You're just hooking me up with a serial killer so you can buy me dinner and a beer, get me liquored up, and get me to do things I'd never do otherwise?" She brushed her hair off the crown of her head. Talking to him like this made her feel strange . . . kind of sexy. It had been a long time since anyone had made her feel this way.

"You found me out. See that, you're already a good investigator. You ever thought about trying to write a different kind of book? True crime always sells, you know."

She chuckled. "Ah yes, of course. I'm sure my publisher would be thrilled with the idea for the new book: *A Fool's Guide to Serial Killers and How to Avoid Them.*"

He laughed with her, his voice rich and husky. "See you Wednesday."

* * *

Marshall hung up the phone and dropped it on his desk as if it had suddenly become too hot to handle.

What was he doing talking to Sydney that way? Flirting with her like that? Where had that come from? He knew he was sexually attracted to her. More attracted to her than he had been to a woman in a long time. Longer than he could remember. But she wasn't his type.

He wasn't her type for sure.

Marshall knew Sydney MacGregor wasn't going to be interested in any quickies. She was a level-headed, well-grounded woman who would know better than to get tangled up with a man like him. A man with serious relationship problems.

He wondered if he ought to call back and cancel. This was crazy. He was going to interview Eshey while she watched from behind dark glasses in the next booth? It was so unlike him.

But how could he abandon her? He knew she was alone in this and he knew now, in his gut, that someone was terrorizing the families of Eshey's victims. He didn't care what the FBI said. He was going with Sydney's instincts and his own. So he'd go to Jersey and he'd meet Sydney and he'd try to talk to Eshey. He walked to his laundry basket and began to pull out dirty clothes and stuff them into a canvas laundry bag.

He stuffed a pair of khaki shorts in the bag and yanked on the tie to close it up. OK, so that was the plan. He'd meet with Sydney, do this interview in case he could help her. In case he could help himself. But he'd definitely stay away from Sydney on a personal level. He'd keep it strictly business.

Someone tapped on his door. He didn't get many uninvited visitors. He dropped the laundry bag and walked to the door to peer through the viewer.

It was Renee from upstairs.

He opened the door. "Hey."

"Hey, yourself." She smiled.

He could tell that she'd just gotten out of the shower. Her honey brown hair was pulled back in a damp ponytail, and she wasn't wearing any makeup. She looked wholesome enough to be in one of those soap commercials.

"My day off. The boys are with their dad's parents. I'm going out for breakfast," she said looking up at him with those big lonely brown eyes of hers. "Want to join me?"

What she meant, of course, was did he want to have breakfast and then sex, or sex and then breakfast. Since she was here at the door, he guessed she was thinking sex first, then brunch, or maybe lunch.

Usually he'd be up for the diversion. He really did like Renee and she was good in bed. Sweet.

But for some reason, it just didn't feel right this morning. He told himself it was because his head was full of thoughts of the questions he would ask Eshey. It had nothing to do with Sydney MacGregor.

"Ah, Renee, I can't." He ran his hand over his forehead, pushing his hair back. He'd need a cut before he headed south. "I'm just getting myself together to make a research trip. I've got a lot to do. Laundry, too."

"Oh, OK." She blinked. "No problem."

He could tell she was disappointed. A part of him wanted to take her in his arms and make love to her because she wanted him. Needed him. She'd certainly been there often enough for him when he needed her.

But having sex with Renee was the last thing on his mind right now. The idea nearly repulsed him.

"So I'll talk to you when I get back," he said, wanting to close the door as quickly as possible. "Tell the boys I said hi. Maybe we'll all catch a Yankees game." Her boys were big fans.

"Sure. Call." Renee waved, still smiling bravely, and then disappeared down the hall.

Marshall shut the door, feeling very small.

Twenty-nine

"What's up?" Carl leaned over the half wall that divided the cubicles in the office.

Jess leaned back in her chair, thankful she had worn a sleeveless shell beneath her jacket this morning. The air-conditioning was on the fritz in the building again and it felt like it was a hundred degrees in the office this morning.

She grabbed a file folder and fanned herself. "I got a call from CASMIRC this morning." The Child Abduction and Serial Murder Investigative Resource Center had been established by Congress in '98 as a new component in the National Center for the Analysis of Violent Crimes. CASMIRC's job was to provide agents investigative support when dealing with abductions of children, as well as serial killers.

"An Amanda Whitehall—know her?"

Carl shook his head.

"The last time I was at Quantico for training, she and I had dinner."

Carl lifted a brow suggestively.

She scowled. For such a straight guy, he dealt well with her homosexuality. "Not *that* kind of dinner. She's married, has a dozen kids or something. Anyway. She's a smart cookie. Very sensible. I liked her."

"What does she say about Eshey?"

"Well, she had one interesting tidbit to offer right off the top. Remember how I told you that Eshey's brother died in a farming accident when the boys were fourteen?"

Carl nodded.

"Well, Eshey was convicted of *killing* his brother. He served four years in a juvenile facility."

Carl cursed under his breath. "And then he was released and his records were sealed because he committed the crime as a juvenile."

"You get a gold star."

"So what else can this wonder woman provide us with?"

"Not sure. She's going to send the pervert's records to the profile geeks. Because the case took place in the seventies, it wouldn't have been done before. She's going to have them look over the Baker case, as well as the other suspected murders, and tell us if they think he could be our guy now."

"How long will that take?"

She lifted a shoulder as she reached for her coffee. "A day or two. She's jammed up; Atlanta's got some joker shooting old folks on their way to church."

"It gets warm and the killers come out," Carl agreed sympathetically. He met Jess's gaze. "So what's the plan for the week, partner?"

"Well, the Pennsylvania state police and two guys out of the field office in Philly are chasing down the Jason lead. It still hasn't been confirmed that this witness actually saw him."

"In the meantime?"

She sipped her coffee. "In the meantime, I'll read all of this crap. You go ahead and do what you need to do. I know you haven't finished that surveillance report that was due last week." Carl nodded, still leaning on the divider. This morning he was wearing a brightly colored tie that looked as if it had been painted by one of his kids. Probably had been.

"I've been hoping the report fairies would do it for me some night, but no such luck so far." Carl stood to leave. "Hey, you talk to Sydney Baker last night?"

"Yup."

"She flip?"

"No. Not at all. She seems like a sensible woman."

"What pretense did you use for making the call?"

She set down her coffee and picked up the folder again. She was beginning to wish she'd worn a tank top and shorts to work. Of course, Carl didn't look a bit overheated. He was still wearing his suit jacket. Was the man a robot?

"I just told her that the Lorenzo boy had gone missing. She's pretty familiar with the whole Eshey case. Knew the boy's aunt's name. She's sending me the book that joker wrote about her sister's death."

"So she was OK with your call?"

Jess tossed the file folder onto her desk and reached for a legal size notepad she'd been using to make notes on Eshey. "She was a little touchy at first, but I think I just startled her. She wanted to know why I was calling if there was no evidence pointing toward Eshey. She calmed down, though. I think she understands our position."

"We going to keep her updated?"

"I don't know." She spun in her chair to face him. "She wanted to know if I was going to contact the other victims' families. What do you think?"

"I don't know that we need to contact them yet. I can tell you that Crackhow's going to say no. The more people we speak to, the better the chance someone will talk to the papers, and we don't need that. I say we get the names and see how everything else pans out." He brushed his immaculate brown hair off his forehead. "Who knows, maybe we'll get lucky. Maybe Jason will turn up alive."

He sounded so hopeful that Jess's heart ached for him. So what if a third child linked to Eshey's victims disappeared? Would she have a serial *kidnapper* on her hands? It wasn't a crime that existed. That left her with a serial killer.

Monday afternoon, Charlie stood at the pay phone, his quarters in his hand. He decided to use the pay phone instead of the one in his apartment in case someone was tapping his phone. The police did that kind of thing.

He had the number on a little piece of paper. It was amazing what you could find on the Internet, especially with a little help from nice piggy fat ladies like Ida Moore. In the end he had decided not to kill her. What if he needed more information at the library?

He stared at the number on the paper, scared and excited at the same time. He wondered how much Dorian knew. In his back pocket he had the Carrie Morris news clipping and then the new one. Somehow, having the kids with him made him feel strong. Like the old days. People always said kids sucked the strength out of you, but not with him. Kids gave him strength. Power.

So many times over the years Charlie had thought about his own kids. Wondered what they were like. Then when he had learned what had happened with the fire and all, his heart had nearly burst with pride. So he had lost one child; he understood. He had understood by the time he was ten or eleven that he and his twin brother couldn't both exist on this earth. Just wasn't enough room. Enough air.

They said kids grew up to be like their folks. Guess they were right.

Charlie wanted to talk to Dorian about Darin. He knew Dorian had killed Darin and the squeaky-shoed old woman. Knew it in his bones.

Now if only he could get up the courage to call.

He took a wheezy breath. The heat bothered him a little. He tugged at the collar of the new white Hanes T-shirt he'd bought at Wal-mart. He might have to take something from his paycheck this week and buy another fan for his apartment.

Charlie stared at the number in his hand for a moment. Then he dialed and listened for the amount of money he had to feed the phone.

He began to drop quarters into the slot.

Thirty

Charlie listened to the hum of the dial tone, feeling a little dizzy. Dorian had hung up on him.

That little ungrateful—

He dropped the handset and walked away from the pay phone, leaving it to swing on its silver metal cord. He started down the sidewalk toward his apartment, head down.

It was hot. Really hot. He could feel the heat rising off the pavement, spreading across his face. His T-shirt was stuck to his chest and armpits, damp with perspiration. And there was that buzzing in his head that he hadn't heard for a long time. It was a loud buzzing, like having a big fat bumblebee in his brain, but somewhere in the buzz he could hear his mother's voice. *Stupid, no good, worthless.* He could almost feel the sting of the razor strop across his bare behind.

Charlie hitched up his drawers and shuffled up the street. He pushed the bee out of his head. Pushed his mother out of his head. He wasn't stupid; he didn't care what she said. A man who had done the things he had done and gotten away with them couldn't be stupid.

Why would Dorian hang up on him? Did the flesh of his flesh, bone of his bones, think he was stupid?

That wasn't it at all. Of course not. Charlie had just startled Dorian.

Charlie immediately started to rationalize. That was how he calmed himself, kept himself in control.

His phone call had been a shock, of course. He'd just caught Dorian off guard. That was all.

Of course Dorian wanted to talk to him. Wanted him to know. Otherwise, why the news clipping?

Charlie wiped the sweat from his brow.

He'd go back to his apartment and make some ice water. He'd park himself in front of that little fan the super had given him and watch some TV. His favorite soap would be on soon. He liked the soaps. He'd gotten hooked on 'em in jail. Been watching the same one for years. Maybe today he'd learn who was the father of Elise's baby.

Charlie would let Dorian be for a while. That's what he'd do. Then he'd call again. That was all Dorian needed. A little time to get used to the thought of, after all these years, having a father.

Instantly feeling better, Charlie picked up his pace a little. Once he and Dorian got to talking, he might take himself a little trip to Baltimore to see his kid. Now that he had made a couple of trips here and there, busied himself here and there, he wasn't so worried about getting caught leaving the state. Charlie knew he was too smart for that little skinny bitch of a parole officer. Too smart for the police.

Always had been. Always would be.

Thirty-one

Sydney rode beside Marshall in his rental car, trying to think about anything but why she was here. They were headed north on the Jersey turnpike and had almost reached the rest stop where Eshey worked.

She stared out the window, watching the scenery go by, thankful she had moved away. Everything here reminded her of her dismal childhood and of Marla: The scrub pines forests, the Garden State license plates, even the signs along the road marking the towns and distances between them.

"You're quiet," Marshall said.

She looked at him and then back at the pavement in front of the hood of the white Chrysler.

"Change your mind?" he probed gently. "Because if you have, it's OK. I'll turn around right now and take you back to your car."

"No," she said softly. "I need to do this. It's just that I'm nervous." She rubbed her sweaty hands together. "So tell me about your phone interviews. What did you find out?"

He kept his eyes on the road, yet he was totally attentive to her. "There's really not much to tell. Let's see, we know that Lorraine Brown Morris and Norma Jean Truitt Lorenzo both had twins. I didn't call them because I'm not sure what we could gain there at this point. I know this sounds silly"—he looked at her— "considering what I do for a living, but I like to try to respect victims' families. Besides, what if it really is just a sick coincidence?"

She knew he was as certain as she was that it wasn't, but she could have kissed him for offering that glimmer of hope. "Monday night I talked to Anna Marie Carpenter's father," Marshall continued. "Remember, her sister was number three. She never married and is presently serving as a missionary somewhere in South Africa."

"Guess we can safely check her off." Sydney wiped her damp hands on her jeans. "No twins born there. She's probably still a virgin."

"Probably. Her father was insulted by even the suggestion of unwed motherhood. I couldn't find any family members of Megan Naples, but I talked to this old geezer who lived in the home the girls had grown up in. He heard she was living in California and had one son. The kid is attending UCLA."

"OK." She nodded.

"And I found info on Spring Jackson, April's sister, on the Internet in a high school search engine. She died in an automobile accident on prom night in 1980."

"So no twins there, either," Sydney said quietly.

"Nope." Marshall glanced at her, then back at the road.

Sydney suddenly felt a tightening in her stomach. She knew the girls' names by heart, just as Marshall did. And she knew them in the order the girls were killed. He had left out Tracy and Terry Ponds. Tracy was the very first to die. "What about Terry Ponds, Tracy's sister? She was the only one in '71."

"Well, the only killing atributed to Eshey in '71," he answered grimly. "I only touched on the possibility in my book, but it is very likely he killed others while working out his MO. I've learned a great deal more about serial killers since I wrote that book. They're like that; they work up to their crimes. *Improve* on their technique."

He was stalling.

"You didn't answer my question," she pointed out.

"Terry Ponds had twins." He said it in one breath. He went on before Sydney had time to respond. "But I talked to Terry's mother, Diana. Terry became a nurse and married a surgeon. Diana, who's in Florida, said that her daughter lives in Newark and that she has twin girls, almost fifteen, Susan and Sarah."

Sydney held her breath.

"The girls are fine. Right now they're spending weekends playing soccer."

Sydney exhaled loud enough for Marshall to hear her. Tracy had been Eshey's first kill. Carrie's and Jason's aunts came after her. Wouldn't it make sense if he was killing the nieces and nephews that he will kill them in order? Especially with Terry Ponds living right in New Jersey?

So maybe it wasn't Eshey *or* a copycat killer. Maybe it had nothing to do with Eshey. Maybe Krista *was* safe.

Sydney looked up as Marshall covered her hand, which rested on the seat between them. "Please tell me you think Carrie's and Jason's disappearance after Eshey was released is just unrelated tragic coincidence. I know I sound like a broken record, but I just need to hear you say it."

"My honest opinion is that I don't agree with the FBI. I understand their legal position. I understand why they can't do anything lawfully without evidence, but I think they're lying if they say they think there's no connection whatsoever."

"Krista was right." She frowned, staring out the window. It had begun to rain and the pavement was slick and black. "They should have fried the bastard when they had the opportunity."

Ten minutes later, they turned off the turnpike into the state-operated rest stop.

He checked his watch. Marshall had actually spoken to Eshey the day before. He agreed to meet with Marshall and talk about his rehabilitation for the so-called article Marshall was writing, but not at his apartment. Sydney wondered immediately if he had something hide there. Eshey told Marshall that he got a half an hour lunch break today at one. It was quarter of.

He parked on the side of the parking lot near the tractor-trailers, out of view of the main building. He cut the engine and reached for his soft-sided black leather briefcase on the backseat. I'm going in ahead of you, taking a seat." His speech was clipped. "I imagine this place is like all the other rest stops on the turnpike. Open seating in a main dining area. You familiar with it?"

She nodded.

"Give me a couple of minutes, and then you come in and take a different booth; sit facing me so that Eshey won't be facing you when he sits down to talk. Keep quiet and don't draw any attention to yourself."

Again, she nodded.

He grabbed his briefcase to go and then set it between them again. "Sydney, can't you just sit here in the car? This is so damned unprofessional of me."

He sounded angry with her now. But she didn't care. Now that she was here, she was even more determined to carry it out. She knew Marshall didn't understand her need to see Eshey. No one could understand. But she had to do it.

"I'm going," she murmured. "See you inside."

He hesitated for a second, then grabbed the briefcase and climbed out of the car. He walked up a long brick sidewalk toward the main entrance and disappeared into the building.

Sydney sat and watched and waited as travelers pulled into the rest stop and got out of their cars. It had been raining on and off all morning and was drizzling right now. There were businessmen and families. Young people and old. Some raced through the parking lot to dodge the raindrops, others got wet, while yet others were well armed with umbrellas and raincoats.

She checked her watch and when five minutes had passed, she grabbed a rain hat and coat she'd brought with her off the backseat and got out of the car. She slipped into the baggy beige trench coat and pulled the floppy hat over her head, thankful for the cover of the rain. Gritting her teeth with determination, she threw her bag over her shoulder, lowered her gaze, and walked up the sidewalk and into the stone building. At the lobby, she turned into the food court, which was bustling with lunch business.

Sydney immediately spotted Marshall, but she made a point not to make eye contact. She spotted several suitable empty tables. Still keeping her head down, she walked to the self-serve soda fountains and made herself a drink. She couldn't bear the thought of eating anything, but she didn't want to draw any attention to herself by sitting alone without seeming to have a purpose there. Besides, it would give her something to do while sitting in the booth. Sydney paid for the drink and slipped into a booth, suddenly feeling a little weak-kneed. She kept her hat on to obscure her face.

Once settled in the booth, she opened her straw

and punched it into the lid of the drink. She took a sip, her gaze straying to Marshall, who was busy removing paper, pen, and a small tape recorder from his briefcase.

Watching him like this, Sydney couldn't help but notice what a nice looking man he was. She definitely had a thing for him. She was rusty with the male-female relationship complexities, but she was pretty sure he was interested, too. She just didn't know if she'd have the guts to do anything about it.

She glanced at her wristwatch. Five minutes, and Eshey would be here in this very room. He could even be watching now. She felt as if she were under water. Sounds were odd, hollow. The people around her appeared to be moving in slow motion.

Would she recognize him? She had been a little girl when he had taken Marla, a little girl yet to mature. He wouldn't know her. She had changed a great deal after puberty. But he had been a man already. Would he just be a grayer version of the man she saw when she closed her eyes at night?

She glanced up to see Marshall watching her.

She looked away.

Her back was to the entrance so that she could face Marshall. She didn't dare turn around again, but she suddenly got a cold feeling. The hair raised on the back of her neck.

He was here.

She watched Marshall. His expression, as he glanced up and beyond her, confirmed that it was Eshey.

Sydney spotted Eshey out of the corner of her eye an instant later. He was an old man; short and walked with a shuffle. She didn't catch a look at his face, but her breath caught in her throat.

Against her will, the black and white images of the

crime scenes in Marshall's book flashed through her head, superimposed over her own memories.

Sydney swallowed hard, afraid for a moment she was definitely going to be sick. She stared at the table in front of her, her head down as she grabbed for the soda. What if he saw her and somehow recognized her? She was being paranoid, of course. She knew Eshey wouldn't catch more than a glimpse of her as he walked by. She knew he wouldn't recognize her. Christ, she'd been twelve, and what had he seen then? A little girl with skinny legs, kicking and screaming?

"Mr. Eshey."

Sydney watched from below her lashes as Marshall half stood and offered his hand to the old man.

Eshey wore a tan uniform and a ball cap. He was carrying a paper bag that was probably his lunch.

"Mr. King." The voice wasn't really familiar. Or was it?

Sydney could see only the back of his balding head now, but he sounded like he was smiling. Bastard. What right did he have to smile? Marla and all those little girls would never smile again.

"I swear by all God Almighty, Mr. King." Eshey still had a slight West Virginia accent. "You don't look a day older than you did all them years ago when you come to the prison to see me."

Marshall indicated with his hand that Eshey should sit, and the man slid into the bench across from him.

Sydney was sitting over ten feet from them; Eshey hadn't even noticed her. Yet it was all she could do not to bolt for the door.

"As I said on the phone," Marshal said smoothly, "I'm working on an article about men who have served prison terms, have been rehabilitated, and now live as tax-paying citizens again." He picked up the recorder. "I can't tell you how pleased I am that you were willing to talk with me, especially since I interviewed you all those years ago. Do you mind if I tape—my memory is getting bad." He gave a little laugh that sounded odd to her. Marshall was nervous, too.

"Don't mind a'tall, if you don't mind if I have a little of my sandwich." Eshey unrolled the paper sack that looked as if it had been used many times before. "I only get a half hour to eat and then I got to get back on the job. Got trash cans to empty."

"Go right ahead. I just have a few questions for you." Marshal hit a button on the tape player and spoke softly into it, for his own record, no doubt.

Sydney watched with a sick fascination as Eshey pulled a sandwich in a plastic bag from the sack. He opened the Ziploc bag and pulled out two slices of white bread pasted together with something.

Her stomach did a flip-flop as he opened the sandwich to reveal some kind of gray-colored potted meat. He then slapped the bread back together and took a bite.

As Marshall began a list of innocuous questions about life outside of prison, Sydney just stared at Eshey. Even from the back, he looked older than sixty-two. Even without seeing his face, he *did* appear sickly and harmless. The way he had walked. The way his hand trembled a little as he raised the sandwich to his mouth.

But he had looked harmless that day he took Marla, too. Sydney could still see him in her mind's eye. He had driven by the car in his tractor. She remembered his smile, his porcupine hair, the way his elbow had rested on the door through the open window as he had asked her for directions.

Eshey was answering Marshall's questions about his

job now. About his apartment, and about what it was like to have all this freedom after being in prison all those years.

Eshey finished the sandwich and then carefully rolled up the Ziploc bag and put it back inside the paper sack.

Marshall moved on to the harder questions. Did Eshey feel he was a rehabilitated man?

Eshey hesitated in his response, and for the first time since his arrival, Marshall glanced her way. Her lower lip trembled and for a moment she was afraid she'd fall apart, but she managed a half smile. If it wouldn't have been so obvious, she might have even given Marshall a thumbs up.

She was OK. Her heart was beating fast, but not too fast. She was going to be fine.

"A re-ha-bil-e-tated man," Eshey said. He pronounced the word syllable by syllable with a long e in the middle. "Now that there's a tricky question." He waggled a bony finger. His stubby-fingered hands were clean, his nails neatly clipped. "'Cause you know, I didn't really kill that little girl." He shook his head. "I was an innocent man servin' a sentence for something someone else did."

Sydney ground her teeth and lowered her gaze to the soda again. She was squeezing the cup so hard that it was a wonder she didn't shoot the soda up through the straw and on to the table.

"So, the question is, son, can an innocent man be re-ha-bil-e-tated?" Eshey went on with the hillbilly accent he seemed to be able to turn on and off. "Now, I'm not a man of a lot of schoolin', but by my definition of the word, I can't be, 'cause I done nothin' wrong."

Marshall scribbled something on his legal pad as Eshey glanced at the cheap Timex on his wrist.

Sydney automatically looked at her own watch. It

was one twenty-five. Had almost half an hour really already passed? It seemed like only seconds.

"Well, sir, it's been real nice talkin' to you." Eshey slid off the bench seat and stood at the end of the table. "But I got to be clockin' back in." He offered his right hand and shook Marshall's. "Now, you got any more questions, you just give me a ring. You got my phone number there and I don't mind ya callin', 'cause I don't get no phone calls anyway. Just got to have that phone for my parole officer to get up with me."

Eshey turned away from Marshall, the paper bag in his hand.

Sydney lowered her gaze, hunkering over the table, and gripped the soda cup. She wished she could will herself invisible.

Eshey was walking past her now, a little closer to her side of the aisle than he had been when he came in.

Sydney held her breath.

Then he was gone.

Sydney looked up to see Marshall watching intently. His eyes were asking her if she was OK. She knew he couldn't get up yet, not until Eshey was gone.

She took a deep breath and counted to ten. Marshall was still putting his things into his briefcase, but Sydney couldn't wait for him. She had to get out of here. She couldn't breathe. She jumped up, grabbed her purse, and then, stealing a quick glance over her shoulder to see if Eshey was gone, she hurried for the exit.

Sydney ducked out of the rest stop and ran down the wet sidewalk. The rain had stopped. At the car, she pulled off the rain hat and took in a deep breath.

Marshall strode down the sidewalk toward her.

"You all right?" He set his briefcase down on the pavement and put his arms on her waist beneath the baggy raincoat.

She nodded.

"You sure?" He caught her chin and lifted it.

She met his gaze, tears in her eyes. "Let's get out of here," she said shakily. "I think I could use a drink."

Marshall gave her a quick kiss on the lips that surprised her. "Me too."

Thirty-two

"You OK?" Marshall slid his hand across the table and covered hers.

"I'm OK. Stop asking me that." Sydney glanced up at him, then back at her beer.

The sound of Britney Spears came muffled and scratchy from a speaker somewhere overhead and mingled with the sounds of conversation and clattering dishes. They had found a little pub just off the turnpike in a little town whose name she didn't recognize. They had ordered some chips and salsa and two beers. She drank only half of hers. She still had to drive home this afternoon.

She lifted her gaze to meet Marshall's. He wore a white and maroon pinstriped oxford and it was nicely pressed. It looked like one of those athletic cut shirts, and she had to admit it did look rather fine on him.

"He seemed harmless, didn't he?" Sydney asked, feeling oddly detached.

"The man didn't look like he could hurt a fly."

"Just an old, harmless, pathetic, sick fuck now," she murmured.

"Hey, remember that New Year's resolution of yours?" Marshall squeezed her hand beneath his, and she was surprised to find that his touch actually comforted her.

She cracked a half smile. "So, extrapolate with me," she said. "If he couldn't harm a fly—"

Marshall lifted one shoulder that seemed to be too broad for a man pushing fifty. "The FBI could be absolutely right."

She leaned forward toward him and the intimacy he seemed to be offering. Her emotions were spent. It had upset her greatly to see Eshey today. She kept telling herself that she should feel better. He couldn't hurt her now. He was a stooped over, fragile shadow of a man and she was a strong, healthy woman in her prime. He couldn't hurt her and he couldn't hurt her baby.

It all sounded so logical, and yet she still couldn't believe a word of it. Not even after seeing him. Sydney was scared and felt so damned vulnerable, and she had no one in the world she could depend on now but this man across the table from her.

"You believe that?" she asked.

He reached for his beer. "I don't know what to believe. I'm a man of facts. That's what I present in my books. It's how I make my living."

"So set aside the facts for a minute and tell me what you feel."

"Not sure," he murmured. "Like we're missing *something.*"

"I know," she groaned, wrapping her hand around her beer. She was having a difficult time here, divided between this whole thing with meeting Eshey, putting herself in possible danger the way she had, and with being with Marshall this way. The pub was dimly lit, intimate. She kept having these feelings, these flickers of desire that had no place here. How could she be thinking of sex with a man who was practically a stranger when she had just seen her sister's killer?

Because, she knew, concentrating on Marshall and

her awareness of him was safer and more welcome than the grisly thoughts that had been haunting her every moment, both waking and sleeping, since she had read about Carrie. Because if she didn't have respite from those thoughts, she would surely go stark raving mad trying to figure out why she was still so afraid of Eshey.

For a while at least, she could escape and find safe haven in Marshall's company.

But should she? As much as she'd like to spend more time with this man, she wasn't sure she should complicate her life any more than it was already. She wasn't sure she could handle it.

"I need to head home," she said, staring into the beer, the glass cool and damp on her fingers, her thoughts so confused she didn't know what she wanted at this point.

"I hate to send you home alone like this. I should have thought this out better."

She smiled. He really was sweet. "I live alone, Marshall, without a man to protect me," she teased.

"That isn't what I meant."

"I'll be fine. Eshey comes after me, I'll run his ass over in my SUV." Neither of them laughed. "Really, I'll be home in two and a half hours if I catch the ferry."

"You sure you don't just want to get a hotel room? Go home in the morning?"

She grabbed a chip out of the basket, waving it at him. "Was that a lewd invitation of some sort?" She couldn't believe such a thing had come out of her mouth.

It was his turn to smile. A sexy smile. Predatory, and yet way too charming at the same time.

"I need to go," she said, reaching for her purse. Suddenly she wanted to be in her own home, in her old ratty gym shorts and T. She needed to talk to Krista, just to get grounded again. Krista and Joel would be headed back toward the beach from the cabin by now. Ball practice was in an hour.

Marshall insisted on paying the bill and followed Sydney out of the pub and into the parking lot. It was still warm out and the sky was hazy. He walked her to her Explorer and she leaned against it, her purse thrown over her arm.

"So now what?" she asked. She meant about Eshey, of course, but about them, too. Was there a *them,* or at least the possibility? She'd been out of the whole dating scene for so long that she didn't even know how to approach the subject.

"I'll keep digging into Eshey. In the meantime, you're going to set this mess aside and get to work on your book. I'm not going to have any missed deadlines out of you."

He poked her playfully, and she surprised herself by catching his hand. "OK. I'll get back to work. I feel better now. Now that I've seen the bastard for myself."

He threaded his fingers through hers.

"Will you call me?" She said it almost shyly and felt silly. Giddy.

"Of course. I have that guy who used to work at the prison who I'm going to call, and then I'm going to get to work on locating Dorian Eshey."

"I didn't mean about Eshey." She didn't know where her boldness came from. Those raging forty-year-old hormones, she guessed.

He smiled. "I was just going to ask you that." He moved closer, dropped her hand, and rested both of his hands on her hips. "It was really good to see you again. I wish it could have been under better circumstances . . ."

"But," she offered, daring to look up at him.

"But I have no shame. I'll use any excuse to see a beautiful woman."

She laughed, raising her hands to rest them on his shoulders. He leaned closer to kiss her, and she lifted her chin hesitantly to meet his lips. Marshall was a good kisser, which really didn't surprise her. He started out gently, but with just the right amount of pressure.

Little tingles of pleasure shot through Sydney as she parted his lips to taste the tip of his tongue.

The kiss ended way too soon, and she was glad she was leaning against her Explorer. Otherwise she might have made a fool of herself right there in the parking lot by falling to her knees. Had to be the beer.

He brushed his lips against hers one more time, but it was a quick kiss. "Right about now I'd ordinarily be asking you if I could come back to your place or if you'd like to come to mine," he said. "Or at least see if you wanted to rent a hotel room."

"But I'm too ugly?" she teased. "Or my life is just too big of a mess and you don't want to get involved?"

Marshall laughed. "Oh, you don't know what a mess is until you've gotten a close look at my life." His dark eyes twinkled. "No, I would try to get you into bed in a second, but . . ."

"But?" She laughed with him, glad this conversation had taken on a playful tone, because she certainly wasn't ready to go to bed with him. Not the first man she'd dated since she was making the rounds at frat parties in college.

"But you, Sydney, aren't my usual kind of date."

With great exaggeration, she lifted an eyebrow as she met his gaze. She could tell by the look on his face that he really did want her. The thought made her feel good. "Oh?"

"And you're no ordinary woman."

She lowered her head, feeling silly again. "Well, thank you."

"So I think I need to go back to my apartment alone and figure out how I'm going to keep from screwing this up with you."

She felt weak-kneed again.

"Because I really like you, Sydney. More than—"

She pressed her finger to his mouth, then replaced it with her lips. Another gentle, quick kiss. "You say another word and you might scare me off," she murmured, gazing into his dark, movie-star eyes. "Go home and call me tomorrow."

"OK," he breathed.

She couldn't tell if he was disappointed or relieved that she was sending him on his way. "I'll be gone in the morning—I have to pick up Krista and take her to a morning ball practice, then I have to see my Mom. Call me in the afternoon."

Still he didn't look away, and she was so damned tempted to kiss him again—to grab his shirt and pull him against her like a scene from the romance novels she liked secretly to read. Worse, she wanted to take him up on the offer of the hotel room. She knew he would be good in bed, and she could feel that ache between her legs that wanted to take over her decision-making process.

Instead, she let go of his hand and reached into her bag for her keys.

Somewhere in her subconscious mind she knew she was thinking about what Joel had said about Marshall, about him wanting to get into her pants to get closer to the story. The man obviously wanted to get into her pants, but she didn't know if Joel was right about the rest. And she wasn't sure that she could make a good judgment right now.

"Good night," she said, unlocking her car and climbing in.

Marshall stood there until she pulled out of the parking lot and onto the road, headed south for home.

Feeling giddy, Sydney grabbed her headphones for her cell phone the minute she was back on the turnpike. She hit the automatic dial for Joel's cell phone.

"Hello."

She felt a sudden rush of emotions, and her eyes filled with tears.

"*Hello?*"

"Hey, you," Sydney said, getting a grip on herself.

"Mom."

"You headed for home?"

"Already been to the house and got my bat bag. I had to change my shorts because they got all yucky crabbing. We're going to practice now. Dad's stopping so I can get a sports drink."

"What, you couldn't find any water at the house?" Sydney wiped her eyes with the back of her hand.

It was one of their small ongoing disagreements. Joel always wanted to buy Krista sugary sports drinks when water was sufficient. It wasn't so much that Sydney cared right now what Krista drank as that she was looking for some normalcy after seeing Eshey. Some normalcy, and she wanted to keep Krista talking. It didn't matter what they talked about; she just wanted to keep her on the line. Hear her voice.

"Mom," Krista groaned. "One won't hurt."

"No, I guess it won't." Sydney changed lanes to get away from a tailgater. "So did you have a good time?"

"It was great! We got crabs and we steamed them and ate them before we left. Oh, and Mom," Krista rushed on, "Dad bought me weighted softballs. They are so cool. They're all different weights and they come in colors."

Krista had been dying to get the training balls that were heavier than the usual seven ounce that she pitched. Sydney wished Joel had asked her about buying them before he'd gone out and done it. From what Sydney had read, the balls were excellent training tools, but they could also be dangerous.

"That does sound cool. I can't wait to see them," Sydney said, unwilling to get into an argument with Krista right now.

"Well, I brought home the nine-, ten- and eleven-ounce ones, but I lost the purple twelve ounce somewhere in the cabin," Krista said. "I can't believe I could be so dumb. But Dad said it's OK because it's really too heavy for me right now anyway. We'll find it next time we go. We're at the market. I have to run in. Here. Talk to Dad."

"No, that's OK. I just—"

"Hey, Syd."

She took a deep breath. She didn't want to talk to Joel, just Krista. Since she had called him about the missing boy and gotten into that argument about telling Krista about Kayla, their conversations had been strained. She didn't want to deal with him right now.

"Hi," she said on an exhalation.

"We had a good time. Thanks for letting her come."

It was the warm, understanding, sober Joel. She softened. It would be so much easier if he were just nasty to her all the time. "She said she had fun," Sydney said. "She's thrilled with the training balls."

"Yeah. I know I should have asked you first. I was ordering on-line those slider shorts she needed and the balls were on special. If you want, I can make her leave them at my apartment. We already discussed the safety issues. I told her she could kill someone with one of those things, as fast as she's pitching these days."

"It's OK. She was probably ready for them anyway. You know me. Always overprotective." She gave a little laugh.

"Hey, where are you?" Joel asked. "There's a lot of static."

She spotted the sign for the Garden State Parkway, the road she needed for Cape May, where she would catch the ferry. "Oh, just out doing some errands." She didn't know what she wanted to hide more, her visit with Eshey or with Marshall.

"Oh, OK. Well, Krista has pitching practice tomorrow. You want to meet me there? I'd sit with her, but I have a morning meeting."

"No, it's fine," she said quickly, feeling guilty for having lied about where she was. "I'll just take my laptop."

There was a pause on his end. "Listen, Syd. I'm sorry about our phone conversation the other day. I understand why you're worried. I think it's unfounded, but I understand."

She took a deep breath. A part of her was relieved, but a part of her would have been more comfortable with him just thinking she was paranoid. "Don't worry about it, Joel."

"No, I'm serious. I acted like an ass. And that threat about family court." He made a sound. "That was really lousy of me. You know I would never do that. You know I know you're a good mother and Krista belongs with you."

Sydney brushed a lock of hair out of her eyes. She wasn't up to having a nice chat with Joel right now. "It's OK. Listen, I have to go. Tell Krista I love her. I'll see her in the morning."

"Have a nice evening."

"Yup." Sydney hung up and tossed the headphones on the seat, wishing Marshall had a cell phone so she could call him.

"Dorian, it's me, your Pap." When Charlie didn't immediately hear the click of the phone disconnecting, he went on excitedly. "I . . . I understand why you hung up when I called before. And . . . and it's okay. Just . . . just please don't hang up on me now."

"Why are you calling me?" Dorian's tone was flat. Angry. "What do you want?"

Charlie's voice trembled. He was scared and excited at the same time. "You . . . you know what I want."

Thirty-three

This case was getting to her big time, and it was only getting worse.

Jess threw her legal pad on the table at the little diner nestled off a side street from the downtown field office. Carl had ordered a caesar salad. She'd ordered a quarter-pound burger with a side of fries. He'd asked for diet soda; she, hi-test. That was why he was going to live to be a hundred and she was going to die before she was sixty, just like her old man.

If cases like this one didn't do her in first.

The Jason sighting had been a false lead. The Philadelphia police had actually managed to track down the vehicle a witness thought he had seen Jason in, accompanied by two suspicious looking males. When the police went to the apartment to investigate the vehicle's owner, "Jason" had answered the door. The little boy turned out to Joaquin Lopez. The two male suspects spotted by the witness were his father and his uncle, who had taken Joaquin out to eat after the boy's evening soccer game. The boy's team had won four to three, Crackhow had noted dryly.

So, just like Carrie, Jason had simply disappeared. No witnesses. No leads.

"Everyone says the same thing about Eshey." Jess stared at her notes on the pad and then glanced out the window at the traffic going by. She'd been making phone calls. She talked to Eshey's neighbors, two of his co-workers—the ones who had phones.

"'Oh, he's such a nice old man. So friendly, so courteous,' this lady tells me." Jess shook her head in disgust. "I wish I could have seen the look on that neighbor's face when I told her he was a convicted pedophile. 'But Mr. Eshey is so nice to little Ashley,'" she mimicked with disgust. "Of course he's nice to your nine-year-old daughter. He wants to—her." She edited her own crude words.

Carl peeled the paper off his straw. "You think about all the hard work people went to get Megan's Law passed. You think about the kids who had to die." He didn't mention Dani's name, but Jess knew he was thinking of her. Dani had been killed by a convicted pedophile who lived in the same apartment building as Carl and Barb.

"Now parents have a way of knowing if there are convicted pedophiles living in their neighborhood, and they don't pay any attention to the bulletins." He poked his straw into his soda and took a sip.

"Well, I don't care what anyone says." She sat back, crossing her arms over her chest. "The sick bastard is up to something. If you ask me, it looks like his behavior is just a little too 'model.' I swear, I think Miss Carmack has the hots for him." She glanced at Carl across the Formica table. "How can that be? She knows what he did. What he was convicted of doing."

"He's a smooth talker." Carl gestured. "The man has some kind of charisma, you have to give him that. That fits the profile of a serial killer."

She picked up her soda and took a sip. She didn't like straws. "I've spent hours making calls, pouring over paperwork until my eyes are crossed, and I'm beginning to think this was a waste of time."

"It's never a waste if you reach the end of the day with a better understanding of your suspect."

Out of anyone else, the words would have sounded ridiculous, as if Carl was reading from an FBI training textbook. But it worked for him. It just sounded like the wisdom of a guy who had been at the job a long time.

She looked up at him over the rim of the yellowed plastic glass in her hand. "You still think he is a suspect?"

"I don't honestly know. But I've been mulling this over and I think we have to assume there is a connection, whether it's directly with Eshey or not. I don't know if we can do anything about it—our hands are pretty tied right now without any evidence. But when we get back in the office Monday, let's start tracking down the other victims we think are connected to Eshey. Get info on married names and locations. We won't contact the families yet, but at least we would have names and locations if we need them. And I want to read Marshall King's book. There might be something to go on there you missed."

"You don't have to," she said studying her hands around the sweating glass. It was too warm in the diner, just like in the office yesterday. Didn't anyone's air-conditioning work these days? "I just started reading it and it made me want to retch. I can give you what you need to know without having to put you through that."

One look from Carl was enough.

She lifted her hands, palms facing out, in surrender. "OK, already. No kid gloves. Read the book. Read it twice, if you like."

"Burger and fries." The waitress with a bouffant hairdo straight out of the fifties sidled up to the table and slid Jess's plate to Carl. "Salad."

Jess waited until Carl's meal glided to a halt in front of her and she switched the plates. It was logical; burger for the man, salad for the lady. They were used to it.

"Anything else?" The waitress chomped on a piece of gum without bothering to make eye contact with either of them.

It was so stereotypical that Jess almost laughed. Real life was, after all, where stereotypes came from, wasn't it? That was what her father used to say. He was man who liked clichés, too.

"We're fine, thank you," Carl said, smiling at the waitress.

She walked away.

"What do you think about going to see Eshey again?" Jess sank her teeth into the rare burger.

"Don't know that it's warranted. You know how Crackhow loves harassment charges."

"I don't want to harass him, just chat. We could run up there and run back in one day. Come on," Jess plied. "A day trip and we don't really need Crackhow's approval. He knows we're still investigating Eshey. No one would blink at a second interview."

Carl stabbed a piece of chicken with his fork and smiled at her across the table. "You're good. Sneaky, but good."

She took a bite of her burger. Some days Carl's confidence in her was all that made her think she could make a difference in this awful world they lived in.

By moonlight, he dragged the rake over the dark, moist soil. It had rained in the afternoon, making the dirt soft and pungent. He raked carefully, dragging the tines in a straight line, making a pattern of a series of lines.

He knew there was nothing left of its body, of any of them, but he was meticulous. There could be no mistakes. Mistakes were what sent fools to jail for a very long time. He was not a fool.

"Clean?" came a voice from over the fence.

It enveloped him, the voice so like his own.

"Clean as a whistle," he answered, smoothing the soil with the back of the rake. "Not a bone to be found."

Their gazes locked, and it was a surreal moment. It was as if they were one and not two.

"Only one left now," he murmured.

"Only one left now," echoed the brother.

Thirty-four

Friday, mid afternoon, Jess sat at a rickety kitchen table in Charles Eshey's pathetic little apartment. It was a single room with a kitchenette table and two chairs, a sink, a small refrigerator, and a two-burner stove. In the center of the room was a plaid loveseat that had seen better days. Only a couple feet from it was a new thirteen-inch TV set up on the box it had come in. Homemade coat hanger rabbit ears rested on top of the TV. On the far side of the room, under one of the three windows in the whole place, was a single bed, neatly made and covered with an ancient patchwork quilt. There were only three doors in the apartment; one led into the outside hall, one to the bathroom, and the other to a closet.

The apartment was amazingly clean for its shabbiness. The yellowed linoleum floor was swept, and Jess could smell the faint scent of floor wax. The stove and countertop were wiped clean, and there was a cup, a plate, a bowl, and some eating utensils lined up neatly in a drying rack beside the sink.

There was something eerie about the place, and she couldn't figure out what.

"Sorry I got nothin' to offer ya but ice water." Charlie sat in the chair across the table from her.

Carl had insisted the old man take the chair. He

stood, leaning against the sink, where he could watch Eshey while Jess interviewed him.

"That's quite all right," Jess said, making a point to try and appear friendly. "We appreciate your seeing us." Once again, they hadn't called to let him know they were coming. Eshey's supervisor had been able to tell them he was off today.

The man made her skin crawl, but Jess forced a smile. "You keep a nice place, Mr. Eshey."

"Pshaw, call me Charlie, why don't ya? All my friends do, and I'm beginnin' to feel like we are friends." He glanced over his shoulder at Carl. "Shoot, you've paid more visits to me since I got out than anyone else."

Jess glanced at Carl and back at Eshey. "All right, Charlie."

Eshey glanced around. "It aint' much, but it's a sight bigger than that cell. Almost too big some nights when it gets all dark and quiet." There was a strange edge to his voice that Jess hadn't picked up before with him. A vulnerability.

Again, her gaze strayed to Carl's. He had heard it, too.

"I guess that's understandable," she said, sliding her chair in toward the table to get closer to Eshey. "I used to get lonely when I lived alone, too. It was always the night that bothered me. I used to put off going to bed by watching TV."

"Not much on that's good." Eshey hooked a thumb toward his TV. "I don't get many channels, not like it was in prison. Just got me rabbit ears, not them hundred and some cable channels."

"So what else do you do to occupy yourself when you're not working, Charlie?"

"Well, I been tryin' my hand at a little readin'."

"Have you?"

He folded his hands on the table. No signs he had

been in a struggle with anyone. No nicks in the skin on his hands or face. No bruises.

"They got a nice library here. Real nice librarian. Friendly."

"And she helped you find something?"

He nodded. "Got me Tom Sawyer. You read it?"

She smiled. "Back in grade school, probably."

"Well, my readin' ain't the best." Again she heard an edge to his voice, but this one was different, almost hostile. Definitely defensive. "My mama took me out of school my fifth grade year. Needed me around the place."

Jess tried to come up with a quick response. She hadn't meant to agitate him. Obviously his lack of education was a sore spot.

"Well, education isn't all school and books, is it, Charlie?" She met his gaze. "A lot of it is about people. About life. You seem good with people."

He smiled slowly. "You think so?" he asked.

"Well, you're friendly. You put people at ease."

She could have sworn his face colored with a mixture of delight and embarrassment. It was so childlike, so strange, that she couldn't take her eyes off him.

"Guess you got that right. I made friends right away with Miss Moore, that librarian."

Jess made a mental note to track Miss Moore down, give her a call. Now what she had to do was shift the conversation. She wanted to talk to him about Marla Baker, see if he'd give anything up after all this time. In all the transcripts from the trial, not a word was recorded as having come from Eshey's mouth. He never took the witness stand and he never confessed to the abduction, molestation, and murder of Marla.

"Listen, Charlie," she said, slipping out of her jacket. Despite the windows being open, the box fan blowing, and the sun beginning to set, it was hot in the second floor apartment. "I apologize for having to bother you again, but that little girl is still missing, and my boss is all over me to bring you in for questioning."

She and Carl had made the decision not to mention Jason's disappearance. It might be a card they could play later.

She shook her head, as if disgusted. "I told my boss about our talks." She gestured toward him. "I told him about how willing you've been to cooperate, and . . . well, about your illness."

Charlie took a white handkerchief from his back pocket and wiped the sweat from his upper lip.

Jess noticed that the handkerchief was folded perfectly into a neat square, so neat that it looked as if it had been pressed. A janitor who'd spent most of his life in jail was pressing handkerchiefs? Eshey was definitely a strange character.

"Well, Miss Manlove, I appreciate you speakin' up for me. Like I said before, I got no way to get nowhere. You know that." He spread his skinny arms. Arms that didn't look strong enough to wrestle a ten-year-old boy into a car. "I'm sorry 'bout that little girl and all, but it's got nothing to do with ole Charlie here."

"My partner and I understand that."

Carl nodded appreciatively.

"But you see, Charlie, my boss keeps reminding me that you were convicted of murdering Marla Baker and that you were suspected of kidnapping and killing at least six others—perhaps more."

Charlie's eyes shifted at the sound of the little girl's name. "I didn't do that," he said softly. He looked her right in the eye. "You know I was falsely convicted of killin' that little girl. I wouldn't kill no child. I like children."

He was a good liar.

She shook her head in feigned frustration. "I hear

you, Charlie. I reminded my boss that you never confessed to that crime." She glanced at him across the table. "But we're in a bad place. We've got victims' families contacting us. Families who say you kidnapped their little girls years ago and now you're after their girls again."

"Terrible world we live in, ain't it?" he remarked settling back in his seat.

He was distancing himself from her. And while his voice sounded relaxed and matter-of-fact, he was definitely nervous now. The question was, why?

"You know, I was in prison with men who did them kind of things," Eshey continued. "Terrible men."

His words were the invitation she was looking for. Jess had learned in training at Quantico that while suspects often won't talk about what they have actually done, they're willing to talk about how crimes *might* be committed. What she wanted to do was try and get Eshey to talk about how a person *might* kidnap a child if he wanted to.

"That's true," she said, as if they were best friends. "You have spent some time with those kind of men, haven't you?" She pressed a hand to the table. "Say, Charlie, if we have some questions about those kind of men, do you think you could help us out?" She tried to imitate his cadence of speech—another technique she had learned in Quantico. "I mean, you having met people like that, talked to them. Mostly Carl and I"—she gestured to Carl—"do surveillance work. Watch buildings, run wiretaps. I have to admit, this child abduction is way out of our league."

She watched his face change. He was taking what she said as a compliment. As with most serial killers, she was guessing that Eshey had self-esteem issues. The way she had put it to him, it sounded as if she thought he was smarter than she was, at least on this

subject. Killers fitting into the profile that was un-
folding with him needed to feel important. They
needed to feel smarter than others, especially figures
of authority.

"Aw, I could tell you some stories, Missy." Eshey wiped
his mouth as if he were disgusted by the thought.
"Gruesome stories. They're clever, those men. Most
people don't give 'em enough credit where credit is
due."

"Well, Charlie, tell me something, if a man did
take a little girl, steal her right out of her back yard
in Annapolis, Maryland, where might he take her?"

He shrugged. "Depends on what kind of man ya
are. What's to your likin'. Some might drive to a
lonely spot in the woods. Do what needs to be done
and dump it."

Jess noted that Eshey didn't say *dump her.* He said
dump it. Depersonalization of the victim.

"But that's not what all men do, is it?"

Charlie paused, as if considering whether or not to
answer. "No ma'am, some like to make it last."

According to her father's records, Charles Eshey
had taken Marla Baker to a dumpy motel in some
hole in western New York. The little girl had wandered out of the motel room two days after she had
been abducted. Eshey had left her tied up while going
to get something to eat, apparently thinking she was
too weak from blood loss to walk. By the time Marla
was found by a passerby on the roadside, she was already unconscious. She never regained consciousness
again.

"If a man was going to *make it last,* where would he
take her?" Jess's head was spinning with possibilities.
She honestly didn't believe Carrie was still alive, but
what if Jason was? Could Eshey have brought Carrie
and Jason all the way back to New Jersey? It didn't

seem feasible, but she knew from past experience that she had to think outside normal guidelines. Obviously men like Eshey were not normal. "I mean these days you've got less privacy than you used to," Jess offered. "People are more curious about men traveling with little girls."

"I don't know that a man could get away with that these days," Eshey agreed. He sipped the glass of water in front of him. "Because you're right. Folks don't mind their business like they used to."

In Eshey's trial, it had come out that he had been bold enough to actually take Marla to a truck stop for dinner the night he kidnapped her. Witnesses saw him with the little red-haired girl. A waitress gave testimony at the trial that she had thought it suspicious. She hadn't called the police, though, because, she said, "It wasn't any of my business."

"So he wouldn't keep her long?" Jess probed.

Eshey shook his head. "Probably not. Probably do his business and then shut it up."

Jess could feel her heart thumping in her chest. Was Eshey trying to tell her something? Had he killed those kids immediately rather than following his old MO of keeping them around a day or two?

"And then he'd just dump the body somewhere?" she asked, trying hard not to hold her breath.

He looked up at her suddenly. "How would I know?" He gave a laugh that could have almost been interpreted as devious. "You know how crazy men like that are? There's no telling what the hell they'll do. 'Scuse my language, ma'am."

And just like that, Jess knew the interview was over. She wouldn't get any more from him, at least not today. She looked down at his hands, the nails neatly clipped at the ends of his blunt fingers, thinking about what those hands had done. Her stomach turned over, but she made herself smile. "Well, listen, Charlie, I think we've taken enough of your time today." She rose out of the chair. "We truly do appreciate your talking to us."

Eshey, always the gentleman, got up. "Like I said, any time, ma'am. Always happy to help, 'cause ya know, I ain't bitter about what happened."

"Bitter about what?" she asked.

"'Bout bein' falsely tried, of course. I understand in this fine country of ours, some innocent folk got to go to jail to be sure we're catchin' all the guilty ones."

She picked up her jacket off the back of the dinette chair. What a clever man he was. He'd probably go to his grave denying he had killed Marla or any of the others. Maybe he truly believed he hadn't done it. It was that way with some criminals, but she didn't think that was the case with Charles Eshey. He was a smart fox for a man with a fifth grade education.

"If we have any more questions for you," Carl said, "maybe if we need some insight into some of those men you did time with, would you mind if we call you?"

Charlie limped toward her, dragging one hip a little as if his arthritis was bothering him. She hadn't heard any wheezing, though. Not like the other times. So was he really feeling well, despite this heat? Or had he forgotten to add the rasping to his performance?

"Feel free. And I got your card. The one ya gave me last time." He pointed to the refrigerator that was bare except for Jess's business card, which was attached with a plastic carrot. "I think of somethin' that might be helpful, I could even give ya a ring myself."

Jess followed Carl out into the dark, hot hallway. "That would be great." She made herself offer her hand to Eshey.

He pumped her hand and then Carl's.

"You have a good day, Charlie," she said as she and Carl went down the stairs.

"You too," he called after them.

Carl and Jess made their way down the dark, stale smelling hallway and into the stairwell. Their footsteps echoed off the metal stairs as they hurried down. "So what do you think, Cowboy?" Jess whispered to Carl as they reached the ground floor landing.

He glanced up the staircase. "I think that was a damned fine interview." His gaze met hers. "And I think we've got absolutely nothing tangible to go on."

Thirty-five

Charlie walked up to the gas pump and rested an elbow on the trash can. The filling station smelled of gasoline and oil and tires. He breathed deeply, enjoying the stench of familiar things. "Good day to you."

The truck driver who was fueling his rig turned to look at Eshey. He was wearing an orange ball cap and an old gray shirt with a big mouth bass on it. "Good day to you, boyo."

Charlie grinned. He'd picked a friendly one; this wouldn't be hard. "I hear you're headed south to'ard Baltimore way."

"You got that right." The driver looked him over.

Charlie hitched up his pants. Despite the heat, he didn't wear shorts. Didn't own a pair. "You lookin' for a little company?"

He gave Charlie another good look, which was understandable. A driver had to be careful picking up hitchhikers. You never knew what kind of crazy you might get. Charlie had once had a friend who had picked up the wrong hitchhiker and ended up dead for the cash in his wallet.

The driver tipped his dirty Orioles ball cap. "You lookin' for a ride?"

Charlie gave a nod. "Got a sister that way. I was

thinkin' I might go see her for a little visit. Maybe get me some tickets to see them Os." He pointed to the hat.

"Well, you're welcome to come along, boyo. Truth is, I could use a little company." The driver offered a meaty hand that was stained with wheel axle grease and thousands of miles on his log. "Name's Chuck. Chuck Boris. I'm runnin' a load of washing machines into downtown Baltimore." He gave Charlie another look as the gas pump shut off. "I'm ready to roll soon as I pay."

"Be right back." Charlie held up a finger. "I just got me a little old bag of things." He loped off, careful not to look too spry.

Charlie had left his cat and a bag of cat food with the little girl down the hall. Nice little girl. Smooth white skin. Pretty teeth. Dorian had invited him for a visit and he wasn't sure he'd be back to Jersey. If he didn't return, he wanted to be sure the old fleabag was taken care of.

Charlie went into the empty employee lunchroom. He felt bad not giving notice to his boss, who had been downright nice to him. But Charlie wasn't stupid. What if his boss called Miss Carmack and told her he'd quit his job? Nope. It was better this way. Charlie had visited his parole officer Thursday and she wouldn't be expecting him until next Friday. By then, he'd be long gone.

"Mom, look what's in the paper!" Krista burst through the door onto the deck, where Sydney was enjoying a morning cup of coffee, taking a few moments to read something that didn't have to do with vacationing with one's family. The book was going well. Sydney felt like she was back on track. And she had talked to Marshall every day since they'd met in Jersey. He was going to Baltimore tomorrow to interview Eshey's only living relative, his daughter Dorian. Then he was talking about coming to the beach to see Sydney and watch Krista's ballgame. So far, the team was in first place in the county.

"You're home early." Sydney folded her page to mark where she left off and closed the book.

"Actually, we just came by to get a few things," Joel said, following his daughter onto the deck. "If you don't mind, I'll take her with me and we'll come back this evening. I'd like to buy both of my gals dinner if you're willing. After that, we thought we'd head to the boardwalk to see the fireworks. There's supposed to be an orchestra to accompany the display this year."

It was a beautiful July morning and the air was warm and smelled of the bay. The crash of the ocean waves was a symphony on the summer breeze. It was too beautiful for Sydney to take offense at being referred to as one of *Joel's gals*. "Dinner and fireworks would be good," she said.

Krista plopped down on the glider beside her mother. "So did you see this? Did you see my picture in the paper? Dad said it was in all the beach papers yesterday." She pointed to one photo and then the other. "It's our All-Star team! And look, that's me pitching!"

Sydney reached for the newspaper article her daughter was fluttering in front of her face. She had seen the photos this morning; in fact she'd already called the paper to get a copy of the picture of Krista pitching, thinking she'd have it made into a poster for Christmas. But she didn't want to take any of Krista's fun away. "Let's see, won game two of the series, led by pitcher Krista MacGregor, who threw a one-hitter for a seven-three game." She nodded her head. "Pretty cool, girl."

Krista bounced off the glider, taking the newspaper article with her. "I have to get my other bathing suit. I left the turquoise one on the bathroom floor and it's still wet." She flew off the deck, sliding the door shut behind her, leaving Sydney and Joel alone.

"Listen, I wanted to talk to you," he said as he sat beside her on the glider.

She wished he wouldn't sit so close.

"I've been thinking about his whole Charles Eshey thing, and I understand your concern."

Sydney listened, not sure where he was going with this.

"I really don't think Krista is in any danger, but I suppose anything is possible." He linked his fingers together, leaning over thoughtfully. "Krista and I were thinking." He glanced over at her. "Maybe it's time I moved back in."

Sydney bolted off the glider, sending Joel swinging backward. "Move back in?" She looked at him as if he had grown another head. "Absolutely not!" She threw up her hand. "And you talked with Krista about this? How could you?"

"Sydney, listen to me." He got off the glider, following her across the deck. "Syd, you know I've changed. I haven't had a drop of alcohol since January, not even a beer."

She wrapped her arms around her waist, shaking her head. "No. Forget it. I don't want you here." Her voice caught in her throat. "I won't go through that all again."

"Will you listen to me for a minute?"

He took a step closer and she took another step back. Now he had her backed against the rail. She couldn't go anywhere unless she hurled herself over it to fall the two stories to the beach. It was a thought.

"Syd, Krista really misses seeing me every day. Having me, having both of us. And I have to tell you, I know you're angry with me for all those things I did, but I still love you. And I think that if you would just give me a chance—"

"No, Joel," Sydney said firmly. "Don't you understand no? You and I are done. Finished. Divorced. You're not moving back in and I have to tell you, I resent the fucking hell out of the fact that you would use Krista this way."

He rested his hands on his hips and scowled. "I thought you were cleaning up your language. Krista—"

"Krista is not here," she said softly. She took a step toward him. "And how dare you patronize me, telling me you understand my concern about Eshey? You have no fucking idea about Eshey. About what he did to my sister."

"All right. All right." He threw up one hand. "Fine. I was just trying to do what I think is best for our daughter."

"Not for our daughter, for you," Sydney snapped. "And you don't love me. I don't know that you ever loved me. This isn't about me. This isn't even about having Krista with you." She could feel the heat in her face as her ire rose. "This is about losing, isn't it?" She stared him in the face. "You've finally sobered up long enough to realize what you've lost and you don't like it."

He turned away, raising a hand as if she were being totally unreasonable. "We're going. We'll be back to get you at six."

"Have Krista call me," she said, backing to the rail again. "Right now, I can't stand the thought of eating with you."

Joel walked off the deck, slamming the sliding door.

Sydney turned away to look out at the ocean, feeling guilty as hell. Joel wasn't a bad person, and he was Krista's father. A good father. Was she wrong not to take him back for Krista's sake?

She closed her eyes for a second. She didn't care what was right. She couldn't do it. She just couldn't.

She walked back to the glider and picked up the phone from the small table beside it. She punched the numbers she now knew by heart and smiled as Marshal picked up the phone.

"Hey, I was just getting ready to call you. I didn't want to wake you if you were trying to sleep in."

"Sleep in, are you kidding? I've already gotten into a fight with Joel this morning."

"Sorry."

"Yeah." She sat down and tucked her bare feet beneath her. "Used the f word and everything. I'm really not doing well with my New Year's resolution. I think half the neighbors on my block heard me." She smiled, feeling better. Just hearing Marshall's voice made her feel better. "So are you coming tomorrow after the interview?"

"I see Eshey's daughter at one. Then I'll be heading your way. I figure I'll be there by four. I already made hotel reservations in Albany Beach, so I'll drop off my stuff and be by."

"Great. I can't wait." She hesitated. "I kinda wish I could go with you."

"That's out of the question. I can't do that to her. Not when she's been nice enough to agree to see me. But why would you want to go?" he asked.

She lifted her shoulder. "I don't know. Sick curiosity. Anyway, I'm going to hang out here with Krista and get her to her noon batting practice. She doesn't play until eight, so you'll have plenty of time to get here from Baltimore."

"Sounds good to me. I can't wait to see you."

Sydney smiled to herself. Marshall was driving from New York City to see her. Did this mean she had a boyfriend?

Thirty-six

Marshall walked up the brick sidewalk to the bungalow where Dorian Eshey lived and rang the bell. As he waited, he took in the little house nestled in a neighborhood in the suburbs of Baltimore. It was neat, with cedar siding, shutters painted barn red, and window boxes with beautiful pink geraniums tumbling out of them. The tiny lawn was recently manicured, with flowerbeds running up both sides of the sidewalk that led to the house. He didn't know that he had ever seen such perfect flowerbeds. There wasn't a single dead leaf or wilted flower, and the mulch was raked as if by a fork.

The door opened and Marshal glanced up. He didn't know what he was expecting, but this wasn't it. Dorian Eshey was inches taller than her father, and though she wasn't yet thirty, she looked twenty years older. She had mousy brown hair, pulled in a bun, and an angular face. She wore so much base make-up that it looked as if it had been applied with a trowel, topped off with unnatural rosy cheeks and lips, and blue eye shadow. Marshall wasn't even aware Maybelline still made eye shadow in that color.

"Miss Eshey," Marshall said. "I'm Marshall King. I appreciate you seeing me."

She raised one hand to reveal a yellow plastic glove.

"I'm sorry, I was washing dishes. You won't mind if I don't shake your hand with these wet things?"

"Certainly not."

"Come in." Dorian stepped back. "I'm just finishing up in the kitchen, so if you don't mind, we'll go there instead of the living room."

"That will be fine." Marshall had to work not to appear to be staring at her. The woman was odd, for sure. She was wearing flowered stretch pants and white leather sneakers that looked to be close to his own shoe size. And the woman was ugly. There was just no way around it.

Marshall followed Dorian into the house. The shades were drawn and the entryway was dim. The house smelled of Pine Sol and mothballs. It had that scent that the homes of the elderly often possessed. Marshall had always likened that scent with the smell of death, but apparently it was just the combination of cleaning solutions and moth repellent.

It was like stepping back in time thirty years as Dorian led him into a kitchen that, though spotless, was in serious need of remodeling. The appliances were all in the avocado green that had been so popular in the late sixties and early seventies, and the countertops were speckled gold Formica.

"Please sit," Dorian said, motioning to a kitchenette table with metal chairs that had red vinyl seat covers. She leaned against the sink, making no attempt to remove her yellow rubber cleaning gloves.

"As I said, I appreciate your being willing to talk to me." Marshall drew a notebook and pen from his briefcase. "I'm doing an article on rehabilitated men and I have a few questions to ask you about your father."

"I'm glad to talk to you, but I'm not sure what I have to offer." Her diction was perfect. Definitely a teacher's tone.

"Do you mind if I record you?" Marshall asked, holding up a small tape recorder. "That way if I miss anything in my notes, I can go to the tape rather than having to bother you again with a call."

"Not at all."

He popped in a fresh tape and hit "record." As he turned to look at Dorian, he realized there was a pig asleep on a dog bed in the corner of the room. A pig on a plaid dog bed? He wouldn't have been any more surprised if there had been an elephant in the kitchen.

He knew his eyes widened, despite his attempt to be professional. Over the years of interviewing people, he'd seen a lot of things, but never a pig in a kitchen.

"That's Jessica," Dorian said. "Pigs make better pets than dogs, you know. They're much smarter than dogs, and they're very clean."

At the mention of its name, the pig lifted its head, its eyes opening for a moment.

"I see." Marshall forced himself to return his attention to the interview and away from the large farm animal. "Let's see, Miss Eshey. As I said on the phone, I have only a few questions. The article is about the released prisoners, but we like input from family and friends." He glanced at his notes and then up at her. "Have you spoken with your father since his release?"

"Mr. King," Dorian said patiently, "my father was arrested before I was born. I have never met or spoken to him in my life."

"I see. So how do you feel about him, now that he's been released?"

"How do I feel?" She frowned, pulling her mouth into a tight pucker. "Why, angry, of course."

"Because he was released without serving a life sentence?" Marshall asked.

"Because he went to jail before I was born. He was never there to care for my sister and me. Instead, we were left with a drug addict mother and then a brutal grandmother." Her tone was thick with hostility, her grip tightening on the rim of the sink behind her.

"We never had a father, and every girl deserves a father, don't you think, Mr. Marshall?" She met his gaze, her eyes the same gray color as Eshey's.

"Do you think it was wrong for the state to release your father on parole?"

"Oh, I don't know about that." Her anger was gone as quickly as it had surfaced. She began to take dishes from the drying rack and slide them onto a stack in a nearby cupboard. "I was told by the FBI that he was ill. An ill, harmless old man."

Marshall paused. "The FBI contacted you?"

"Oh, I think it was just routine."

Marshall wasn't sure he agreed, but he didn't say anything.

Dorian waved a yellow hand. "Some kind of background check or something. I imagine it's done anytime a man like my father is released."

Marshall scribbled on his notepad. "Miss Eshey, do you intend to ever see your father?"

"I'm not sure that I could." She carried two coffee mugs to the dish cupboard and lined them up so that they matched the others on the shelf, handles to the right.

He watched with fascination as Dorian fiddled with the cup handles until she had them positioned just so. When Marshall had first walked into the house, he had decided Dorian was a neat freak. Now he was beginning to wonder if she was some kind of obsessive compulsive. Of course, how could a woman emerge unscathed from the past she'd had?

"So you wouldn't see him, even if he asked to meet with you? Even knowing that he is ill with a heart condition?"

She lowered her gaze. "My father made my life very difficult for me. I've worked hard to erase the shame of his imprisonment." She lifted her gaze. "No sir, I have no desire to meet my father, except perhaps in hell." She lowered her voice thoughtfully. "Where I'm certain we will meet, indeed."

Her words echoed oddly in Marshall's head. This woman was just as creepy as her father. It certainly gave some food for thought to the nurture versus nature argument.

Marshall scribbled something else and flipped the page of the notepad. "I think that's all." He glanced up at Dorian, who was again standing against the old two-tub-style porcelain sink. "There's one more thing, Miss Eshey. I understand that the year you graduated from high school, your twin sister died in a house fire along with your grandmother."

"The old woman didn't understand the importance of functioning smoke detectors," Dorian said sadly, hanging her head. "No batteries. They died in their sleep. I was able to get out only because I woke to use the restroom."

Marshall made another note and looked up. "I'm sure you were aware that your father was a twin. Did you know that his twin brother also died in an accident?"

"My family has certainly had its tragedies, hasn't it?"

Marshall slipped his notepad back into the briefcase and clicked the tape player off. "I think that's it. If there's anything else you'd like to tell me, anything you'd like me to express in this article I'm writing, I'll leave you my name and number. I'll be on the Delaware shore for a few days, so I'll leave that number, too. It's the Ocean Sands in Albany Beach." He copied the phone number from his Day Timer to his business card. "Again, I thank you for your time."

Marshall left his business card in the center of the

table and rose from his chair. "One more thing, Miss Eshey. Would it be all right if I took your photo?"

"Oh, goodness." She brushed her slacks with her hand. "I hadn't realized you wanted a picture." She was obviously flattered. "I'm a mess."

"How about just a head shot?"

"Well, I suppose." She was already posing before he got the camera out of the briefcase. She smiled.

He took two pictures. "Got it. Thanks so much. I'm not sure if the article will include photos, but it's always nice to have them."

"Let me walk you out," she said.

Following Dorian out of the kitchen, Marshall took one more look at the pig. *A pig in the kitchen.* As he shifted his gaze back again, he noticed refrigerator magnets attached to the freezer door that seemed to have been placed there randomly. It was of no importance, except that nothing else in the house seemed even slightly out of place. Everything, like the cup handles, appeared to be placed precisely by the schoolteacher. Odd.

"Have a safe drive, Mr. Marshall." Dorian opened the door for him.

When he was gone, Dorian closed the door behind the writer and leaned over to realign the strawberry floor mat, which was slightly askew.

Dorian had read *Twin Murders* and while some colleagues at work might have thought King a bit of a hack, Dorian thought the man had talent. The question was, would he live to write another book?

The jury of two was still out.

He pulled back the mini blind and took a quick peek out the window. He saw the feet first as the writer stepped out the front door. He had known they were leaving the house by the sound of their footsteps overhead.

The writer walked down the sidewalk toward the white sedan on the street, and he watched him get into the car. The man was leaving now, but perhaps he would see him soon.

He dropped the blind and gazed at the newspaper clippings on the bed, hastily taken from the refrigerator door. On the top was the photo of a team of smiling girls, all dressed to play softball. Krista MacGregor smiled out at him, holding up one finger to tell him she was number one.

He smiled back.

Thirty-seven

"A pig?" Sydney laughed as she walked out onto the deck, a beer in each hand. "I can't believe she had a pig in the house!"

"They're really very clean, you know. They make better pets than dogs." Marshall accepted his beer as he slid over on the glider to make room for her. "Or so she pointed out to me."

Sydney laughed again, sat down, and gave the swing a push. It was late, after eleven. The rain had cleared up and Krista had gotten to play her softball game. Marshall had gone with Sydney to watch and that had gone relatively well, aside from some nasty looks from Joel. Krista's All-Star team won again and was declared the district champion. Krista had been so excited about the win that she had actually been pleasant to Marshall. After a team pizza party, Krista and Katie had come home with Sydney, and Marshall had driven over in his rental car. The girls, worn out from their exciting day, had retired to Krista's bedroom half an hour ago and were probably already asleep.

"Damn, she sounds pretty strange," Sydney said, sipping her beer as she thought about all Marshall had told her about Dorian. "Looked pretty strange from those photos you took, too."

"She didn't behave any stranger than a lot of people I've interviewed over the years." He slipped his arm around her shoulders and she slid closer. "Come to think of it, not nearly as odd as some. I've met some incredibly bizarre people."

"Well, I don't know that we've gained anything by your talking with her. It doesn't sound as if she gave you any insight on her father."

"I think I knew more about him than she did." He sipped his beer. "Though I definitely sensed some serious hostility there."

"That right?"

"Can't blame her." Marshall rubbed her shoulder. "It had to be hard growing up knowing your father had killed those little girls. Knowing he ruined your life and your sister's."

"Still, can you imagine always knowing where your father was, yet never meeting him?"

"Can't blame her there, either. I'd never want to step foot in my father's presence if he'd done something like that."

"Now you see, there's a difference between the two of us." She looked at him. "I'd have had to go see him. Tell him what I thought about him. Tell him how much I hated what he had done and what he had done to our family."

"I think that's one of the things I like so much about you, Syd. You're a woman with serious balls."

She turned to look at him and he caught her by surprise. He pressed his mouth to hers, and she responded with the pent-up emotions of the day. She rested her hand, still holding the beer bottle, on his shoulder and let go of her thoughts of Eshey and of Marla. Of Joel. She let herself feel . . . and she had to admit Marshall felt damned good.

The kiss ended too soon, and she licked the bottom of her lip, gazing into Marshall's dark eyes. The deck was cast in shadows, lit only by the security lamp at the edge of her property, but she could see that he was studying her.

Her whole body was revved up and she suddenly felt jumpy. She could taste sexual tension in the air between them. A million thoughts were rushing through her head, but one prevailed. She wanted to put down their beers, take Marshall's hand, and lead him to her bedroom.

Did she dare? She'd been a virgin when she met Joel and had never slept with anyone else. Never really wanted to until now.

Marshall waited, and she knew he knew what she was contemplating. This had been building since he arrived in Delaware. She had felt it when she first met him in the hotel parking lot, when he had brought her a soft pretzel at the game this evening, and later when they had sat here in the dark and glided on the swing in silence while Krista and Katie chatted about the game.

She held his gaze, wanting to say something, but not sure what. Mostly because she didn't know what she wanted. "I think we're thinking the same thing."

"Oh, yeah?" His voice was husky and so damned sexy. It felt so good to be wanted by someone who wasn't just trying to manipulate her. Joel had always used sex as a reward, or lack of it for punishment.

Marshall took her beer out of her hand and placed it on the deck along with his. He reached out to brush a lock of hair off her cheek. It was an innocent enough gesture, but it sent her blood pulsing.

God, she needed to get laid.

But Krista and Katie were asleep upstairs. And Marshall lived in New York. She wasn't going to sleep with him just because she was horny. She wasn't that kind of person.

She smiled tentatively, knowing she had made her decision . . . at least for tonight. "You need to go."

He smiled back with an "I almost had you" grin, and she laughed.

"OK. You almost had me swayed," she murmured, her own voice lower than usual.

He brushed his fingertips against her cheek. "But no go tonight, eh?"

She leaned toward him and kissed him lightly on the lips. "No go tonight, Marshall." She rose from the glider, leading him by the hand. "But I'm thinking about it. Thinking hard."

He grabbed her around the waist. "Let me help you, then." He covered her mouth with his again, and didn't let up until she swayed in his arms, dizzy from lack of oxygen.

"Marshall," she panted, resting her hands on his chest. She was pushing herself away from him as much as trying to push him away from her. "You have to go."

"I'm going." He let go of her, raising his hands in surrender. She was relieved he was taking her rejection with a sense of humor. "I'm going, already. I just wanted to let you know what you'd be missing."

She walked him to the door. "When are you going back to New York?"

"I don't know yet. I've got to be back Saturday to give my landlord the rent check." He leaned against the open door. "But I thought I'd hang around here for a few days. Try some of those famous blue claw crabs. Get some caramel popcorn on the boardwalk."

"You don't have to stay to protect me," she said quietly, wishing right now that he could stay forever, or at least long enough for her to figure out how she felt about him. "I'm not afraid of him, you know. Not now. Now that I've seen him and know what a sorry son of a bitch he is."

"I understand." He kissed her on the cheek and gave a wave. "That's not why I want to stay." He brushed his fingertips over her lips and walked out. "Talk to you tomorrow."

Marshall backed out of Sydney's driveway and wound his way out of the neighborhood. The hotel was a few miles away on the bay side. As he signaled to turn left, he shifted in his seat. He was so hard for Sydney that he couldn't get comfortable. He had really wanted to stay and make love to her. If he had pushed, he knew he could have won her over. But for once, this wasn't about winning the girl. It wasn't about laying on the charm and getting her into the sack like all the others. It was something else.

Marshall groaned aloud. He was fifty years old. He'd been married twice and made a mess of both marriages. Then there was the long string of affairs before, during, and after his marriages. He obviously wasn't cut out for monogamy. He wasn't convinced any man was.

But he knew it was the only way he could have Sydney. He could see it in her clear blue eyes, taste it in her kiss. The funny thing was, for the first time in his life, the idea appealed to him.

Thirty-eight

Tuesday mid afternoon, Jess walked into Marvin Crackhow's office. "You wanted to see me, sir?" She hoped this wasn't about what she thought it was. Yesterday she'd turned in a preliminary report on what she and Carl had found on Eshey.

The file was on his desk, but he didn't glance at it.

"Good work on the Eshey follow-up." Her supervisor glanced up at her over his reading glasses.

She stood in front of his desk because he didn't offer a chair. This was going to be short and sweet and it probably wasn't going to be anything she wanted to hear.

"Thank you, sir."

"You and Steinman make a good team." He removed his glasses to look at her. "You're smart to latch on to a man like Steinman. He has a superb record."

The fact that Carl had only four years more with the Bureau than she didn't seem to matter to Crackhow. Neither did the fact that she didn't need to latch on to any man to do her job well.

"Yes, sir. He's a good man. We mesh well." *Mesh?* Where the hell had she come up with that idiotic word, and why did Crackhow make her so nervous? Even if he didn't care for her sexual preference, he had nothing on her here in the office. He couldn't argue that she wasn't a good agent. She met his gaze, tucking her hands behind her back. She waited for the shoe to fall, because fall it would. He hadn't called her in here to give her an "atta girl."

"I've looked over your report," the balding man went on without further preamble. He was so thin, his cheeks so sunken, that in his straw-colored suit, he reminded her of a scarecrow. She heard he ran five miles a day, rain or shine. She wondered if he was running toward something, or away from it.

"Yes, sir."

"And I think we can go ahead and shelve this one, at least for the time being."

She frowned. "Sir?"

He blinked. "I've read your report. We haven't got enough evidence to connect this old man and the two missing kids, and I've got a stack of assignments waiting for agents to free up. Someone else will keep up to speed on the kidnappings and you'll be reassigned."

"But, sir, didn't you read my notes on the interview with the librarian? Eshey was looking up old records. He wanted to know how to use the Internet to find people."

"Everyone else in the free world uses the Internet to find people. It's the new national pastime. You've got nothing concrete, Manlove." He almost sneered her last name. She knew what he was thinking. People were always joking about her last name. A lesbian called *Man*-love.

"What about the medical report on Eshey?"

"What about it?" He smacked his lips together as if she was now boring him.

"They were inconclusive. It was never determined that he definitely has a heart condition."

"So? I never see a friggin' doctor that he doesn't tell me the tests are inconclusive. Manlove, in case you didn't know it, the science of medicine isn't a science." He set his jaw. "We've got nothing on Eshey, and it's time we move on." Crackhow said it as if it needed to be repeated, and then he waited for her to disagree with him again.

But what was she going to say? He was right, of course. There was no evidence beyond shaky circumstances to point to Eshey. It didn't matter if she thought Eshey a suspect. Didn't matter if she *knew* he was killing kids again. She needed evidence and had nothing to support her suspicions but her dyke intuition. She almost laughed aloud.

"Something funny about what I said?" Crackhow snapped.

She wiped what smile must have appeared at the corner of her mouth. "No, sir."

"So you agree with me?"

"I agree that we have no tangible evidence, sir, but I feel we need to further investigate Mr. Eshey. There was something about him in our interview that didn't sit right with me."

He reached for his reading glasses. She was about to be dismissed.

"Of course he doesn't *sit right with you*, Manlove. The man raped, tortured, and murdered seven little girls." He reached over her Eshey file for another manila folder. "But in these United States we only convict and punish a man once for the same crimes. "He flipped open the new file, burying Eshey's on his desk. "Left up to me, they'd all fry, but it isn't left up to us, is it?"

"No, sir." She paused. "If Eshey is not connected, sir, I wonder if we should be looking in another direction for a possible link between the missing boy and girl beyond what took place in the seventies. A copycat crime, perhaps?"

"There's no such thing as a serial kidnapper."

"If they're dead and we just haven't found the bodies—"

"Exactly, we have no bodies," Crackhow snapped. "No bodies. No evidence against Eshey. Just missing kids. Shelve your investigation of Eshey and let the local police continue theirs; they'll call us if they need us or someone digs up something more."

Something more? Jess wanted to scream in frustration. *Like another missing kid?* But she kept her mouth shut because she knew that she had to remain within the parameters of the law. The FBI's hands were tied concerning Eshey until evidence turned up.

Crackhow flipped through sheets of paper in front of him. This time he didn't even bother to look up when he spoke to her. "I think we have a surveillance team going into one of the harbor warehouses next week. Possible money laundering. Connect with Bottleman and see what you can do for them."

Jake Bottleman? In the office, he was the asshole among assholes. He knew hundreds of dyke jokes and told her every one while sitting in close quarters on surveillance. He farted a lot, too.

"Yes, sir."

"Have a good day, Special Agent Manlove."

Like that was going to be possible now. "You, too, sir."

Jess waited until she was out of his office, the door closed, before she let loose a blast of foul names for her supervisor, all cleverly rhyming with the word pucker.

"What's the matter, panties in a twist?" Carl met her in the hall as she retreated to her cubicle. He followed her to her chair.

Jess wanted to throw something, but because she had nothing in her hand, she smacked the back of her chair instead. It rolled forward and slammed into the desk, making a satisfying clatter. "Crackhow is pulling us off Eshey. The state and local police will continue their investigations on the missing kids. We'll continue to run info for them through our computer banks, but Crackhow wants us to move on."

"I'm sorry," he said quietly.

She looked at him, knowing her face was red. "He says we have no evidence either to indicate Eshey is responsible or that the two kids could be connected beyond their obvious link."

"He's right."

"He says we can be better used elsewhere."

"He's probably right about that, too."

She jerked her chair away from her desk and sat down. "I think he's wrong, Carl. I've got this bad feeling in the pit of my stomach that won't go away."

He brushed his sandy hair off his forehead as he leaned against her partition. "So give it a few a days to sit and simmer. Take the work home and go over it. There's nothing wrong with your rethinking the case on your own time. You find something, we can always go back into Crackhow's office together."

She sighed. "No, he's probably right." She picked up her Eshey file and threw it down. Papers flew out and across her desk. "We need to concentrate on the cases we can solve." She leaned on the desk and covered her face with her hands.

He reached out with one long arm and closed his hand over her shoulder. The contact lasted only a second, but it was long enough.

"If you'll excuse me, I have to make a phone call." She reached for the desk phone.

"Who you calling?"

"Sydney MacGregor."

* * *

Sydney hung up her office phone and immediately dialed Marshall at the hotel. She'd already talked to him once today and he was coming over to dinner tonight, but she couldn't wait until then to talk to him.

"Hey," she said when he picked up.

"Hi there. I was just getting ready to call you. I wanted to give you time to get home. How was your mom today?"

"Her usual charming self."

"And batting practice this morning?"

There was no rest for the weary. Because Krista's team had won for their district, they would be playing for the state championship the following week.

"Good. Well, Krista got beaned on the head at the plate, but other than that she had a good day."

"Ouch," he said.

"Yeah, but she's like her mother. She's got a hard head. Besides, she was wearing a helmet."

Sydney could hear him smile.

She took a breath and exhaled. "Marshall, I just got off the phone with Special Agent Manlove. The Eshey case is closed."

"Closed? How can it be closed? The kids haven't been found."

"The cases on Jason and Carrie haven't been closed. There are others working to find them. Agent Manlove just isn't investigating Eshey any more." She swept her hair off her face. "Manlove says there never really was a case, per se. Her job was to investigate Eshey to see if he was a possible suspect in the missing children's cases. Her supervisor looked over the file and decided there was no evidence to link Eshey to the disappearances of Carrie and Jason. She says he says there's no link between the two cases either other than the obvious. Just . . . bad coincidence."

He was silent for a moment, giving her time to think. She had been intensely relieved when the agent had called. After all, if the FBI didn't even consider Eshey a suspect now, if they thought there was no connection between the cases, that meant Krista was safe, didn't it? It meant she could stop worrying about the safety of her child's life and get on with her own life. Didn't it?

Sydney wanted desperately to believe the FBI. But already her doubts were creeping in. It just didn't *feel* right. The question was, could she trust this feeling? Or was it unfounded? Would she have it until she knew Eshey was dead?

"What does Special Agent Manlove say?" Marshall asked.

"What do you mean?" She brushed her hair out of her face again.

"I mean, you said she said her supervisor determined there was no case. What does she say?"

"Well, I didn't really ask. I suppose she agrees with him. I imagine she thought it would sound better if I knew the FBI brass believed Krista was safe." She walked back to her desk and flipped on her computer monitor. "So I guess there's no need to pursue Eshey anymore."

There was a pause between them.

"Marshall?"

"No. I guess there isn't."

"You believe that?" She felt as if she were on a roller coaster, one she desperately wanted to get off.

She heard him sigh. "I don't know what to believe, Sydney."

She was quiet for a moment, wishing he was here. "I don't know what to do," she murmured. "I want to believe them. I want my life back. I want to go to bed at night believing my daughter is safe from that monster."

"Let's talk tonight," Marshall said gently. "We'll both think on it."

"You're still staying a little longer anyway? If the FBI says there's no case, there's no book."

"I don't care about the book. I care about you and Krista. I'm not going home until Thursday. Now tell me what time is good for you for dinner. I found a place that sells crabs by the dozen. Do I buy them steamed or unsteamed?"

"Unsteamed. I have my Old Bay in the cupboard. Come around six-thirty." She sat in her chair behind her desk and stared at her computer monitor. "I have got to get moving on this book, or it's not going to be done in time. I was actually thinking about heading to our place down on the Maryland peninsula for a few days. It's quiet there. I always seem to get a lot done when I'm there." She hesitated. "Is that a crazy idea?"

"To want to get away? Of course not."

"No . . . I meant is it crazy to go to my cabin? It's pretty isolated." She gave a little laugh. "Of course, maybe that makes it even safer. No one would know to look for us there." She didn't wait for him to speak. "And if the FBI says Krista's safe, I can believe them, can't I? I mean, I can't spend the rest of my life thinking Eshey's in every shadow. I can't never go to my cabin again. I can't never let my daughter walk to the market again."

"I think going might be a good idea. Sometimes a change of scenery is the best thing you can do for yourself."

"Well, if I'm going to meet this deadline, I've got to do something drastic," Sydney admitted. "Even just a day away from here and I think I could make some headway."

"We can skip dinner if you want to write into the

evening. I'm a big boy. I can go out to a restaurant for crabs by myself. I'd rather eat with you, but if you need to leave me hanging—"

She laughed. "No, it's OK. I'll need a break by then."

"I'll see you at six-thirty."

"See ya." She hung up and stared at the computer screen, still frightened for her daughter, but relieved she had found Marshall King.

Jess turned in the shower stall, pressed her palms to the wall and let the warm water run down her back. This afternoon she'd hooked up with Jake Bottleman as instructed by Crackhow and had gotten the scoop on the surveillance assignment she'd been transferred to. It looked to be a long, boring task, made even longer by Jake and his juvenile behavior.

Jess heard the shower door open. "Mind if I join you?"

She smiled to herself, her back to Meagan. "Nothing like a shower party."

"My thoughts exactly." She stepped inside and closed the door.

Jess could smell the faint scent of her perfume.

"Want me to do your back?"

"Sure." Jess heard her unhook the bath sponge from the faucet and squirt shower gel from the dispenser. She moaned with contentment as Meagan dragged the rough scrubby sponge down the center of her back.

"Another bad day?" Meagan scrubbed her shoulders vigorously.

"I don't want to talk about it. I've got my application in for that job flipping burgers down the street."

Meagan chuckled, scrubbing methodically. "It can't be that bad."

"Oh, it is. Crackhow pulled me off the Eshey investigation. He says we have no evidence. Our hands are tied until we find bodies, I guess. And my new buddy, beginning next Monday, is Jake Butthead Bottleman."

"Oh God," Meagan moaned. "Not the lesbian-hating fart machine."

"The very one." Jess closed her eyes and groaned. As Meagan washed her back, she could feel her knotted muscle relaxing.

"How can Crackhow say you have no case?"

"Because he's right." Jess stretched her shoulders forward and back, pressing her hands to the slippery wall. The warm water running over her skin mingled with the light caress of Meagan's bare hand, sending ripples of pleasure through her.

"I don't understand. The man killed the girl and the boy's aunt. The kids disappeared within weeks of the kook getting out of jail. Sounds like a suspect to me." Meagan rested her hands on Jess's hips and Jess turned in her arms to face her.

"I know, I know," Jess said, opening her eyes. "But that's not how it works. As I was sharply reminded today, evidence is what we go by." It was reassuring to see Meagan. To have her here close like this. Jess reached out and rubbed a smudge of mascara from under her lover's eye.

"Unfortunately"—Jess continued blinking as spray hit her in the face—"that's been our case from the start. We have absolutely nothing to go on with the two missing kids, which means we have absolutely no way to tie them to Eshey or anyone else other than their dead aunts." She lifted her hands and let them fall to her sides. "Coincidence, nothing more."

"And what about that dyke intuition of yours, huh?" Meagan caressed one of Jess's buttocks and then gave it a playful slap.

Jess laughed, and the release felt so good. "I don't know. Did I read it wrong? I mean, how often do you pick an old case that was once your father's? He died haunted by the fact that he could never pin the deaths of any of those other girls on Eshey. Isn't it natural that I would want to get the bastard for my dad?"

"Maybe." Meagan leaned forward and brushed her lips against hers.

"Anyway, it's over." Jess gazed into Meagan's dark eyes. "Crackhow has partnered me up with Bottleman on a surveillance gig and I called Sydney Baker and told her the investigation on Eshey had been dropped. I more or less told her that her little girl was safe." Her voice caught in her throat and the last words were ragged. "Only I'm not sure she is safe, Meg, and I don't know what the hell to do about it."

"Ah, sweetie." Meagan pulled her against her thin, lean body and hugged her tightly, their breasts touching. She caught a lock of Jess's wet hair between her fingers and tucked it behind her ear. "It's going to be all right." She held her gaze. "You gave it your best shot. That's all you can do. You didn't kidnap those kids and you can't control the people who commit these crimes. Surely you know that by now."

"I know. I know. I do." Jess tightened her grip around Meagan's waist and rested her cheek on her shoulder. "I would just hate it if we were wrong. I read part of that book, Meg, and the man is as sick as any I've ever seen."

Meagan caught Jess's chin between her thumb and forefinger and tilted her head back to gaze into her eyes. "You're a good cop, Jess. You do the best you can, and sometimes you save people and sometimes you don't. You have to accept that or you need to start flipping those burgers."

Jess smiled, sad and yet momentarily content. She

was so lucky to have Meagan. "I love you," she whispered.

Meagan smiled and brushed her lips against Jess's. "I love you too, babe. Now, come on, let's get in bed." She winked. "And let's seriously forget our troubles."

Thirty-nine

"Dad, please, she's doing it again. Can't you make her be reasonable?" Krista whined.

Sydney, Joel, and Krista all stood in the parking lot after Krista's softball practice Wednesday afternoon, at an apparent stalemate. Krista was going home with Joel to spend the night, but Sydney wanted her back in the morning so they could head south for a few days at the cabin. She had decided that Marshall was right; she needed a change of scenery. After all she had been through in the last couple weeks worrying about Krista, it would be good to get away from the phone, the newspapers, and the television.

She still had a niggling fear in the back of her mind about going where she would be so isolated, but she was almost sure it might always be there. She really needed to go to the cabin, to see the marsh, to feel the trees around her. She needed this time away if she was ever going to get this book done and if she was ever going to move on with her life.

Sydney rested her hand on her hip. "I'm not talking about moving to Bangladesh, Krista. I just want to go to the cabin for a couple of days. It won't kill you to go with me. You can start your summer reading assignments, which I know you haven't looked at."

"I want to stay with Dad." Krista stuck out her lip

stubbornly. "I can practice my screw ball if I stay with Dad."

"There are no scheduled practices until Sunday. You heard your coach. Everyone needs a break. That means you, too." Sydney looked to Joel for support.

Joel scowled. "I hate it when the two of you put me in the middle of these arguments."

Sydney ground her teeth. "No one is putting you in the middle of anything. We're just sticking to our schedule. She's with you tonight. I'll bring her back in time to spend the day with you on Sunday. I'll see Ma and then we'll go back Sunday night."

"Mom," Krista groaned.

Joel looked at his daughter, whose frown nearly reached the pavement. "How about a compromise?"

"I don't want to go at all," Krista grumbled.

"That's enough." Sydney eyed her daughter. "I've had it with the sulky teenager face for the day."

"Don't you think you're being a little hard on her?" Joel said quietly.

"No, I don't! She's been like this since she got up this morning."

"I've been like this because you *said* you wanted to go to the cabin," Krista snipped. "And you *said* I had to go with you."

Sydney didn't want to fight, not with Krista or Joel. What she really wanted to do was get home and get in the shower before Marshall arrived at eight. She'd been thinking about him all day, about them, and she was seriously considering broaching the subject of their relationship before he returned to New York tomorrow.

"How about you? Would you be willing to compromise?" Joel asked Sydney.

She was caught between wanting to keep Krista with her every minute of the day and wanting desperately to move on. The agent had *told* her Krista was safe from Eshey. "I'm listening." Sydney leaned on the back of her Explorer.

"How about if Krista stays tonight and tomorrow night, and I bring her down after work on Friday?"

"What are you going to do with her during the day while you work?"

"Tomorrow morning she can go to Katie's, which was already planned and approved by you. The whole family is going to that water park in Ocean City. Friday, she can go to work with me and do some of that summer reading." Joel glanced at Krista. "I'll take off at lunch and she and I will go kayaking in the bay or something. We'll be at the cabin by eight, eight-thirty."

"Come on, Mom, please? I really should get a start on that reading." Krista's tone was instantly sweet. "And Dad's been promising to take me kayaking. You hate kayaking in the summer."

Bugs. She hated the bugs, not the kayaking.

Joel brushed Sydney's elbow. "It will give you some time to yourself," he said quietly. "Your friend still in town?"

She met her ex-husband's gaze. She wasn't sure what he was suggesting, and she didn't want to think about it. It was none of his business if Marshall was still in town.

"Please, Mom?"

Sydney could think of no good reason to say no. With this plan, Krista would never be alone for a minute. She threw up her hands. "Fine. Go."

"Yes!" Krista leaped into the air, pumping her arm.

"Thanks," Joel said.

Sydney looked at her daughter. "Do you need to come home and get anything?"

"Nope. I have my overnight bag in Dad's car already. I've got some shorts and my old bathing suit there. If I really need anything, Dad can run me home. I have my key."

Sydney grabbed Krista's arm and gave her a kiss on the cheek. Because she obviously wanted to be with her father, Krista let her. "I'll see you Friday night, sweetie."

"See you Friday night. I hope you get a lot of work done on your book." Krista bounced across the parking lot toward Joel's Jeep.

"You'd better bring her Friday night," Sydney warned Joel with her finger.

"Scout's honor."

Shaking her head, Sydney climbed into her SUV and headed home.

"I could get used to this," Marshall said, taking a deep breath as he leaned over the deck railing.

The waves crashed in the distance, a sound Sydney never tired of. She stood beside him and breathed deeply. The air was thick with the scent of the salt water and the incoming tide. It had rained earlier in the evening and the beach was empty. Quiet except for the rhythmic sounds of the waves.

Earlier in the evening, they had talked about the FBI's decision to close the Eshey case, and Sydney felt better. This was the FBI, for heaven's sake. If they said Eshey couldn't have taken Jason and Carrie, she should believe them. Sydney didn't know that she could go overnight from fearing for her daughter's life to not thinking about Eshey again, but she thought she could begin to distance herself from the man who had taken her sister from her. She could begin to put her life back together. Maybe better than it was before.

Sydney eyed Marshall. "So you think you might be back this way soon?"

He slipped his arm around her waist. "I think so. If nothing else, to get some of those steamed crabs again."

She laughed and let him pull her into his arms. All evening they'd been dancing around the issue of sex. They'd kissed, touched a little, and Sydney's entire body was hypersensitive. Every smell, every color, every taste seemed magnified to her. She felt as if she had way too much caffeine . . . or way too little sex.

"I'd like you to come back," she said, suddenly feeling vulnerable. It was hard for her to tell him that she was interested. But she was determined not to miss this opportunity. She and Marshall connected on many levels, and she really didn't want to see him walk out of her life.

Marshall covered her mouth with his and she clung to him. She parted her lips, welcoming his tongue, swaying in his arms.

When they were both breathless, he lifted his head, gazing into her eyes. She loved his eyes, dark, mysterious, and yet there was something boyish about them. Needy, even.

"You going to kick me out now?" he whispered. He brushed his hand down her rib cage, his thumb brushing her breast.

She bit down on her lower lip. Last chance. "No," she breathed, certain of the decision the moment she made it. "I want you to stay a while."

He smiled and swooped down for another kiss, but she stopped him.

"But I have to tell you now, Marshall. I'm not a woman who takes relationships lightly and that's exactly what I'll be expecting. *A relationship.*"

"I know," he said quietly. "I've been thinking about that all week."

"I realize you have other girlfriends. How many, I don't know and don't want to know." She continued to study his face. "But that isn't going to sit well with me. I don't care how far away you live."

"That's fair."

"No." She brushed his cheek with her palm, feeling the evening beard stubble. "It's probably not, but it's how I need it to be."

"Done."

He kissed her again, and this time she gave herself fully to him. She let go of all her perceived notions of the way things should and shouldn't be and she just let herself enjoy the taste of him, the touch of his hand on her breast.

Hand in hand, they walked down the hall to her bedroom. They made love and she was shocked, not by how well he pleased her or how easily, but how she responded to him. Marshall wasn't Joel, and that was, at last, fine with her.

After they both came, they lay naked in each other's arms, not saying anything. Not feeling the need to. Then they made love again and she came three more times.

She hated saying good-bye to him at the front door.

"I'll call you in the morning before you leave," he said.

She remained in the shadows of the front hall, because she was still stark naked. "You'd better."

Marshall disappeared in the dark night and she closed the door, setting the lock. "Yes!" She jumped into the air and pumped her arm.

Thursday morning, Marshall called her at nine, and she was just packing up the car. "Morning," she said. She couldn't stop grinning like a Cheshire cat . . . or a fool.

"Morning."

She knew he was pleased with the previous evening, too.

"So, you headed back to New York?" she asked as she slid her laptop case in the back of the SUV.

"Yeah, I need to get back to work, too."

She laughed. "So I suppose that means you wouldn't like to join me for dinner and a sleepover at my cabin tonight?"

Sydney wasn't sure where that had come from. She hadn't even considered inviting him to spend the night until she heard his voice on the other end of the line. Suddenly she wasn't ready to let him go yet.

"I could be persuaded."

"Give me the day to work and come about seven. We'll have dinner outside on the deck and we'll watch the sunset on the bay."

"Wouldn't miss it."

Sydney gave him directions to the cabin south of Princess Anne, Maryland, and he repeated them back as he jotted them down. They were tricky, so she hoped he'd be able to find the place.

"So I'll see you tonight?" she asked, going back into the house to grab a case of sodas and a couple of bottles of wine from the kitchen pantry.

"Wouldn't miss it for the world. Now get going. I expect a full report tonight on vacationing with the family in the northwest."

She laughed and hung up, amazed at how terrible life could be sometimes and then how it could become so sweet.

By the time Marshall arrived at the cabin nestled in a crook in the creek three miles off the main road, Sydney had marinated steaks, chopped up fresh veggies for shish kabobs, and written nineteen pages of her book.

"You made it!" Sydney called from the front porch of the log cabin. She'd been watching for him through the picture window for the last half hour.

"Well, three wrong turns onto the wrong dirt roads and I made it. But you had me scared for a minute there." He rose out of the car carrying a gym bag and a big bouquet of tiger lilies. "I thought I was going to have to park the car and hike in when I saw that river running across the road."

"That's not a river, it's a ditch." She came down the steps to meet him in the driveway that was really just a mowed area. "And I'll have you know we're having a dry year. You won't need a four wheel drive to get in here until fall, when it starts to rain."

She looked at the flowers that were not from a store, but had obviously been picked along the road, which made them all the more special. It was hard to imagine Marshall, in his pressed khaki slacks and close-fitting polo shirt, parking along the road to push through the weeds of a ditch where the lilies grew. "Those for me?"

"They are. I had to fight some cows up the road for them."

She laughed. "Come on in." She hurried up the dirt path that led to the front porch.

"Wow, this is great." He looked up at the cabin as he followed her up the front steps.

"Yeah, Joel and I bought the land and had the cabin built after one of my books hit the *Times* bestseller list. We had this foolish idea that it would fix our marriage."

"You didn't have to give it up in the divorce settlement?" He followed her into the great room that sported a stone fireplace and a comfy denim couch and loveseat.

"When I started making serious money, my accountant suggested that I keep everything in my own name." She led Marshall into the kitchen and grabbed a salt-glazed pottery vase off the top of the re-frigerator. "I think he knew Joel was screwing around on me. He probably saw the divorce coming before I did." She ran water from the kitchen sink into the blue vase. "Master suite is through the dining room." She pointed. "Leave your bag there."

He grinned lasciviously.

She grinned back. "There's a bathroom there. Come out onto the back porch when you're done." She pointed to the French door in the great room as she poked the orange lilies into the vase. "I'll pour the wine."

He stood for a moment, his bag in hand, his gaze meeting hers. "I know this was hard for you to do, and I want you to know it means a lot to me."

"What was hard?"

"Having me here. Taking this step away from Joel."

"Not as hard as you might think." She kissed the air, but the kiss was meant for him. "Meet me outside for the best sunset on the Eastern Shore."

The next few hours were magical. Sydney felt as if there was no one in the world but the two of them. They shared a bottle of wine and dinner on the open-air porch that faced the creek which lead into the Chesapeake Bay in the distance. After dark, they sat on a cedar swing and stared out at the tall waving grasses and the eerie lights that were phenomena of the salt marsh. They retired early and made love twice before falling into a peaceful sleep, only to make love again in the morning. Together they made a big breakfast of blueberry hotcakes and scrapple and then they made love again.

It was close to noon by the time Sydney agreed that

Marshall had to go. After all, she'd come to the cabin to write, not frolic.

She said good-bye to him on the front porch, wearing nothing but silk panties and an old T-shirt. Her closest neighbor was two and a half miles away overland, so there was no one to see her but the croaking frogs and the mournful marsh birds that flew overhead.

"I'll call you when I get back to New York tonight."

"You can try my cell. Sometimes it works, sometimes it doesn't. Not enough antennas out here in the boonies." She grabbed him by the collar of his buttondown oxford and kissed him one last time. "But I'll be back in Albany Beach on Sunday morning. I'll definitely talk to you then."

Marshall grabbed one more kiss and headed down the driveway to his rental car.

She waved and walked back into the house to get dressed and get to work.

Forty

Cynthia Carmack chewed on the cap of the pen and stared at the phone on her desk. She needed to call the FBI, but she was nervous. She hadn't cared for Special Agent Manlove; her kind scared her. And she had gotten the distinct impression that the agent didn't like her any better. But that didn't matter. It was Cynthia's responsibility to call the agent, and she'd be remiss if she didn't. She had already screwed up a couple of things, already had her supervisor breathing down her neck, and she couldn't risk losing her job. She had too big a student loan payment to risk unemployment.

She took a breath and dialed the number she found in Charles Eshey's file.

"Federal Bureau of Investigation, Baltimore Field Office. How may I direct your call?" the operator said in a mechanical voice.

Cynthia's mouth went dry. She reached for her Diet Coke. "Extension 411, please."

The phone rang only once, not giving Cynthia time to chicken out, hang up, and go home to start reading the want ads. "Special Agent Manlove."

Cynthia pulled her tongue off the roof of her mouth. "This is Cynthia Carmack, parole officer for the state of New Jersey. We've met."

"Hello, Miss Carmack," the agent said in that icy voice of hers that intimidated Cynthia. "How can I help you?"

"Agent Manlove, I'm sure that this situation I have has nothing to do with your missing kids cases, but I knew I should call you." She gave a little nervous laugh.

"Yes?"

"Charles Eshey didn't show for our weekly appointment this morning. I get no answer at his place of residence and . . ." She nibbled her lower lip tasting her lipstick. "When I called his employer, I found that he missed work this week. As far as I can tell, no one has seen him since he was in my office last Thursday."

"Actually, I interviewed him Friday."

"Well, he is required to be here today. I'll have to have a judge issue a capias."

"Shit," the agent said. Then, "Excuse me, Miss Carmack. I apologize for my language."

"That's all right." Cynthia smiled a little. She could hear Manlove shuffling papers. The agent didn't seem to be upset with her, only the situation.

"Have you sent anyone to his apartment?"

Cynthia hadn't thought of that. "We . . . we don't usually do that."

"*Can* you send the state police out? You have that authority, don't you?"

"Of course."

"Then do it," Manlove ordered. "Send them to the apartment. If there's no response, I want them to get inside. I don't care how they do it. I want to know if Eshey is there, dead or alive."

"Dead?" Cynthia's word came out like a squeak. God, she hadn't thought of that. She immediately felt bad. She'd been sitting here all morning feeling guilty because she was afraid her client was out on some rampage killing little girls. What if the poor man had died of a heart attack and lay rotting in his bed?

"Well, it is possible. He's supposed to have a heart condition," the agent muttered impatiently.

"All right. I'll send the police. I'll call you as soon as I hear from them."

"Thanks for calling." Manlove surprised Cynthia with a civil tone. "You did the right thing in not waiting any longer, Cynthia."

And she called her by her first name. "Thanks . . . Agent Manlove."

Jess hung up the phone and stood up to dig through the piles on her desk in earnest. Hell, where were her Eshey files? She knew she'd left the packet of old photos at home, but the main file had to be here somewhere.

She tossed files aside, ignoring flying sheets of loose paper. Her heart pounded in her chest. The son of a bitch was gone. The question was, where?

"Yo, Candy-striper, you coming, already?"

It was Bottleman. He was always calling her by idiotic nicknames. What was it with men and nicknames, anyway? She didn't even bother to turn around. "Nope."

"What do you mean, no?"

"I mean I'm not taking my shift with the surveillance unit. Do it yourself. I just had something come in that needs my immediate attention."

"Crackhow isn't going to like this," Bottleman, whined. "I'll have to speak with him, of course."

"Of course." She nabbed the file, obscured by a Baltimore *Sun* newspaper. "You know where Steinman is?" She glanced over her shoulder at Bottleman as she crammed stray pages back into the fat Eshey file.

"In the coffee room, I think." His television screen

forehead wrinkled. "What do I care where he is? I don't want to go on this surveillance gig alone. It's boring."

She brushed by him. "Sorry, buddy. I'm going to miss you, too." She offered a fake smile. "Take Portsmouth."

"Portsmouth? Talk about friggin' boring. All he wants to talk about is his colonoscopy." Jess kept going. She found Carl in the coffee room, spreading a file over the worktable. "He's gone, Carl," she said anxiously.

He looked up. Gray suit, red tie today. Nice. "Who's gone?"

"Eshey." Jess could feel her adrenaline pumping. Her dyke intuition was going full tilt. Eshey was gone and she knew as well as she knew her own name that he was up to no good. "Cynthia Carmack from the parole office just called. When Eshey didn't show up for his appointment, she checked up on him." Jess paced in front of the table. "No answer in his apartment, and he never showed up for work this week. As far as she can tell, no one has seen him since we saw him last Friday."

"Think he croaked?"

"I don't know. My guess is no; in this heat, the stench gets pretty strong pretty quickly. But Carmack sent the police over to his place to look for a body. We should hear something within the hour."

"So what do you think?" Carl spoke calmly as he stacked his work to put it away.

"I think we need to find him. I think we need to talk to the daughter again"—she hesitated—"and I'd feel better if I called Sydney and warned her that we've lost tabs on him. I implied that her little girl was safe, and now I'm not sure I can say that."

He looked up. "Jason and Carrie were both twins, Jess. I don't think we need to scare Mrs. MacGregor quite yet."

Jess grabbed a sheet of paper from inside Eshey's folder. Once Crackhow had halted the investigation, reports she had previously ordered from various agencies had still trickled in. Jess had read this one just last night. Why she had run a check on Sydney, she would never know. She slid the paper in front of Carl.

He glanced at the fact sheet, nodding as he scanned the information. He stopped at just the place where Jess knew he would.

"The little girl, Krista, is a twin," he said, his tone grave.

Jess nodded. "I don't know why the hell she didn't tell us."

"People are funny about talking about babies that die," Carl murmured.

Jess grabbed the fact sheet on Sydney Baker Mac-Gregor. "I'm going to call her."

Carl pushed out of his chair, headed for the door, leaving his file. "Let's hold off a little longer. If Eshey's dead, this is all a moot point. I'm going to see Crackhow and let him know we're both back on this. I won't take no for an answer. You go back to your desk and wait for Carmack. Come up with a plan."

Jess watched Carl's broad back as he turned the corner and strode down the hall, long legs pumping. She was glad he was on her side.

Jess sat at her desk with a legal pad in front of her and zoned in on the task at hand, filtering out the ringing phones, the chatter, and the click of the copy machine around the corner. She was attempting to get creative and think outside the box. Her father had always been a pure facts man—one of the old school, a J. Edgar Hoover man. But she liked to think that her femininity brought something to her job that her father hadn't possessed. Carl teased her about her dyke intuition, but truly, she thought of it as genetic feminine intuition.

Jess made headings of all of the people involved in Eshey's case so that she could jot down notes. She created headings for Carrie's and Jason's families. A heading for Sydney and her surviving twin daughter. And one for Eshey.

She gripped her pen in frustration, staring at the names. There was something she was missing. Something that was right in front of her.

She stared at Eshey's name. She thought about her meetings with him. About his apartment. What had bothered her about the apartment. The cleanliness; it had been weird. Single men that age didn't scrub floors.

And Dorian's house had been even cleaner, if that was possible.

She added a line below Eshey's name and wrote Dorian.

Dorian had struck her as odd, too. Real odd. The pig. The obsessively clean house.

She groaned. But none of it was connected . . . was it? Just odd ducks, both of them. Was cleanliness inherited?

Jess reached for a diet soda on her desk, letting images of her interviews flash through her mind like photo pages in an album. Her brain kept shuffling the images. Her interviews with Eshey . . . her interview with Dorian. What was alike? What was different?

She flipped through the images in her mind of her interviews with the father and daughter.

Dorian's grass was so neatly manicured that it looked as if it had been cut with scissors.

The dish rack on Eshey's sink. The cup and plate placed so precisely.

The refrigerator magnets in both kitchens lined neatly along the freezer.

Dorian's trowel that looked as if it had never touched the soil.

Her gloves.

It was as if there was something right on the tip of Jess's tongue, and yet she couldn't say it. She couldn't figure out what it was that she was missing.

She drew more lines.

Charles Eshey had killed his brother.

Dorian's sister had died in a fire. She added Darin to the Eshey family grouping on her paper. She made a note to order a report on the fire. *Think outside the box.*

Her phone rang, startling her. "Special Agent Manlove."

"It's Cynthia Carmack again."

Jess almost felt sorry for her. She sounded petrified. "Yes?"

"He's not in the apartment," she rushed. "The police checked with his neighbors. He's gone. Been gone since Saturday. He left his cat in the care of the little girl next door."

"Damn it," Jess groaned. "Did he tell the neighbor where he was going?"

"He apparently mentioned Baltimore. I believe my records show that his daughter Dorian Eshey lives in—"

Jess hung up the phone before Cynthia finished her sentence. She located the information she had on Sydney Baker MacGregor and dialed the number she had penciled in. Baltimore was too damned close to Delaware to take any chances.

She got Sydney's answering machine. *Please leave a name and number and the time you called.* Yada, yada yada.

Jess was suddenly so frustrated that she wanted to scream. "Mrs. MacGregor." She took a breath. "Sydney, this is Special Agent Manlove. I need you to call me at my office immediately." She looked at her watch. "It's four-thirty on Friday afternoon." She left her number at the office as well as her personal cell.

She hung up and dialed the second number she had for Sydney—a cell phone.

A recording came on saying the number Jess had dialed was presently unavailable. She disconnected and dialed an interoffice extension. She ordered phone records from Eshey's New Jersey apartment and from Dorian Eshey's house and asked that she be contacted by radio as she would be out in the field. She hung up the phone a little harder than she meant.

"Easy there." Carl came around the cubicle. "I talked to Crackhow. He's reluctantly released us from our current assignments to locate Eshey."

"Prick." Jess grabbed her soft-sided briefcase from under her desk and began stuffing everything she had pertaining to Eshey into it. "Let's go," she said, grabbing King's book from the floor where it had fallen.

"Where we going?"

"Dorian Eshey's place. I talked to Carmack. I'll fill you in on the way."

He hooked a thumb. "That's a long hike out of town. You want to call her before we go?"

"Nope." She walked so fast that he had to take a running step to catch up with her. "Because I think he's there."

Forty-one

Marshall opened his apartment door with his keys and pushed in with one foot, a gym bag in each hand. He had parked the rental car on the street. He'd decided to wait and return it tomorrow. He was going to have to pay for the extra day anyway, since it was after noon.

He dropped his bags by the door and went to the fridge. It was nearly bare, and what was there didn't look safe for human consumption. He grabbed a can of diet soda, always a safe bet.

He popped the top. It was almost five. He'd made a couple of stops along the way and still made good time coming home. He grimaced, thinking about his week. He didn't know if he was happy or sad, angry or content. He wished the FBI hadn't pulled off the Eshey case so quickly, yet he was delighted with the turn of events with Sydney MacGregor. He prayed to God he could help her, whether that meant getting to the bottom of these missing kids or helping her cope with her fears that, though perhaps unfounded, might never go away.

He walked over to his computer and flipped on the power switches. Maybe he would work a while. While the computer went through the loading screens, he hit the answering machine message button. He sipped the cold soda while he listened.

A hang up.

His mother asking him when he was coming for a weekend. She needed the powder room toile plunged.

A call from Renee to see if he was back yet. He would have to return her call, but he needed a plan He didn't want to hurt her feelings, but he wouldn' be sleeping with her anymore. This thing with Sydney was too important to him to screw it up with a quickie with the neighbor.

"Message four," said the mechanical voice in the an swering machine.

"Mr. King . . ." It was a woman's voice. Older. She sounded upset. "Mr. King, this is Diana Ponds, Terry' mother. We spoke about two weeks ago."

Marshall set down his soda, staring at the answering machine.

"Mr. King, I told you that my granddaughters were fine. That Susan and Sarah were fine." She paused again and when she spoke, she was obviously crying "I found out this morning that Susan is missing. She' been gone more than two months."

Two months. Marshall did the math. Gone since be fore Carrie Morris was kidnapped. For a second he felt as if his heart had stopped beating.

"Diana says that Susan probably just ran away again That's why she didn't tell me sooner. They didn't wan to worry me. Susan's done it before. The girl has al ways been high-strung. Always resented authority Only now she's been gone so long. No one has seer her." A sob caught in the older woman's throat. "Wha if she didn't run away? What if—" She cut herself off "If you will call me, Mr. Marshall, I'd appreciate it."

Marshall stared at the answering machine, unable to

believe what he had just heard. Susan, daughter of Terry Ponds, whose sister Tracy was the first to die, had disappeared. Then Carrie. Then Jason. There was only one twin left.

He grabbed the phone, read the number off his blotter, and dialed Sydney's cell phone. The number wasn't in service.

He cursed.

Now what? Keep trying Sydney and hope she turned her cell on? Hope it worked? Call Joel? The FBI? Go back to the cabin where he left her?

It only took him a second to decide on all of the above. He ripped the June and July pages off the desk blotter he used as an address book and sprinted across the apartment, leaving the soda behind. He grabbed his keys off the counter and ran out of his apartment, slamming the door behind him. The knob self-locked. To hell with the deadbolt.

Marshall hurried up the stairs to the next floor, praying Renee was home. He banged on the door. He was sweating hard. Scared, sick to his stomach. He couldn't let Eshey get to Sydney or Krista.

The door opened and sweet-faced Renee appeared. "You're back."

He pushed through the door. "You have a cell phone, don't you?"

She blinked. "Yes. Why?"

"Is it good nationwide? I mean, can you call anywhere in the US? Receive calls from anywhere?"

"Sure." She stared at him in confusion. "Why?"

"Can I borrow it?"

She walked across the living room area to the counter that separated it from the kitchen. She reached into her purse. "Of course. What's wrong? Marshall, are you in some kind of trouble?"

He must have looked wild-eyed or something, but

he didn't have time to explain. The moment she lo cated the cell phone, he grabbed it out of her hand "I'll tell you later. I have to go. I'll pay for any calls make." He ran for the door and burst into the hal headed for the stairwell. "Thanks, Renee."

"Call me," she hollered over the rail as he took th steps down, two at a time

On the street, Marshall hopped into the rental an headed for the Holland tunnel. He'd thrown out hi directions to the cabin when he'd stopped earlier i the day. He hoped the hell he could find it again, an now in the dark.

Once on the road, he dialed Special Agent Manlov and got her voice mail. He left a message. He calle Susan and Sarah's grandmother and got an answerin machine. Then he tried Sydney's cell again. "Com on, Syd. Come on girl," he groaned. "Turn on you damned cell phone."

As he cursed aloud, he couldn't resist a bitterswee smile. He sounded like her.

"Bingo," Jess said dropping her two-way radio ont the car seat. Carl was driving. She had just talked t someone at the office who had the phone records sh requested.

"So Dorian never spoke to her father, huh?" Car said dryly.

"Well, she may not have called him, but he sur called her. Last call was last Wednesday night."

"I've been thinking." Carl glanced at her, the turned his attention to the road again. "We need t call for backup."

She eyed him. "Yeah?"

He nodded. "Call into the office. Bottleman an

hoever is on surveillance with him are probably the
losest on-duty agents."

She groaned. She hated to call in Bottleman, but
Carl was probably right. She had enough circumstan-
ial evidence now to suggest that father and daughter
vere up to something.

Jess radioed in and received confirmation that
omeone would be sent for backup. Five minutes
ater, across the crackling radio, Bottleman called in
o say that he and Portsmouth were on their way and
hat they would bring the warrant Carl had requested.
He thanked Jess for breaking up what looked to be a
boring evening. He gave half an hour as his ETA.

Twenty minutes later, Jess and Carl parked a few
houses down from Dorian Eshey's house and walked up
he street to the little bungalow. As Jess strode beside
Carl, she reached under her coat and unfastened the
afety strap that kept her Thompson .45 in place. In all
her years with the Bureau, she had drawn her weapon
only twice and never had to fire. She hoped this wasn't
going to be the day to test her marksmanship. She
hated the idea of killing anyone, but she knew she
could do it if she had to. She knew she would.

"Car's gone," Carl said quietly as they walked up the
sidewalk to Dorian's house. "Everything looks quiet."

Jess tried to take everything in at once. A morning
newspaper in the driveway. Closed drapes in the windows. Grass cut, but it wasn't as short as it had been
he day they paid Dorian a call.

"Want to wait for Bottleman?" Carl walked up the
steps to the door as he looked over his shoulder.

She shook her head, glancing to the left and then
to the right at the nearly identical bungalows on each
side of the property. No nosy neighbors in sight.
"Nah. Let's go in. He and Portsmouth will be here any

minute." She knew she was fudging the rules a little but that feeling in her gut just wouldn't go away.

Carl met her gaze. "You want to go around back?"

"In case he tries to run?"

"In case anyone does."

She nodded. "Give me a couple of minutes. Keep your ears open in the meantime." She checked for her radio in her jacket pocket. "I'll give you a ring when I'm in place."

"You be careful, babe."

She grinned. "You too, Cowboy."

Jess hurried around the side of the house, keeping an eye on the windows. There were basement windows, too, which she hadn't really noticed the first time she was here. She eyed them. Mini blinds closed. She got to the six-foot plank gate and lifted the latch.

It wasn't going to be that easy. Locked.

She peered through the crack between the fence and the gate. She had a pretty good view of the tiny back yard. Nothing. She glanced behind her, again looking for an audience. When she didn't see anyone she gave the gate a hard kick.

It popped open without even splintering the wood.

Jess slipped inside the backyard and eased the gate shut. Still no sign of anyone.

She heard Jessica the pig snort.

A friggin' pet pig. She spotted it as she cut across the lawn. It was in its pen.

Jess walked up onto the back porch, her hand on the pistol on her belt. The green umbrella over the patio table flapped in the warm, light breeze. She pulled her radio out of her jacket pocket and spoke softly. "In place."

Her muscles tensed as she heard Carl knock on the front door. She tried to take everything in at once as she waited, holding her breath. The pig was still mak-

ıg oinking noises, but there wasn't another sound. In
yard a few lots down, someone was mowing the lawn.

No answer at the front door. Carl knocked again.
They both waited.

"Gretel doesn't seem to be home," Jess murmured
nto the radio.

"My door or yours?" His voice was as calm as if he
were ordering his lunch.

She glanced over her shoulder toward the pigpen.
essica really seemed to be wound up about some-
hing. But there still wasn't another sound. "You stay
here. I'll go in this way. We go busting down front
loors and you'll have the neighbors breathing down
our back."

"Roger that."

Jess eased open the old storm door, checked the
nob to be sure the wooden door was locked, and
hen took a deep breath. She wasn't a tall woman, but
he was strong. She kicked it hard with the heel of her
ensible loafers. The door popped open, splintering
vood on the second try.

She burst into the kitchen, drawing her weapon.
'FBI," she shouted.

The first thing that struck her in the clean kitchen
vas the stench of rotting flesh. Once you knew that
mell, you never forgot it. The second thing she no-
iced were the newspaper clippings neatly lined up on
he refrigerator door. And the smiling face of star
ɔitcher Krista MacGregor.

Forty-two

Jess followed procedure, identifying herself again. She swung her handgun in one direction and then the other, running into the dark living room. Instead of hurrying down the short hall to check the bedroom and bath, she rushed to the front door and let Carl in.

"What's that smell?" he said, drawing his own weapon as he stepped over the threshold. "Dead rat?"

"I'd like to think so."

He met her gaze. "Or something worse?"

Jess shook her head. "Christ, I don't know. You think Eshey killed his kid?"

As they spoke, they walked out of the living room and inched down the hallway. Jess covered Carl as he kicked open each door. The bathroom was empty. The first bedroom was small and dark, with only a neatly made single bed and a nightstand. It didn't look as if it were ever used. There was nothing in the closet but some old drapes hung on plastic hangers. In the second and larger bedroom there was a double bed, a vanity-type dresser, and an easy chair. On the nightstand was a stack of teacher's guides. Dorian must have been doing a little summer reading to prepare for the next school year.

Jess and Carl cautiously walked back up the hall and into the living room.

"There's a basement," she whispered.

"Of course there is." He wrinkled his nose at the smell that was definitely stronger at this end of the house. "Where the hell is Bottleman?"

"He'll be here. Come on." Jess walked to the paneled wooden door between the kitchen and living room that she suspected went to the basement.

Carl whipped opened the door. No one there. "You first or me?"

"Me. You're taller. You can shoot the bastard right over my head if you need to."

Jess held her Thompson directly in front of her with her right hand as she stared down into the darkness of the stairwell and felt for a light switch. "B-I-N-G-O," she murmured as the basement flooded with light.

"FBI," she called as she eased down the steps with Carl right behind her. As she stepped down into the cooler room, she heard nothing but the slight echo of her own voice.

There was one large room in the basement where cardboard boxes were neatly stacked and methodically marked with a black magic marker. *Winter Sweaters. Winter Skirts. Fun Days,* the boxes said. They looked as if they had been lined up with a measuring stick. Jess's winter sweaters were thrown on the bottom of her closet floor. She had no "Fun Day" clothes. "Sick chick."

"Nothing wrong with a little organization," Carl teased as he approached a door in the corner of the storage area.

Jess came up beside him. They had their timing down pat. He opened the door and she burst in, weapon drawn.

It was another bedroom. One that looked as if it were used regularly. Her skin crawled. The whole room, at least upon first glance, appeared identical to the master bedroom. The double bed was made with a spread matching the master bed upstairs. There was an easy chair identical to the upstairs chair. There were even teaching manuals stacked beside the bed. She didn't take the time to see if they were the same books.

Creepy. Very creepy.

"Now this chick is really freaking me out," Jess muttered. "What the hell is this? Never got over her twin sister dying or something?"

Carl shook his head. "I don't know. But no one is here. The place is secure. You want to go upstairs and see what the sweet smell is?"

"Do I have to?"

He grinned. "This is your ballgame, babe."

She hurried up the steps. Confident no one was here, she holstered her pistol. Bottleman and Portsmouth were just walking in the front door when Jess and Carl stepped into the living room.

"What the fuck is that smell?" Bottleman groaned, whipping a handkerchief from his pocket to cover his nose and mouth.

Portsmouth said nothing, but he pressed his lips together, looking a little green.

"We're secure here," Jess glancing around the dark, neat living room. Here, mingled with the odor or rotting flesh, she could smell furniture polish. "No one home." She spoke to Bottleman. "I want you and Portsmouth to go out into the backyard and have a look around. There's a pig in a pigpen."

"A pig?" Bottleman looked at her as if she had grown another head.

"Through that door." She pointed to the kitchen.

"Sure. Christ. Anything to get out of here."

Jess and Carl let the other two pass and then walked into the kitchen.

"Ah, no," Carl groaned as he looked at the newspaper clippings on the refrigerator. "You see this?"

"Yup."

He brushed his fingertips over Carrie's and Jason's photos, then Krista MacGregor's photo. "What's going on here, Jess? Eshey bring his photo gallery to show his daughter? His daughter keeping her own?"

"Don't know." Jess opened a broom closet. Nobody there, just a mop and a broom and a dustpan that looked brand new, or scrubbed clean, hanging from a hook. "But I'd sure feel better if Sydney would call me back."

Carl stood in front of the fridge staring at the clippings. There was Krista, Jason, Carrie, and a Polaroid photo of a teenage girl with long brown hair. She looked frightened. "You recognize the girl in the picture?"

"Nope." Jess opened another door. A small pantry. Dorian's body wasn't there, either. Just canned goods, neatly stacked, front labels facing out. She didn't have time to check, but it looked as if the cans were in alphabetical order by contents. She closed the door.

Jess stood in the middle of the room, thinking hard. "So where's the smell coming from?"

"I don't know. It's here in the kitchen, though." Carl opened the cabinet beneath the sink. A trashcan and cleaning products, all lined up neatly, of course.

They both began to open dish cabinets, leaving the doors open as they went. Still nothing.

Carl went back to the refrigerator, stared at it. "What do you think?"

Jess lifted one shoulder. "Shouldn't be a smell coming from there, but go for it."

Carl took a breath and eased open the refrigerator door. Nothing but condiments, diet soda, and cleanly wiped shelves. "It looks like she was going away on vacation," he observed. "Barb always cleans out the fridge before we go away."

Jess walked over to the dishwasher—avocado green like the one her mother had once had. She popped open the latch and lowered the door.

"Ah, fuck," she groaned and turned away.

"What?" Carl spun around.

Jess wiped her mouth with the back of her hand and swallowed the bitter bile that rose in her throat. She looked up at Carl. "I think we've got a problem with our present theory."

He stared at the dishwasher, which she had partially closed when she stepped back. She took a cleansing breath and touched her finger lightly on the dishwasher door, opening it for Carl.

On the bottom rack was Charles Eshey's severed head.

Forty-three

Carl gagged and covered his mouth with his hand.

Jess slammed the dishwasher door shut. "So where's the rest of him?" she panted as she reached for her radio to call for more backup and the body guys. Now that a body was discovered—or at least a piece of one—she knew she would have to back off until forensics arrived and did their thing.

Jess and Carl moved toward the back door, away from the dishwasher, as she checked in with the office. She was told the forensic team would be there half an hour to forty-five minutes. She also got an urgent message from Marshall King. He'd left a cell phone number.

"King?" Carl said, the color slowly returning to his face. "What does he want?"

"I don't know. You have your personal cell with you? I left mine in my car at the office."

They stood in the kitchen speaking as if there wasn't a head in the dishwasher.

"I'm going to call King. Maybe he's calling for Sydney." Jess kept her tone all business. It was the way it was done in situations like this. "Then I'm going to try to get hold of Sydney again. I don't know what the fuck is going on here, but no one can argue that Sydney and her girl don't have a right to protection until we figure it out. We just have to find them."

Carl handed her his phone from his suit pocket. "So now what do you think is going on here? Who—"

A strangled cry rent the air. Bottleman.

Carl, closest to the back door, wrenched it open and sprinted toward the back yard, Jess right behind him, drawing her .45. As she stepped onto the porch she spotted Portsmouth standing near the shed, staring at her in horror. Bottleman was on his hands and knees puking his guts out in the neatly manicured grass.

"You don't need your firearms," Portsmouth croaked as Jess and Carl sprinted across the lawn.

They halted in front of him.

"Portsmouth, what the hell—"

He lifted his hand, pointing toward the pigpen beside the shed.

Jess looked at Carl. Carl looked at her. They took the couple of steps to the fence and peered over it.

Jessica, the pig, was snorting happily . . . chewing on a human hand. "Oh, God," Carl moaned, looking away.

Jess took enough time to look over the entire pigpen. The dirt was damp, muddy in places, but the edges looked raked. Was that an arm bone protruding from beneath the feeding trough? She swallowed and turned away.

"Carl, call in and let the office know we're going to need more help here." She glanced down at Bottleman who was still on all fours, panting. "You OK?"

He wretched again.

Jess walked toward the house.

"Where you going?" Carl asked, pulling his radio out of his pocket.

She looked at Portsmouth. "You'd better have a seat

up on the porch for a minute, buddy. You look like you're going to pass out on us."

Portsmouth staggered away.

Jess checked out Carl. He was pale, but he was OK. "I dropped your phone on the kitchen floor—I have to get it. I'm calling King. Hopefully he'll know where Sydney and her daughter are." She glanced at the pigpen in disbelief. "You know, I've read about pigs eating bodies; it's supposedly a common way to get rid of them in Ireland. But I've never believed it."

She walked away, shaking her head, thankful she had an iron stomach.

A short time later, Dorian Eshey's house and yard was flooded with cops, FBI agents, and forensic scientists. It was almost seven by the time Jess gave a full report of the situation and could search the yard to find Carl.

She tugged on the sleeve of his pressed white shirt. He'd actually removed his suit jacket and rolled up his sleeves. "Let's go."

"Where?"

"Delaware."

"Delaware?"

"We have to find Sydney MacGregor. I've tried her number and her ex's—no one is answering at either place. I tried the number Marshall King gave me. It's busy. But he must have called because he knows something is going on. I'm not playing Crackhow's coincidence game any more. More than intuition tells me she and her daughter could be in big trouble."

Carl followed her out the back gate. They stepped over the crime-scene tapes that blocked off the sidewalk in front of Dorian's house. The news stations with their vans and their intrusive reporters were already lining up and down the quiet street. There were people everywhere, all gawking, trying to find out what was happening behind the wooden fence of the teacher's house.

Carl and Jess passed two uniformed cops. Everyone nodded.

"I understand we need to find them, but we don't know where they are." Carl pulled the keys from his pocket.

"It's at least a two-hour drive to the shore. If nothing else, if we don't talk to her or King, we'll go to her house. It's as good a place as any to start. Just head for the Bay Bridge."

Carl slid in behind the wheel; Jess got in on the passenger's side.

"Bottleman in control here?" Carl asked.

She laughed, though she wasn't in a humorous mood. "Not hardly. Last I heard, he still had the dry heaves. Crackhow called Lockhart in."

Jess grabbed a notepad off the back seat and began to scribble down notes. "OK, partner, let's think this through. The twins born of Eshey's victims are now missing, except Krista—who we now know is a twin."

"And she's the last in order," Carl offered.

"But Eshey is dead, and as far as we know Krista is still all right. If it was him, she's safe. A dead man can't kill a little girl."

"You think Dorian discovered what her father was doing and killed him?"

"Possibly." Jess wrote it down under another heading. "Keep thinking out loud. I'll keep trying to get hold of King. Eventually, we'll get through."

The moment the phone rang, Marshall picked it up. "Yeah?"

"Mr. King?"

"Yes?"

"This is Special Agent Manlove returning your call."

She sounded agitated, probably because it was after hours. He didn't care. "Thanks for getting back to me. I called because I have some information for you that I think will make you reconsider closing the Eshey case."

"Yes?"

"I guess you know I've been doing some investigating of Eshey on my own." He didn't wait for her to comment. "Well, I was in Delaware for a few days with Sydney MacGregor, and when I got home, there was a message on my answering machine from the grandmother of Terry and Tracy Ponds."

The agent didn't say a word.

"You still there?" Marshall switched lanes. The speed limit was sixty-five on Route One, the bypass through Delaware. He was driving eighty. If he had one of the cell phone earpieces and could have put both hands on the wheel, he might have gone faster. At this speed, he thought he could reach Sydney by nine. It was almost eight now.

"I'm listening, Mr. King," Manlove said tightly.

"Apparently the surviving twin, Terry, has twin daughters about fifteen years old."

"I'm aware of that."

"Are you aware that one of them has been missing since early May?" he snapped.

He heard her exhale. "I was not. I had the family's names and their whereabouts, Mr. King, but we hadn't contacted them. I know this is hard for you to understand, it's hard for me to understand," she muttered. "But legally we have to be careful who we talk to and why."

"Well, you missed the boat on this one, Agent Manlove," Marshall said angrily. "Because, by my calculations, this girl, Susan Catcher, disappeared the first week of May. Carrie Morris disappeared the last week of May and then—"

"Then Jason. In order of Eshey's kills," Manlove said.

"So can you arrest the bastard?" Marshall glanced in his rearview mirror. "Can you go to his apartment, to his job and arrest him? Because I don't know if you know this or not, but Krista MacGregor is a twin. The last twin."

"As far as you know, is she all right?" the agent asked.

"As far as I know, yes. But I left New York a little after five. If Sydney has tried to get me since then, she couldn't have reached me."

There was another pause before she spoke again. "Mr. King, I can't give any details right now because I'm presently involved with a crime scene, but I can tell you that Mr. Eshey will not be committing any more murders."

"He's dead?"

"I can't say."

He had to be dead or already arrested, and Marshall suspected Manlove would have told him if Eshey was in jail. He was stunned. "I don't understand. Are you saying I have no reason to be concerned for Krista MacGregor's safety?" He switched lanes, switched back, not even bothering to signal this time.

The agent groaned into the phone. Marshall hadn't a clue what was going on, but he was becoming more frightened for Sydney and Krista by the moment.

"I can't tell you what's happened, Mr. King," Manlove said. "What I need from you right now is any other possible locations for Mrs. MacGregor and her daughter other than their home. I had local police go by there and the ex-husband's place, and nothing seems amiss. Do you know where they are? I tried Sydney's cell phone number, but it isn't in service."

Marshall didn't need specifics after that request. If the agent was looking for Sydney, then Sydney and Krista were in danger. Marshall pushed his hair off his forehead, trying not to panic. If he panicked, he'd be no help to anyone. "Sydney's at her cabin on the Maryland Peninsula. Alone. Joel, her ex-husband, is on his way there, with Krista. It's an isolated area, Agent Manlove."

"Son of a bitch," she mumbled. "Do you know where the cabin is? I need an exact location. Is there a phone there?"

"Just her cell. I keep trying to call it, too, but she must have it off."

"Give me the location."

"I'll try. It's hard to find and I don't know any road names," Marshall said. "I'm on my way there now and I think I can be there in an hour."

"Mr. King, you can't go there."

Marshall pressed the gas pedal down further. "You want the directions or not, Agent Manlove?"

Forty-four

Sydney poured a glass of wine and walked out onto the back deck of the cabin. The sun was beginning to set over the marsh, promising to be yet another best sunset on the Eastern Shore. She sat on one of the cedar deck chairs and tucked her bare feet beneath her. She'd pulled on a pair of gray gym shorts in honor of Joel's impending arrival with Krista, but other than that addition, she hadn't changed her clothes since Marshall left. There was something deliciously decadent about sitting around the house all day working in your underwear and a T-shirt with no bra.

Sydney had had a good writing day. The book was definitely taking shape, and she was certain she could have it on her editor's desk on August first. She was glad she had come here. Glad Marshall had encouraged her to come.

The thought of Marshall brought heat to her cheeks. She was too old, too jaded to think he might be falling in love with her, but for now, she was content to have him in her life like this. He was a good lover and a good companion. She could just imagine intimate weekends away from home. Visits to New York City. She wanted to take Krista to New York; they hadn't been in years.

Sydney sipped her Merlot and wondered where Joel

and Krista were. She had been listening for the sound of the car in the driveway. She didn't know what time it was, because she had purposely left her watch at the beach house, but she knew it had to be eight-thirty by the position of the sun. It was beginning to ease below the horizon, a great ball of burning yellow and orange light, and it would soon drop fast. It was a truly a magnificent sight, with a great blue heron in flight painted against the backdrop of water, waving marsh grass, and cloudless silver sky.

She watched as the sun slowly descended below the horizon and darkness enveloped the marsh, the cabin, and the little porch where she sat. For a moment it seemed as if she were the only one on earth, just she and the impending darkness.

Sydney took a sip of wine and her stomach grumbled. She'd been so busy writing all day that she hadn't eaten a thing since she and Marshall had shared hotcakes this morning. Suddenly she was starving. She left her wine on the table beside the chair and stepped into the house. She'd make herself a bag of popcorn.

By the light of the lamp over the sink, she retrieved the box from the beneath the cabinet, tore the cellophane wrap off a bag, and stuck it in the microwave. As she hit the buttons, she heard a floorboard creak in the living room behind her.

Had Joel and Krista arrived and she'd not heard them? She pushed start on the microwave and turned around. No one was there.

Sydney frowned. "Krista? Joel?" she said aloud. She stood for a moment and heard nothing but silence and the whir of the fan inside the microwave. The interior of the house was cast in shadows, lit only by the small copper lamp over the kitchen sink and by a nightlight in the hallway near the master bedroom.

She walked into the dark living room that opened directly into the kitchen, where she halted and listened. She could see out the front picture window to the driveway. Even in the falling darkness, she could see that Joel's Jeep wasn't there.

She cautiously reached out and turned on the floor lamp beside the overstuffed chambray couch. Something popped behind her and she jumped.

The microwave. She pressed her hand to her left breast and her skipping heart. The popcorn began to pop and the room filled with the delicious smell of it.

She glanced at the digital clock on the back of the stove. It was eight-fifty-three. Joel and Krista weren't terribly late. There was a lane closed on Route 13, so traffic could be slow.

Sydney went to the kitchen counter and unplugged her cell phone from the wall where it had been charging. She turned it on and the message screen read that she had received six calls. Who could have been calling her cell? She brought up the phone log, but it only said that the numbers were not listed in her private mailbox. Wrong numbers? Maybe just Marshall checking to see if he could get through.

She punched Joel's cell phone number and waited. All she got was static. Damned reception seemed worse at night. She thought she could hear it ringing, though.

The microwave beeped, startling her yet again. Suddenly she was skittish and she didn't know why.

Still no answer on Joel's phone. Was the call even going through? She groaned and disconnected, leaving the phone on the counter beside the corkscrew she'd used to open the wine. Even if Joel or Krista did answer, they wouldn't be able to hear each other anyway.

She glanced around the cabin. Something didn't feel

right. Was it just that Joel was running late and she was being paranoid?

She stood quietly and listened again. She tried not to think about Eshey. He was in New Jersey, a feeble old man. He couldn't hurt her now.

Sydney heard nothing but the sound of a frog croaking outside the window.

She walked through the kitchen into the master bedroom. Nothing there, just a king size bed with the bedcovers still rumpled, the way she and Marshall had left them.

She returned to the kitchen and pulled the popcorn out of the microwave. She'd just go out on the deck, eat her popcorn, and wait for Joel and Krista. They'd be here any minute. She looked into the living room again. Was that a moving shadow?

She dropped the popcorn on the center island, rounded it, and stepped into the living room. She continued to the front hall, where there was a staircase directly across from the front door, a powder room to her right, and the living room to her left. She stared up the dark staircase that led to two bedrooms and a full bath. Could someone be upstairs?

Her head filled with images from horror movies. Halloween. Freddy Someone. The images were superimposed with Eshey's face.

Could he be here?

Cold fear seeped down her spine. She rested her hand on the rail. Did she go upstairs? Did she run out the front door and down the drive? Joel would be here any minute. Surely they would run into each other.

Sydney caught movement out of the corner of her eye and she screamed. She ducked left as a figure came out of the powder room.

"No!" She scrambled to escape.

The intruder caught her forearm in an iron grip and she screamed again, jerking her arm so hard that it felt as if she had pulled it from its socket. As she turned her head, struggling to escape, she saw his face for the first time. *Her face.*

Dorian Eshey.

She recognized her from the photo Marshall had taken in his interview. She screamed again, suddenly in a frenzy. Dorian? Was the killer's daughter kidnapping the children so her father could kill them? Had they come here to kill her Krista?

The possibility hit Sydney with a fury she hadn't known she possessed. Instead of fighting to get away, Sydney turned on Dorian, screaming like a madwoman, pummeling her in the chest, arms, face.

Dorian howled as Sydney caught her jaw with a punch. "You can't have her. You can't have her," Sydney screamed.

Sydney kneed the woman so hard that they both fell off balance and tumbled to the floor. She had Sydney by the bare leg. Sydney grabbed a hank of Dorian's hair and, to her shock, it came off in her hand. A wig?

She threw the thing in repulsion. She gave a hard kick and exhaled in a great whoosh as she broke free.

"Get back here," Dorian commanded and Sydney realized that without the wig, she looked like a he. She sounded like a he.

Was Dorian a man?

Sydney scrambled off the slick wood floor and flew around the corner, headed for the open French doors that led onto the back porch.

"All I want is the girl," Dorian called after her as she ran across the porch and into the darkness.

"You can't have her," Sydney shouted. All she could think of was that Krista would be here any moment.

She had to get down the driveway, had to stop Joel before he reached the cabin.

Dorian walked to the edge of the porch and leaned on the rail. Sydney hid behind a boxwood, staring through the darkness at her . . . or him.

She remembered what Marshall had said about the error in his book. He had said that Charles's girlfriend had given birth to boys. Later, the only information he had found was that Eshey's children were daughters. How was that possible?

It didn't matter, of course. All that mattered now was getting to Joel and Krista.

"You can't win, you know," Dorian called into the darkness, making no attempt to come after her. "We're good at this. In the end I'll have her . . . and you, too." She made a clicking sound with her mouth as if chastising a naughty student. "If you hadn't insisted on looking over the entire house, if you'd sat on your porch and drank your wine like a good girl, Sydney, you'd never have known we were here."

We? Who was we? Charles Eshey, of course, his father. Charles Eshey was inside the house, too. Sydney crept around the bush, thankful for the cover of darkness. Her heart pounded in her ears. She had to get around the house, down the drive. She had to get to Krista before Dorian and Charles did. She hunkered down behind the bush as she tried to catch her breath.

Fear threatened to strangle her. Incapacitate her. She remembered the taste of her fear when Eshey had tried to pull her out of the car. But now her fear seemed even greater. But it wasn't for herself. It was for her daughter. If Joel came down the drive, if Krista got out of the car—Sydney darted out from behind the bush and ran, her bare feet smarting from the tiny sticks and dry leaves in the grass.

"You can't escape us," Dorian called into the darkness.

Sydney kept running.

She cut into the field beside the house and circumnavigated it. She kept looking back over her shoulder. Lights were coming on in the house. Was Dorian turning them on, or was it Charles?

Why hadn't Dorian chased her?

She pushed through the high weeds of the field that had gone untended this season. She ran parallel to the dirt road, ignoring the pain in her bare feet and the weeds that snagged her hair and her clothing. Crickets chirped and she heard the rat-a-tat-tat of a pileated woodpecker in the distant twilight. A branch snapped off to her left, and her blood froze as she heard the rustle of a large animal moving through the underbrush. She would not let them have Krista. She would not let them have her. She would die protecting her baby. Charles had taken Marla from her, but the bastards would not have Krista.

Once Sydney was a safe distance from the cabin, once she was fairly certain that Dorian wasn't following her, she cut out of the field and onto the rutted lane. Her bare feet were bleeding. She was breathless from running and her lungs were bursting. She hadn't run this far in years. She pushed harder. It was easier to run on the dirt road than in the field.

A little more than a half mile from the cabin, Sydney spotted something big in the road. It was dark now, but she knew it was a car. She dived into the cover of the weedy field. Her head pounded with pain and she shook all over. If only she had gotten that gun, taken those firearm lessons. She crept through the weeds, crouching low. She recognized the car and her heart tumbled. Dorian and Charles must have followed Joel here.

The woods, the field, the dirt lane were so quiet. There was no movement inside or around the car. It looked unoccupied.

She crept closer and her breath caught in her throat. There was someone in the driver's side, leaning back, appearing to be part of the seat—

"Joel?" she cried, bursting out of the field. She rounded the front of the Jeep. Why wasn't he answering her? Even in the dark, she could see it was him. She pounded on the window, then reached for the door handle. Where was Krista?

Terrified, she yanked the door open. "Joel—"

The interior light flooded the car.

Blood. Blood on Joel's T-shirt. On the steering wheel. She could smell it, thick and primal. It was Joel in the driver's seat and yet it wasn't. His face was pale, his eyes half open, but unseeing.

A single neat hole marred his forehead.

A strangled cry bubbled out of Sydney's throat and for a moment she feared she would faint. "No. No!"

Joel was dead.

Where was Krista?

She ripped open the back door to be sure Krista wasn't hiding in fear in the back seat. No Krista, only her purple bat bag.

"God, no, no, not again," Sydney sobbed, tears blinding her vision. A white T-shirt lay flung on the back seat. She grabbed it and lifted to her face. It still smelled of Krista, of shampoo and powder and the scent Sydney had recognized as her daughter's since the moment the OB nurse had placed her in her arms. Another sob bubbled up.

For a moment Sydney stood in the darkness looking up the road toward the cabin, down toward the highway. She trembled as she walked over and placed her hand on the hood. Christ, it was still hot.

She panted, trying to catch her breath, trying to make herself think. It was another two miles to the paved road. There was a house on the corner. She could call the police. How far away was the nearest state police headquarters? How long would it take them to get here—if they even believed her?

The thoughts raced parallel to possibilities as to what she should do . . . now, before it was too late. What good had the police done her before? No one had helped her when she had told the FBI that Charles Eshey was killing again. No one was going to help her now.

She placed her hand on the hood again, thinking clearer with every second that passed. She had to reason through this and be smarter than Dorian if she was going to save Krista.

She looked in the direction of the cabin. She had to be right. There had to be two of them. Charles had to be here, too. How else could someone have gotten to Krista? Sydney walked to the rear of the Jeep, reached into the back seat, and grabbed Krista's bat bag. She jerked open the zipper and pulled out her daughter's favorite bat, a thirty-inch Red Line softball bat. Joel had paid over two hundred dollars for it, giving it to Krista for Christmas.

Gripping the blue aluminum bat, she gave one hard swing and then bolted up the driveway, back in the direction she had come. She didn't have time to run the two miles to the corner house to get help. She had to get to the cabin. Get Krista. The idea that the madman probably had Krista at this moment made her run faster. She sprinted up the lane, the lights from the cabin coming into view around the bend.

Her cell phone was still in the house on the kitchen

counter. If she could get to it, if she could dial 911, maybe the call would go through. Even if no one could hear her, couldn't they trace the phone call? She didn't know enough about cell phones to be sure, but it was worth a try.

Forty-five

"What do you mean they can't find the place?" Jess barked into the cell phone at poor Lockhart, who had taken over the crime scene at Dorian's place. "I don't have a friggin' address. The guy who gave me the directions was only there once and it's out in the middle of nowhere. They don't even have paved roads."

"The Maryland state police are looking over maps now," Lockhart said contritely. "They know the area, of course, but they say there are a lot of back roads along the marsh."

She groaned. "So tell them to run the name through a computer for property owners in the area; the ex-husband's name is Joel. Joel MacGregor."

"Not sure if they have that capability on hand, but we'll give it a try. Maybe our office can do it faster."

Jess pushed her hair off her forehead as she peered out the car window in the darkness. "I want you to make the police understand that when they arrive at the cabin, they are to hold their position until we get there. We don't know who we're looking for. We don't even know who's at the cabin. It could just be this woman and her kid, safe and sound. I don't want to scare the crap out of them, Lockhart."

"I've already made that clear. Surround the property and stay put until you and Steinman get there."

"Call me back as soon as you know something." Jess disconnected and tossed the phone on the car seat. Her stomach was in knots. She felt as if she had failed this mother and child, and she was determined to make it right. She just hoped she wasn't too late. She glanced at Carl. "Can't you drive faster?"

Sydney reached the front lawn and dropped onto all fours, the softball bat in her right hand. She could see through the big picture window into the living room and spotted Dorian standing near the couch. She didn't think Dorian could see her outside in the dark, not with it being so bright inside, but she wasn't going to take any chances. She crawled up the steps, dragging the bat behind her, and scurried across the porch. At the front door, she stood up, her back to the wall, and inched over to the window. She peered around the corner and then immediately drew back. She had to cover her mouth with her hand to stifle a cry of fear.

Krista was there. Oh, God. Dorian had her.

She fought not to hyperventilate. Krista was there, but she was unharmed. She looked scared and small. She looked pissed off, too. Sydney almost smiled.

She dared another look.

Krista was sitting on the floor in front of the couch. Dorian stood threateningly over her. He . . . she . . . it . . . had put his wig back on. Sydney could see now why Marshall had thought him so odd looking. He was wearing navy stretch pants and a flowered shirt. He looked like an ugly woman. But now that Sydney had seen him with his wig off, she saw the masculine features Marshall must have missed. Even from this distance, she could see his Adam's apple. He had the hands of a man, too.

There was no sign of Charles, but Sydney knew he was here. Here with a gun. Probably the only reason he hadn't killed Krista was in the hope of luring Sydney in. Then he could kill them both and there would be no living witnesses.

An image of Joel dead in the car flashed through her head, but she pushed it away. She couldn't think about him now. Couldn't grieve for him now. Krista was all that mattered. If Joel were here now, he would say the same thing.

Sydney pulled away from the window, forcing herself to breathe slowly. She had to get into the house to the cell phone. She looked at the cumbersome bat in her hand. Maybe in the kitchen she could find a better weapon; a knife or something. She crawled down the porch steps, wincing as she scraped her bare knees on the wood. Once in the shadows against the log cabin, she jumped up and ran around to the back. She crawled under the railing of the back porch, dropped to her hands and knees, and crawled again. The French doors were still open.

"I'm coming, Krista," she whispered. "Mom's coming. Just hold on there, sweetie."

Sydney peered around the open doors into the living room. She saw Dorian standing over Krista. He was speaking quietly to her. Krista had her arms crossed over her chest, her jaw thrust out in anger.

"Atta girl," Sydney whispered. "Don't be afraid. Be angry." Sydney's own anger, she knew now, had saved her from Eshey all those years ago, and from Dorian earlier.

Keeping one eye on Dorian, Sydney peered around the corner, into the kitchen area. She didn't know where Charles was, but he wasn't in the kitchen.

Rather than standing and risking tall shadows, she crawled in through the door, praying as she crept forward, trying to keep the aluminum bat from hitting the wood floor and making any noise.

"Please God, please God, help me save my daughter. He can have me, but don't let him have Krista."

Sydney slid on her belly across the plank kitchen floor. On the far side, she could see her cell phone on the counter. Another foot and she would have the center island to block her from Dorian's view. She scrambled forward, her gaze locked on the cell phone. Another six inches—

A hand came out of nowhere and grabbed the phone. Sydney shrieked as a foot in a large white sneaker caught the bat and kicked it out of her hand. "How did we know you would come back?" Dorian said sarcastically. He had a small black automatic pistol in the other hand.

Sydney jerked backward, sitting up as the bat, her only weapon, rolled out of her reach. She bumped the back of her head hard on the cabinet. Dorian? How was that possible? Eshey's daughter, son, whatever the hell it was, was in the living room with Krista. She had seen him—it—only a second ago. "Get up," he ordered, waving with the gun. "Into the living room."

Now that she was caught, all she wanted to do was get to Krista. She'd figure this out. She'd find a way to save them from this lunatic.

"Where is he?" she asked, getting to her feet, backing against the counter with both hands behind her. She felt dizzy. A little disoriented. She was breathing hard again. As she drew back, her thumb hit something metal. Hard. Cold. Oh, God. The corkscrew from the wine bottle she'd opened earlier in the evening.

"Where is who?" Dorian poked her with the pistol "I said, into the living room."

Sydney managed to cup the small corkscrew into her palm as she drew away from the counter. "Charles."

Dorian smiled. "Oh, I'm afraid our father won't be able to join us."

Our father?

Sydney stared at Dorian in confusion.

He waggled the gun. "Come on, we've been waiting for you. We knew that after you found the husband you'd be back."

Sydney stepped around the corner of the kitchen into the living room and halted in shock. Dorian was still there with Krista, just where she had seen him a moment ago. Yet he was also standing behind her pressing a gun barrel into her back.

Then it hit her. "She didn't die in the fire," she whispered. As she spoke she brought her hand to the front of her baggy shorts. She had no pockets, no place to hide the corkscrew.

"Mom?" Krista looked up at Sydney with big frightened green eyes. Marla's eyes.

Sydney ran across the room and fell to her knees to hug her daughter.

"Mom, Daddy," Krista sobbed, pale with shock. Fat silent tears ran down her cheeks.

"I know," Sydney whispered, careful to hide her weapon behind her back. "It's going to be OK." She kissed the top of her sweet head, murmuring in her ear. "We're going to get these fuckers."

"To answer your question, I did not die in the fire. The Dorian who had been guarding Krista had smiled. "I'm Darin."

Sydney stared at one Eshey and then the other as it slowly came together in her rattled mind. They were identical twins, down to the same stretch pants and short mousy woman's wig twisted in a bun. Sydney couldn't believe it. Charles Eshey's twin girls were both alive, only they weren't girls. They were boys, as Marshall had originally reported.

"Why are you dressed as women?"

"A question to ask our grandmother." Darin frowned. "She got it in her head that if she pretended we were girls, if we were raised as female, we wouldn't behave as our father had."

Sydney wanted to say how sick that was, but she didn't. Her head was spinning with all the information suddenly bombarding her. She still didn't understand. "But how can there still be two of you? Darin died. A body was found," Sydney said, remembering what Marshall had said. "You and your grandmother's. How—"

"The body in my bed was that of a poor, unfortunate hitchhiker we offered a ride to." Darin smiled at Dorian. "Tests are rarely run when it's obvious who the victim is. Charred in my bed, poor dear. Already dead, of course, but who could tell in such a terrible fire?"

"I still don't understand," Sydney whispered. "Why would you fake your death?"

Dorian, with the pistol, lifted his shoulder. "We know. It *is* hard for someone to understand, but if anyone could, it would be you. It's difficult to be a twin, always half of something, isn't it? Never your own person. Our father solved the problem by killing his brother. We decided to join forces instead . . . act as one."

Sydney eased her arm around Krista who was trembling. Their backs were against the couch. "As one?" she said, trying to keep the brothers talking. "What do you mean?"

"It wasn't hard to fool anyone. We took turns going

to our college classes," Dorian explained in a very teacher-like tone. "We both interviewed for positions after we graduated."

"We keep each other well-informed," Darin continued. "At the end of the work day, we tell each other everything. It's really quite refreshing not to have to work every day. It gives us the energy we need to tackle those fourth graders. They can be quite a handful, you know." He smiled almost lovingly.

The thought that these animals had been teaching someone's children made Sydney ill. It seemed impossible to her that both could be sharing one life, and yet she believed them. The whole premise was so bizarre that it had to be true.

"So now what?" Darin looked to Dorian.

"Kill them both, of course." Dorian glanced at the living room. "We could make it look like a robbery."

"Like we did that time in Alexandria," Darin said cheerfully.

"Mom," Krista whimpered.

"Shhhh," Sydney soothed, getting a good grip on the corkscrew. She was trying to figure out who to go after, the one with or without the gun. She had to keep them talking. "I still don't understand who you are. Why you're doing this." She met Dorian's gaze. He seemed to be the dominant twin. "You took the other children, didn't you?"

He smiled proudly.

Sydney's lower lip trembled and she fought to keep her emotions in control. It was her and Krista's only chance. "Why?" she asked. "Why did you do it?"

Again the smile. "Because we could," he said arrogantly. "Because it amused us. We outsmarted the police, the detectives, even the FBI. Our father was an idiot. He got caught. We're far smarter than he was. And"—he looked to Darin—"we have each other."

Dorian cocked his head, lowering the pistol slightly. "You hear something?"

Darin turned his ear toward the front door.

Sydney had been so caught up with what was happening that she hadn't heard it before, but now the sound was clear. Police sirens.

"How did she call them?" Darin's face was awash with alarm. "We have to go. We'll have to leave them here now."

"But not alive."

"No, not alive."

"What a mess," Dorian snapped. He turned to look at Sydney, every bit the annoyed schoolmarm. "Get up."

When Sydney didn't immediately obey, Darin stepped in front of her and Krista and grabbed Sydney's arm, hauling her to her feet.

"Mom," Krista wailed.

At the same moment that Krista cried out, the front door burst open. It was Marshall. He had something in his hand. A fire extinguisher. He barreled forward, aiming the extinguisher at Dorian, and pulled the trigger, shooting foam into his face.

"Marshall! He's got a gun," Sydney screamed.

Jess flung off her jacket and ran through the darkness to the nearest state police car. The night air was thick with the sound of insects and the smell of the bay. "Cut the damned sirens!" she choked.

The trooper turned to look at her by the light of the interior of his car.

Jess flashed her badge. "Special Agent Manlove." She motioned to Carl. "And Special Agent Steinman. You were supposed to surround the place and wait for us. What the hell are all the sirens?"

A dog barked in the weeds behind them as a po
lice officer led him onto the driveway.

"And where did the dogs come from?"

"We weren't told no sirens."

Jess looked at Carl. "We didn't tell them no siren
because we thought they would figure it out."

Carl drew his weapon, gazing at the cabin fifty yard
away. Light spilled from the large picture windov
There were people inside, just who they couldn't te
from this distance. "Let's go, Jess," he murmurec
"With the ex-husband already dead, I'm afraid w
might not have much time left."

"Stay put until we call," Jess ordered the closest stat
policeman as she unhooked the safety strap on he
weapon. "And radio in to cut the fucking sirens."

Jess hurried after Carl, approaching the cabin, rur
ning in a half crouch. "Who's in there?"

"I can't see," he said, craning his neck, while tryin
to stay down.

As they approached the front porch, they saw a fig
ure run along the front of the house.

"Halt, FBI," Jess called.

"He's got them!" the figure hollered as he burst i
the front door.

Gunfire exploded in the night air, coming from ir
side the cabin.

"Jesus," Jess swore as she drew her weapon and ra
for the house.

Marshall flew backward under the impact of th
bullet as Krista's scream filled the air.

Sydney lunged at Darin, hitting him as hard as sh
could in the stomach with the corkscrew. Darir
howled with pain as Sydney twisted the weapon, he
hand covered with wet, warm, blood.

"Get away from my mother, you son of a bitch," Krista shrieked, coming up off the floor.

"No, Krista," Sydney cried as she tried to pull loose from Darin. The stench of gunpowder and blood and popcorn was thick in her nostrils.

Instantly, everything seemed to move in slow motion. Even the sound of her own scream seemed out of sync with the rest of the universe.

Sydney watched in horror as Dorian aimed the pistol at her and Krista flew forward toward their attacker, swinging one arm in a windmill pitching motion. To Sydney's shock, her daughter had something in her hand, something big and purple. Krista released the object and it hurled through the air toward Dorian.

A softball.

The twelve-ounce weighted softball hit Dorian Eshey from less than ten feet away, going fifty miles an hour. It struck him squarely in the temple, shattering his skull.

Dorian went limp and fell to the ground as the pistol hit the hardwood floor and slid away.

"Mama!" Krista cried, throwing herself at her mother.

Sydney scrambled away from Darin's dead weight, her arms open to her daughter.

"FBI!" a woman shouted, bursting through the open front door, pointing a gun.

The agents raced into the living room, weapons drawn, as Sydney closed her arms around Krista's shoulders. "It's all right, baby. It's all right."

"Mom, I'm sorry. I was afraid she was going to shoot you."

"Special Agent Manlove. How many more in the house?" the woman demanded.

Sydney kissed the top of Krista's head. "I don't

know. We never saw anyone else, but Charles could be here somewhere."

Agent Manlove stopped beside Marshall and the male agent went around the corner into the kitchen weapon still drawn.

"I don't think that's going to be a problem, Mrs MacGregor," Manlove squatted down to check Marshall's pulse.

Afraid to let go of Krista, Sydney looked to the FBI agent. "Is he dead?" she asked, fear overriding anger for the first time that night.

"No." State police poured into the house through the front door. "We're going to need the EMT's and some ambulances here," Agent Manlove called.

Agent Manlove stooped over Darin next. The corkscrew still protruded from his abdomen. Blood pooled beneath him on the floor. "This one is still breathing, but he's not going to make it." She eyed Sydney.

Still holding on to Krista, Sydney staggered the distance between her and Marshall and knelt beside him. "Marshall?" She brushed his cheek with her hand. He didn't respond, but she could feel his warmth. She could see his chest rising and falling. He'd been hit in the right shoulder. There wasn't too much blood. He was going to be all right. She just knew it.

Sydney threw both arms around Krista, not sure if she wanted to laugh or cry. Her daughter was safe. "Where did you get the ball?" she murmured.

Krista clung to her mother. She was laughing, but tears ran down her cheeks. "It was the weighted ball Dad bought me." She sniffed. "I told you I lost it here at the cabin. It was under the couch. I found it when that bastard made me sit on the floor."

"Hey, watch your language," Sydney chided.